THE THREE *Week* DEAL

HANNAH SHIELD

THE THREE Week DEAL

1

Angela

"I am *not* going in there."

Neve tugs my arm. "Come on, Angie. You promised we could do whatever I want."

"Including torturing me?"

"Hey, you said *anything*. What I want for my birthday is to buy *you* a present. Of my choosing." She drags me forward.

She's won, and she knows it.

Grumbling, I let her pull me through the doorway of a high-end lingerie boutique on Ocean Lane, the busiest commercial strip in West Oaks.

"You're the worst best friend ever. And technically, it's not even your birthday yet."

"When have I ever been persuaded by the word 'technically'?"

The wealthiest residents of our town come to this street to drop their discretionary income. I'm not usually one of them. For one, because my salary doesn't leave much room for discretion.

And two, because I'm a practical girl.

As a West Oaks PD detective, I have to be sensible

when it comes to clothing. On any given day, I might be chasing down a suspect, testifying in court, or standing in on an autopsy. My fashion needs are particular, to say the least. And I'm not talking about those yoga pants that pretend to be work appropriate. My standards are higher than that.

This is one of those stores where they have a sparse collection of items arranged artfully on modern tables. The sizes are small, tiny, and tinier. "I don't even know how to put this on," I say. I pick up the nearest negligee with way too many straps hanging from it. "The lace would probably rip at the slightest pressure."

Neve winks. "Exactly the point. Never had your man tear your undies off in a fit of passion? You're missing out."

I glance at the label. "At two-hundred bucks a pop?"

Also—what man? I have no man.

"It's my credit card, not yours," she sing-songs. "My birthday. Remember?"

I'm not saying I wear granny panties, not that there's anything wrong with those. I enjoy dressing up and treating myself to a little pampering. I put in my time at the hair salon so that I can look my best. But I want it to be my choice. I don't appreciate anyone telling me what I *need*, not even my bestie.

"I want you to have something special that you'd never buy for yourself," she says.

"Why, exactly?" I ask, smelling a trap.

And her answering smile is devious. "You'll find out."

Neve's birthday is next week, and I did promise to do whatever she wanted tonight. She'll be leaving town in the morning for a month, so this is our only chance to celebrate until she's back.

But a girl has to draw the line somewhere.

"Oh, no. You are not fixing me up with someone. Absolutely not." I'm using my detective voice, which is loud and commanding.

The other customers eye me, and Neve pulls me by my elbow to a corner before I make a scene. "I was going to work up to this, but fine. If you're determined to skip ahead. This is an intervention."

"A *what?*" I know what the word means. But I certainly don't need one.

Neve's forehead creases, which is saying something given how she loves her Botox. My friend is gorgeous, but she's been sensitive about aging since we both hit our thirties.

"It's been almost *two years*, Angie. Don't you think it's time?"

"I don't know what you're talking about."

"Ha, nice try."

"If you're referring to Rupert, I've already forgotten about him."

My last boyfriend. He was exactly my type. Sophisticated, soft-spoken, fifteen years older than me. A man with a handle on his life. Unfortunately, he was so established that he was already married and didn't bother to tell me.

"You know I'm not talking about Rupert," Neve says.

Uh oh. This isn't a conversation I want to have.

A distraction. That's what I need.

I pick up a matching bra-and-panty set in red satin. I hold them up in front of me. "You know, I think I like this one."

"Nope, you wanted to have this chat here and now. So we're doing it." She rests a hand on my arm. "Angie, there's no shame in struggling, but you gotta do what you need to do to get better. You can't just ignore the problem and assume it'll go away."

I want to argue she's wrong. I am a hard-ass cop who never lets fear get the best of her.

But then, the truth wells up inside of me. And more than

anything else, it pisses me off to know how right she is.

Neve is talking about what happened to me one year and ten months ago. When I was shot in the line of duty. I have a scar running along my collarbone, both from the gunshot and the surgery afterward. But the scar doesn't bother me in the least. That's not the issue.

When I'm at work, I've got everything together. I've completed my official therapy sessions and mandatory psych evaluations. I'm the same old Angela Murphy as far as my coworkers are concerned.

But my personal life?

What personal life?

I guess that's the problem.

I don't fully understand it, but I've withdrawn into myself since getting shot. The thought of getting out there, meeting someone new… It's so much effort.

I'd rather face a nasty crime scene.

"Oh no, are those sirens I hear?" I cup my hand around my ear. "I'd better see what that's about." I make a move toward the door, and Neve pulls me back.

"Not falling for it. You already told me you're not on call tonight."

I roll my eyes. Where's an emergency when a girl needs one?

"Look, there's nothing wrong with living a solitary existence," Neve says, "if that truly suited you. But I know you. Maybe nobody else will call you on this, no one except your best friend. But your grump score has gone off the charts, lady. You're practically a hermit. You need to have some fun. Be kind to yourself. Will you do that for me?"

I stare at the rainbow of fancy underwear draped over a glass table. "I guess I could pick out a few things here. Just to make you happy."

"So accommodating of you."

Half an hour later, I've got a bag full of pricey lingerie, and we're sitting at the bar of a sushi restaurant down the street. I fit right into the after-work crowd here. I'm wearing my usual on-duty uniform: suit pants, a button-down. Pumps because they look good, but with sensible low heels.

Meanwhile, Neve's T-shirt and jeans are both ultra-casual and effortlessly fashionable at the same time. Her outfit is oversized, yet somehow shows off all her curves.

"So, what's next on your torture agenda?" I ask.

"Give me your phone."

Ugh. What now? I unlock the device and hand it over. "I'm going to regret this, aren't I?"

She smiles wickedly, sips her Moscow mule, and starts tapping at my phone screen. "You need to get back on that horse. Post Rupert, and post injury. Preferably a horse with a really big dick."

I snort a laugh. The bartender walks by and arches an eyebrow at us, though he looks more intrigued than shocked.

"You need to shake something loose," Neve says. "Do something different. Because you're languishing, and I can't stand to see it anymore. Your mouth might claim you're fine, but your soul says otherwise."

Her eyes meet mine, and it's one of those best-friend moments. If our souls are conversing, then hers is saying, *Trust me. Give it a shot.*

"Okay," I whisper. "I'll try."

Her grin could power the western seaboard. "So here's what we're going to do." She turns my phone screen toward me, showing the new icon waiting there.

"A dating app?" Sweat rolls down my sides.

"A hookup app. We're shaking things up, remember? Sex can be a form of self care. Self love. As long as you and your partner both know the score, it can be empowering and cathartic and *all about you.*"

"Can't I stick with the fancy underwear? I'll wear it while I'm watching Netflix."

"Just make the profile with me. You could always delete it tomorrow, but for tonight, I want you to keep an open mind."

I wave at the bartender. "Another scotch and soda, please." I'm going to need it.

It's one night, I tell myself. How much harm could it do if I let my guard down? I've already been through plenty. Getting shot. Struggling to heal. But I made it. I'm here.

There's not much more the world could throw at me.

Right?

SIRENS AREN'T unusual in West Oaks. My hometown might look like a sleepy seaside tourist destination, but I never forget for a moment how close we are to Los Angeles. On any given night, there can be something shady going down.

It's my job to head into those dangerous situations instead of away.

But still, I'm shocked when I hear sirens on my way home. My first thought is about my bad joke from earlier.

Where's an emergency when a girl needs one?

Every muscle in my body tenses.

I'm sitting in the back seat of an Uber. Neve and I stayed at the sushi bar for hours. Much later than I intended. Finally, she had to run off for some last-minute packing. She's taking a town car to Los Angeles tonight, where she'll stay in a hotel so she can catch her early morning flight to Italy. Such a tough life she leads.

I'm supposed to be in bed for a bright-and-early wakeup tomorrow. Gym, then work. Back to my usual programming of solving crimes.

But a West Oaks PD cruiser roars past in the direction of my apartment building. And there are more red and blues up ahead. I tap my fingers anxiously on the passenger door.

"Huh, something going on," the driver mutters.

Yeah. No kidding. I squeeze my phone in my hand, wondering if I should check in with dispatch. Find out what's up.

We go a few more blocks, but that's as close as we can get. "The road is blocked," the driver says.

I'm already opening the door and getting out. "That's okay. I need to... I need to go." I almost forget my shopping bag and lean in to grab it before I slam the door shut.

A terrible feeling is creeping up my insides.

Smoke. I smell smoke.

Please, please say it's not... I rub at the scar at my collarbone and start jogging, then break into a full-out run. And with every step, it's more obvious.

My apartment building is on fire.

Actually *on fire* right now.

You'd think that with all the crime scenes I've attended, a moment like this wouldn't throw me so much. But I'm suddenly choking on bile and fear. It's the utter shock of it. How fast everything can go to hell.

Just like almost two years ago, when I was completely blindsided at my own home. *A dark figure lurching toward me. Raising a gun.*

But this isn't like that day. It's a coincidence. A really freaking bad one, but still. I need to get my act together and think about my neighbors. Figure out what I can do to help.

Breathe.

I race across the parking lot. Smoke pours from the northwest corner of the building, third floor—where my unit is located. My chest tightens even more.

Two trucks have responded, and firefighters are guiding

residents out of the building's exits. Fire hoses snake from the trucks. The West Oaks PD units have only just arrived, but I head for my neighbors rather than the patrol officers.

I see Hazel, the woman who lives down the hall from me. She stumbles as she rushes down the front steps. A huge, burly firefighter points her to the far side of the parking lot, where other neighbors and onlookers are gathering. The firefighter is shouting commands, a gruff scowl on his face, and I'm instantly on edge.

Hazel is a sweetheart. The resident grandma of the third floor. She brought me cookies last Christmas and always has a kind word. Any given afternoon, you'll find her taking her fluffy Pomeranian for a walk.

And she looks *terrified*.

I rush over to her, wrapping an arm around her waist. My eyes lock with the burly firefighter for a second, but then he turns his focus to shuffling more evacuees from the building.

"Angela," Hazel says. "Oh, we had to get out so fast. I, I couldn't…"

"It's okay. Come on. We need to get away from the building."

"But wait, *please*. Listen. I told that firefighter, but he wouldn't *listen*." I've never heard her so insistent. "Daisy is still inside!" Her Pomeranian. "I tried to go back for her, but they wouldn't let me. You're a police officer. They'll listen to you. Please, Angela, tell them to get my baby out of there."

I feel sick at the thought of anything happening to her beloved pet. When something like that is taken from you— your sense of safety, of stability—I know what that can do to a person. How it can break you.

A dark figure lurching toward me. Raising a gun…

I force down my fear and dismay. My training takes over. The experience that I've built over the last decade as a cop.

I can handle this. In fact, *I need* this. A job to do. A mission. Or I might end up panicking just as much as Hazel.

I hand her my shopping bag. "I'll see what I can do, okay? You wait with the other neighbors. *Do not* approach the building. I'll be back."

I leave her and walk along the perimeter, studying the scene as quickly as I can. Firefighters are still evacuating the apartment residents, but the trickle has slowed. From what I can tell, the fire hasn't spread from the northeast corner yet. The building is three stories tall, but it looks like the flames are isolated on the third floor.

Hazel's unit is at the far opposite end. Away from the fire.

I weave through the crowd to get closer to Hazel's side of the building. The firefighters' main priority is human life, both the residents' and their own. The sad reality is that they can't save pets until they're sure the other dangers have passed. But fires are unpredictable. The flames haven't reached Hazel's side yet, but who knows what will happen?

That little dog could suffer from smoke inhalation before anyone can get to her. Hazel would be heartbroken. It's just too awful to think about.

I crane my neck to scan the patio doors to the third-floor apartments. Then I spot movement, just visible through the metal rails of the balcony. A tiny blond puffball, jumping up and down behind the glass. It's Daisy, right there at the door to the balcony, probably desperate to find her momma and get out. I'm religious about locking my balcony doors, but Hazel's could be open. If not, I'll try to break the glass.

I could reach her. I could do it.

It would be madness for a civilian to go back for a pet. I'd never advise it. But me? This isn't anywhere close to the worst danger I've faced.

So I'm not going to think about it anymore, whether it's a bad idea or not.

I keep that burly firefighter in my peripheral vision, but he's busy talking into his radio over near the building entrance. I bite my cheek and move, striding confidently to the perimeter.

There's a patrol officer here, stationed to keep the crowd under control. Officer Evans. Brand new on patrol, baby-faced and blond. I remember meeting him when he made the rounds his first day. He looks like he's straight out of high school, though he must be at least twenty-one. Was I ever that young?

His eyes widen when he recognizes me, and for good measure, I take the badge from my pocket and flash it. "Detective Murphy?" he says, my name sounding like a question.

"Evans, keep the residents back." I don't mention to him that I'm technically one of them.

"Yes, ma'am. But—"

I don't stop to chat. I have no idea if he realizes I'm not on call tonight, and it's definitely not normal for a detective to approach a fire while it's still active. Not with firefighters in charge of the scene. But Evans doesn't try to stop me.

There's a scaffolding attached to the building here for some ongoing stucco repairs. I clamber onto it. It's stronger than it looks, but the metal still creaks as I scale it as fast as I can. Good thing I've been putting in some hours at the rock climbing gym. I never want to be one of those detectives who can't keep up with a fleeing suspect.

Somehow, I'm fearless when it's time to protect and serve. Yet the idea of dating a new guy makes me break out in a sweat. Don't ask me to explain it.

Once I reach the third floor, it's a bit of a leap to reach Hazel's balcony, but once again I don't let myself think.

I just jump.

2

Matteo

I blink my eyes in case I'm hallucinating.

Nope, I still see her. Some chick just climbed up a scaffolding to a third-floor balcony. Of a building *that is on fire*.

She vaults over the railing like a gymnast at the Olympics.

Oh, hell no. Not on my watch. I'm not going to allow this nut to get herself—or one of my teammates—hurt. Or make *me* look like an incompetent idiot who couldn't handle an evacuation.

Barking into the handset of my radio, I hurry toward her.

Tonight was supposed to be my chance to prove myself to my superiors. At our morning briefing, Battalion Chief Ross announced that one of the captains is out sick today. Ross surprised me by saying, *De Luca, you've been asking for more responsibility, right?*

And what did I say? *No problem, sir. I've got it. You can count on me.*

Famous last words.

As it is, I'm lucky that Ross put me in charge of anything. Just because I've been late a couple of shifts. And then there was the time I was dancing around with one of the fire hoses at the station, and Ross walked in and didn't see the humor in my antics. Which were completely harmless, by the way. I was building morale.

But anyway. Station Two—ours—is already smarting from bad press last week, when some of the guys were seen on social media posing with girls in bikinis when they were supposed to be running a training exercise. The men were flashing their six packs, and one of the bikini girls turned out to be the fifteen-year-old daughter of a state senator.

It wasn't my shift, and if it had been? I wouldn't have been dumb enough to pose for those pictures or flirt with some teenager. Because, contrary to popular opinion, I'm actually a very responsible and stand-up dude. Even if my past reputation suggests otherwise.

So I don't want to add to our station's negative publicity. But more than anything, I'd never want someone hurt if I could've saved her.

Which is all a long way of saying—I'd better get Spidergirl off that flipping balcony before she roasts in a burning apartment building or falls to her death.

But damn, that woman is fast. As I run toward her, she's already opened up the patio door of the balcony. A ball of fur bounds out to meet her. In the blink of an eye, she's over the side of the railing.

I nearly swallow my tongue when she jumps onto the nearby scaffolding with a tiny dog in her arms.

Holy shit. The chick really is nuts.

I'm a little impressed.

I reach the base of the scaffolding. "Stay there!" I shout. "Do not move another—"

She starts to climb down. One hundred percent ignoring me.

"Hey, I'm talking to you!"

"And I'm trying to concentrate," she calls down. Like *she's* the one in charge.

I don't have time to request a ladder or anything. "Un. Freaking. Real," I mutter.

Do I start up the scaffolding myself? Or just stand here like a piece of furniture, gawking at her?

Apparently, it's the second one.

Somebody's talking to me over the radio, and I respond. I'm still supposed to be coordinating the evacuation and managing crowd control. The good news is, my team has reported that they've cleared the apartment building. And it sounds like the fire is pretty well under control, too.

Too bad there's a one-woman disaster over my head, working her way down that scaffolding. It doesn't look easy juggling a squirmy fur ball.

I have to do something.

I climb up onto the first level of scaffolding. "Lower the dog to me!"

This time, she listens. She stops at a platform, lies on her stomach, and lowers the animal down. I reach up using all of my wingspan. Which is a lot, since I'm six-five. I grab hold of the fuzzy little fur ball, who nestles right against my chest.

I bend over, extending my arms, and the fur ball jumps happily to the ground and darts away.

I hear the metal creaking. Spidergirl is descending again. This woman seems determined to either give me a heart attack or get me fired by the end of the night.

Then, her foot slips. And everything stalls into horrifying slow motion.

My arms stretch out. I don't so much catch her as break her fall. The two of us land in a heap on the ground, a pile of squirming limbs and shouts and growls.

She ends up on top of me, pushing her hands against my

chest. The rest of her is settled between my legs. And she's scowling at me like I'm the problem.

"Lady, are you *insane*?" The words just fly from my mouth. I can't hold them back.

"Let go."

I realize I've got one hand gripping her waist. And the other is cupped around a shapely, firm ass cheek. I release her, holding my hands at my sides.

She scrambles upright.

"Ow, *careful*," I say. Her knee just came awfully close to my junk. And I'm not so sure it was accidental.

"Calm down. Everything's fine."

"*Fine*?" I jump up to standing. "You were scaling a burning building!"

"Well, I've handled more than a few dangerous situations before. And I've dealt with bossy men who think they're in charge of a scene."

"*I am* in charge of this scene. You're leaving." I take her arm and march her across the parking lot, where the fur ball has reunited with its owner. At the same time, I check in with my teammates via radio. They've noticed something's up and are asking if I need help. Which makes me look super competent.

Chief Ross may never let me play captain again.

"I could have you arrested. For… interfering with fire-fighter business."

She snorts. "Really? You think so?"

The apartment's residents are watching us with wide eyes and open mouths. Along with a blond patrol officer who was supposed to be keeping my perimeter secure. *Thanks, man.*

Her cavalier attitude is grating on my last nerve. "I don't have time for this," I growl.

"Look. I realize what I did was risky. But I got the dog, and I got safely down."

"Barely."

"I don't see why you're in my face about it."

An older white-haired lady pushes her way toward me. She's cradling the fur ball in her arms. "You leave Detective Murphy alone!"

Whoa, wait. *Detective?*

"She's a hero for saving Daisy," the woman says. "Far more than you did, *sir*. I told you Daisy needed help, and you ignored me."

"Ma'am, I didn't ignore you. I passed along that there was an animal in jeopardy, but I wasn't able to prioritize—"

"That is *animal cruelty*."

There are gasps and frowns from the other neighbors. Oh, jeez. They think I'm some dog hater? I have pets too. I'm not a monster.

Oh, shit. Somebody's got their phone up. Recording this.

Spidergirl, aka Detective Murphy, is giving me a smug smile. She knows I'm beat.

"I'll let you off with a warning this time," I say to her.

"Kind of you."

"You know, I didn't have to catch you when you fell. You're welcome, by the way."

"Thanks for helping with Daisy. But I wouldn't have slipped if you hadn't distracted me."

"*What?* That's—" I barely manage to hold back the curse that's on the edge of my lips. Chief Ross would not appreciate seeing that on social media.

She smirks and arches a well-shaped eyebrow. The fact that she's a knockout just makes my skin burn hotter with frustration.

It's time to cut my losses and walk away with the little authority and dignity I have left.

∿

I HEAD over to talk to my friend Danny Bradley. He's applying a bandage to the arm of an apartment resident. Looks like a scrape sustained during the hasty evacuation.

Danny looks up as I approach, saying a few more words to the woman before patting her on the arm and sending her on her way. Danny's one of our trained EMTs. He was a line medic in the Army. I was a Marine myself, but I know how tough any combat medic has to be. Smart, too.

I've gone to Danny a time or two when my niece was sick, because doctors' visits can be damned expensive. Yes, emergency medicine is different. But Danny is the next best thing to a pricey urgent care appointment when Natalie has strep or swimmer's ear.

"Hey, *Captain* De Luca."

"Don't even," I say. I'm not in the mood for his chirping.

"Not enjoying command?"

I frown at him. "You saw some of that mess, I assume?"

"A little. I heard the rest from McGill and Shinoba."

"Great. Everybody knows."

"Some lady was saving a dog?"

"Yeah, and she turned out to be a detective," I say. "West Oaks PD, I'm guessing." That must be how she got past the patrol officer.

"Everything else went smoothly though," Danny says. "Right?"

"Like clockwork." But that won't matter if Detective Murphy complains about me to the chief. Or if that video of me makes the rounds. *West Oaks FD: front-line heroes or hotbed of animal cruelty?* Fuck me, I can see it now.

I didn't get the sense that she was here doing her job. She seemed like a resident of the apartment building. In a way, that's more forgivable. She was probably upset and stressed.

Maybe I shouldn't have lost my temper.

Coulda, shoulda, woulda. Story of my life.

"She's a detective, huh?" Danny looks past my shoulder at the crowd. "Dang. Maybe I should get myself arrested, because it might not be so bad if she's the one throwing me up against the wall."

"Say that to her face and see what happens," I warn. "That chick has a short fuse."

He's right, though. She's beautiful. If you're into well-dressed women who can save a pet from danger while wearing heels and not smudge their eyeliner or ruin their hair.

And she smelled like expensive perfume or bath products. I give my arm a sniff and find the soft feminine scent lingering. My lungs inhale deeply, and my cock gives an interested twitch.

Don't get any ideas, fella.

Lady like that? She wouldn't look twice at a ruffian like me. Besides, I don't need her busting my balls.

Though strong, feisty women are my catnip. Because I do so love to get them begging underneath me.

"Hey, did Emily find a new place?" Danny asks.

My naughty fantasy vanishes with a pop at the mention of my sister-in-law. "Um, no. Not yet."

Emily and my niece are currently in between housing arrangements. Emily is a second-grade teacher. I don't make much as a firefighter, and Em's salary isn't any better. And rent prices have only been going up in West Oaks. Unfortunately, her lease wasn't renewed because her landlord is selling, and she couldn't find anything else on short notice in her price range.

"I'd offer up my couch if I didn't have two messy roommates of my own," Danny says.

"I know you would. It's nobody's fault. Just life."

"Except maybe the pencil-pushers who refuse to pay teachers enough."

"Yeah, that too." I smirk. "Emily and Natalie are going to crash with me for a bit. Just until I can find something more permanent for them."

I meant to spend last weekend apartment hunting for her, but I got behind on my property manager duties. That's my second job. I get my rent for free in exchange for handling my roommate's investment properties around town. Plus, watering her insane number of houseplants during her frequent travels. She could afford to live alone, but she says I'm like a permanent house sitter.

Neve is a great boss and a low-key roommate. Too bad she doesn't have any rental vacancies Emily could afford.

But since Neve is out of town as of last night, there's room for Emily and Natalie at my place until my roomie returns.

Danny looks pensive as he organizes his medical bag. "It's not all on you though, is it? Emily's looking too, right? You have a lot on your plate. Three jobs, dude. I don't know how you do it."

The third job is bartending at the pub near my house. But it's not a regular thing. I pick up shifts whenever I can.

"Of course Emily's looking," I say. "But she's wrapping up teaching a summer school class, and she's got Natalie. She needs my help."

Emily's had a rough time since my brother Brent—her husband—passed. And that was after the hellacious years of him being sick. Natalie's only seven and has to move on from losing her dad. Who's supposed to take care of them if not me?

"You're the one who was telling me how hard it is to juggle everything," Danny says softly. "You said you forgot that loan payment thing last month. And you were late on shift last week because you were so exhausted, you slept through your alarm."

Like I needed *that* reminder.

"If you'd tell Chief Ross what's going on with you—"

"I can manage it," I snap.

I've never been the best with numbers or details. That's why I became a Marine and then a firefighter instead of an accountant or scientist or whatever. I'm not the genius my brother was. The shining star we all looked up to. The best damn guy I ever knew.

But I'm not the fuckup that people seem to believe, either.

"*De Luca,*" a voice says over the radio. One of the guys who was inside fighting the fire. "*You seen Buc? He's not answering.*"

I glance around for Bucanan, the other captain on-scene. "He's probably busy. What's up?"

"*We found some weird shit, and we need to know what to do.*"

"What does that mean?"

"*Uh. You'd better come in and see it.*"

3

Angela

I wake up in a cozy nest of blankets.

Usually, after I've had a bad night, I feel better in the morning. But not today. Today, I feel just as unsettled as I did the evening before.

I sit up as my partner, Detective Beau Grayson, pads into the room in his socks. He's wearing his suit pants and his undershirt, and there's still a couple of spots of shaving cream on his chin.

"Hey, Murphy. How are you feeling?"

"I'm just peachy."

I smell coffee, and I hear his wife humming over in the kitchen of their cozy bungalow. The place is so new I can practically smell the paint drying.

Grayson has been my partner for the last year. He's junior, new to the major crimes department after spending his time in property, just like I did as a young detective.

At first, he was intimidated by me, though I'm only a year or so older than him at thirty-two. He would hardly say a word to me when we were in the car together. But he's warmed up. I know he loves Chinese food, went to USC, and is obsessed with both the New York Yankees and college basketball. We don't have much in common, but at least we can always agree on a lunch place. I like Chinese too.

Grayson's wife Nora comes into the room, rubbing her giant belly. I think she's about eight months along now. "Breakfast is ready, if you're hungry. Toast and eggs. Easy to make a sandwich if you want it to-go."

"Thanks, hon." Grayson turns to me. "I wasn't sure what you wanted to do. If you were planning to go into work this morning, or—"

I stand up and start folding the blankets. "I'm going into work."

"Nobody would blame you for calling in. Maybe you should. If my place burned down…"

"It didn't *burn down*," I say, a little too sharply. "I'm displaced for the moment. Shit happens. I'm fine."

Being temporarily homeless doesn't mean I have fewer cases needing my attention. Work is the only place these days where I feel like I know what I'm doing.

I'm still wearing my wrinkled suit from last night. Grayson doesn't comment on it or give me any more advice.

He drives us to the station, tapping his fingers against the steering wheel. It's a habit of his.

"*Grayson*," I say, and he stops.

"Sorry," he mumbles.

Gah, I'm acting like such a harpy right now. And after the guy took me in last night? Neve would be scolding me about *self care*. I need to make an effort.

"Did you finish writing up that Geo-fence warrant?" I ask.

We chat about the cases we're working. But really, my mind is on what happened last night. The fire at my apartment building.

And for some reason, that big, burly firefighter with the sexy beard who couldn't leave well enough alone.

The guy was just trying to do his job, and I realize that my behavior might've seemed slightly reckless. I guess, technically, he caught me when I slipped off the scaffolding. But I'm sure I would've caught myself if he hadn't been there getting in the way.

And the guy didn't have to yell at me. That seemed unnecessary.

After Mr. Sexy Firefighter—arg, no, Mr. *Arrogant* Firefighter—left, Detective Sean Holt showed up. He's a senior detective in major crimes, like me, and he was on call. I ended up giving him a quick rundown of what I knew, which was basically nothing, and then he got radioed into the building.

That's when I texted Grayson and asked if I could crash here.

I don't know how much damage my unit sustained. I'm not looking forward to finding that out. Nobody from our building has been allowed back just yet.

But the fire was definitely close to my apartment.

At least Hazel and my other neighbors found shelter last night. I was up late texting to check up on them. Several reported seeing an unfamiliar man in a hoodie and sunglasses hanging around the building shortly before the fire, which has me wondering if arson could be a factor.

Grayson pulls into the station. Once I'm inside, I grab an extra suit out of my office that I keep here for court appearances. I head into the locker room to get showered and cleaned up. It does *a lot* for my mood.

Score one for self care.

After that, I plop into my desk chair with a sigh and wake up my computer. I just need to get on with my usual daily activities. Get my mind off my personal mess.

But the top email I see is from Alex Liu. Chief of Police. He's asked me to come to his office for a chat.

I groan. Maybe this is about some other case, and not about my issues. But the fact that he didn't just knock on my door, which is literally next to his, suggests this is something a bit more formal.

Guess all I can do is go over there and find out what fresh hell awaits me.

Alex's door is open. I knock on the frame. "Come in," he says, glancing up from his desk. "Close the door?"

I come inside, and the door snicks shut. "Morning. What do you need?"

"I hear you had a rough evening."

I sink into the chair across from him. "You could say that."

His eyes soften with concern.

Alex is in his early fifties, and he's got a silver-fox vibe, with plenty of muscle filling out his tall, lean frame. He was a Marine Force Recon operator before joining West Oaks PD way back when, which not many people realize. They see him as the consummate police-politician. Tailored suits, an elegant watch on his wrist.

But I know Alex better than most.

We've been close since I joined the force. He was a mentor when I was a new detective and he was a senior. Later, when he made chief, he promoted me to my current position, even though I was still in my late twenties and by far the youngest detective in major crimes. I'd already made a name for myself as an ambitious up-and-comer by then, so I think I earned my spot on pure merit. But I've always wondered if Alex's personal connection to me influenced his decision.

The fact that, before he was my direct boss, we were sleeping together.

I might know how he looks with sex-mussed hair or how he sings pop songs in the shower. But our history is just that, and we're nothing more than friends now. I worked my ass off to earn my place here, regardless of *anything* in my past or where I come from.

"Is there anything you want to tell me, Angie?" Alex asks.

He only calls me Angie when things are getting *very* real.

"No, *Alex*. What's this about?"

He studies me, that strategic mind chewing on something. "Have you spoken to Holt about the investigation into the fire at your apartment building?"

"Not since I left the scene. Why?"

He taps his finger against his chin. "I spoke to the fire investigators this morning. I have some preliminary info on the incident. The fire started in the unit next to yours, north side. A gas stove left on, apparently, near a dish towel."

I groan. "Are they okay? The couple who lives there?"

"They are. No one was hurt. But there was damage to your apartment."

My stomach wrenches, though I knew this was coming. "I figured. Any word how bad it is?"

"Not yet." He picks up a pen and fiddles with it. He pauses, and it goes on way too long. "Are you sure you have nothing to share? Anything at all?"

I have officially lost my last shred of patience. "If you need to say something, say it."

He glances at the closed door. "What I'm about to tell you doesn't leave this room. You never heard these words from my lips."

I stand up, crossing my arms. Bracing myself for whatever he's about to hit me with. I haven't got the faintest clue.

But the way he's acting? He's acting like somebody died. No, worse. He's acting like *I* killed someone.

"There was contraband found in your apartment last night."

I replay the words in my head, but they still don't make sense. "Contraband? What do you mean?"

"I can't get into specifics." Alex swallows. "There's going to be an investigation."

"An investigation?"

He nods, eyes intent on mine.

Chills cascade over my skin. "Okay. Wait a second. Are you talking about IA? Am I *accused* of something?"

"Not yet."

Yet. *Yet?*

"There's got to be a mistake."

I'm racking my brain for what kind of "contraband" could've been in my apartment. But there's literally nothing. Marijuana is legal under California law, but it's still off limits for law enforcement officers like me because of the federal prohibitions. I don't even have old prescription drugs hanging around.

The only thing in my place that could be considered "contraband" is that shitty Halloween candy from last year that I dip into whenever I'm desperate for a sugar fix.

"Who found this supposed contraband? The firefighters? It was something in plain view in my apartment? Because I'm telling you Alex, I didn't have *anything*." Then, with a lurch, I remember what my neighbors reported seeing before the fire. "My neighbors saw someone suspicious around our building that day. Who knows what the guy was doing?"

"You know I can't discuss any of these details with you. You're a cop being accused of wrongdoing, and that means there's going to be scrutiny. Media attention. Even if I think this is bullshit, which I'm sure it is, there can't be any appearance of bias."

"Who's going to run the investigation? Someone from in-house?" West Oaks doesn't have a dedicated Internal Affairs department. We aren't big enough for that.

His jaw tenses. "We're figuring that out."

"I guess it doesn't matter. Once they investigate for five minutes, they'll see this has nothing to do with me."

"I'm sure you're right. We're going to do this by the book, and that starts with you heading home. Wait to be called in for your interview."

I don't bother to point out that I can't go "home," because my apartment building has been evacuated and is now apparently a crime scene to boot.

"What about my cases?"

"I'll sort that out. Treat this like a vacation. You're way overdue for one."

I grip the edge of his desk. "I swear Alex, if you say the words *self care…*"

"That's not a bad idea. You'll hear from your union lawyer, and they'll instruct you on what's next. Let this die down."

"Easy for you to say."

None of this is making sense. I'm struggling to even process it.

"Angie, I know this is tough. But we are going to get to the bottom of it." He pauses. "Are you going to call your father? Let him know what's going on?"

Ugh. That would be as fun as an ice pick to my temple. Not because I don't adore my dad—I do—but because I'd hate to hear the quiet disappointment in his tone.

"That won't be necessary. I'll be fine." I'm not convincing anyone, least of all me.

"Let me know if you need anything else that's not related to the IA investigation. Use my personal cell. I'm here for you."

He's launched into politician speak. *This* is why Alex and I didn't work out as a couple. I'm sure he'll find the perfect woman someday. But she won't be me. I grew up a politician's daughter, and I got sick of the need to play nice.

This is why I don't date anymore, I say to Neve in my mind. *Because I can't stand being patronized, and the men I pick always seem to do it.*

I spin around and get the heck out of that office.

I TAKE an Uber back to Grayson's house, where I left my car. The trunk of my Honda holds a box with everything I could pack up from my office—spare toiletries, a change of clothes. My extra phone charger. It's pretty much all I have in the world until I can get my belongings from my place. Assuming I can salvage any of it.

Everything is just… *gone*. In the blink of an eye. My home. My job security. Maybe I'll get it back, but that's little consolation in this moment.

My nose stings as tears rise in my throat.

A dark figure lurching toward me. Raising a gun…

No. Don't go there now. My chest is seizing. I rub it, trying to get my lungs to work, but they won't. I'm gasping for air.

Breathe. Breathe.

I take out my phone and call my best friend.

"Hey, lady," her cheerful voice says. "I just arrived at JFK. I'm heading to a lounge for the layover, and my second flight is tonight. Next stop, Roma! Did you get any messages on the app yet?"

"Neve." My voice sounds all choked up. Wrong.

Instantly, she turns serious. "What happened, Angie?"

I tell her as much as I can in a flood of words. The fire, the contraband. Within minutes, my chest loosens up knowing my friend is listening.

"I'll head straight to the ticket counter," Neve says. "I could be there by this evening."

"No. Absolutely not. If you cancel your trip because of me, I'll feel even worse."

She sighs. "I really don't mind. I can book another Italian magazine spread. But you are one of a kind."

"Please don't."

"All right. But you're staying at my place. Do not even *think* about arguing with me. I need to check with my roommate, but he can't really say no. I'm the landlady, and he gets free rent anyway for managing my properties."

"I don't want to put anybody out."

"You won't be. You can sleep in my bed, and Matteo works super long hours anyway. I hardly ever see him as it is. He's easy-going, I promise."

"This is the guy who waters all your plants?"

"Exactly. He's a life saver. And he's hot, too. Huge and hot. I don't know if he's single, but—"

I smother a smile. "I'm not sleeping with your roommate."

"You wouldn't be stepping on my toes. He's too old for me."

"Because he's older than twenty-five?"

"You got it. I want to be able to bounce a quarter off dat ass."

My best friend is ridiculous, but she's right. I need a place to stay, and for the next several weeks she's got a room lying empty. A room full of reminders that there's at least one person out there that I can count on and trust.

"Thank you," I say.

"Don't mention it. I know you would do the same for me. You still have that key I gave you, right?"

"On my keychain." Neve gave me a spare to her house in case of emergencies. I've never used it, but I guess this situation qualifies. I just didn't realize the emergency would be mine.

"Then get to my place and settle in. You don't have to worry about a thing while you're there, okay? Wear my clothes. Use my dang toothbrush if you need to."

I snort. "I don't need to use your toothbrush. I had one at the office, and I'll swing by the drugstore for everything else." Like my hair products. Ugh, that's going to cost me.

"You know what I mean. Lady, you can wear my underwear. That's how much I love you. Wait, what about all those undies I bought you last night?"

Now I'm full-on laughing. Of course she's worried about the lingerie. "I've got them. No shopping bags left behind."

"Then you should be good to go. You've got the run of my bedroom for the next few weeks. And when I'm back, we'll figure out a permanent solution."

"I certainly hope I'm back in my own apartment by then," I say. "But thank you again. Really."

"Matteo takes good care of my plants. If he's single, I bet he'll *take care* of you, too. If you ask nice."

"Would you stop?"

She snickers. "Everything is going to be okay."

I exhale, doing my best to believe it.

4

Matteo

*D*anny aims an egg at me and throws. My hands dip as I gently catch it. *Yes*.

"That's half a dozen, baby," I say. "Keep them coming."

The rest of our teammates cackle.

"We gonna eat anytime soon?" Bucanan asks. But there's a smile peeking through that scowl.

It's morning, and we're coming up on the end of our twenty-four-hour shift. Our schedule is twenty-four on, forty-eight off. As usually happens, Danny and I are providing some entertainment. Danny bet me I couldn't catch a dozen eggs without any breaking. I have to keep them all in my hands, so each successive one is harder and harder to manage.

He doubts my skills. But I've got this.

Danny lobs another at me, the seventh, and I have to dive to the side to get it. There are gasps and shouts. The game is getting intense.

On Danny's next throw, the egg smashes at my feet.

"Boom," he says. "I win."

"That throw was shit!"

"Buc, it was fair, wasn't it?"

The captain shakes his head. "If I say it was fair, will that get us closer to food?"

Scoffing, I start breaking the eggs into a bowl. I don't really care who won anyway.

Today, I'm making a spinach and bacon quiche. Well, three of them, in store-bought pastry shells. I'd prefer to make the dough myself, but in a pinch I go for convenience. Danny and the other guys on kitchen duty chop veggies while I mix the eggs.

One thing all the guys know about me is that I can cook, but I hate recipes. All those instructions and fractions. I'd rather wing it. Comes out better, anyway. When I have the time, I can spend hours trying things out in the kitchen.

When I have the time. Hasn't happened much lately.

I've been a West Oaks firefighter for almost five years, ever since I left the Marines. Before my brother moved to California, I'd never even heard of this town. But even when we were kids growing up in Missouri, Brent talked about coming to the West Coast someday. Unlike my brother, I never thought much about settling down. Brent did all the grown-up stuff, and I just tagged along.

When he got into UCLA for medical school, I sent him a bottle of champagne. The fancy kind.

Shortly after I moved out to California, Brent got sick. Then, after he passed, there was no question of me leaving and going anywhere else. West Oaks is home now. Plus, I have Emily and Natalie to look after. I'm determined to hold things together now that Brent is gone.

You can see why I need to blow off some steam by kidding around.

Ross, our battalion chief, strolls in. The air in the kitchen instantly turns stifling, and it ain't the heat coming from the oven.

"De Luca, Bucanan. Come with me."

Danny lifts his eyebrows slightly at me, like he's asking, *What's that about?*

All I can do is shrug.

I rinse off my hands and someone else takes over my egg mixture. "Don't forget to add the cream," I mutter, drying my hands on a towel.

I follow Buc into Chief's office.

I've been dreading this since last night. Did Chief hear about the apartment residents ganging up on me about "animal cruelty"? Did that video of me wind up on social media?

Chief sits, but he doesn't invite us to do the same. Buc perches casually on the edge of the desk, arms crossed.

"De Luca," Chief Ross says, and lets my name hang out there. Just twirling in the breeze.

My phone rings, and I fumble around trying to silence it. "Sorry."

Chief frowns at me before finally saying, "Good job last night."

I want to dance around pumping my fist, but I restrain myself. "Thank you, sir." *Yes. Yes. Hell, yes.*

Chief rubs his eyes, which are bloodshot. "Unfortunately, this mess with West Oaks PD is causing all sorts of headaches. The discovery in that apartment? I've already fielded three calls from the media this morning."

"Really?" I ask. "Why?" Buc's eyes shoot to me. His head shakes in a tiny movement.

I guess I wasn't supposed to speak right then. But I'm surprised it's such a newsworthy story.

Last night, the fire started in a third-floor unit. The investigators are still analyzing the evidence, but it looked like it was inadvertent. A stove left on.

The guys went into the apartment next door to fight the

flames, which had spread along the shared wall. They walked into a bedroom. That's where they found an overturned box, contents spilled over the floor.

Bricks of what appeared to be a Schedule Two narcotic. As in powdered and white.

I know, it sounds pretty insane. But I've seen some really weird shit in this job. Still, those drugs just sitting out in the open like that? It was obvious enough that we had to send it up the chain. I told the guys not to touch anything else and called Chief Ross. I'm pretty sure I did what I was supposed to do.

From there, it was up to the police to deal with it. It's not even the first time we've found illegal drugs at the scene of a fire. Meth labs are a crazy kind of mess all their own.

Why is the media so interested in a minor drug bust?

"This is going to be a mess," Chief Ross says, "and we don't want to be in the middle of it. West Oaks PD will call you both in to answer some questions at their station tomorrow, along with the guys who first found the drugs. You're going to tell the investigators exactly what you saw, but don't volunteer anything either. We're neutral."

"What's so special about this incident?" Buc says.

Oh, so it's fine when *he* asks.

"That apartment belongs to a West Oaks PD detective. Angela Murphy."

My eyes bug. Detective Murphy? *Spidergirl*? Savior of pets and nemesis of innocent firefighters?

Not to mention a stone cold fox of a woman.

Those drugs were *hers*?

Damn. She's more unpredictable than I even imagined.

"There's an internal police investigation," Ross says. "The media will try to make it seem like we're closing ranks, protecting a West Oaks officer. We don't want anywhere near that. We tell them what we saw, and otherwise, we stay out of it."

My brain is fast at work. Do I mention my run-in with Detective Murphy last night? Is it important, or totally irrelevant?

"De Luca?" Chief Ross's voice rings out. "Are you listening?"

"Of course, sir. Yes. Understood."

He heaves an exhale. "Don't gossip about it. Don't talk to any damn reporters. Hopefully, after all of you give your statements tomorrow, that'll be the end of it as far as we're concerned. If I hear about this from *my* bosses—like the Fire Chief—I'm going to be pissed."

After Chief dismisses us, I grab Buc in the hallway while I've got the chance. "Hey Buc, can I speak to you for a sec?"

He turns around. "Sure. What is it?"

"Uh, I was wondering about that captain spot opening up soon. I'd like to be considered." One of the older guys is retiring in a couple months. It would probably mean switching to another shift, away from Danny and my closest friends, which is a downside. But it could be worth it.

Buc is quiet a moment, studying me. "What's your pitch? Tell me why you're a strong candidate."

"I think I'd do a good job. These guys mean the world to me."

"And the higher salary sounds nice?"

"Sure." The extra money could do a lot for Emily and Natalie. "But I wouldn't go for it unless I thought I'd do it right."

Buc perches his hands on his hips. "De Luca, you're a great worker. When you're focused, there's nobody who can rival you. I love having you on my team. And the guys love you, too."

"Thanks."

"But you have to show that you're serious and ready for more. Because a promotion means more responsibility. You can't show up late anymore. You can't piss off the chief. You can't be the class clown."

Fuck. My face heats as I nod.

"Keep doing what you're supposed to, and you've got a shot at captain." He claps me on the shoulder. "I'll be rooting for you."

THE QUICHE IS ONLY SLIGHTLY overdone. Everyone else raves about how delicious it is. But my talk with Buc left a bad taste in my mouth.

When I first left the military, I wasn't great at being on time. You'd think it would be the opposite. But for me, the loss of that structure made for a rocky start. I slipped too easily back into the role of little brother. The fun guy who nobody expected much from. Even though I was old enough that I should've known better.

But I've gotten my act together. I've been late only twice in the past six months. Last week, I did oversleep because I'd been tending bar the night before. But the other time, I was staying over at Emily's because she and Nat both had the flu. When I drove in for my shift at the firehouse, I hit a snarl of traffic from an accident. It was bad luck. When I got in that day, I took my lump and worked twice as hard.

I *don't* make excuses.

But if Chief Ross expects perfection, I'm not sure I can deliver that, either.

After breakfast, while Danny and I are getting ready for the shift change, he nudges me. "What did the chief want to talk to you and Buc about?"

Discretion, the chief's voice repeats in my mind. "Can't

talk about it. It's sensitive, so we're supposed to keep our mouths shut."

"That's no fun," Danny grumbles. But he doesn't keep pushing.

I remember how my phone was ringing earlier. I step away to check the voicemail. And as I listen, I can feel the blood draining out of my face.

It's Neve. My roommate. My *boss*. I have a lot of those.

Neve says that a friend of hers is going to stay in her room while she's gone. Which is a serious fucking problem. Because Emily and Natalie moved into that room this morning. I haven't been home, of course, but my sister-in-law has my spare key.

I was supposed to ask Neve if it was okay, but... yeah, I know. I'm the idiot who forgot. *Fuck.*

Why am I constantly two steps behind where I'm supposed to be?

Neve owns the house, and even if she didn't, she has every right to decide who stays in her room. Now, it's too late for me to say my family has nowhere else to go. I'll seem like a complete asshole. Not only taking advantage of Neve's absence to get free rent for Emily and Nat, but also trying to edge out her friend.

I try calling Neve's number, though I have no clue what I'm going to say to her. But she doesn't answer. So I text my sister-in-law instead.

Me: Put your stuff in my room. You can't stay in Neve's room after all.
Emily: What? Why?
Me: She's got a friend who needs the room.
Emily: ?????? But didn't you clear this with her first?
You forgot, didn't you?
This was your idea. You insisted it would be okay.

Me: I'm sorry. I'll figure it out. Just switch your stuff to my room, okay? You'll stay there.
Emily: But where will you sleep?

Shit, good question.

Me: The floor.
Emily: But you snore.

I feel my teeth creaking, I'm clenching my jaw so hard.

Me: The couch in the living room then. [Shrugging emoji]

Danny wanders over. He must see the frown on my face, because he asks, "Everything okay?"

I put my phone away. Nothing else I can do about this now. "Yeah. Family stuff."

If my brother were here, Emily and Natalie would be living in a comfortable house. Not shuffling from one borrowed bed to another. They'd be happy. And damn, it sucks.

Don't get me wrong, I love my sister-in-law and my niece dearly, and I'd go to the ends of the earth to protect and provide for them. But I'm the consolation prize. They didn't *pick* me.

Maybe I wouldn't pick me either.

"Need to get your mind off things?" Danny asks. "You should come out with us tonight. It's been a while."

It's one of our WOFD rituals. Every week, our shiftmates gather at a dive bar called The Shore Lounge when we're off duty. And I want to say yes, I really do. I want to forget my troubles and kick back like I don't have a care in the world. The way it used to be.

But I can't do that anymore. I've got that stack of bills

waiting for me. It's not just the physical one on my nightstand.

There are debts that I owe.

I don't resent the responsibilities that are on my shoulders. It's the opposite. I want to be worthy of them. There's no way I could replace my brother, but shouldn't I at least try to make him proud? I'm the one standing here, *alive*, while he's fucking *gone*.

"I can't. I might be bartending tonight at the pub."

"We could all meet up there instead. Keep you company."

"Do not do that. I'm going to be working, not goofing off." If my friends are there, I'll be tempted. Buc's words from earlier keep repeating in my head. *You have to show that you're serious.*

Danny holds up his hands. "Okay, sheesh. I miss the Fun Matteo."

"You can kiss Fun Matteo goodbye, 'cause his ass is history."

Danny chuckles like he doesn't believe me. "But we're still going out on your birthday, right? You can't miss that."

I'll be turning thirty-six. I could've sworn I just turned twenty-five, and people certainly accuse me of still acting like it. "I won't miss it."

"Don't be too hard on yourself, yeah?" He pulls me into a back-slapping hug.

Danny's my closest friend. But he doesn't get it. If I'm not hard on myself, who will be? Nobody else believes I'm capable of more. All I can do is show them.

But before I can do *anything*, I have to get home and deal with my new roommate.

5

Angela

*U*sing Neve's key, I unlock the door to her house and step inside.

"Hello," I call out, "anybody home?"

There's no answer, but I hear water running. Maybe her roommate's in the shower.

Closing and locking the door behind me, I carry my few belongings into the house. And the first thing I see is *green*.

There are plants everywhere. On tables around the living room, perched on windowsills, and on the mantle above the fireplace. On the shelves in the kitchen. A couple of honest-to-goodness trees grow in pots, basking in the sunlight shining through the large windows.

Neve has always loved plants. That was my first impression of her when we moved into our room freshman year of college. The tiny pots of succulents and vines, making our space both lively and comforting before I'd even met her.

If I could keep anything alive, my home would be filled with plants too. But I killed even the zero-maintenance ones that Neve has gifted me over the years. I've had to settle for a few plasticky-looking fake cactuses, which Neve hates. She claims they smell weird.

I set my cardboard box on the kitchen counter and drop my shopping bag of lingerie to the floor. I haven't been to this house since right after Neve bought it. Neve thrives on the energy of other people, so she always wants to go out. Museums, restaurants, even just walking on the beach. Neve likes to see and be seen. When I'm with her, I don't mind it.

But if I'd known how adorable her house is, I would've insisted on coming over here more often. I finger the shiny, bouncy leaf of a vine trailing from a shelf in the kitchen. Her roommate must be doing a great job, because these plants are so dewy and lively I'd swear they're sparkling.

My gaze sweeps over the cozy, open-plan living area. But I do a double take at what I spot in one corner.

There's a scruffy gray dog and a black and white cat sitting in a little bed. As in, cuddling up on each other.

This could be a viral video. It's that adorable.

And they're both watching me. The dog has his tongue out and his mouth open like he's smiling, while the cat has a quintessential grumpy frown. Then they glance at each other, like they're wondering who the heck this weird lady is who just walked into their house.

I set down my things and walk over to them, crouching next to their bed. "Hey, cuties. You're a pleasant surprise, aren't you?"

Neve didn't mention anything about pets, but whatever. I assume these belong to the roommate. I don't have pets of my own, but I'm not allergic or anything. It's just that care-taking gene I seem to be missing. I like other people's pets, though.

"I'll be staying here a few weeks. Hopefully we can be friends?"

The dog comes right over, sniffs my hands, and accepts my rubs on his head. Or her head? I'm not sure.

The cat flips her tail, undecided.

"I get it," I tell her. "I don't always warm up quickly either."

After that greeting, I grab my box and head to the open doorway of a bedroom. I'm pretty sure this is Neve's, and the sight of more plants confirms this is the right room. That, and the crystals hanging in the window catching the light.

I bring my sad little box to the dresser. Then I sit on her bed and just breathe. I can almost taste the oxygen flooding into my lungs. *Ahhhh.*

Thank goodness I'm here.

This has been one of the worst days in recent memory, possibly even worse than the day I got shot, because I don't actually remember too much from that day. Just scattered images. Impressions. Today has been all too vivid.

But I'm here now, surrounded by my best friend's aura, as she would say.

Neve and I were assigned as roommates freshman year of college. She was an outgoing general studies major, more interested in partying than going to class. And I was the introverted criminal justice major with a politician father and a socialite mother.

But despite our differences, Neve and I became inseparable. She dragged me along to social events, and I had a blast. Specifically, I hooked up with a lot of guys. And so did my roommate. We had a whole scheduling system for who got to use the room when. Afterward, we shamelessly shared all the dirty details.

For a hot minute back then, I was almost as wild as Neve. I got a Marilyn Monroe piercing on my upper lip. A line of tattoos down my bicep.

It was a good time, I'm not denying that. But I outgrew it.

I never wear the piercing at work, and I keep my tats covered. Many people who know me as Detective Murphy would be shocked that I have a sense of humor, much less a wild-child past. Even Alex doesn't know me like that.

Could I ever go back to that carefree version of me? As I look around Neve's room, I think... probably not.

My phone chimes, and I tense up again.

I've mostly been ignoring my notifications all day. But Alex said a union lawyer would be contacting me, and I need to deal with that. Biting the bullet, I open up my phone and glance through what's waiting. Some texts and emails from colleagues, asking what the heck is going on. And the union lawyer who's been assigned to me.

But there's also a few notices from that app Neve downloaded last night on my phone. Before my life went to shit.

The hookup app.

Because I'm just that desperate for a distraction, I thumb over to the app icon and click on it.

There are a couple "hey girl, you dtf?" and the inevitable dick pic. But most of the messages are friendly. The guys might even be normal. Their profile pictures are kind of cute.

Am I seriously considering this?

I swipe back over to the dick pic. I tilt my head, taking in the view. It's... Huh. Not bad. I'd never respond to the type of guy who would send this without any preamble.

But my lady parts aren't all that offended. Which surprises me. Interesting.

Maybe it's just been too long since I saw one up close. The last was Rupert's, the secretly married guy, and his dick wasn't worthy of any close-ups. I guarantee that.

"Whatcha doing?"

My head whips to the doorway, where a little girl of six or seven is standing. I jump and gasp slightly, fumbling my phone, rushing to darken the screen before she can spot what I was looking at.

"Um, nothing."

Ha. I sound so guilty right now.

She takes a step into the room. "Are you a robber?"

"You're lucky I'm not. You shouldn't come near people if they could be robbers."

"I know that. I was just kidding." She walks over and sits beside me on the bed. "I like you. What's your name?"

"My name's Angela. What's yours?"

"Natalie. Why is your hair like that?"

She points at my head. Lately, I'm wearing tiny cornrows in a geometric pattern near my hairline, with the rest of my hair falling in curls.

I arch an eyebrow at her. "Because I think it looks good, and it suits me."

"It does," she assures me.

"Oh, good. Why is *your* hair like that?"

She sighs wistfully, like this will be a long story. Her hair is chin length and dark brown. "It used to be long. But Mommy says that I cry too much about combing out tangles, and that makes *her* cry. So I cut it with some scissors at school. But when I'm a grown-up, I'm going to grow my hair long and leave the tangles. I'm going to do whatever I want when I'm a grown-up."

"It's not as great as you might think," I murmur.

Natalie gets up and wanders around Neve's bedroom, examining the space. She stops at a framed photo on the dresser. "That's you with Miss Neve."

"She's my best friend."

Natalie looks at the photo again, then at me. "Why don't you have that gold dot on your face anymore?"

My Monroe piercing. I touch the left side of my upper lip,

where I can feel the hole under my skin. "You're very observant."

"That's what my mommy said when I told her she should get new pants 'cause her old ones were too tight."

Another head pops into the room. Her eyes go wide when she sees Natalie in here with me. "Oh my gosh, Nat, there you are. I'm sorry. I thought she was taking a nap."

I'm guessing this is Mom. She must've been in the shower. Her damp hair is making water spots on her shoulders. Unlike her daughter, she's blond and blue-eyed, pale-skinned with lots of freckles.

"It's no problem." I stand and offer my hand. "I'm Angela, Neve's friend. I hope I'm not intruding. Is Matteo here?"

"His shift should be over by now. I'm sure he'll be here soon." She takes my hand. "I'm Emily."

"Nice to meet you. Neve didn't mention she had so many roommates." Neve is my ride or die, but she's flighty as hell sometimes.

Emily's face burns crimson. "Oh, um…"

"Mommy, can I show her my coin collection?"

Emily runs her fingers through her daughter's hair. "Of course you can, Natty-bear. If Angela doesn't mind?"

"Not at all."

Natalie scampers off. Emily turns back to me, eyeing me nervously. "How do you know Neve?" Emily asks.

"We met in college and have been close since. She's got her exciting fashion photographer lifestyle, and I'm serious and boring, which is why you haven't met me."

"I'm sure that's not true."

"Oh, it is. I'm a detective with West Oaks PD."

"I teach second grade."

Her hands are twisting like she's nervous around me. But I'm not sure why. Is it the cop thing?

"Guess we'll be roomies for a bit," Emily says. "Let me know if you need anything. Or if Natty is bugging you."

"I don't mind. Not like I have much else going on." That's all the hint I want to give about my current situation. "Are you Matteo's—"

I'm cut off when Natalie dashes back in, holding a plastic bag. "These are my coins, Angela."

Emily excuses herself, and Natalie proceeds to show me her nickels, dimes and pennies. Each one has a story that I suspect she's making up on the fly. And I gotta say, I'm liking it.

I'm curious about the real stories around here, though. It's what makes me a skilled detective. I like digging into people's histories, learning what makes them tick.

"Is Matteo your dad?" I ask.

Natalie considers my question longer than seems necessary. "Sort of. Yes, he's my dad."

I suspect I can't believe everything this girl says. So the jury's still out. Maybe he's her stepdad?

"He's really nice and fun and smiles a lot. Even when he's sad. And he has drawings all over his arms and some on his chest too."

Out in the living area, the front door opens and closes. "I'm home," a voice says.

A familiar voice, oddly. Though I can't place it.

"That's him!" Natalie says, scooping her coins into the bag. "Come on." She grabs my hand and pulls me into the living room.

And the contents of my stomach immediately curdle.

"*You,*" I say.

The burly, obnoxious firefighter who yelled at me yesterday drops his gym bag to the ground with a thunk. He's wearing jeans and a WOFD T-shirt, but I'd recognize that scowl anywhere.

"You?" he says. "You've got to be kidding me."

Natalie's eyes bounce from him to me. Emily emerges from their bedroom and stands frozen in the doorway.

"You're Neve's friend?" he asks incredulously.

"*You're* Matteo?"

Emily walks toward us. "You know each other?"

He aims an accusing finger at me. "Yeah, she's a detective. And she's trouble."

"*Matteo*," Emily hisses, moving closer. "You're being rude."

I aim my next comment at Emily, because she's the only adult in this room I can deal with talking to. "Look, there was a fire at my apartment, and that's why I need a new place to stay. Matteo and I met there, and we had a mild disagreement. But I can keep to myself. That's what I usually do anyway. I promise I won't get in your way."

I head back into Neve's bedroom, a whole firestorm of emotions running through me. This day has just been *too much*.

I close the door and nearly jump out of my skin when I find Natalie sitting on the edge of the bed.

How does she do that? Appear places without making a sound?

"Why doesn't he like you?" she asks.

Now that I've seen her and Matteo in close proximity, the resemblance is striking. Their hair and skin tone, their strong features, though Natalie's are more feminine. I guess she was telling the truth, and he's her dad. Which makes this even more awkward.

Because the guy hates me.

"We had a misunderstanding." I was taking care of business, and he was mistaken in thinking he could boss me around.

Does he know about the "contraband" found in my apartment? He probably does. I'm so sick of that nonsense.

"Why?" Natalie asks.

"It just happens with grownups sometimes." I sink down beside her on the bed. "Want to tell me more about your coins?"

She pulls the bag out of the pocket in her shorts. But instead of pouring out the coins, both of us just sit there listening to the whispered argument in the kitchen.

"They fight when they're stressed," Natalie says. "A lot of the time, it's about money." She shakes the coin bag. "I'm saving these up to help with the bills."

"That's very thoughtful." But I make a mental note not to tell this kid my deepest secrets, because she'll spill them in no time. "Money can be stressful for adults. That's for sure."

She nods sagely. "When I'm a grown-up, I'm going to have lots of money."

"That would make things easier, wouldn't it?"

"And I'm *never* going to get sick and go to the hospital."

"Did you know someone who went to the hospital?"

She gets quiet then, so I don't press. We play with the coins instead.

A few minutes later, the arguing stops, and there's a knock at my door. It opens, and Matteo is standing there. "Natty-bear, can you go see your mom for a sec? She wants to talk to you."

"But I'm being friends with Angela right now."

Matteo puts a hand on his hip. "*No*, you're doing what I say."

She scampers away, sticking out her tongue at him as she passes. My sentiments exactly.

Matteo hulks in the doorway, not stepping into my room, but blocking the only exit. He's tall. Huge, really. Twice the size of me, and I'm not tiny.

His arms fold over his broad chest, biceps bulging. As Natalie mentioned, colorful tattoos criss-cross his olive-toned skin. He's got thick, tousled dark hair that I didn't see last night because of his helmet. A strong jawline visible beneath a full, trimmed beard.

A man that obnoxious has no right to look so... edible.

"I assume you heard about the investigation against me?" I ask. He probably knows more about it than I do.

His nostrils flare as he inhales. "Whatever your drama is, I don't want any part of it."

"I didn't ask you to be a part of it. This is just a shitty coincidence."

He glances over his shoulder, then comes further into the room and shuts the door. I get a whiff of his scent. Cedar, woodsmoke, pine.

"I can't have drugs and shit around my family," he hisses.

"*Excuse* me?"

"You heard what I said."

"Drugs? Is *that* what they found?" That must be the "contraband." Oh my God. This man thinks I'm a drug dealer. No wonder Alex was worried about the media. *A dirty cop selling drugs.* Doesn't matter that anyone who knows me wouldn't believe it. I've never been so mortified. Or pissed off, because I want to know how those drugs got in my home.

Matteo's glaring at me, those sexy lips all twisted up.

"I have no idea how anything illegal got into my apartment, but I can assure you that whatever you're thinking, it's not true. I do not use or peddle illicit drugs."

He holds up his hands. "Whatever. All I know is what I'm told."

"And that is?"

"To steer clear of you."

"You know what? Go through my stuff. The whole damn box of it! There it is." I grab the box and overturn it on the bed. Then, for good measure, I up-end the bag of lingerie. Rainbow colored scraps of satin and lace fall over the bed.

He shifts and clears his throat. "That's... an interesting assortment."

I look at the bed, and yeah, maybe dumping everything out was a mistake. It's almost all underwear. Very skimpy, scandalous underwear.

"I went shopping just before the fire. That's not important. As you can see, nothing illegal."

He lifts a black mesh garter belt by one finger. Neve must've snuck that in. "Maybe this one should be illegal. A guy with a weak heart might keel over seeing you in this thing."

I snatch it away from him. "Just... *nevermind*. I'm basically homeless at the moment and almost all my stuff is ruined. God forbid you could manage a tiny shred of sympathy."

He gives me a sheepish frown. "Okay, I'll back off. Whatever you do outside these walls is your business. Not mine. Let's just not discuss it. All right?"

"Fine by me. Give me my space, and I'll give you yours."

"Excellent."

Matteo throws open the door. Emily and Natalie are standing on the other side, eavesdropping. He glares at them both.

"What's going on?" Emily asks.

Matteo storms past her. "*Nothing.*" He stops in the kitchen, glancing around. His eyes have darkened to almost black with fury. Natalie claimed he smiles a lot, but I have my doubts.

He grabs a windbreaker from the hall closet.

"Are you going out again?" Emily asks.

"Yes. I'll be late. Don't wait up."

Matteo storms out the front door. But surprisingly, he doesn't slam it. Just pulls it gently closed.

Natalie sits on the couch, looking at her coins. Emily and I glance at each other. Then she looks down at the kitchen tile. "Sorry to hear about the fire at your place. That's rough."

"Thanks."

"Not sure if you're hungry. I was going to make Nat and me some pasta for lunch."

"I appreciate that, but I'm not hungry. Maybe I'll grab something later."

I duck into Neve's bedroom, then close and lock the door.

This is why I don't do roommates. While I enjoy examining human dramas at work, I'd rather do it from a distance. Here, I'm smack dab in the middle of it.

My fingers trace the outlines of my scar.

I don't normally let arrogant a-holes like Matteo get to me. But somebody out there is trying to fuck me over, and I've never felt so powerless.

I spend that afternoon bingeing reality TV. When I emerge to collect a DoorDash delivery, Natalie is playing with the pets and Emily's taking care of dishes. It looks like Matteo is really out for the day. Clearly avoiding me.

That night, as I get ready for bed, my insides twist and shift with uncertainty. Never in my life have I felt this unmoored from everything I know. Not even when I got shot. Being in my best friend's space helps, but I don't see how I can stay here with someone who thinks I'm a danger to his wife and kid. Or I suppose Emily is his girlfriend, since they weren't wearing wedding rings.

How did Neve miss the fact that her property manager has a longterm girlfriend and a kid? My best friend is clueless sometimes. She has a tendency to get wrapped up in her own life. Which is probably how my self-isolation slid under her radar for so long. But I still miss her. So much.

I hug Neve's pillow as my whole body starts to shake. Tears stream silently down my face.

Breathe. Breathe.

I still don't want Neve to cancel her trip for me, but I wish my best friend were here. For the first time in ages, I wish I had someone next to me. Holding me steady.

Those are my thoughts as I fall into fitful sleep.

I'M NOT sure how long I manage to rest before I'm jolted awake.

It's pitch black. And there was just a crash from somewhere inside the house.

I think someone just broke in.

Heart racing, I throw back the covers and grab my phone. It's after three a.m. Everyone else must be sound asleep by now. And my brain is spinning out terrible images.

A dark figure lurching toward me. Raising a gun…

No. No, no, no.

I need a weapon. I have to do something. I can't let this happen. Not again.

6

Matteo

*W*hen I get back to the house, everything is dark. As it should be. Because it's past three in the morning.

I ran a few errands, then went in to the pub, but it turned out they didn't need me to bar-tend after all. So I ended up at The Shore Lounge with Danny and our friends. Better than getting yelled at any more at home.

I didn't drink, though, volunteering as DD instead, which meant staying until after final call. I gave every last one of those jerks a ride home, even though Danny kept calling me a grumpy bitch the whole time.

It's the stress, man. Just… all of it.

I shut the door and hang my keys on the hook. I don't turn on any lights, navigating instead by the moonlight and the microwave clock in the kitchen. The fridge light blinds me as I take out the milk carton. I pour myself a glass.

Sometimes, when Natalie's staying with me, she gets up in the night and nudges me awake. She knows I'll make snacks and let her watch movies on my iPad. To me, it's being a good uncle. Nat needs comfort, and I remind her of her dad. But Emily thinks I'm reinforcing bad habits.

More often than not, Emily and I don't see eye to eye.

Earlier, she was lamenting that she'd let me talk her into staying with me. *I could've figured something else out, and then we wouldn't all be crammed in here.* As if I somehow did a bad thing by putting a roof over their heads. I would live with them full-time if Emily and I could get along and make it work with my property manager gig.

It bugs me when somebody obviously needs help, yet is so difficult about accepting it.

But at least I had a good conversation with Neve, via text. She was using the airplane WiFi on her way to Europe. I came clean about Emily and Natalie staying here and explained that they'd had some trouble finding a new place after their old lease ended, and that I was going to sleep on the couch. And of course, she was completely understanding. She just asked me to make sure Angela is comfortable, and I said I would, leaving out any of the conflict between us.

Neve is good people. Which makes me think I was a little too mean to her friend. I don't know what Angela's deal is, but she's obviously going through some shit. I can identify with that.

I might, perhaps, owe her an apology.

Still carrying my milk glass, I step into the living room. I squeal when a plastic dog toy sinks into the soft arch of my foot. It's got spikes all over it, and I curse, hopping.

The milk glass slips from my hand and shatters onto the floor. *Fuck.* Can I not catch a break for five minutes around here? I plod back to the kitchen and grab paper towels and a dust bin to clean up.

When I turn around, a dark shape suddenly rears out of the shadows. Wide eyes meet mine. I choke back a scream.

It's Angela, and she's holding a cast-iron skillet in her

clenched fists. Holy crap, she could've taken me out with that thing.

"What the hell?" I hiss, switching on a floor lamp, but keeping the dimmer low.

She's glaring like *I'm* the one with a deadly weapon. "I thought you were an intruder. What're you doing sneaking around?"

"I live here."

"It's the middle of the night!" she whisper-yells. "I assumed you were in bed asleep. I heard a noise out here, and it freaked me out."

I stomp over and start cleaning up the spilled milk and broken chunks of glass. "I'm not going to ask your permission every time I enter or leave the house, you know. I said I'd be back late."

"This is typical for you? Coming and going at all hours?"

"I didn't ask for some crazy, paranoid chick to move in with me."

"That is offensive in *so* many ways."

"Then stop talking to me. We'll get along better."

So much for apologizing. But this lady really knows how to get on my nerves.

Fuming, I finish cleaning, then stalk over to the couch and drop my weight onto it. Angela follows me into the living room. "What're you being so salty about? Your apartment didn't burn down."

I want to roll my eyes. I do feel sympathy for her, but it's not fair to use her bad luck as the ultimate trump card. *And that's setting aside the whole drug bust thing.* Maybe she's innocent, and maybe she's not. How would I know?

But, whatever. She's not the only one with issues.

"I was the designated driver tonight, and drunk people are annoying when you're sober." I had a couple sips of Danny's craft beers, but that was it.

"You don't smell sober."

"I don't have to explain myself to you," I mutter. But then I do. "The server spilled a drink on me."

The waitress also offered to take me home to her place and wash my clothes for me. She was hot. Tits half out of her tank top, cheeks peeking below her cut-off shorts in the back.

I politely declined because I needed to drive my drunk friends home. But I think she would've taken me into the bathroom for a quickie if I'd asked. In the old days, I would've gone for it. Life was so carefree back then that I had to seek out reckless thrills just for kicks.

But tonight, I wasn't feeling it. Oh, how my life has changed.

Guess that's why I was being a grumpy bitch.

I close my eyes and lay my head back, hoping Angela will get the hint and leave me alone.

I don't know how I'll get decent sleep out here. The couch is way too short for my height, and I'm supposed to go down to West Oaks PD headquarters for that interview tomorrow. After that, I'll be watching Natalie. I usually look after her on my days off. Emily's going to notice me yawning and make comments.

Fuck. How'd I end up surrounded by women who are constantly pissed at me?

At least Natalie is easy. Candy and a screen and she's set.

The couch cushion shifts. Angela must've sat down, which infuriates me. I want this conversation over. But for some reason, I go and ask another question. "Did I wake you coming in, or were you already up?"

"I'm not a great sleeper. I get nervous being in a new place. I like to check that I'm secure."

I open my eyes and look at her. "Because you're a cop?"

"That's part of it."

I adjust my weight on the couch, trying to get more

comfortable. "Sounds like you've had a stressful couple days. I know how that is. That's probably why I was a little testy before. Sorry."

"A *little* testy?"

"I'm trying to apologize here."

"All right. Then I apologize too. I haven't been at my best."

Suddenly, I'm exhausted. And I just can't deal with fighting anymore. "I'll make you an offer. While you're staying here, it's neutral territory. No more fighting."

I hold out my fist. After some deliberation, she bumps it. "Good by me."

She chews on her lower lip. I see a glint of metal and realize it's a small piercing. Like a little beauty mark. I don't think she was wearing that before.

She's got a silky scarf wrapped around her hair, which accentuates the beautiful features of her face. Large, distinctive eyes, brown with hints of green and gray. Elegant cheekbones, full dark-rose lips.

My eyes drift downward further. Over her tank top, which reveals a line of tattoos on her right bicep, black ink against bronze skin.

I wouldn't have expected the ink and the piercing. She seemed so uptight before. But maybe she's not so easy to pin down or figure out.

Warmth blooms in my low abdomen. Blood rushes to my cock and thumps in my balls.

"What're you looking at?" she asks sharply.

I shift on the couch. I must be wired from lack of sleep, in addition to being stressed and generally unsatisfied. That's the only thing that could explain this flare of attraction to the woman who has been nothing but a thorn in my side since I met her.

Her hand goes to her collarbone, and I notice the puckered lines in her skin there. It's a scar, a big one. It didn't stand out to me before in the low light. Not until she drew attention to it.

"Is that why you have trouble sleeping? Whatever caused that scar?"

Her mouth twitches, and I figure I've said more than I should. But she nods. "I was shot."

Oh, damn. "On duty?"

She nods again, lips pressed together.

"I'm sorry to hear that." Being a firefighter is dangerous, but we don't usually have people trying to hurt us on purpose. That's something I don't miss from the military. I'd prefer to go the rest of my life without anybody shooting at me. "I had buddies in the Marines who were wounded."

"You're a vet?"

"Yeah. Been out for five years. Joined West Oaks FD not long after." I'm not sure why I'm telling her. Maybe because she's being vulnerable, and it sucks to feel alone in moments like that.

A furry head sneaks up and rests on Angela's knee. "Hey there," she says softly. "You thought I could use some comfort, huh?"

"That's Pretzel," I say. "And the cat is Chips."

Angela pets Pretzel's floppy ears, and his tail wags. Chips slinks over, not intending to miss out on the lovin'.

"Did you name them?" Angela's large eyes are animated with amusement. Arousal zings through my veins. I like seeing her happy. Those eyes. *Damn.*

"No, not me. They're Natalie's pets. I took Nat to the shelter to find a dog, but these two were inseparable. Seemed mean not to take them both."

That was right after my brother died. The pet was my idea, and Emily went along with it. She was annoyed when we came back with two animals instead of one. But now, she adores them.

Angela gives some attention to Pretzel's belly, then rubs Chips between the ears for good measure. They're going to be in love with her in no time. We sit in silence for a while, and it's nice. Relaxing. But somehow energizing at the same time.

When we stop sniping at each other, it's easy to talk to her. My shitty mood from earlier has softened into almost contentment. I'm not so interested in sleep.

I keep sneaking looks over at Angela, and find her sneaking looks at me. Assessing.

Then Pretzel wanders over to the back door, and I go to let her out. Angela gets up and follows me. It's a warm night, so we stand with the door open while Pretzel does her business in the yard. Chips has disappeared. I assume she made a detour to her litter box in the laundry room.

Angela crosses her arms over her chest. "I wanted to say, I understand your concern from earlier. About the drug stuff. You don't know me, and—"

"We don't have to talk about it. I'll take your word for it." In fact, I *shouldn't* be talking about it. Chief Ross's warning from earlier echoes in my brain. I'm supposed to stay out of this investigation. Chief would probably tell me to stay away from Angela Murphy, too. No way am I going to mention she's my new roommate. That wouldn't go over well, especially with me trying for captain.

Pretzel trots back inside, and I close and lock the back door. The dog heads to her water bowl. Angela crouches beside her, petting her back. Chips appears, snuggling in between the two of them.

It's pretty damn cute.

"I just need you to know that I wouldn't bring anything

dangerous around your family," she says. "Or around any kids, for that matter. I always keep my gun locked up."

"It's all good." I sit on the tile floor beside Angela and scratch Pretzel's ears. With two humans petting her, she looks blissed out.

I nudge Angela with my elbow and smile. "You know, if you have some time off, you could hang with me and Nat tomorrow."

Her eyebrow arches. "You'd want that?"

"Sure. Why not? Natalie loves making new friends. So do I."

She sits back from me. There's a challenge in her gaze.

And it's turning me on.

In my wilder days, before my brother died and life got so damn serious, I could peacock with the best of them. I'd whip off my shirt at any excuse to show off my tats, because women fucking love my ink. They loved my facial hair, my muscles, but most of all, my cocky, flirtatious attitude.

I don't know if I'm that guy anymore. If I even *want* to be that guy.

But there is no denying this woman is stunning. With each passing minute I spend in her presence, it's more obvious how much my dick likes her.

I'm not supposed to talk about the investigation with her. But who says we'd need to talk?

"We can start with friends," I say, "and go from there."

Her eyes narrow. "Are you flirting with me right now?"

I let my gaze drag over her, admiring every curvy inch. "Would it be so bad if I was?"

"Really." The look of pure disgust sweeping over her features tells me I've screwed up. Big time. "Your girlfriend is asleep in the next room, the mother of your child, and you're coming on to a woman you just met?"

"Hold on, my *what*? She's not my—"

Angela grabs Pretzel's water dish and dumps it over my head. Cold water and dog slobber cascade over my hair, my face, trickling down my neck. "You should be *ashamed*."

I'm sitting there frozen, utterly bewildered by what just happened. Angela gets up and stomps off to Neve's bedroom.

Pretzel comes over and licks the water from my face.

I'm not even sure what I did. But Detective Murphy just made me look like an asshole. *Again*.

Maybe I should learn my lesson this time.

7

Angela

$\mathcal{I}$ stroll into West Oaks PD headquarters with my head held high, ready to take down my detractors. I get a few looks on my way in.

"Morning, detective."

They all know. Of course they do. It's been less than two days since the fire, and I've been summoned to speak to the IA investigator. They always try to complete this initial interview as soon as possible after the incident.

When I left this morning, Matteo was in the shower. I spotted a pillow and blankets on the sofa, so I'm guessing he slept out there. Wonder if he's in the doghouse with Emily. Does she know he came on to me?

Last night when we talked, I thought he might be a decent guy. Turns out, he's an even bigger asshole than I imagined.

But it's not like I would've responded to Matteo's overtures in a positive way if he were single. The man is good looking—*very* good looking—but he's nowhere near my type.

Then why can't you stop thinking about his stupidly sexy body and his obnoxiously handsome face?

Those aren't things I have the energy to deal with, and it doesn't matter anyway. I just want this IA investigation cleared up so I can go back to my normal life. No, it wasn't all that great, but I could tolerate it. I was surviving.

This mess of confusion I'm living in now? I cannot take it. Without my work to focus on, I don't feel like *me*.

At least I've got a clean suit on. I went to a dry cleaner with a one-hour turnaround.

I head down the corridor, planning to grab a cup of coffee in the break room before it's time for my meeting. I'm supposed to meet with my lawyer a few minutes before-hand to go over some things, which I'm not looking forward to.

But when I turn the corner, I come face-to-face with Detective Cassidy Diaz.

"Murphy," she says. "You're early for your interview."

"How do you—" My brain catches up. "You've been assigned to the IA investigation?"

She scrutinizes me. I don't want her to notice I'm squirming under her gaze. "Is that an issue for you?" she asks.

Cassidy Diaz is ambitious, just like I am. I haven't got a problem with that. But she has an issue with *me*. I have a year less experience than her, yet the chief picked me over her for major crimes. It was after my relationship with Alex had ended. But I'm sure Cassidy would've made a big deal out of it if she'd known.

She remained in property crimes, and in the years since, she's made it known she dislikes me. I have to wonder if Alex chose her to lead this investigation to avoid any appearance of bias.

I don't like thinking there are politics involved in my case. But of course there are. Just like Alex said. When a cop has been accused of wrongdoing, it's inevitable.

"I haven't got an issue," I say. "Just eager to get this over with."

"Since you're here, we might as well get started. Assuming your lawyer's available?"

"He should be around here somewhere. Let's do it."

We head to an interview room, and my lawyer catches up with us, looking a bit panicked and breathless at the change in schedule. I feel just as nervous, but I don't dare show it.

I settle in as Detective Diaz opens her file and glances over it.

And the seconds... tick... by.

I know exactly what she's doing. I know every single trick in her arsenal. Frankly, it's insulting. This is just supposed to be an interview, not a full-on interrogation.

I know I sound like a hypocrite. It's not an investigator's job to make the witness comfortable, especially if that witness is a potential suspect.

But that doesn't mean I'm enjoying this.

"Are you going to give me my advisement?" I say, running out of patience.

"I was just getting to it."

When a police officer is suspected of a crime, they don't get the typical Miranda warning. Detective Diaz informs me I have a right to a lawyer and to remain silent, and that I also can't be fired for refusing to speak.

Then, the real questions finally begin. "Could you tell me what happened at your apartment the night before last?" Diaz says.

It's strange to be on this side of the table. I've sat in this room so many times, but never as the target. I've never run into an IA investigation until now, despite a few use-of-force inquiries and the occasional hiccup with Alex when I've bent the rules. But now, I am clearly in their sights. I don't like how nervous it makes me.

I go through that evening, step by step. How Neve and I went shopping, then out for drinks and sushi. The sirens on the way home.

"I saw my neighbors when I arrived. I went over to talk to them."

"Was that before or after you tried to get into the building?"

My pulse picks up. "I didn't try to get into the building."

Detective Diaz stares at me. Why would she think that, unless... Someone told her. Who? One of my neighbors?

I swallow down my annoyance. If I lose my temper with her, it's just going to make this worse. "My neighbor Hazel had left her dog inside. I was able to climb up to her balcony and get the dog out. Then I climbed right down. I never went in or even tried to go in. There was a firefighter. He saw me." I decide not to volunteer any more about Matteo. She can ask me about him if she wants to. But Diaz keeps up with her accusations.

"So you weren't trying to reach your apartment?"

"Absolutely not."

"You weren't worried about what the firefighters could discover inside your unit?"

"*No*. And I still don't know what that was."

"I think she's answered the question," my lawyer says.

"My neighbors reported seeing a suspicious man in a hoodie and sunglasses shortly before the fire. I assume they told you the same thing when you interviewed them. Have you bothered to find that guy?"

"We don't even know he exists. What is it you think he did?"

"I don't know yet. I haven't got enough information. Would you like to share?"

"You keep asking me for things." She folds her hands on the table. "I think you're deflecting."

I bite the inside of my cheek. "How can I deflect when I don't know what I'm being accused of?" It's true that Diaz doesn't have to tell me anything unless—or until—I'm formally charged. But this is getting ridiculous. "I don't even know what was found in my apartment. All I've heard are rumors about some kind of contraband. But if that's true, it wasn't mine. Somebody must've planted it."

"Isn't that what they all say, Angela?" She smirks. "I'm sure we'll have more questions for you soon. For now, you can go."

OUTSIDE, my lawyer advises me to cooperate and be patient. It's the same things that Alex told me yesterday. And I don't want to hear it. "Maybe you can find out more about this 'contraband'," I say to him. "Because it's a mystery to me."

I can't understand why Cassidy Diaz is holding her cards so close to the vest. Why not just tell me it was drugs, if what Matteo said was true?

Then, like I've summoned him straight out of my thoughts, I glance down the hall and see my new roommate.

Matteo is wearing a long-sleeved T-shirt today, covering his tattoos. But it's snug enough to show off that burly physique. He spots me, and our eyes lock.

He must be here to talk to Diaz about the investigation. About *me*. A fact that he failed to mention last night when he was *hitting on me*.

Is Diaz questioning every firefighter who was at the scene, or does she have some reason to believe Matteo has particular knowledge?

Did he volunteer for this?

The man is unbelievable.

My lawyer finishes whatever he was saying—not that I was listening—and tells me he'll be in touch. The two men pass in the hall.

And now, Matteo starts walking toward me.

Oh no, I have had enough of my obnoxious, devious roomie.

"What are you doing down here unescorted?" I ask.

"They said I could use the bathroom. Lucky I saw you."

"Not lucky for me." I turn away, and he grabs my arm.

"It's not what you think."

"Really? You're not here to tell them how unstable I am?"

Honestly, I don't want to hear it. I'm done. I'm out. It doesn't matter if I stay in a hotel or my damn car. I want nothing more to do with him.

"Give me a chance to explain," he says.

"I have nothing to say to you."

"Then just listen."

I glance up and down the hall, wondering who might see us and report back to Diaz. "You're a witness against me. Right? I can't be seen talking to you."

"All right, fine."

But instead of leaving me alone, he pulls me into the nearest empty room.

"Wait—" Before I can stop him, he shuts the door. "You just locked us in here, idiot."

He frowns at the door. Then jiggles the handle.

"This is an interrogation room. They lock from the inside. Because they're supposed to keep suspects *in*."

"But you work here. You can get us out."

"Not unless I call somebody. We're trapped." We're going to look like we're colluding. Every single thing I do is going to be scrutinized. There are cameras in here too, which Diaz could switch on at any moment if she wanted to.

Plus, if I was colluding? I'd be a lot smoother about it than this.

He throws his hands outward, an exasperated gesture. "Good, then you'll have to listen to what I've got to say. I would've said it this morning, but you avoided me."

"Wasn't hard. You were showering, and I wasn't going to pop in and say goodbye. Is this about the investigation against me? Because I guarantee, you're not supposed to be talking to me about that."

"I know. That's not it."

I arch an eyebrow, waiting.

"Emily is not my girlfriend. She's my sister-in-law. We were never together. And never will be."

My indignant expression freezes in place. "But Natalie said you're her dad."

"She thinks of me that way sometimes, but she doesn't mean it literally." He rubs his eyes. "Natalie is my brother's daughter. Or was, I guess. He died."

I open my mouth, but I have no idea what to say. I was puffed up on moral superiority a moment ago, and now I've deflated. "I'm sorry."

"Me too." He nods. "But you can see now, I'm not a cheater. I would never do that. Not to Emily or anyone else."

"Okay. I should've let you explain. Before dumping a water bowl on your head."

A giggle sneaks past my lips. I was pissed off at the time, but in hindsight, it's an amusing image.

His mouth slides into a lopsided grin. "Like I should've waited to hear your side about the drug thing?"

I put my finger to my mouth, shushing him, afraid someone will overhear. "Yeah. Like that."

"No one's listening to us. Are they?" He steps in closer to me.

"They could be."

"Well, let them. I'm not going to say anything but the truth. To you or the detective who I'm supposed to meet with."

"Diaz. She's in charge of the internal investigation. You haven't met with her yet?"

"No. I doubt it'll take long to tell what I know. After the fire was out, I got radioed to come inside. I did. I saw the drugs. I passed it on to the chief, and he called in the police. That's it. End of story."

"Have you told anyone I tried to get into my apartment?"

His brow creases. "You didn't, not that I saw. When you climbed up to the balcony, I wasn't sure what you were doing at first. But then it became obvious. You were saving that fur ball."

"You mean Daisy?"

He shrugs. "I'm not into tiny dogs."

"Imagine if Hazel heard you say that."

"Don't tell her. She'll file a complaint against me."

I try to hold in my smile, just because we're discussing something serious. I'm not supposed to be enjoying this.

I bite my thumbnail, trying to think. But the man in front of me is distracting. All big and masculine and impossible to ignore. Every breath I take, I inhale the heady scent of cedar.

Focus, I tell myself.

"What did the drugs look like?" I ask. "When you saw them in my apartment?"

"Thought we weren't supposed to discuss it."

"Just answer the question." I'm tired of waiting for information. I need something to go on.

"They looked like bricks of white powder in plastic. Like heroin or cocaine. They were scattered on the floor, and it looked like a cardboard box had been overturned."

"What room?"

"The bedroom."

My bedroom. My skin creeps as I think of some weirdo planting drugs in my bedroom, and I rub my arms. "Who knocked the box over?" I ask. "One of your teammates?"

"That's the odd thing. The guys were talking about it last night at the bar. Loose lips after a few beers. And they swore the box was turned over already when they entered the room. The drugs were just there."

In plain view. I stop my pacing. "Like someone wanted the drugs to be seen. They had to be out there in the open. Obvious." It would look like the firefighters had knocked it over by accident and happened to see something incriminating. As if it was all a coincidence.

But it wasn't an accident at all.

"It was staged," I murmur. The whole thing. At some point before the fire, that box of drugs turned up in my apartment. *Unless it was planted during the chaos right after the fire started.* My brain is moving at light speed.

"Staged?" Matteo asks.

"Whoever planted the drugs must've set the fire next door intentionally. To draw the fire department. No clear signs of arson, but—"

"That would be an elaborate set-up."

"And what's the alternative? That I had a bunch of heroin in a box in my bedroom, and didn't realize it?"

He presses his lips in a tight line.

"Or do you think I'm a liar?"

"I don't think you're a liar." He stops me when I start to pace, his hand resting on my arm. "Angela, I'm just trying to get my head around this. If somebody put drugs in your apartment and set a fire, that is majorly fucked up."

"No kidding."

"They must hate you. *A lot.*"

"You think?" I deadpan.

"They've already gone to significant lengths to ruin your reputation. They could do a lot worse."

"If you're afraid they'll come to Neve's house—"

"I'm worried about *you*."

His voice is soft. Deep. Rumbly in a way I can feel in my chest. His big hand is still on my elbow, and he tugs me closer. I can feel the heat radiating from his body. See his pecs move as he breathes. I look up at him, and he peers down at me, his dark lashes heavy.

"Why? You don't even like me."

He seems surprised. But I'm not sure if it's the question that caught him off guard, or the fact that I'm right.

Suddenly, the door opens. And Alex is standing there.

His gaze misses nothing. How close we're standing, Matteo's hand on my arm. The intense way we're both breathing. "What's going on in here, Angie?"

Matteo and I break apart. Matteo's spine stiffens. He takes a subtle step, angling himself in front of me. As if he's determined to shield me.

"Thanks, *Chief*," I say. "Got stuck in here. I was about to call someone."

I'm not sure if Matteo would have recognized the police chief on his own. But either way, he gets the message and retreats a few inches, standing down. Though his fists remain clenched.

"How'd you get stuck in here, exactly?" Alex asks.

"Long story." I push Matteo past Alex through the door. *Get out of here*, I command silently, and he knows what's good for him, because he does. But he still gives Alex a hard glance on his way out.

"Was that one of the firefighters who's here to speak with Detective Diaz?" Alex asks after Matteo is gone.

"We were just clearing up a small misunderstanding."

"Please tell me you weren't tampering with a witness."

"Tampering is a strong word." I'm just making Alex angrier with my flippancy. I realize that. But it's hard to care. I'm angry too. I rub the puckered skin at my collarbone.

"*Angie*," he warns.

"I'm sorry. It won't happen again."

"I should hope not. I don't want to take sides against you. But if I have to?"

He doesn't finish because we both know the answer.

8

Matteo

"Please state your name for the record."

"Matteo De Luca."

"Your occupation?"

"Firefighter. West Oaks Fire Department, Station Two."

I'm stuck in another interview room, but this detective isn't nearly as alluring as the last one.

Detective Diaz is asking me questions about what went down at the fire. And I'm doing my best to concentrate. But my nerves are still on edge after what happened with Angela. It's one step forward, three back with her. I told her I'm worried about her, because it's true, and she threw it back in my face.

She's right that I didn't like her at first. The feeling was mutual. And I didn't like when she assumed the worst about me last night.

But I can't restrain the protective instinct that roars to the surface around that woman. At least when she's vulnerable or in danger, which seems to be every five minutes.

It's like when I saw her climbing down that scaffolding

the night of the fire. Was she making my day harder than it had to be? Yes.

Was I going to stand there and let her fall if I could step in and catch her?

Hell, no. Of course not.

She still infuriates me with that air of superiority. Yet the more she pushes me away, the more I want to prove that I can help her if she'd just let me. I'm a lot more than she thinks.

I've spent so much of my life accepting other people's expectations, and that's not enough for me anymore.

Guess that explains why I was ready to deck the chief of police just for looking at me crossways.

"Mr. De Luca?" Detective Diaz says.

I clear my throat. "Sorry, what was the question?"

"I said, did you witness Detective Murphy attempt to get access to her apartment building during the fire?"

I explain exactly what happened, as I told Angela I would. But inside, I'm wondering how Detective Diaz got that information. I don't think any of the other guys knew Angela was a detective. I didn't repeat her name to anyone except maybe Danny, and as far as I know, he hasn't been called in as a witness.

"So Detective Murphy claimed to be saving a neighbor's dog."

"I wouldn't say she *claimed* it. That was what she was doing. She got the dog, climbed down. She needed some help, and that's when I stepped in."

"Were you upset about that? Did you accuse Detective Murphy of using poor judgment? Putting people in danger?"

"I probably did. In the moment. I was a little worked up."

And now I'm being called in, expected to talk shit about her. Just because I might've been slightly antagonistic toward her that night. I don't like being used that way, regardless of how pissed I may have been at Angela in the moment.

"Excuse me," I interrupt, "but can I ask a question? Was it heroin in those packages, or what? Because it's weird that a detective would leave stuff like that out in the open for anyone to see. Right? Doesn't that seem hard to believe?"

Diaz sets down her pen. "No, Mr. De Luca. You may not ask a question."

I shrug. "Whatever. Just curious."

She rolls her eyes a little, and I know that look. It's the, *look at this meathead trying to use his brain* look. I'm never going to win any Nobel Prizes for physics, but I've got plenty of street smarts and common sense. Not to mention years of military and firefighter training.

Sometimes, though, there are benefits to being underestimated.

I think that's why, twenty minutes later, Diaz answers a call and tells me she needs to step outside. And leaves her notes there, right on the table.

Right where I can see them.

I know there are cameras watching me. But all I have to do is lean forward onto my elbows, craning my neck. She's got messy handwriting, but I can make out a lot of it even reading upside down.

See folks? De Luca isn't so dumb after all, is he?

Heroin matches the Volkov case.

I have no idea what that means, but I bet Angela would.

WHEN I GET HOME, I find Angela sitting with Emily and Natalie at the kitchen table. Natalie's coloring, and when I walk in, the two women stop talking and look at me.

"Complaining about me?" I ask.

Emily smirks. "Angela was just telling me that she thought I was your girlfriend. Ew. Like that would ever happen." She gets up and punches me lightly on the arm. I assume this means our disagreement from yesterday is over, and I'll take it. If Emily needed to vent her frustration with me to Angela for her mood to improve, I've got no problem with that.

I'm less excited to think that Angela was venting about me. I have no idea where I stand with her.

She's looking at me like she's dying to know how my interview with Diaz went. And I'm willing enough to tell her. But I figure we shouldn't discuss it in front of Emily and Nat. They don't know anything about the investigation against Angela, and I assume she'd rather keep it that way.

"I need to run some errands," Emily says. "Have you got Natalie for the rest of the day?"

I ruffle my niece's hair. "You know it. We're going to have a great time."

"Can we go to the park?" Natalie asks, not pausing in her mission to shade every curl of Moana's hair in the coloring book.

"The one by the beach? Your favorite? Of course, Natty-bear."

"Can Angela come with us?"

I look over at the woman in question. "If she wants."

"Sure," Angela says. "Thank you for the invite, Natalie." She's being all mysterious and hard to read.

I have no idea why that gets me going so much.

This will give me a chance to tell Angela about what I learned from Detective Diaz's notes. And to convince her that, even if we're not exactly friends, she can trust me. I don't screw over people who need my help.

I change into shorts and a tee, and we head out. Angela's switched into a sundress I recognize as Neve's. It looks great on her. The skimpy straps show off both her tats and her scar, which I dig. And she's put that sexy piercing back in after leaving it off this morning at the police station.

Natalie is pushing her scooter about a half block ahead of us. "Wait at the curb, Nat," I call out. I get nervous whenever she nears an intersection, but she's pretty good about stopping.

"Diaz asked about you trying to get into the building during the fire," I say. "Like you expected she would."

Angela's mouth tightens. "I didn't ask you for a rundown of what happened during your interview."

"Nah, but you wanted to."

"I got another talking to from Chief Liu. I'm trying to stay out of trouble."

"Yeah, what's the deal with your chief anyway? He seemed jealous when he found us together. Why is that?"

"I shouldn't be telling you this," she murmurs. But she doesn't follow her own advice. "He's my ex. Ancient history. But we're still friends. Most of all, though, he's my boss. I can't be accused of tampering with a witness. I shouldn't have been asking you those questions earlier."

I fight back a rush of annoyance at the image of her and the police chief together. Is that her type? Impressive politicians who wear expensive suits?

"Then blame me," I say. "Diaz left the room, and I looked at her notes. Don't you wanna know what they said?"

Angela bites her lip. Huffs. She's struggling over this. Then finally, she shakes her head. "I really don't get why you're trying to help me. Don't you have enough problems of your own?"

So she and Emily *were* talking about me.

"Maybe I like your problems better."

"That's idiotic."

"Jeez, can you give me a sliver of credit here? I believe

you're innocent, and I don't think it's right for someone to mess with you like this."

"I do appreciate the sentiment. But you need to get over it. I don't need your help."

"Oh really?"

"Really. I'm not dragging you into this. You've done enough."

"Who said you're dragging me? You don't think I'm a big boy? I can't make decisions for myself?"

We catch up to Natalie and cross the boulevard, entering the path that runs along the beach. The playground equipment is visible up ahead, and Natalie speeds toward it.

Angela hasn't answered. As if she thinks refusing to talk about this means it's over. Like it's her choice to make.

"Ms. Murphy," I say lightly, "you seem to think you're the alpha around here. Nobody tells me when I've had enough. Nobody but me."

Her eyebrows slowly raise, and her mouth drops open. Like she doesn't know what to say to that.

"Detective Diaz had written something in her notes about the name Volkov," I go on. "That the heroin matched the Volkov case."

Angela's eyes flash.

"Clearly that name means something to you."

It takes her a moment to speak again. "I was the lead detective on the case about a year and a half ago. My first murder investigation after I returned to work from being shot. But I think of it as the Rossi case, not Volkov. That was the victim's name. Stefanie Rossi."

"What happened to her?"

She exhales.

"Stefanie went to my high school. West Oaks Prep. Over a decade after I did, but still. It's a private school, and Stefanie won a scholarship. She should've had a bright future. Then she got mixed up with Luke Volkov. Older guy, charming. Not every woman who likes older men has daddy issues. But Stefanie? She did."

"Her dad wasn't around?"

Angela nods thoughtfully. "And her mother was absentee. Volkov was exactly the type of guy her family should've warned her away from. A drug dealer, and that was bad enough. But he also had ties to the Bratva, Russian mafia. Stefanie was with him for years. He got her into prostitution."

"That's rough. What happened to her?"

"When she was twenty-two, she decided she wanted to leave Volkov. She'd met someone else, a guy who promised her a different future. But Volkov wasn't having that. So he gave her an overdose of heroin laced with fentanyl. Killed her."

I curse under my breath.

Natalie shouts for us to watch her cross the monkey bars. I wave at her, getting closer in case she needs a quick rescue. Then I glance back. Angela is still standing frozen behind me, her expression hard.

"Why would the heroin found in your apartment have ties to that case?" I ask.

"I don't know."

"Really? Or you just don't want to share?"

"I don't know. Truly. But thanks for telling me."

"Anytime."

I want to ask more questions. Find out why she's got that haunted look on her face. But Angela jumps onto the swing set with Natalie instead and paints a smile over her features.

I can't stop noticing other details of her. The flexing of her small, lean muscles. The rise and fall of her breasts with every pump of her legs on the swing. Around Natalie, Angela's feigned smile turns real, lighting up her eyes.

What else are you keeping hidden? I ask silently.

When we get home, I tell Natalie to go change her sandy clothes in the bathroom. Angela lingers in the kitchen, elbows on the counter.

"Emily told me why she and Natalie are staying with you," Angela says. "It's kind of you to take care of them."

"Glad somebody thinks so."

"You shouldn't have to sleep on the couch because of me."

"Are you offering another arrangement?"

I'm kidding, but she sputters and coughs. "*No*, I meant I can find another place. Or a hotel."

"Not necessary. It might not be so bad after all, having you here."

A hint of a smile plays at her lips.

Angela said I have enough problems of my own, and I guess I do. But today is the first time in a while that I haven't felt like I was suffocating. The only thing that's changed is her. It was the same last night, when I came home in a terrible mood and it turned around when we got to talking. That conversation went off the rails because of a misunderstanding. But that's beside the point.

I can't seem to stay away from her, and I no longer see the point in trying.

That's why I open my mouth and say the first thing that comes to mind.

"My birthday is next weekend, and I have the day off. I'm getting together with some people to celebrate. Or commiserate, maybe. It's no big deal. But you should come."

"Why should I do that?"

"Because you have nothing better to do."

She flips me off, and I laugh.

"And it'll be fun," I add. "You're not against fun, are you?"

"Not in theory. But I shouldn't draw attention to the fact that I'm living here."

"Because of the investigation? You can't live your life in hiding."

"Can't I?"

I really can't tell if she's kidding.

"I'm not cowering in *fear*, all right?" she adds defensively. "Whoever's targeting me is trying to destroy my reputation, not harm me physically. If I thought there was real danger, I'd leave here right away rather than put Emily or Natalie at risk. But I still don't want them drawn into this mess."

"How about this? If the rest of the week is quiet, you should come out. Live your life. Fuck anybody who has a problem with that."

"Maybe."

"Come on. Just say yes."

Without answering, she spins and walks toward her room, hips swaying. I watch her as I shake my head and grin.

She's so saying yes.

9

Angela

*C*rime scene tape flutters at the entrance to my apartment building.

Somehow, I've found myself parked across the street. I know how bad an idea this is. But maybe I just need to take stock of my life right now.

It's been a solid week since the fire. And today is Matteo's birthday. The past several days, I've gone back and forth on accepting his invitation. I even mentioned it to Neve, who encouraged me to say yes. *Matteo's birthday is the day before mine. With the time zones, it'll be like you're celebrating with me!* Not entirely accurate, because by tonight, it will only be morning in Italy. But who knows, maybe Neve will start her birthday party early.

But since my frustrating IA interview with Cassidy Diaz and the mysterious revelation about ties to the Volkov case, I've gone into full hermit mode. I've burrowed under the covers of Neve's bed and hidden from the world.

From Matteo especially. Which isn't too difficult given how much that man works.

Despite our differences, he's a decent guy. I had a great

time with him and Natalie at the park a few days ago. But that's just it. He's got a recklessly heroic streak. What the heck was he thinking, spying on Cassidy's notes? I can't be responsible for messing things up for him with his job or whatever else just because he can't resist a woman in distress. Forget the fact that I *hate* being in distress.

I'm just not good at accepting the kind of help that Matteo wants to give me.

That's how I found myself perusing that stupid hookup app this morning. Not because I want to meet up with a stranger, but to get Matteo *out of my head*. And that was the last straw for me. If I had spent all day staring at dick pics, I wouldn't have been able to face myself in the mirror.

I had to get out of Neve's house. Do *something*.

Then I heard a rumor—from one of my friends on patrol —that there was a search warrant being executed today. On *my* apartment. I have no idea what kind of shoddy investigation Cassidy is running, because she should've wrapped up any searches days ago. It's like she *wants* the evidence in my apartment to be tampered with.

But that's how I wound up in my car, driving down familiar streets.

I shouldn't have come.

And yet, here I am. Just sitting in my car. Not like a guilty person returning to a crime scene. Not like *that* at all.

According to my neighbors, they've been able to get in to gather belongings, but the fire caused some sort of damage to the plumbing. They haven't been allowed to move back in yet, which is awful. But I haven't been inside my apartment once.

I want to, though. I want to see if my stuff is salvageable. And I'm grasping for any scraps of information. Some sign of who could've planted the drugs there.

Ugh, what am I doing? This is a terrible idea. I need to get out of here before Cassidy Diaz and her minions show up.

Then I see movement over by the apartment building. I have to blink a few times for my brain to adjust to what I'm seeing.

Someone just stepped out of a set of balcony doors on the third floor. And he's dressed in a hoodie with dark sunglasses.

He climbs over the railing and onto the repair scaffolding, just like I did a week ago when I was carrying down Hazel's Pomeranian.

Could this be the same guy who was spotted before the fire?

Did he have something to do with that heroin planted in my apartment?

The whole idea is farfetched. But I want to talk to Hoodie Guy out there. I want to know what he was doing sneaking around the third floor. *My floor.* If he's a fellow resident, then he can explain why he's in a building that's still closed off pending repairs.

Hands shaking, I use my keys to unlock my glove box and pull out my handgun and holster. Then I'm out of the car, pulling the holster into place as I dash across the parking lot. My footfalls are silent.

The guy makes a beeline for the side of the building. Like he's trying not to be seen. But he hasn't spotted me, either. I try to close the distance as fast as I can.

Ideally, I would call for back up. I wouldn't be here alone. But I'm not supposed to be here anyway, and there's no time to call anyone. I'll lose him.

When I'm just a few feet away, I bark, "West Oaks PD. Hands where I can see them."

Without a single glance at me, the guy sprints away.

Dammit.

I hate when they do this. Now I've got to catch him.

I race after him. The guy is *fast*. I'm in good shape, but he's leaping over recycling bins like this is parkour.

He cuts through an alley between my building and the next, and I follow. He knocks a trash can in my way, and garbage spills across my path. My shoes squish through days-old food containers and crunch through broken glass. *Gross*. These are the white sneakers that I never wear anywhere except the gym.

This guy is *really* starting to piss me off.

I need to work smarter, not harder.

Hoodie Guy rounds the corner of the next-door building. It's another apartment complex. I'll bet he's heading back to the main boulevard, hoping to lose me amidst the late-afternoon traffic.

In my head, I visualize where he's probably going. Two parts instinct and logic, one part luck.

I race to a side entrance for the next building and wrench it open. My shoes pound through the lobby. I fly out of the front doors onto the pavement, ready to cut him off.

But instead of the guy in the hoodie, I almost collide with a blond in a patrol uniform.

"*Whoa*," he says, arms out to ward me off. "Slow down!"

It's Officer Evans, the brand new patrol officer.

"Evans." I'm panting, trying to catch my breath. "What're you doing here?"

He points at his squad car, which is parked on the curb. Several more units are just pulling up. "We're executing a search warrant. What are *you* doing here?" He squints at me, like he knows I shouldn't be in this vicinity, but I'm not about to take attitude from a baby cop.

"There was a man. He was in my apartment building." I gesture at it. We're standing on the sidewalk that crosses in front of both my building and the one I just cut through. "He was running. Refused to stop when I identified myself."

"Shit, really?" Evans's head swivels like he's checking for threats. His chest lifts, and he takes a shaky breath. "I didn't see anyone. Maybe he went a different way?"

My eyes are still scanning the street, hoping for a sign of a hoodie. But I think the guy's gone. Dang. I made a gamble, and I lost.

"The search warrant is for my apartment?" I ask.

His skin was already pink, but now it's going crimson. "Uh. I can't talk about that."

Evans must be on Cassidy's internal investigation team. He was at the scene of the fire, too. In fact, he saw me save Hazel's dog. Did *he* report to Cassidy that I tried to get into the building?

An unmarked pulls up, and a detective from property crimes steps out. Cassidy Diaz. Her eyes narrow when she sees me. She heads over, face stormy as a thundercloud, and I hold up my finger.

I take out my phone and call Alex. "Chief? It's me." When I try to explain, he's nowhere near happy.

"Detective Murphy," he says. No more *Angie*. "I told you to stay away from the investigation."

"I wasn't trying to get involved. I saw some shady guy sneaking out of my building."

"You shouldn't have been there in the first place. Detective Diaz is in charge now. Not me, and certainly not you. *You* are on leave. Go to your rock climbing gym. Go to the spa. Hell, send me the bills. But stop pushing your way into this investigation. Are you hearing me?"

Diaz and Evans watch from a few yards away.

I say, "Yes, sir."

But I've got plenty of fight left in me. I'm nowhere near finished. I'm going to figure this out.

Even if it means going it alone.

10

Matteo

*M*y birthday officially sucks.

I'm sitting at the bar with Danny, my friends all around, laughing and toasting. And I'm pissed. Because I'm thirty-six, and that sounds so much older than thirty-five.

Also, because Angela hasn't shown.

"Darts?" Danny asks me. "Or a round of pool? Come on, you can't sit there on your ass on your birthday. You promised Fun Matteo was coming tonight."

"I don't think I promised that."

True, Angela never said for sure she'd come. I haven't seen her much since I asked, and she didn't give me a definitive answer. But I thought that was a formality. I thought something had changed with us.

Guess I was wrong.

I can't even explain why that bugs me so much. We don't really like each other. But this still feels like a rejection. And it stings.

"Man, you've been such a buzzkill this week," Danny says. "Buc and Chief Ross aren't here. You're allowed to let loose without killing your chances for that promotion that you *supposedly* want."

"I do want it."

My friend harrumphs. "You should be a front-runner for leadership, with that stick that's working its way up your ass."

Danny and some other guys head over to the dart board. I remain on my bar stool, sipping the pale ale they bought me.

Alone.

On my birthday.

I glance up at the mirror above the bar, wondering who the hell this guy is in my chair.

I just can't figure out where my head is at these days.

The past several have been more chaotic than usual, even setting aside my roommate drama. I pulled extra shifts bartending nearly every night off, had repair work to do at several of Neve's rentals. Plus two more twenty-four-hour shifts at Station Two.

Whenever I had a free moment in between all that, I hung out with Natalie or walked Pretzel or hit the gym. Angela remained in her bedroom, as if she's grown roots in there like one of Neve's plants.

I see Emily approach behind me in the mirror. She grabs my shoulder, and I feign surprise.

"Happy birthday!" she squeals. "Having fun yet?"

"Me? Always."

Emily sticks her lower lip out, an acknowledgment of the lie behind my statement. She's not usually this jubilant. I credit the martini in her hand. I'm guessing there was some pre-partying as well. "Girls' night?" I ask.

"*Ladies'* night. Matteo, this is my friend Harper. She's the new art teacher at my school."

I greet the pretty redhead beside Emily. I'm nervous it's

some kind of setup until I spot the simple wedding band on her ring finger.

"I've heard a lot about you," Harper says. "Especially from your niece."

Emily snickers. "Natalie's hanging out with Harper's step-kids tonight."

"My husband Jake offered to babysit so we could have a night out," Harper explains.

My sister-in-law shimmies, arms up in the air, almost spilling her drink. "We haven't had that many chances to celebrate lately. Didn't want to pass this up."

The truth of her statement strums against my heart. I take a sip of my beer. "Did you see Angela before you left home?" I ask. Totally nonchalant.

"I did. She seemed upset this afternoon when she got back to the house. I invited her to come along tonight, but she said she shouldn't be seen in public with WOFD fire-fighters at the moment. For, you know, *reasons.*"

I don't like hearing she was upset. But I guess she and Emily have been talking more while I've been away from the house. "She told you about the investigation against her?"

Emily nods. "She's pretty freaked out, though she's trying to hide it. But hiding your pain and fear happens to be my specialty, so... yeah, I get it." She downs her martini and sets the glass on the bar counter.

Harper looks confused. "What investigation?"

"Matteo's new roommate is a West Oaks PD detective," Emily explains, before I can stop her.

Harper's eyes widen. "Angela? Angela *Murphy*?"

"We're supposed to be keeping quiet about it," I say.

Harper holds a finger up to her lips, then lowers her voice. "I'm just surprised. She's a friend of my husband's, and I hadn't heard a word about Detective Murphy having issues. She helped us out in the past. Long story, but she's a kickass lady."

"No kidding," I say. "Prickly though."

Harper laughs, though her frown returns as she thinks. "I'll have to reach out. I'm sorry to hear she's got troubles."

"Don't we all," I mutter into my beer. "Good luck, because Angela hates people trying to help her."

Harper and Emily share a look. Emily whispers something to her, and Harper goes to the far end of the bar to order another drink.

Emily leans her elbow against the counter, crowding me. "Okay, what's your deal with Angela? You're acting weird."

"You should know. You've been talking to her about me."

"Hardly. I know you clashed a little with her, but she hasn't said a thing against you since then."

There's a flicker of warmth in my chest. I guess it's the beer starting to work on my mood.

"This is as good a moment as any to give you your present," Emily says. "Natalie and I are going to stay at Harper's place. You can sleep in your own bed instead of the couch."

"That sounds nice. My back will thank you."

She doesn't seem to like my muted reaction, because she heaves a sigh. "Matteo, please don't stress and worry tonight. I need this break too. Okay? I'm so tired of fighting and struggling and just..." She swallows. "Please have some fun. Be the old Matteo. Even if it's just for me."

She hugs me, then wanders over to Harper, who hands her a fresh martini.

My bedroom to myself tonight. It's a nice gift. Maybe nicer than Emily realizes.

We don't discuss our respective sex lives. Or lack of sex lives. But I can't remember the last time I brought someone home. Even when I could have. My libido hasn't been the same since Brent died.

But my blood's been pumping hotter the last few days. My dick's been perking up, showing interest in getting a workout.

It might be slightly awkward with Angela in the other room. But she's just my roommate. A temporary one, at that. I need to get her off my mind. Find somebody else to take my attention, at least for tonight.

Getting laid might just be the birthday present I need.

After a glance around the bar—nah, no prospects—I open up my hookup app and start swiping. But everyone I see is just too... something. And not enough of something else.

My thumb swipes again, and I almost choke on my beer.

This profile pic is zoomed-in so you can't see the top half of the person's face. Not unusual. But she's got a tiny gold piercing above her upper lip. Like a beauty mark.

It couldn't be. Could it?

She's got Angela's narrow waist, round hips. This picture doesn't show her tattoos, but this sure looks a hell of a lot like her.

There's a funny feeling spinning out through my limbs. It makes my head fuzzy. My skin heats all over my body. I haven't had nearly enough alcohol to explain this reaction.

My eyes move down the profile. It says a few vague things about her. Thirty-two years old. West Oaks native. *I like Hitchcock movies, red wine, and creamy desserts.* Does she know how sexual that sounds? She's probably been getting a lot of dick pics from that line.

That thought makes the temperature in my body skyrocket.

It says she's active right now. Fuck. Is she looking for a guy to hook up with? Is she perusing said dick pics like a fucking takeout menu?

I read the last bit of her profile. *Looking for a mature guy for fun and satisfaction with mutual respect and no other expectations.*

Mature? What does mature mean? A much older, successful man like the police chief? Does it mean, *Not you, Matteo?*

I'm older. And I'm mature, damn it. I'm responsible. I went out of my way to help her, even though she hates me, and I'm not her biggest fan.

I realize I'm trembling a little. My heart's thumping, and so are my balls. Equal parts indignation and arousal. And something that's a whole lot like jealousy.

I invite her to my birthday, and she sits at home swiping for other dudes to hook up with? In the house where I'm supposed to sleep tonight?

Oh, hell no. That's not going to fly.

IN THE LYFT on my way home, I try to reason with myself. I'll be cool about this. Just let her know I'm not comfortable with some random dude showing up at my house to bang her. She'll have to go out for that.

Except I don't want her to go out for that.

By the time I walk up to my house, I'm coming in hot.

I storm inside, letting the door slam on my way in. I go straight to her room and rap on the door.

The door cracks open, and Angela's large eyes peek out.

"I know what you're doing in there," I say.

Those beautiful eyes narrow. "Are you drunk?"

"A few beers does not equal drunk." I nudge the door, and she steps back, letting me widen the gap. "Let's see your phone," I demand.

"What? *No.*"

She hides it behind her back. So I hold up mine. I've got

her profile all cued up, because I may have been studying it on the ride home. Just for informational purposes.

"This you?"

She shrugs. "I'm not admitting to anything. What is this, a bust? I'm the cop, not you."

"Ha ha. Very funny. But I know for a fact you were just trawling for a hookup. Creamy desserts and Hitchcock? *Really?*"

She scowls. "Shut up. You can go now." She tries to push me out the door, but I don't budge. It's like a cute little squirrel trying to uproot a tree.

"Thought I'd make sure you knew all your options. Call it a benefit of being roommates."

I switch the screen to my own profile pic. It's me shirtless, all my best assets on display. Most of my assets, anyway. I keep the below-the-belt action in-person only.

This was *not* my plan when I walked in here. But I guess the old Matteo has shown up tonight after all. "This guy's looking for a good time. No strings attached. Just hot, dirty fun."

And from the way her eyes bug, I suspect she's not opposed to what she sees.

"Well, what do you say?" I ask. "Do you swipe left? Or swipe right?"

11

Angela

I stare at the phone in Matteo's hand. More specifically, at the photo there.

Holy... wow.

I'm still counting the abs, because there's a lot of them. And tattoos, golden skin, a broad chest that a girl could snuggle up to and use as a pillow...

"Like what you see?" he asks smugly.

"Uh." My mouth has gone dry. Probably because it's hanging open like one of those old cartoons when the alley cat sees a sexy female.

I didn't even realize the hookup app was open on my phone. I've been poking around online, my poor excuse for "research" since all my usual investigative resources are off-limits.

And after what happened at my apartment earlier, chasing the mysterious guy in the hoodie, I was in no mood to party at some bar.

But now that Matteo's right here in front of me, all woodsy-smelling and indignant, it's impossible to focus on anything else.

I school my features, hoping to be less obvious. "The view's not bad, I guess."

"Not bad? It's better in person."

He whips off his shirt, inked muscles flexing as he tosses the cotton to the ground. He's in low-slung jeans, a Calvin logo waistband showing beneath.

And he's right. This view is better in person.

It's spectacular.

I for sure never saw Matteo's profile on the app, because that stunning torso would've caught my attention. I'm not saying I would've hit him up. But there would've been a sustained amount of ogling.

Exactly like what I'm doing now.

I'm face to chest with a torso that could've been cut from honey-colored stone. My eyes don't know where to focus. The veined, bulging muscles, the intricate tats. The dusting of dark hair. In addition to the colorful designs on his arms, the words *Semper Fidelis* are marked in cursive on his upper left pec.

And the *scent* of him, God. It's more intensely smoky than ever. Musky and manly. I swear I can feel heat rising from his skin in waves. If I had my glasses on, they'd be steaming.

My gaze traces the V leading into the waistband of his jeans, and moves back up to spot his nipples hardening. A fevered flush burns me from the inside out.

I want. Those are the barely coherent thoughts that rise to the surface of my desire-addled mind. *I want. I want.*

A smirk spreads his mouth wide. Like he can see straight into my head.

"You're not my type." But the tone of my voice says that's a lie. I sound all breathy and desperate. Not like myself.

I'm used to being the one desired. The one *in control.*

And my control is barely hanging on.

"Your body thinks I'm your type." He advances slowly, and I back up until my legs hit the edge of the mattress. "Tell me your panties aren't damp right now."

I swallow. "They're not."

He leans over and whispers in my ear. "Liar. I bet they're *soaking*." His beard brushes my cheek oh so faintly. A breath of a touch. But I gasp in response.

"If you don't want my help with the investigation against you, fine," he says. "But I could help you in other ways. You want something. So do I. *Fun and satisfaction with no expectations.*"

He's using the words from my profile. I didn't even write those. It was Neve.

Do something different, she said that night. *Get back on that horse.*

A horse with a really big dick.

And now, my eyes are shifting downward before the rest of my brain can stop them.

From the shape of that bulge, I'd say it is *very* big. I hold back my whimper.

Matteo gently takes my hand. He lifts it up, his fingers delicate against mine, though his skin is rough. He presses a kiss to the back of my hand. In contrast to his state of undress and his visible erection, the move is almost gentlemanly.

He lets go, but instead of withdrawing my hand, I let it rest on the warm, firm curve of his shoulder. I drag my fingers down to his left pec, over the *Semper Fidelis* tattoo, pausing at his hard nipple to give it a tug. He groans.

And that's when the dam *breaks*.

We launch ourselves at each other.

His hands move to my face, and his mouth slants over mine. I grab hold of his denim-clad ass cheeks and squeeze his rock-hard glutes. His tongue lashes over my lips, seeking entrance, and I open up like he just found the secret password. His hot tongue fills my mouth.

My knees go weak. I nearly fall backward onto the bed, but Matteo's arm circles my waist, holding me to his washboard abs. He sucks my lower lip, giving it a nip between his teeth, then sucking it again.

My brain has lost all semblance of rationality. This is just instinct and desire and sensation.

Matteo breaks our kiss with a small pop of released suction. "Pace yourself, angel," he says. "We've got all night. If you want it."

A shiver passes through me, and he grins wickedly when he sees it.

"You make me feel crazy," I murmur.

"Then don't fight it. Let's be crazy together."

His tongue pushes into my mouth again. He explores with confident strokes, and it feels like he's laying claim to new territory. My tongue responds, dancing with his, and he gives me another of those guttural groans.

Matteo's hands cup my behind and lift me up, tossing me slightly in his palms. I grasp him around the neck and try not to break our kiss as my legs clamp down on his hips.

None of the men I've been with have been as strong as Matteo. There's latent power coiled up in his huge body, yet the way he's touching me is the perfect balance of roughness and ease. Like he's got this, got *me*, and I'm in very good hands.

He kneels on the bed, crawling us both toward the center of it while I cling to him like a greedy little koala, sucking on his tongue.

He lays me down and presses his hard body onto me. His kisses shift to my ear, tugging the lobe between his teeth. My moan is breathy and totally out of my control.

"You like that, don't you? My mouth on you."

"Mmmm."

"You want it all over you?"

"*Yes.*"

"We'll get there."

With every move of our lips against each other, we somehow draw even closer. Until my legs and arms are tangled up with his. There's a pulse of need between my legs. My fingers wind into his hair and grip the strands tight.

"I'm going to get you naked now, angel. I can't wait to see how beautiful you are."

"Wait," I blurt, and he stops, eyes fixed on me.

This is like a rush headlong off a cliff. Overwhelming and exhilarating, but now reality is looming, and it's all a little too much for me.

He props up onto his hands. "You want to stop?"

"No. Don't stop." I grab onto his neck, keeping him from pulling away further. But I need to get back a little bit of my control. My veins are flooded with adrenaline, and I'm starting to shake.

I don't want to stop. But I'm scared. Not scared of him, but of this free-fall feeling.

Now that we've slowed down, I'm remembering the reasons I shouldn't do this. He's my roommate for the next few weeks. I don't want things to get awkward. In fact, I don't want my best friend to know about this at all.

Then there's the fact that he's a witness against me in the internal investigation.

And we don't even get along. You don't like him. He doesn't like you. Remember?

"Tell me what you're thinking." He lowers his head and kisses my neck. I close my eyes. It feels so good. Scary good.

"Can I be on top of you for a while?" I ask.

He looks down at me, grin widening. "Of course, angel.

Show me what you've got." Matteo flips onto his back. The mattress bounces under his weight. I climb onto him, straddling his middle. I love how he feels between my thighs. Solid. The bulge in his jeans nudges my ass, but he doesn't try to rut against me or make any other move to take his cock out.

His hands caress my thighs, eyes sweeping hungrily over me. The pulse at his neck is jumping. "What do you want?"

I grip the bottom of my cropped tee and pull it off. I'm wearing the red satin bra and panties Neve bought last week. Matteo's lips purse, eyes zeroing in on my chest.

"So pretty."

His fingers hook the waistband of my knit shorts, and he gives me a questioning look. I nod. He pushes down the fabric, leaving my panties in place. I wiggle around so he can get my shorts off.

Then I'm sitting on top of him in my bra and panties, my palms resting on his abs.

"Damn, you are smoking hot," he says. "Five-alarm fire, right here. Careful or the smoke alarms will go off."

I roll my eyes. "Shut up. You're so ridiculous."

"I am. I have a tendency to run my mouth when I'm turned on." He holds my chin. "But I mean every word. You are extremely sexy. I want to taste and touch every inch of that body."

His praise sets off a glow of pleasure in my chest.

His fingers trace up my thighs. Then both of his thumbs run beneath the edge of my panties at the crotch. I tip my head back and moan.

His hand dips further under the damp scrap of satin. His thick fingers stroke and tease, and I fall forward, shocked by the groan that falls from my lips.

"Like when I play with your pussy?"

My eyes snap open at his blunt wording. He grins like he's pleased with himself. "That's what I'm doing, isn't it? It's okay to say it."

"I know that." I'm not a prude. I'm just not used to my partners being so... literal.

But second by second, my self-consciousness fades as Matteo strokes and plays with me. My hips rock against his hand.

"What do you want next, angel?" I try to move his hand to hit me in just the right spot, but he won't do it. "Nope, you have to say it. Tell me where to touch you."

I grumble at him, then give in. "My clit. Please."

His talented fingers massage my clit, slipping and sliding even more inside the crotch of my panties. I keep rocking, moaning. It feels so incredibly good.

Then a thick digit pushes inside of me, followed by another. I gasp, my nails digging into his abs.

"Like when I finger-fuck you?" he whispers.

Heat floods my body. I can barely manage to nod.

"Do you like what I'm doing? Yes or no."

"I like it," I grind out.

"You like me doing what?"

"I like... your fingers. In me. In my pussy." Saying those words rockets my arousal to a new level. I had no idea how hot it would make me to say that aloud.

It's insane how this feels. Pleasure is blooming at my core and racing up and down my limbs.

"Now, beg me to make you come, angel. Say it."

I don't even get the words past my lips. I cry out, my orgasm ripping through me. I ride his hand through it, shaking and convulsing and gasping uncontrollably. When it's over, I'm barely sitting upright.

Matteo reaches down between us and undoes his fly. He

shoves his jeans and briefs down past his hips. His hard length pops out, slapping onto his stomach.

His thumb traces the vein on the underside, his other hand brushing my lips. "You want to suck my cock, angel?"

I nod.

"Then get down here on my dick."

I shiver with an orgasmic aftershock at his filthy bluntness. No man has ever spoken to me the way he's doing. In that rough, demanding, vulgar way.

I don't even know what's happening right now. This is already the most intense sexual experience I've ever had. But once again, I don't hesitate, even though going down on men isn't usually my favorite thing. With Matteo, I'm shocked how desperate I am for this. I want my lips around him, tongue pressed to his hot skin. I want to feel and hear how much he's enjoying it.

I move down his gorgeous body to bring my mouth to his crotch. My lips press to his tip. It's shiny and smooth, the skin deep pink.

I sweep my tongue around his glans, tasting his salty skin and breathing in the musky scent of him, before I suck the blunt head into my mouth.

"Just like that," he babbles.

My hands tug his jeans down further and then land on his muscular thighs, his leg hair tickling my palms. I nurse his tip for a while, wrapping my hand around his base. When I taste a pulse of salty precome on my tongue, I slide his hot length further into my mouth. And Matteo keeps up his naughty ramblings.

"You look so beautiful sucking my cock, angel. You take me so well. Feast on my dick like it's your last fucking meal."

I pull off. "The things you say." My heart's racing so fast that I'm lightheaded.

He grins. "I thought you were enjoying me talking dirty. You don't like it?"

"I didn't say that." I pump his cock in my fist. My head lowers, and I run my tongue along his slit.

"Damn, that feels good. But wait a sec." He caresses my cheek with his thumb until I pull off of him again and meet his gaze. His smirk is gone. "Angela, in all seriousness. If you're not feeling the dirty talk, I'll stop. I don't wanna do a single thing you don't like."

Somehow, this show of concern after his filthy words just makes my heart beat faster. What we're doing is thrilling, but I feel safe. And the part of me that was still holding back lets go a little more.

"I like it," I murmur, unable to get my voice over a whisper. But he grins.

"Good, because unless you gag me, I'm going to keep talking. And bondage isn't my thing." He looks thoughtful. "Unless I'm the one tying you up. I could dig that. You'd look incredible spread out on this bed. Like one of those fancy, ten-course menus that's more expensive than a car."

I roll my eyes and laugh. This man truly is ridiculous.

"Now get back to it," he says. "I want to see those pretty lips stretched around my prick. If anyone's going to be gagging, it should be you."

My face floods with heat again. "Your mouth is shameless, you know that?"

I decide to tease him instead, just to prove I don't have to take his orders. Even though, at this moment, I want to. I want him to keep saying filthy things. It's not something I ever expected to get off on.

Guess I've been missing out. Who knew?

I trace my tongue up and down the underside of his shaft, looking up coyly at him. His groans and whimpers and lusty facial expressions are my reward. "I'm going to be dreaming about that tongue," he says. "Taste me. Get me all wet."

I take him fully into my mouth. Matteo thrusts upwards, finding a rhythm while I bob up and down. I love the noises he makes, the naughty words spilling from his lips.

He's getting close. His cock swells, the heat and the slide of him against my tongue all so vivid that it overwhelms me. I can't believe how much I love it.

"I'm coming, angel. Suck it out of me."

I whimper as another shiver cascades through my body. He explodes into my mouth, pulse after pulse of hot creamy release coating my tongue. I moan through it like I can feel his pleasure inside my own body.

As soon as he's finished, I crawl up him. I'm burning up all over from wicked, unfettered desire. "Touch me," I say. "Please."

His hand moves between my legs, pushing the panties aside once again to stroke my clit. "Can I go down on you?" he asks. "I want to taste you when you go off again."

But he doesn't get the chance. I'm already reaching my second climax after a few seconds of his fingers on me. He pushes his tongue into my mouth, kissing me hungrily as I cry out against his lips.

After, I go limp and slump onto his chest.

Matteo draws circles on the skin of my back. "We're going to have fun together, aren't we?"

He wraps me up in his arms, and it's so warm and comfortable. I curl up against his side, crashing into sleep.

～

IN THE MORNING, I wake up clinging to Matteo like an octopus. He's snoring lightly, his face peaceful against the pillow.

His body makes hills and valleys under the blanket. I lift the corner and peek beneath. He must've kicked his jeans off, but his briefs are still pulled down below his ass, revealing his thick, toned butt cheeks. I guess he crashed out as hard as I did.

It should look silly, but it's Matteo, so of course it's one of the sexiest sights I've ever beheld. I'm tempted to bend down and sink my teeth into that muscle. Which is an impulse I have never had before.

Last night... I can't believe the things I said. And did. I was desperate for his cock and fingers and whatever he'd give me. And I *liked it*. Maybe too much.

I'm not going to judge what other people prefer in bed. But after almost two years in my celibate hermit shell, that was a lot for me. Being so *exposed* to him.

I have no idea what else this man could get me to do.

I shouldn't let it happen again. I really shouldn't. It's the kind of thing I could get addicted to, whether it's good for me or not.

Matteo grunts and rolls over, and the view gets even more enticing. My eyes greedily study him, and I notice a scar a few inches below his belly button. I didn't see it last night, but my focus *may* have been elsewhere.

My focus was on his giant, erect cock. That's what I'm saying.

I'm about to look closer at the scar. Then voices startle me, and my hand slips, dropping the blanket. Emily and Natalie must be home. Matteo shifts, his heavy arm draping across my bare stomach.

Oh, shit. I don't think we locked the bedroom door.

I push Matteo's arm off me and scramble out of bed. I can't let his family find us together like this. Sticky and half naked. The thought is mortifying.

I jump up and throw Neve's silk kimono over my underwear. Somehow, I have to get Matteo out of here without them knowing.

There's a small knock at the door.

"Angela?" Natalie says. "Are you awake?"

12

Matteo

a puffy cloud slams into my head, jogging me out of
sleep.

Wait. That was a pillow. It smells like Angela. I think she
just tried to smother me with it.

"Hi," Natalie says from somewhere nearby. "What are you
doing?"

I peek out from beneath the pillow. Angela's blocking the
doorway, her back to me as she looks out at my niece.

"I'm not doing anything," she says to Natalie.

Ha, I think. *We both know what we've been doing.*

"Have you fed Pretzel and Chips yet this morning?"
Angela asks. "I'll bet they're hungry." She sneaks out of the
room, closing the door quickly behind her.

She's probably afraid Natalie will see me in here. I'd just
tell her we were having a little sleepover. Natalie would never
know the difference.

Doubt Emily would approve, though.

I push the pillow behind my head and yawn. It's morning,
apparently. I kick away the blankets and realize my briefs are

pushed down to my thighs, which is not the most scandalous state of undress I've ever found myself in.

But last night? That was blow-the-roof-off hot. I loved watching Angela grow more and more eager under my hands. I don't think I've ever been with a woman who's so responsive to me.

And so different in bed from how she is at other times, when she seems to be fighting everyone and everything, including herself. We didn't even go very far yet.

I can't wait to do it again.

My cock plumps at the thought, and I tug my briefs up. *Later*, I tell it.

Voices come from the living room. Natalie's telling Angela about playing with her friends. Harper's stepkids, I'm guessing. Since that's where Emily and Nat spent last night.

And there's Emily's voice, too. I catch the word *Bakersfield*, and my ears perk up.

"I've decided to take Natalie to Bakersfield for a few days," Emily is saying.

Wait, *what*?

Emily's parents live in Bakersfield. But she's not close to them at all. They never liked Brent, and they're always complaining about the way Emily lives her life.

Why on earth does Em want to go there?

I'm worried this has something to do with me and the fact that I haven't found her and Nat a better living arrangement yet.

I jump out of bed and grab my clothes, which I tossed all over the floor last night. Good thing Natalie didn't spot them. I'd prefer to just go into the living room right now and find out what's up. But Angela doesn't want them to know I slept in here.

What to do?

I glance over at the window.

It takes half a second to slide it up and pop out the screen. I jump out into the side yard. Pretzel finds me immediately. Guess Natalie let her out. She woofs a greeting. I bend over to pet her while she sniffs at me. "Don't tell on me, okay?" I whisper. "Sorry I didn't let you out first thing."

She follows me through the gate and around to the front of the house. Then I waltz inside, like it's totally normal for me to show up disheveled, no wallet, doing an epic walk-of-shame.

Emily's eyes zero in on me immediately. "Matteo. We were just talking about you."

"That right?" I ask.

Angela crosses her arms over her robe, glaring. Guess she didn't expect to see me out of her room.

"You clearly enjoyed your birthday." Emily gives me a once over. "Where are your *shoes*?"

My niece saves me by running over and jumping into my arms. "Matteo! Look what I did!" Natalie shows me her arms, which are covered in colorful marker drawings. "I have tattoos now. Just like you."

"Wow. Beautiful. Excellent work."

"I know. I gave some to Riley and Hudson too. Harper is their stepmom. They're twins, and they're my friends."

"They must love you."

"Yep, they're only six, so I have lots to teach them. Did *you* have fun last night?"

I smile, my eyes flicking to Angela. "I did, yeah. Lots of fun."

Angela subtly shakes her head. But I can tell she's hiding a smile.

I set Natalie down, and she runs back over to Angela, grabbing her hand. "I'll show you the paintings that Harper helped me make," she announces.

While Angela and Natalie huddle in the living room,

Emily corners me in the kitchen. "You're chipper. I would've thought you'd be hungover."

"Nah, I didn't drink that much."

"Yet you stayed out all night and came back like *that*?" Then she holds up her hands, palms out. "Sorry, not my business, and I don't want to know. You deserved a night out."

Emily pours me a mug of freshly brewed coffee and hands it to me.

"Thanks," I say. "Hope you had a nice night, too. *You* deserve it."

"Look at us, getting along so well." She smiles carefully.

"I thought I heard something about Bakersfield just before I walked in the door? Something going on?"

Her mouth drops into a frown. "I've decided to take Nat to see my parents for a bit. They've been asking for a visit, and I'm sure you could use the space."

"I'm fine on the couch."

"It's already decided."

"But you can't stand them. They talk shit about Brent. And that dog of theirs? The one that knocked Natalie down?"

Emily grips the skin between her eyes and makes an exasperated sound.

Nat and Angela both look over at us from the living room.

"Look," Emily whispers. "It's just a few days. Please don't take this personally. I'm trying to take responsibility for Nat and me."

"So am I," I hiss. "Aren't we supposed to be a family? Isn't that what Brent wanted for you and Natalie? Me looking out for you? His *last damn request*."

Her eyes flood with tears. "Matteo, don't. Please just don't."

I'm getting choked up too. We don't usually talk about this. Not so directly.

"I'll text you when we get there." She walks into the living room. "Hey, Natty-bear? Come help me pack, okay?"

Natalie scampers off into the bedroom with her mom.

I stroll over to Angela in the living room, all casual like I'm not burdened with survivor's guilt at all. Nope, not me.

She crosses her arms as I approach. "I can't believe you climbed out the window."

"It was that or walk straight out, and Emily and Nat would know we had a sexy sleepover. Or was I supposed to hibernate in your room? Like I'm your sex slave or something?"

"Hardly," she scoffs.

I pull her close, cupping the back of her neck beneath her soft curls. "Nope, you own me now. Come here so I can serve you." I bend to kiss her.

Angela pushes against my chest, glancing at the door to my room, where Emily and Natalie are talking. "We can't."

I bring my lips to her temple. "Fine, let's go to your room then."

"No. Last night was a onetime deal."

I smirk. "Why is that?"

"It's too complicated. I'm not interested in anything... serious."

"Neither am I."

"It's still a bad idea." She wriggles out of my grasp and heads to her room. But I'm right on her heels. I follow her in and quietly shut the door.

"You didn't enjoy it?" I ask.

Angela's digging through the clothes in Neve's dresser. "I did enjoy it. That's not the issue."

"Then you're embarrassed we hooked up?"

"Not *embarrassed*. But there might be uncomfortable questions if you have to testify against me."

"Testify? Like at a *trial*? You think it would come to that?"

"I don't *know*. That's just it." She pushes the drawer closed with a thump. "I don't know what might happen. My life is a mess."

Her hands are shaking.

"Hey. Come here." I wrap my arms around her and tuck her head beneath my chin. "My life's messy, too. But we still have needs. Right? We have chemistry. We're already living together. Hard to get more convenient."

"For three more weeks."

"Then for the next three weeks, we can have a little fun instead of only heavy shit in our lives. *Mutual respect, no expectations.*" I use the words from her app profile. Driving home the point.

Angela's hip brushes my half-hard cock. Then she presses into it again, her hazel eyes darkening with lust. I touch my thumb to her lower lip.

"You want this just as much as I do," I murmur.

She takes an unsteady breath, sinking against me. There's something so sweet about Angela when she's not fighting me. There's vulnerability in her large eyes. Makes me want to cuddle up to her. Keep her warm and cozy.

"Enemies with benefits?" she asks. "Is that what you're proposing?"

"*Enemies*? That's overstating it. But if you're so resistant to us being friends, fine. Call it roommates with benefits." I drop kisses down her cheek to her jaw. My hand rests on her hip, my fingers tightening to hold her there.

"And it ends after three weeks?"

"A clean break. No muss, no fuss."

Her mouth finds mine again, and she opens right up. My tongue nudges hers.

Angela's phone buzzes on top of the dresser, and I grumble at the interruption. "Ignore it." I walk her toward the bed. I don't intend to get naked with Emily and Natalie in the house, but some horizontal kissing would be nice right now.

We both need this. A way to get our minds off the shit we're dealing with.

The phone buzzes again. Angela spins away from me, grabbing her device. She swipes and checks the screen. "Crap. I need to go."

"What is it?"

She grabs fresh clothes from the dresser. "I have to meet someone about the investigation."

"You okay?"

"Don't worry about it."

I hate when people tell me that. My fingers close around her arm. "Wait. I'm not letting you go until I get an answer. Do we have a deal or not?"

She hesitates. "We have a deal."

WHILE EMILY and Natalie finish packing, I clean myself up, brushing my teeth and changing clothes. A few minutes later, Emily's pulling away from the curb, Natalie waving to me from the back seat. I smile at her even though my heart feels like it's being pulled along with her.

They'll be back soon. I'll figure this out.

I go back inside, checking my email on my phone. I've got several responses from landlords, but they say they can't come down on their listed price for Emily. Dammit.

I hate dealing with money, but not because I can't do the math. It's because I can't get the numbers to magically add up to something different when the columns are lacking.

I look up from my seat at the kitchen counter as Angela slips through the door.

She didn't even say goodbye.

But she doesn't take her car, turning on the sidewalk and walking toward the beach instead. I think of the stress in her tone when she saw whatever was on her phone. My instinct is to go after her. Make sure she's truly all right.

On the one hand, it's an invasion of her privacy. On the other, she's got unknown people targeting her. Would it be so bad if I keep an eye on her?

My sister-in-law doesn't think much of my assistance. But that doesn't mean I'm useless.

Without thinking much more about it, I grab my wallet and head out the door.

13

Angela

When I reach the seaside path that runs alongside Ocean Lane, I turn and follow it. I've got half an hour until my appointment.

Earlier, I got a text from an unlisted number. *We need to talk.* But I knew it was from Sean Holt, my good friend and the other senior detective in major crimes. He's used that number to message me before when he wanted to be clandestine.

The guy thinks he's a secret agent sometimes. But he's dealt with his own issues in the past, so I guess I can't blame him for a healthy dose of caution.

I showered and left the house quickly, avoiding Matteo's questions. Just because we now have an arrangement doesn't mean he's entitled to every detail about my life. Nor should he want it.

I really don't know what I'm doing with this roommates-with-benefits… *whatever*. This deal between us. I've never done anything like this before.

But the way I reacted to Matteo last night also surprised me.

He brings out sides of me that I didn't even know were there. Part of me wants to explore it because it felt so incredibly good.

But the more rational part of me is terrified. Even when I've been in serious relationships before, I held those men at arm's length. It always helped when the guy had a demanding career, so he didn't have time to demand too much of *me*.

Matteo isn't demanding anything of me except pleasure, at least in theory. It's supposed to be no strings. But when we were together last night, I felt like he could see through me, see past my defenses to what I really wanted.

I liked it. But I also *didn't*. I know, it's confusing. I don't get it either.

One thing I do know? I can't lose my head over sexy, tattooed muscles and a big dick. Matteo's not a bad guy, but he means nothing more to me than that. I can't let him.

I reach my destination, a smoothie place that's right on the beach. Students on summer break are chatting in line and sipping on juice drinks.

I picked this place for our meeting because it's one of Neve's favorites. I'm living at her house and I'm wearing her clothes, so it seemed appropriate.

Plus, this isn't the kind of hangout most people would expect to find me. Add that to the colorful, flowing caftan I'm wearing, and I'm nearly unrecognizable.

Or I assume so, because when Sean walks onto the patio, his eyes go right past me.

I walk over and tap his shoulder.

"Murphy. You look different." He squints at me. "Your face is pierced."

I snort. "You've just never seen me on my day off."

"This is what you wear on your day off?"

I shrug. "Not really."

I was working on a case of Sean's when I got shot. The case involved him personally, and I know he still blames himself for my injury, even though it wasn't his fault. I consider Sean a friend, but I haven't shared the difficulties I've had.

I don't want him to see me as anything other than Detective Murphy, fearless and unflappable.

After I was wounded, I sold the house where it happened and moved closer to the station. It felt comforting to be surrounded by people instead of out on the edge of town, alone. Yet at the same time, I didn't want to let anyone close enough to see into my head.

"What did you want to discuss?" I ask.

"We'll get to that. We're waiting on one more." Sean nods to another man who's just arrived. It's Jake Shelborne, an agent with the DEA. Quite the coincidence, considering that Emily and Natalie stayed at their house last night. I had no idea until this morning that Jake's wife Harper is Emily's co-worker.

Perhaps this isn't such a coincidence after all.

"Jake," I say. "I didn't know you were coming."

"I heard rumors about what was going on. From various sources." Jake winks. "Then this morning, I texted Holt about setting something up with you."

"Which I was already planning to do," Sean adds, "considering the timing."

"Timing?"

Sean and Jake exchange a loaded glance. "We have a lot to discuss," Sean says.

"Sure you both want to be seen with me?" I ask them. "I thought you were steering clear of me as Chief Liu instructed."

Suddenly, Sean's sweeping me into a hug. I'm not really a hugger at work, but I gratefully accept this one. God, I need it more than I wanted to admit.

This is completely different from having Matteo's hands on me last night, as satisfying as that was. Sean Holt is a friend, and he understands what I'm going through. And what I've been through in the past.

I'm getting choked up, tears flooding my eyes.

Sean gives me a minute, then steps back. Jake squeezes my shoulder. We're not on hugging terms, but he's a good guy, and we've been there for each other in the past.

Way back when—before Harper—Jake used to flirt with me. But I don't think he meant anything by it. That's just how he is. Or was. Nowadays, Jake is strictly professional, except for gushing about the love of his life any chance he gets.

"Could we order smoothies now?" I ask. "Before I start crying and embarrass myself?"

We reach the front of the line and order. I get a strawberry with mint. Sean and Jake place their orders after me. Once we've got our drinks, we walk off the patio into the sand to get some distance from the crowd. Sunlight glints off the water, seagulls scream overhead, and little kids chase each other, jumping over low waves.

"What's the urgency to meet today?" I don't think they know about the Hoodie Guy I saw at my apartment yesterday, or the search warrant. But maybe gossip is spreading.

Sean doesn't answer, going for small talk instead. "How've you been doing?"

I smile and sip my drink, enjoying the cool rush of strawberry. "Pretty much how you'd expect."

"Janie's available if you need representation. She wanted me to pass that along. She would've called, but we're all trying to be careful."

"As am I."

Sean's fiancee is a prominent defense attorney. I like Janie, though we're usually on opposite sides of the courtroom. I'd consider hiring her if I'm actually charged—ugh, if I'm *arrested*—but if I need Jane Simon's bulldog legal skills, I'll have far bigger problems than I've faced so far.

Then I notice a bulky figure over on the patio. He's wearing a ball cap pulled low over his eyes, but I recognize him in an instant.

What is Matteo doing here?

He's not close enough to be listening. But he *followed me*. That man does not understand boundaries.

Jake and Sean follow where my gaze is directed, and I quickly look away. "And what about you, Jake?" I ask, opting to distract them with a new subject. "I hear congratulations are in order?"

I've worked with Jake as part of the regional drug and organized crime task force. He took some time off in the last year after a difficult assignment, but his turmoil had a happy ending. He and Harper got married a few weeks back in a quiet ceremony.

An ecstatic grin brightens his face. "Thanks, I appreciate it. Harper and I are very happy." Then his expression sobers. "These accusations against you are ridiculous."

Sean nods. "There's got to be something shady going on. We know you would never have done what they're saying."

I couldn't agree more. "What *are* they saying?" I ask.

They share another uneasy glance. I'm getting tired of those.

"I guess you haven't checked the news?" Jake asks.

My stomach falls. "What is it?"

Sean scrolls through his phone and then holds it out to me. "This posted last night. That's why I got in touch. I was trying to stay out of it before, but with these kinds of accusations? It's bullshit."

It's an article from a local news outlet. The headline reads, *Daughter of former mayor Waylon Murphy suspected in police corruption scheme.*

My tongue feels like it's lodged in my throat.

Detective Angela Murphy, the daughter of former West Oaks mayor Waylon Murphy, is under internal investigation after a significant amount of heroin was allegedly found inside her residence.

Anonymous sources report that the drugs were stolen from West Oaks PD evidence, accessible only to police department employees.

"Other items found at the scene tie the heroin to a West Oaks PD investigation," a source shared. "It appears the heroin was actually diverted from our evidence department instead of being destroyed. This stuff should never have left official custody."

"This is ludicrous." It was one thing to imagine somebody had planted drugs in my apartment. I've made plenty of enemies in this job. Put away hundreds of criminals, many of them drug traffickers.

But this? Stealing drugs from evidence to sell it on the street? My chest aches like I've taken a punch to the solar plexus. I can hardly breathe.

"Who are these sources?" I ask. "Who's been talking shit about me?"

"No idea," Sean says. "But we're looking into it."

He and Jake regard me sympathetically. They said they don't believe any of this stuff, but could there be even a shred of doubt in their minds? It makes me sick to think of it.

"Oh my God," I say, making the connection. "The Volkov case."

Jake's brow creases. "Volkov? The murder from last year?"

He already knows the case because of the drug trafficking and organized crime connections.

"Exactly. Cassidy Diaz thinks the heroin found in my apartment is tied to Volkov somehow."

"Where'd you hear that?" Sean asks. "Diaz has been tightlipped about your investigation. She's not talking to anybody."

I hesitate. I can't tell them that Matteo is helping me. While I can trust Holt and Shelborne, I can't risk word getting out and blowing back on Matteo.

"My source is reliable. Let's leave it at that. But this means that, whoever is setting me up, they chose the Volkov case because it was one of mine. They're trying to make sure I look guilty."

"They'd have to be someone with access to West Oaks PD evidence," Jake points out. "A cop. Which narrows the field."

And is beyond disturbing. One of my colleagues could be behind this? Who could hate me that much?

Sean rubs his chin. "I can look into it. I doubt the culprit signed the evidence register, but maybe the cameras picked up something." He waves his hand at the phone that I'm still holding. "You should read the rest of the article. There's more, unfortunately."

I brace myself and keep reading.

The article accuses me of being an unusual choice for senior detective, considering how young I was at the time of my promotion. It implies that I got this job because of my father. Then, as if that's not bad enough, the article says that defense attorneys around the city are looking into my past convictions, since they could all be put into question if I'm a corrupt cop.

My heart seizes. My knees buckle, and I have to rest a hand on Sean's arm before I fall.

This is bigger than just my career prospects. Every conviction I've ever helped make could be jeopardized because of this.

That's assuming I don't wind up in jail.

Plus, the part about my dad is a low blow. I've never taken a favor from my father, despite all his political connections. I didn't even take my parents' money for college. I took out loans and paid for it myself. Because I always knew people would say things like this.

When I started my career, I even wondered if I should move to a different city to get out of my father's shadow. But that didn't seem right, either. Why should I leave my home because of other people's assumptions?

I guess it could be worse. These anonymous "sources" could've figured out about my past relationship with Chief Liu.

My past is a freaking mine field.

"You shouldn't get mixed up in this," I say. "You'll get smeared along with me." And Lord knows Sean Holt has broken rules in the past. I've helped him do it.

"I promise, Murphy, if you were really up to no good, I'd help nail you myself," Sean says. "We're not going to get in the way of this investigation. We're not covering up a damned thing. We're going to find the truth and expose it. The only people who could have a problem with that are the ones setting you up."

I exhale, nodding. When my head's feeling steadier, I let go of his arm.

"Be careful who you share this information with," he says. "We don't know who you can trust, aside from the three of us standing here."

"I agree," Jake says. "We don't know who's behind this, if it's one person or more. If they're West Oaks PD or what. What about West Oaks Fire? Any possibility a firefighter was in on this?"

My eyes dart to Matteo, who's still sitting on the patio. "No, I can't imagine."

"I think that's worth looking into," Sean says. "It could be anyone. You know it's not just my paranoia talking." He gives me a meaningful look, and I nod, showing that I understand.

He's seen firsthand that the people you trust might betray you. I'm not quite as cynical as he is, but I am far from naive.

Sean finishes his smoothie and tosses it into a trash can. "It sounds like we have our work cut out for us. We need to start narrowing down suspects. Shelborne, you look into Luke Volkov's Bratva connections, in case they're trying to get revenge for his conviction. I'll check on the missing evidence at West Oaks PD and put out some feelers about West Oaks Fire. Just in case."

Anxiety flares in my stomach. For multiple reasons. "Chief Liu is going to be furious if he finds out you're running a separate investigation on my behalf."

"It's not on your behalf. It's on behalf of the truth. We'll turn over everything we find to Cassidy Diaz when we're ready."

"And what am I supposed to do while you two are doing all the work?" I ask. I'm not some junior detective they can shuffle aside. I'm just as experienced as they are.

"We'll worry about that later. Your job is to keep your head down. Do you have someplace safe to stay out of sight for a while?"

"I do."

"I know the woman she's staying with," Jake cuts in. "A co-worker of Harper's. Emily De Luca. She's a second-grade teacher."

I try not to roll my eyes. I don't need Jake's approval of my living situation. Or Sean's.

I'm not sure what they'd say if they realized Matteo is a

West Oaks firefighter. And a witness against me. And… that I'm hooking up with him.

"Nobody knows where I'm living right now. I'll keep it that way." I suppress a shudder, rubbing at the scar near my collarbone.

"Take care of yourself, Murphy," Sean says. "We'll be in touch."

14

Matteo

I sip my mango smoothie as I keep one eye trained on Angela. She looks good in that dress thing she's wearing. It's nearly translucent in direct sunlight, and I wonder if she notices.

If one of those men she's with stares at her in a way I don't like, I just might have to go over there. I'm sure she'd *love* that.

On my way here, I got a text from Danny.

Danny: Did you see this? It's about the detective who had the drugs in her apartment. The one Chief told us not to talk about.

His text included a link to an article. *Daughter of former mayor Waylon Murphy suspected in police corruption scheme.*

I read through the article while I was sitting here, and I'm still pondering what it said. The claims that Angela's a corrupt cop, that she stole evidence. I don't believe it.

But some pieces of it track. Like the fact that her father was the mayor. No wonder she dated the chief of police.

I bite the straw of my smoothie, watching her touch the brown-haired guy's arm.

The men she's meeting give off a cop vibe, which means they're probably her coworkers. I'm sure it's all professional. But with a woman as beautiful as Angela, I don't see who wouldn't want her. Unless they were intimidated by her. But a man like that wouldn't be worthy of her, anyway.

Jeez, I've already got it bad.

That should be my cue to pull away. Whatever's going on between us, it can't be more than what it is. Something fun and convenient. But I feel a pull toward her that I can't deny.

After several minutes of intense discussion, she gives the brown-haired guy another hug. Then, after a one-armed embrace from the blond dude, which seems to surprise her, they part ways.

Angela lingers by the water for a couple more moments until her friends are out of sight.

Then she storms straight toward me.

I get up, sucking down the last drops of mango as I walk onto the sand to meet her.

"Hey, angel."

"Don't 'angel' me. Do you think you're sneaky?"

"I wasn't trying to hide."

She sighs, shaking her head. "What are you doing here, Matteo?"

"Looking out for you."

"That's not part of our deal."

"It has nothing to do with our deal. This is a free bonus. What were you meeting those guys about?"

"They're friends of mine. Which is none of your business."

"It's a little bit my business. Considering what we were doing last night." At just the mention of it, I'm half hard.

"'Those guys' are Detective Sean Holt and Agent Jake

Shelborne. They were concerned about new accusations against me. There was a news article."

"I know. I saw it. Mayor's daughter, huh?"

She groans and rubs her face. "The article is full of lies. Somebody is out to make me look as corrupt and useless as possible."

"Your father's *not* a former mayor of West Oaks?"

"That part is true," she mutters. "I... need to leave." She turns to go.

"Not so fast. Where are you going?"

"Back to the house. There aren't many other places I can go at the moment. Even my friends agree I should be *keeping my head down*." She spits out the words like she hates them.

"Then I like your friends a little more than I thought. They're right. I drove here. Come with me."

I'm glad when she doesn't argue. We head over to the parking lot. I toss my smoothie cup in a trash can, and we get in my truck. "I'm sorry about what the article said. It must've been hard to read those things about you."

There's a sheen to her eyes when she looks at me, but she blinks it away. "It's fine."

"The article claimed you stole the heroin from West Oaks PD evidence," I say.

"It's not—"

"Not true. Obviously." Everything about Angela speaks to her concern for others. She's not a selfish person. Maybe she held back details of her history, but that was probably more a lack of trust in me than an effort to conceal. She's private, and I'm trying to work with that.

But I want her to let down her guard with me like she did last night.

"Are you and your cop friends going to investigate the Volkov connection? See if the heroin came from Volkov's case?"

She looks impressed that I made that logical leap. "Jake and Sean are. I want to be involved as much as I'm able."

"I could help with that, too. I'm smarter than you might think."

"I didn't say you weren't. You're the one who snooped on Detective Diaz's notes."

"Did you tell your cop friends about that?"

"I didn't mention your name."

I huff. "I don't even get the credit?" I don't have an inferiority complex. But it dings a guy's ego a little to be a dirty secret.

"I'm trying to protect your reputation."

"My rep isn't as squeaky clean as you seem to think."

"Trust me, I didn't think you were innocent." There's a glimmer of something I saw last night in her eyes. A hint of how naughty she can be when she lets herself. I slide my hand onto her thigh. But I don't escalate things. I want to keep talking, not get distracted.

Maybe she's slumming it with me, and that's why she doesn't want anyone to know. The firefighter with the filthy mouth. Good for a few weeks of fucking around, and that's it.

There's no way she'd want to hear this, but us getting intimate? It just made my protective instinct that much more insistent. Call me arrogant. Or a guy with something to prove. It's all true.

She's in trouble, and I can't suppress the urge to catch her. *Save* her. Because, for all the barriers she puts up, for all her strength, I get the sense that she's waiting for a hero.

Well, here I am. I'm involved now, and I can't turn away.

"Tell me about being the former mayor's daughter. How does that fit into this story?"

She cringes. Then her expression darkens further when her phone buzzes and she sees what's on the screen.

"What is it?" I ask.

"Just more people wanting to talk to me about the article. Word about it is spreading. Chief Liu, plus my partner in major crimes. My lawyer." She hesitates again. "And Detective Diaz. I've been summoned for another IA interview."

"What do you think she'll ask?"

"I'd rather not think about it right now."

That, I can understand. I start the engine and pull away from the curb.

She notices pretty quick that I'm not heading back to the house. "Where are we going?"

"On a drive. I thought you might need to get away. Even if it's just for the afternoon."

"I'd still like to know where we're going."

"Of course you would. But it's not so bad to give up control every now and then."

"I've never had a roommate with benefits before," she says. "I don't know how this goes."

"The benefits are many."

She snorts. "I'm getting that sense."

"Will you trust me?"

She takes a long time to respond. Finally, she says, "I already do."

I smile at her and hold out my hand. She takes it, our fingers sliding together.

We drive up into the hills. Once we're off the main roads, I roll down the windows. The sky's a rich blue, and the summer jasmine is blooming.

Angela's watching through the window. "I grew up in West Oaks, but I've never been down this road before. I thought I knew every corner of this town."

There are fancy houses nearby, but this is a stretch of road in a subdivision that never got finished. "The developer might've gone bankrupt?" I say. "I'm not sure. Probably tied up in court or something like that. Before my brother died, we used to come up here sometimes. Whenever he needed to get away. I still do when things feel too heavy."

"Is your family from here?"

"Nah, Missouri. Brent's the one who chose West Oaks. After I left the Marines, I followed him here."

We reach the overlook, and I park the truck. There are a few empty lots here, probably intended for big houses, but since nothing got built, the views of the ocean stretch in a panorama.

We get out and walk over to a shady spot beneath a tree. Blooming bushes add splashes of color. Angela's curls shift against her cheek in the breeze.

"When did Brent die?" she asks.

"Nine months ago." It's gotten easier to talk about. But I don't much. Danny and the other guys at WOFD know the whole story because they witnessed most of it. But they rarely bring it up.

Emily doesn't like talking about Brent. I think for her, it's still too fresh.

"Brent was a year older than me. A doctor. Such a damn overachiever. Always making me look bad." I laugh, remembering the shit I used to give him. Of course, we both knew that I admired him more than anybody in this world. "I was the idiot little brother who nobody expected to do much of anything."

"I don't believe that."

"No, it's true. It's okay. I deserved that reputation back then. But even if I didn't, there's no way I could've competed with my brother for hero points."

People would laugh about how the De Luca brothers were such opposites. Brent was the smart one. I was the class clown. They respected Brent, made him president of all the academic clubs, while I was the guy who got invites to all the parties.

Nobody knew what we were dealing with at home.

Our parents didn't beat us. They just didn't give a shit. Sometimes they'd be gone for days, or wouldn't buy groceries to stock the fridge. Brent would trek to the store for milk, bread, eggs. Basics to keep two growing boys fed. He did our laundry, checked over my homework. I'm sure I would've flunked high school if not for him.

After Brent got a full ride to college for pre-med, I managed to get my diploma, but I wasn't sure what to do with myself. I wasted a lot of time in those years. Being the wild man, out late with my friends any night I wasn't waiting tables. I had a tendency to pick up the sad, pretty girls at the bar. If you needed a rebound to build your confidence post-breakup, I was your guy. A night of sweaty fun, and then I was out.

It was Brent who told me I should make more of myself. I chose the Marines, and though I worked hard, I was still the good-time guy. The one who kept the mood light when we all felt like shit.

Meanwhile, my brother had blown the socks off everybody in college. He got into UCLA for medical. I was so proud of him. By the time I left the military, Brent had married Emily and they'd had Natalie. He'd finally gotten through his residency and was working at a research hospital, finding treatments and cures for diseases. Saving lives. Winning awards.

He was the kind of person anybody would look up to. Especially me.

"What happened?" Angela asks.

I ignore the burning sensation in my nose. "Renal cell carcinoma. Kidney cancer. It doesn't usually hit people as young as Brent, so it was shitty luck. He fought it hard, but he ended up on dialysis. I gave him one of my kidneys."

She stares at me. "The scar on your stomach?"

"Guess you saw it. Yeah." It was a few years ago, and I had to go on medical leave from West Oaks Fire at the time. "We were all hopeful. He seemed like he was better, and for a while things were pretty good. Then the RCC came back, and everything went downhill fast."

I'd been so proud, thinking I'd helped save Brent. Giving him my kidney. Providing for him for *once* instead of the other way around. But it wasn't enough. I maybe bought Brent an extra year or so with Emily and Natalie, but that's it.

I know it wasn't my fault, but it felt just as bad. Fucking brutal. Watching my brother die was the hardest thing I've ever had to do.

Angela's still sitting there. Listening. Her fingers are linked with mine again, though I don't remember when that happened. Her shoulder leans into my side. "I'm so sorry. He sounds like a beautiful person."

"He was. Emily misses him even more than I do. And to add insult to the whole heartbreaking thing, she's still stuck with Brent's medical school loans. At that point in their marriage, she had more money, and she co-signed. That's why money is so tight for her now. She refinanced, and I'm helping her pay them off, but it's going to take years."

"You're trying to take care of her and Natalie."

I flinch at the way she phrased that. She didn't mean any offense. I know that. If anything, it was too accurate, and that's why it hurts. "*Trying*, yes. Meanwhile, things keep coming up."

"And I'm making it harder for you."

"No, the money stuff is hard but that's not the biggest issue for Emily and Nat. It's losing the person who meant everything to them. Someone who could never be replaced. Who was a far better man than me."

"But you lost him, too."

I squint at the water.

"Now you know practically everything about me," I say. "Tell me about you. It's only fair."

Her curls ruffle in the breeze. "I'd rather kiss you."

"Oh. Then why the hell aren't you?"

Her plush lips meet mine. I could get lost in those lips. I roll the lower one between my teeth, and the hungry sound she makes goes straight to my balls.

My hands wander down her sides. Kneading her hips. My mouth trails down to her neck. I lick her warm skin, enjoying the faint salty taste. The hint of floral scent in her hair.

"Take me home?" she asks.

"You don't want to get naked right here?" I'm only half kidding. "There's nobody around."

"Just what I need," she says. "Corrupt cop arrested for public indecency."

"Mmm. You're getting me hard."

"Then take me home and do something about it."

I release her and stand up, offering my hand. But she just gives me a sardonic look and gets up on her own.

"Let's go, De Luca. For a guy in such good shape, you're way too slow."

15

Matteo

We make eyes at each other the whole drive back.

Once we're inside the house, we can't keep our hands off each other. Our tongues stroke and teeth nip. I can't wait for more of her. I didn't get nearly enough last night, and tomorrow morning I'll be off on another twenty-four-hour shift. I want to make sure she's thinking about me the entire time I'm gone, looking forward to when I'll be back.

If we only have a few weeks of this, I'm going to make it count.

"My room," I say between kisses.

"Good idea. I doubt Neve minds if we use her bed, but it is a little weird."

I pause and cock my head. "Unless it's hotter that way. Fucking around on your best friend's bed? Maybe we should go back to Neve's room after all."

She squeezes my ass. "You're incorrigible."

I grunt, pretending to be offended. But I like when she uses big words. Never knew that would be a turn on.

Wait, who are we kidding? Most everything this woman does turns me on. I'm hardly discriminating.

Ha, see? I can use big words too.

She grabs my hand and drags me toward my doorway. "I want to see where you live. I haven't been in here yet."

"What happened to jumping on my cock?"

"You can't wait five minutes?"

"Pretty sure *you* were the one demanding we get home," I mutter.

We go into my room, and she studies my space. I cross my arms and watch her from the doorway. Pretzel edges in past me, followed by Chips. They're curious about what we're doing in here. The cat jumps up on my bed to watch Angela make her rounds.

I haven't done much as far as "decorating." Pictures of our family are scattered all over, most not in frames yet. Just stuff Emily's printed out for me. A set of shelves occupies one wall, mostly filled with Natalie's toys and coloring supplies. Emily or Nat's suitcases are stowed in a corner since they took only backpacks with them to Bakersfield.

Chips waves her tail from my king-sized bed, which is currently made because Emily was the last to sleep here. There's a big TV on one wall with an easy chair, perfect for Natalie to curl up in. A haphazard assortment of dumbbells lie in a corner, and my video game consoles are piled beneath the TV, wireless controllers charging in their cradles.

Angela rearranges Natalie's toys on the shelf, lining them up into neat rows.

"Let me have it, detective," I say. "What's the verdict?" This probably looks more like the room of a college frat guy rather than a supposed grownup of thirty-six.

"I don't issue verdicts. That's a judge's job."

"You know what I mean. Honest opinion."

"Looks like the room of a guy who loves his family."

I walk over and slide my arms around her waist from behind, my chest pressing into her back. She carefully picks up a photo that got buried beneath a stack of Barbies.

"Is this Brent?"

"Yeah. That's him." He, Emily, and Natalie are cuddled together on Brent's hospital bed. He was skinnier than a guy of his frame should ever be, but in this shot he's smiling with his arms around his girls.

"Did you take the photo?"

"I did."

She nods. "I can tell."

"How?"

"The way they're looking at you."

A knot forms at the base of my throat. I don't know where the sexy mood went. I can't find my jokes either.

Angela turns around in my arms and kisses me softly. "You're all right, Matteo De Luca."

I smile, peering down at her. "Hold up. Are you saying you wanna be friends?"

"Let's not go crazy."

I pull her closer. "See, that's where you're wrong. When you and me are together, things are bound to get crazy."

I put my hands on her hips and walk her toward my bed. Our lips and tongues move together. Gently at first. Like we're both rubbed raw by the truths we've been sharing today, and we're caressing away the sting.

Then I realize the dog and cat are still staring at us.

"Okay, both of you out." I hustle Pretzel out the door, and Chips darts away. The door shuts.

When I turn around, Angela is laughing silently.

I shuck off my tee, tossing it to the floor. Then I slide her delicate dress over her head. "Been wanting to take that off you since I saw you in it this morning. It's see-through from the right angle. Bugs me that those other guys saw you in it."

Her bra and panties are yellow lace today. Pretty as icing on a cake. I want to bite them off of her.

"Holt is engaged and Shelborne is married," she says. "And even if they weren't, I wouldn't be interested."

"But you said I wasn't your type either." I kiss along her neck to her scar. "While we're doing this, I don't share."

"Noted."

I like that response, but I kinda want her to demand exclusivity from me, too. To show just a bit of possessiveness. I'm on that hookup app, and my party-boy reputation hasn't faded entirely. Doesn't she want to lock this down?

I probably don't want an answer to that.

She spins us and pushes me, and I sit on the mattress, bouncing a little. Angela drops to her knees between my legs, unbuttoning my jeans and tugging them down to my thighs along with my Calvins. My cock springs up, long and thick and raring to go.

"Hungry for me?" I ask.

"Starving." She blinks her long lashes, somehow shy despite that naughty glint in her eyes.

Angela dives onto me. She swipes her tongue from my balls up the underside of my shaft, then sucks me in past her lips. Then pulls me into her mouth until I'm nearly touching the back of her throat.

Wow. That escalated fast, and I'm so here for it.

I lay back on my elbows and watch her going to town on my dick, slurping and sucking. The sounds she's making are driving me out of my mind. I'm harder than a pole at the firehouse.

"Oh, hell yes. Suck that cock, angel. You go down so good."

Her eyes grin up at me.

My thumb traces along her jaw. Her eyes drift closed, and she moans around my shaft. I wonder who else has gotten to see her like this. Blissed out on cock. I'd like to think that she hasn't been this wild for anybody else.

After bobbing her head up and down my length for a while, I'm nearly there. My muscles clench, the tension in me winding higher, so close to the edge.

"I'm going to come, baby," I murmur, my voice deep and rasping. "The things you're doing to me. I can't hold back."

She pulls off, licking her swollen lips. "I want to see it."

I growl, standing and kicking off my clothes the rest of the way. "Up on the bed," I command, stroking my wet shaft. She obeys, climbing up. "On your back."

Her chest heaves as she stares up at me. I kneel over her, straddling her middle.

"Take your bra off. I need to see your pretty tits."

I love how she doesn't hesitate. Just arches her back to reach the hooks, and then the yellow lace is thrown aside to the floor.

Mmmm. Angela's breasts are petite, yet still full and soft. First time I've gotten to see them. Her hands trace over her curves, the rosy nipples jutting in small peaks. My swollen shaft throbs in my fist. I swirl my hand over the head, capturing the precome that's leaking like a damn fountain.

"Want to watch me come for you, angel? You want to see my cock erupt?"

"Yes," she moans. "Show me."

I take her hand and wrap it around my length. Then I cover her hand with my larger one. We stroke together, working up to the fast rhythm I need. It doesn't take long. She already got me so worked up with her mouth.

Within seconds, pleasure blasts through me, racing down my thighs and along my spine. My cock pulses out hot jets of release on both of our hands, onto her stomach and breasts. Her eyes are locked on my throbbing dick, and I can't take my eyes off *her*. This absurdly sexy woman in my bed.

I grab my sheet to wipe us both off. As I do, I bend down to suck and lick each of her nipples. I hadn't gotten to do that yet, and I could spend the rest of today right here, suckling at her curves. She seems to like it.

But I'm just as hungry as she was. Hungry for more.

I kiss my way down her belly. My hands scout the way, exploring the soft skin of her inner thighs as I shift so I'm kneeling further down the bed.

Her panties are held together by thin, silky straps at her hips. I grab onto the delicate fabric to tug them down. But I guess I'm too rough, because the things freaking snap under my hands.

"Oops."

Hope those weren't expensive.

But Angela doesn't seem to mind. She's staring down at me with those dark hazel irises, her pupils almost swallowing up the color.

I fling her ruined panties over my shoulder. And now she's finally naked. Spread out for me. The scent of her makes my eyes roll back and my spent cock twitch, trying to rise to the occasion.

I press a kiss to her pussy lips. It's almost chaste. But she's so damn pretty.

"*Matteo.*" Her fingers dig into my hair, trying to hold me there. I smile against her.

"So eager for me. What should I do?"

"Fuck me with your tongue. Please."

My grin widens. I'll make a dirty talker of her yet. "I will, my angel. Since you asked so nice."

Gone is every shred of inhibition from last night. She's fully in this experience with me. Not even trying to pretend she's in charge. I wouldn't mind if she wanted more back-and-forth. I'm not intimidated by a strong, commanding woman.

But she wants me to direct this. To take care of her. Even if I doubt she'd ever admit it when we've got our clothes on.

I press another kiss between her legs. Then I lay down next to her on my back. "Straddle my face, angel. Up here." My hand nudges her leg.

She crawls up my body until she's positioned over my mouth. Her fingers grip my headboard. I touch her thighs, feeling her muscles quivering with anticipation.

My tongue darts out over her folds. Tasting. Her cry is desperate. "Yes, *please*."

I suck on her with my lips, then pulse my tongue in and out of her opening. Her clit gets attention next with rapid flicks of my tongue. My hands grip her hips, encouraging her to move as she chants my name.

"Matteo. Oh. *Oh*. Your tongue is magic."

I smile. Does she even know what she's saying? I don't care. I just don't want her to stop.

"Ride my tongue, angel," I choke out. "Wanna suck you dry."

She gasps and looks down at me, eyes flaring with lust. But we've established I have no shame, haven't we? She's still surprised by what I'll say?

Good girl that she is, she does exactly what I asked. Her movements get wilder. Her full breasts sway. I hold on to her hips, helping keep her right where I want her, fused against my mouth.

She screams when she comes, writhing against me. I *love* it. Her noises. Her shudders. Sweetness rushes over my tongue. I try to lap up every drop.

Angela slides off of me, collapsing onto the mattress. I pull her down to me, arms cradling her, and I tuck her head beneath my chin.

We're quiet for several minutes, breathing, exchanging lazy kisses every once in a while. Angela's eyes are hooded like she's half asleep. Or just more relaxed than I've ever seen her.

My stomach grumbles, and I groan. "I don't want to leave the bed, but I might have to eat." It's past lunchtime, and that mango smoothie isn't cutting it.

"No." She shifts and burrows her head between my pec and my shoulder.

"You ready to tell me more of your secrets? It's that or food. A man can't live on pussy alone."

She swats my chest while I laugh.

"You stay here. I'll get us some lunch, and then we'll continue our conversation from earlier."

I scoot off the bed and swipe my boxers from the floor, dancing from one foot to the next as I pull them on.

Pretzel needs to go outside, so I take care of that. In the kitchen, I put together a plate. Some cheese and olives, baby carrots, crackers. A pile of deli meat because, protein. Then I add a few protein bars for good measure.

I'm doing the best I can, here. I'm not about to stop and take the time to cook up a full meal. There's a naked woman waiting for me in my bed. Can you blame me?

I hear a buzzing noise. It's Angela's phone, which she's left right here on the counter. And I can't help seeing the preview pop up.

It's from someone named "Grayson," asking how she's doing and wondering why she hasn't texted him back. I assume it's a him.

Another work colleague? Or something... else?

I'm not jealous. I have no right to be. But there must be a deeper reason Angela keeps even her friends at a distance. I mean, I never even met her until recently, despite the fact that she's Neve's best friend.

She certainly wasn't shy with me just now. But I wonder what it would take for her to truly let me in.

"TELL me more about the Stefanie Rossi case." I set the plate of foot in front of her. She gives me a sardonic look and pops an olive in her mouth.

"You're that determined to get involved in this mess?"

I shrug. "Just trying to understand you. And what you're up against." I sit against the headboard beside her, and our shoulders push together. I drop a kiss onto her head. "You said it was your first big case after you got back from leave, right?"

Her eyes flick up to mine. "Yes. I was thrilled to be back at work. I dove straight in. And it was the kind of case that gets my blood up, you know? A young life cut way too short because of someone's selfish cruelty."

Angela settles in closer to me, resting her head on my shoulder as she speaks.

"Stefanie was headed down the wrong path for a while, but she finally wanted to change things. The day she broke up with Luke Volkov, he screamed at her on her front lawn. Hit her. A neighbor called the police."

"Was Volkov charged for assaulting her?"

"No, Stefanie chose not to press charges. She refused to cooperate any further, probably too scared, so West Oaks PD dropped it. But a few weeks later, a neighbor saw smoke coming from the house that Stefanie was renting. Called in a fire." Angela clears her throat. "Emergency teams responded and found Stefanie's body."

"A *fire*? Really?" I don't remember hearing about that—a fire at a murder scene—but maybe another West Oaks fire station responded. About a year and a half ago, I was taking a lot of days off to spend with my brother. Not reading much news.

"The coroner ruled the cause of death was an overdose,

which could've been accidental. Then we found the syringe with Volkov's fingerprints on it. He became our top suspect."

"Was there any question?" It sounds to me like there could be no doubt about his guilt.

"Well, the evidence wasn't all cut and dried. Certain things bothered me. When we searched Volkov's home, we found heroin packaged for sale."

"The same stuff later found in your apartment?"

"That's what it looks like. But anyway, Volkov's supply was pure. Yet Stefanie overdosed on heroin laced with fentanyl. Volkov also claimed to have an alibi, but his corroboration was shaky at best. The district attorney went forward with charging him."

Angela winds one of her curls around her finger, her dark hazel eyes unfocused. "Volkov didn't present a sympathetic picture, that's for sure. Aside from the domestic violence call, when he'd hit Stefanie before, he had a history of drug arrests. Always managed to squeak by with the help of some mob lawyer and those Bratva connections. At trial, Volkov denied every last accusation. He pushed a theory that Stefanie's new boyfriend had really done it. The boyfriend we never managed to locate or even name."

"Did Volkov have anything to support that theory?"

"Not much. Stefanie had left a diary where she mentioned a new guy. Of course, the prosecutor turned the whole thing around on Volkov, used the 'mystery man' to suggest Volkov was jealous enough to kill her."

"Did anything else bother you about the evidence?"

She sighs. "There were a few pages ripped out of her diary, and I wondered if they could've mentioned the new man. Then, there was the crime scene. The fire destroyed a lot of the physical evidence. Forensics still got plenty. But did they get everything? I don't know."

"Pretty big coincidence that your apartment had a fire, too. And ties to Volkov."

"True. I don't know what to make of that."

"Is there any way Volkov was right? The other man killed her, and now…" I shake my head, trying to puzzle it out. "Someone blames you for not finding him?" I hold her a little closer.

"I don't have a clue what's going on. But the jury had all the evidence and heard all the arguments, and I believe they got it right. If anyone wants revenge on me, it would be Volkov, and he knows exactly what he did." She frowns. "I read Stefanie's journal entries from the months before she died. She was so *hopeful*. Almost innocent, despite all she'd been through. She'd soured on Volkov and thought this new guy could save her. I remember thinking, *save your own damn self, Stefanie.* Don't wait for somebody else to come along and do it. Because usually, no one does."

Her voice breaks on the last part. There's an ache in my chest.

But I'm not sure she was thinking only of Stefanie just now.

"Angel." I caress her cheek, gently turning her head until her eyes meet mine. "What are you thinking about?"

"It's not important."

"Are you kidding? Yeah, it is."

Angela rubs at her scar, staying quiet.

"You do that a lot," I say. "You touch your scar. Are you thinking of when it happened? When you were shot?"

She drops her hand. "I don't know."

There she goes again. Putting that guard up. "New term for our deal. When we're together, we say whatever we're really thinking. No need for a filter."

"You already say whatever you want. You've got the filthiest mouth I've ever heard."

I give her a lopsided grin. "Then we're already halfway there. We'll be totally honest. And whatever we say, it's in the vault. Circle of trust, baby." I close my arms around her and cinch them tight, just to emphasize the point. "Here's a truth. We should be friends. For real."

"You can't say your opinion and declare it's the truth."

"It's *my* truth. Come on, angel. Don't you want to be my friend? It's fun over here. Join me."

She laughs and tries to push me away, but she's nowhere near strong enough. "I'll consider it. But I'd rather hear more of your dirty talk."

She's still playing hard-to-get on the friends thing. Fine. I'll wear her down. I kiss her temple. "Don't get shy with me. You watched me come a little while ago. I had my tongue in you."

"We could do that again."

"And we will. But I asked you a question before, and you have to be honest. New term of our deal."

She exhales, eyes roving toward the ceiling. "You and your new terms. I don't like this deal after all. Three weeks is too much."

"Nah, you can't get enough of my cock." I cuddle her closer, dragging my nose down her cheek.

She sighs again, shifting in my arms. "It's a nervous habit. Touching the scar. It's a reminder, but somehow it soothes me too. It makes me feel *here*. Not in the past. I don't always know I'm doing it."

"Makes sense." After Brent died, I had this thing where I'd tug at the threads inside my pants pocket. I didn't even realize until my wallet fell through the hole I'd made. "Does it feel good?" I ask.

She glances at me like she's surprised by the question. "I've never thought about it. The scar tissue doesn't have the same sensation as regular skin. But it doesn't feel *bad*."

Slowly, I bring my fingertips to rest on her collarbone. She doesn't say anything. Just watches. I drag the pads of my fingers across the puckered skin. Her lips open, chin trembling.

"Okay?" I whisper.

Her eyes are shining. So intense on mine. "Yes."

"Do you like it?"

She answers on a breath. "*Yes.*"

We're quiet for a bit. My fingers brush over her skin. Back and forth.

Angela's gaze goes distant. "While I was recovering, I kept touching the sutures and nearly opened up the wound. I picked up knitting to give my fingers something to do, and that hit of tactile sensation. I kept it up after. When I was off duty, at least. But my knitting probably got ruined in the fire."

"Why haven't you bought more supplies? You could knit all you want around here. Just keep your yarn away from Chips."

"There's been so much else in my head. I haven't thought of it until now."

I keep touching her. And her hand wanders over to my chest, fingers playing with my chest hair. I make a rumbly sound to show her I like that, too. This isn't exactly sexual. But it feels almost that good.

Angela's eyes drop closed as we caress one another. I see tears glistening on her eyelashes.

"I've relied on myself for so long, I don't know how to rely on anyone else."

Her whisper was so quiet I almost couldn't hear it. But I keep listening. Waiting for her to say more. Her eyes remain closed.

"You know what's ridiculous? Neve calls me a hermit, and it's true. Didn't start when I got shot, but it got worse. The truth is, I don't like being alone anymore. It scares me. But I'm also scared of *not* being alone, of letting other people close. How impossible is that? Who would be able to stand me?"

"I can stand you. I might even like you. But don't tell anyone."

"It's in the vault." She buries her face against my neck. But I feel her smiling.

"Will you be okay tomorrow while I'm on shift?"

"Of course," she says immediately. "I can look out for myself."

"You can. But you shouldn't always have to."

16

Angela

$\mathcal{T}$he next morning I have to go in for my second internal affairs interview. Cassidy Diaz gives me a *look* when I come in. "Have a seat, Detective Murphy. I like the outfit. Seems like time off agrees with you?"

Or having multiple orgasms with a sexy-as-hell firefighter. I smile serenely, deciding not to call her on her sarcasm.

I've kept my piercing in, and I dressed in Neve's bright, slouchy clothes instead of a suit. And I left my hair down instead of twisting it up. I'm not here to work, so why should I dress like it?

Or perhaps it's Matteo's influence, making me want to relax into myself. Not be so prim and proper all the time. To hell with my colleagues' expectations. Especially Cassidy's.

As usual, my union lawyer is here with me. He and Cassidy both take out notepads. It makes me think of Matteo, spying on the notes Cassidy took and passing along the info to me.

If I'm being honest, nearly everything has been reminding me of Matteo this morning. Last night, he cooked Fettucine Alfredo for dinner. And then he put on a Hitchcock movie playlist that he found streaming. We ended up watching a movie marathon and curling up on the couch together until late, Pretzel and Chips snuggled on our laps. There wasn't any more hanky-panky, and I can't complain. It was the kind of fun that you can just enjoy and don't have to think about.

Afterward, he argued our roommates-with-benefits deal should include nighttime cuddling as well. It didn't take much convincing. I got another night of restful sleep beside him, minimal wake-ups. His chest does make an ideal pillow.

Now, Matteo's gone for the rest of today and tonight. I can't wait until his shift is over tomorrow and I can see him again. Which shocks me. He's exactly the distraction I feared he would be.

We both know this arrangement can't go anywhere. Neither one of us is in the right place for a relationship. And the thought of me and Matteo trying to make this something more serious, more permanent, just seems ludicrous. We're so different. In such disparate places in our lives.

But he's like a song that you don't like at first, yet soon you find the deeper meaning and nuance to it. The melody catches. And then you can't stop singing.

Cassidy makes a show of studying her notepad. "When's the last time you requested items from the evidence archives?"

"I haven't got a clue. I'm in charge of a lot of cases in major crimes. I don't have my every movement memorized."

We keep evidence for open cases at the station, and once a case is finished, the evidence gets moved to a local warehouse for storage. But drugs are destroyed as soon as possible. They're *supposed* to be, at least.

If drugs from the Volkov case wound up in my apartment, then I'm sure Cassidy wants answers as much as I do. The first step is finding out what *she* knows.

She shouldn't forget for a moment that I'm the senior major crimes detective in this room, not her.

"I'd like to discuss the news article that's making the rounds about me," I say. "I assume you've seen it?"

Cassidy sits back. "You're not directing this interview."

I plow right past her. "Do you know the identity of the anonymous source they quoted?"

"Why would I?"

"I wondered if it could be you." The accusations about me using my father's position to get ahead? Those could've come straight from Cassidy's mouth.

"Murphy, I'm taking my duty to this investigation seriously. I hope you can say the same."

"The article suggested that the heroin found in my apartment was connected to a West Oaks PD case. That it came from evidence."

Cassidy taps her pen on her notepad. "How do you know for sure it was heroin?"

"Let's not play games," I reply.

My lawyer cuts in. "Detective Murphy will be able to respond more helpfully if you share information with us. You'll have to do it eventually anyway."

I flinch at that suggestion, because the only way they'll be required to share info is if I'm formally disciplined or charged with a crime. I hope it doesn't come to that.

But his argument seems to convince Cassidy to open up, just a bit. "The news article was correct. Heroin was found in your apartment. When we searched more thoroughly, we found evidence envelopes with traces of the same heroin inside. Clearly, the drugs were stolen from West Oaks PD. What can you tell me about that?"

"Absolutely nothing. What case did the evidence envelopes come from?"

Cassidy doesn't answer. Just stares and taps that pen. She's playing chicken.

"Was it the Volkov case?" I ask.

Her eyes flash like I've just made a damaging admission. And who knows, maybe I have. But at least we're going to get somewhere.

"In case you were wondering," I say, "I haven't touched the Volkov case in a year. Not since the trial. Check the logs. Any drugs seized from Volkov would've been destroyed over a year ago, too."

She sorts through the file in front of her. "Well, let's talk about Volkov. Shall we?"

I spread my hands. "I'd love to. Because the way I see it, those evidence envelopes are the key. Someone planted that heroin in an obvious attempt to discredit me."

Cassidy is flustered, though she's trying to cover it by looking annoyed. "Fine. Sketch out your theory for me. Tell me all about how someone's out to get you."

While Matteo and I were watching Hitchcock movies last night, my brain was working. Picking up small pieces and clues, rearranging them to make them fit.

And what Matteo said about the fire brought it all together for me.

"Are you familiar with the details of Stefanie Rossi's murder and Volkov's trial?" I ask.

She flips through her pad again, clearing her throat. "I pulled the file, but I haven't had a chance to memorize it. Why don't you give me the background."

"Happy to." I give her the same rundown that I did for Matteo yesterday. Stefanie's tragic murder, Volkov's denials.

"Right, Volkov claimed he was set up," Cassidy says. "He believed the overdose syringe was planted by the real killer to implicate him. You don't agree with him, do you?"

"Of course not. But did you notice the details about the murder scene? After he killed her, Volkov set a fire at Stefanie's home to destroy evidence. What are the chances that a fire was used to muddy the scene of Stefanie Rossi's murder, *and* also used to draw attention to *Volkov's heroin* in my apartment?"

"I'm still not following. You're claiming you were set up by someone who was upset about Volkov's conviction?"

"It's possible."

"A person with access to our evidence?"

"Now you see why this is so concerning."

The pen taps. "You sound like Volkov did. Blaming some mysterious conspiracy for the existence of damning evidence against you. A mystery man, pulling the strings to frame you. It's an interesting theory, Murphy. Now I'll share one of mine. You're used to having things handed to you. That article online spelled it all out. You've been riding Daddy's coattails since you started at West Oaks PD."

And there it is. "I've never relied on my father for anything."

"And when the going gets tough for you," she goes on, "you look for a shortcut. If you're so innocent, how did you know the heroin had come from Volkov's case anyway? Either *you stole* it from evidence yourself, or someone with eyes on my case slipped you that info."

I grit my teeth.

"Was it Chief Liu?"

"Alex would never—"

"He's *Alex* to you? Funny, the chief has never asked me to call him by his first name. But you're close to him, aren't you?"

My lawyer finally decides to chime in. "I don't see how that's relevant, and it's extremely inflammatory. Could we get back to the issue at hand?"

I force myself to remain calm, though I'm tempted to

launch across the table at her. "Cassidy, I get that you don't like me. You think I got my promotion because of who my father is. But why would I risk all of that to resell some drugs that came from evidence?"

"Unless it wasn't just a one-off." Her mouth twists into a self-satisfied smirk. "What if I were to tell you that evidence has gone missing from *numerous* cases? Not just Volkov's?"

"*What?*"

"This goes far beyond Volkov, Murphy. Beyond just drugs. But do you know the common factor in these cases where evidence mysteriously walked off? *You* were the lead investigator in all of them."

My lawyer glances at me as if he expects me to provide an explanation. But of course, I can't.

I may have had the advantage for a moment. But Cassidy's now regained it, and then some. And I've once again lost sight of the bigger picture, all my clues and theories lying useless in my hands.

~

I HAVEN'T SMOKED since college. But dammit, right now I need a cigarette.

I bum a couple from a patrol officer and head out to the back of the station. The burn of the first drag feels good, like it's singeing my lungs. Focusing the whirlwind of my thoughts.

I'd rather avoid the rest of my colleagues today. I don't want to see the doubt on their faces. Or worse, smugness, if they share Cassidy's view that I don't deserve my spot as senior detective.

I might not be everyone's favorite around here. I'm prickly. I know that. But I had my coworkers' respect. I was like the grumpy auntie everyone might be scared of, but they still loved.

Will I ever be able to get that back?

After Cassidy ended our interview, I spent some time conferring with my lawyer. He said he's been trying to get more information, but *this can't be rushed*. He's not telling me anything I don't know. Sometimes, a major investigation can go for months. Even longer. Especially one as sensitive as this.

I've already had to silence my phone and ignore almost all incoming calls the past couple days because of media requests for comment. I've kept an eye out for updates from Sean and Jake, but they need time, too.

All I've got right now is time. And I hate it.

"Murphy?"

I turn my head and find Detective Grayson approaching. My partner.

"I worried you'd fallen off the edge of the earth," he says.

"Sorry. I meant to write back." I haven't spoken to him in days. Haven't even thought of him, honestly. His texts asked about the article and about how I've been doing, which was kind of him. I just didn't have the energy to respond.

"It's okay." He slides his fingers into his thick, dirty-blond hair, flopping it from one side to another. "I'd heard you were spotted this morning, and I'm glad I caught up with you." He nods at my cigarette. "Any chance you've got an extra?"

I hand him the second cigarette I bummed. "Didn't know you smoked."

"I don't really. But lately…" He uses my lighter and inhales gratefully.

"*Lately*," I agree. As if that word says it all, though I'm sure our sources of stress are radically different. He's getting ready to become a father, while I'm mourning the possible death of my career.

We puff in silence until Grayson stubs his out on the back wall of the station. "Want lunch? I was just heading home, and I could pick your brain on the way. I'm sure Nora would enjoy seeing you too."

"Sure. That would be nice." Otherwise I'll be going back to Neve's house, all alone, to sit and stew over the new information that Cassidy revealed. *More evidence has gone missing.* Am I suspected of stealing *that*, too? Is that what she meant?

Was something else found in my apartment when Cassidy executed that search warrant?

Why did I even bother to share my Volkov theory with her? She's never going to believe me. And I'll be honest, I might not have believed it either in her shoes—that Volkov or one of his allies wants some kind of revenge on me. But I'd at least look into it. I doubt Cassidy will.

I'm lucky to have Sean and Jake helping me, but am I proving her point about having unfair advantages because of my friends?

Grayson leads me to his car, and we drive toward his house. "How's Nora feeling?" I ask.

He tilts his hand back and forth. "It's getting really hard for her to sleep. She's got this pillow thing she puts under her belly, but she hates not being able to lay on her back."

I make a mental note to send Nora a care package. Pregnant women should get more praise and acknowledgment for what they do.

Could that be me someday?

I shake my head, clueless as to where *that* thought came from. If I can't take care of a plant, how would I handle a baby?

"What about you?" I ask. "Nervous about the new addition coming to your family?"

He already looked ashen today, but his skin pales further.

"It's a lot. Nora's constantly upset with me about something, and honestly, I haven't been sleeping all that well either."

"I'm sorry."

"And I sound like an asshole, because you've got problems too." He works up a smile. "Can I ask your advice about some of our investigations?"

"Go for it."

Grayson catches me up on how he's running our cases without me. He's been getting help from the other major crimes detectives. It sounds like Sean Holt is way overtaxed, and that's not even counting his efforts to help *me*. Our department is underwater with me gone. I don't want it to be this way, yet I can't help feeling like I'm letting them down.

"How have things been otherwise at the station?" I ask.

"Well…" Grayson glances at me sidelong. "There are rumors going around. Everyone's on edge."

"Has anyone been talking about the Volkov case?" I ask.

He wrinkles his brow. "Not that I can think of, why?"

Grayson was my brand-new partner when we investigated that case. It was his first murder. He knows it as well as I do.

"Detective Diaz told me the heroin found in my apartment was linked to that case. It came from West Oaks PD evidence." Technically it was Matteo who told me first, but I'll continue keeping that to myself.

"Are you serious?" Grayson turns his head to face me, then brings his eyes back to the road. "Wow. That changes things. Doesn't it?"

"It's certainly not good. Do you know Officer Evans? He was at the scene of the fire at my apartment, and I think he talked to Cassidy about it. Made it sound like I'd been trying to get inside the building to 'save my drugs.'"

"Braden Evans? The new kid? I know he's assigned to property crimes with Detective Diaz, so she probably works with him and trusts his word. But it's nuts for anyone to think you took drugs out of evidence. You would never be that stupid."

"Thank you for the vote of confidence."

He shrugs sheepishly. "I'm not the one who makes the decisions. But Diaz will see reason. She'll have to. It's just impossible for her to think anything else."

I wish I was as idealistic as my partner. Maybe I've been doing this for too long.

We turn into Grayson's neighborhood. It's new construction, not far from where I lived before moving to the apartment building. Kids play in sprinklers on lawns.

He pulls up to his house and parks in the driveway. We head inside, where Nora's made reuben sandwiches for lunch. Grayson kisses her cheek and rubs her belly. He's worried about fatherhood, sure, but his love for her is obvious. I feel like a raincloud hovering and threatening their sunshine.

After we eat, we say goodbye to Nora and return to the car. "I'm going back to the station, but I can give you a ride wherever on my way," he says.

"That's all right. My car's parked at the station anyway. I'll go back with you."

Unlike the drive here, we ride in silence. I wonder what Matteo's doing right now. If he's gotten any emergency callouts. He could be in danger at a moment's notice, and I wouldn't even know.

I realize I'm rubbing my scar, and I stop.

"I wish there was something more I could do to help," Grayson says, interrupting my thoughts. "You're my partner. I feel like I'm leaving you high and dry."

"You've got plenty to deal with, between Nora's pregnancy and our cases. Besides, there's not much you can do without getting in hot water yourself."

He nods and turns at the next intersection. "Where are you staying these days?"

"With a friend."

The light turns red, and we stop. Grayson gives me one of those side-glances of his. We've been on countless car rides together in the last year. Hours of learning each other's mannerisms. And it seems like he's unsettled about something.

"What's up?" I ask.

"Just thinking." Grayson purses his lips. "Last year, Nora and I went through a rough patch in our marriage. I slept on some couches at friends' homes. It was awful. So I know what it's like. Feeling like you're untethered. If that's the right word."

"I'm sorry to hear you went through that."

The light turns green, and he accelerates. "But we've been working it out. We have to, right? With the baby coming." He laughs nervously. "Things will turn around for you, too. Just let me know how I can help."

"Thanks. Keep me posted on Nora. Let me know when the big day comes."

"I will." We reach the station, and Grayson lets me out beside my car. "I'll see you, Murphy. Be careful."

"You too."

17

Angela

*A*fter Grayson drops me off, I sit in the front seat of my Honda and text Sean Holt, asking him for an update and summarizing what I learned from my interview with Cassidy.

Then, I tip my head back and sigh.

When I'm working a case, I use every resource available. Background research. Interviews with neighbors and witnesses. Wire taps if I can get a warrant. But right now, I haven't got access to anything. In fact, the closer I get to this investigation, the more it could blow up in my face.

I'll just have to be patient and wait to hear back from Sean or Jake. I happen to think patience is overrated.

Meanwhile, I still have the rest of today and all of tonight. *Alone*. I need to find a way to occupy myself.

My thoughts go straight to Matteo, once again. He took me on that drive yesterday. Cooked last night. Maybe I should do something nice for him in return.

That's it, I'll return the favor and make dinner for him tomorrow.

I've never been much of a cook, but that seems like a

natural thing to do for your roommate. Right? Cook dinner. It doesn't have to mean anything big.

The next question is, what would he like?

Me: Dinner tomorrow. What sounds good to you?
Matteo: Do you mean a restaurant? Are you asking me on a date, angel? [Heart eyes emoji.] [Eggplant emoji.]

I drop my head against the steering wheel. This man. He's impossible.

Me: I'm making you dinner because I'm a solid roommate. Tacos? Steak?
Matteo: [Thinking emoji.] Steak tacos.
Me: Done. Heading to grocery.
Matteo: What if I change my mind and want chicken instead?
Me: No backsies.
Matteo: Trying not to make that into something dirty... [Peach emoji.]

I'm smiling in spite of everything that's gotten me down today.

I've been thinking of Matteo as a distraction, as if that's necessarily a bad thing. But he's a *good* distraction as well. Keeping me from getting too bogged down in frustration.

I open a different text thread.

Me: How do you make steak tacos?
Neve: You mean, how do YOU make steak tacos? I will find an easy recipe for you. Please don't burn down my kitchen.
Me: I won't. You should be happy I'm doing something different. I never cook.
Neve: I know. Thankful that you live with a firefighter. [Fire emoji.] Speaking of, how are things going with Matteo? [Fire emoji.]

Arg. I am not spilling my secrets to her. But it's hard to hold back entirely.

Me: He's growing on me.
Neve: I'll bet he is.
Me: Tell me all about Italy.

I tuck my phone away, secure in the knowledge that she'll switch our conversation to her trip. I'm sure Neve has all kinds of exciting stories to share about her location shoots.

I think back to what Neve said before the fire started and all this began. *You need to shake something loose. Do something different.*

That was before I met Matteo, though he's been Neve's roommate and property manager all this time. Would we have eventually met? Maybe. But I doubt we would've clicked. We're too different, at least on the surface. Matteo and I needed a spark to ignite our chemistry.

We got an actual fire.

I'll never be happy about this awful situation and the accusations against me, but at least I got a silver lining to make it bearable. A little over two weeks until Neve returns, and I'm no longer counting the days. I'm looking forward to this time with Matteo instead.

But what about after? When you have to find a new place, and this arrangement is finished?

Then we'll have pleasant memories. It can't be more than that, and that's all right. I'm allowed to make the most of it while it lasts. Matteo and I both know what this is.

I can almost hear my best friend's voice in my head. *It's okay to enjoy this.*

I put the car in gear and pull out of the station parking lot. There's a grocery store not far. But the fancier one is across town. Why not? I'll do it up right. Hit the swanky grocery for supplies. I might cook something tonight, too. Just for myself.

Self care, Neve says in my head.

I want to make something I've never tried before. Neve would be so proud.

But it's not just her inspiration behind this. It's Matteo's. Making me crave more excitement than I thought I wanted. A *different* kind of excitement—the excitement that comes with expressing myself. I think those parts of me were always present. It's why I got the piercing and the tattoo in college. Why I've spent so many hours at the hair salon in the past getting my hair braided or done *just so*. Why not lean into it?

I find myself full-out grinning, bobbing my head to the upbeat song on the radio. I enter the freeway, keeping an eye on my surroundings as I always do.

Everything seems fine until I notice the gray sedan with tinted windows.

It seems to match every lane change I make. In fact, I think I noticed it in West Oaks too. It was a few car lengths behind me at the lights.

Ever since I left the station.

I take the next freeway exit, and the gray sedan follows. And when I go through the light and take the next on-ramp to re-enter the freeway, that gray car is still a few lengths back.

I'm being followed. That thought makes me want to hyperventilate. *A dark figure lurching toward me. Raising a gun...*

I swerve in my lane before quickly recovering. Shit. I have to focus.

I'm Detective Murphy. I'll use my training. Do my job. I can handle this.

I press the gas pedal and scan ahead of me for openings in traffic. A glance in the rearview tells me the gray sedan is keeping pace. He's not trying to stay hidden anymore. He knows that I see him.

And he's gaining.

There's a man in a hoodie in the driver's seat. Dark sunglasses. His fists clench the steering wheel. My heart rate skyrockets.

It's him. The same guy I saw leaving my apartment building last week. Who I tried to chase down.

Now, I'm the one being chased.

"Call 911," I say aloud, using the Bluetooth voice settings on my phone.

"911, what is your emergency?"

"This is Detective Angela Murphy. West Oaks PD. I'm heading south on Highway 101 through West Oaks and need assistance. I'm being pursued by a gray Buick sedan." I recite the license plate.

My heart rate climbs again as my tires roar across the concrete. The sedan edges closer. I switch lanes at the same time as another car, and I'm forced to punch my brakes.

The gray sedan clips my bumper. My engine whines, and I grab tight to my steering wheel, struggling to keep control of the car. I don't take a breath until I've straightened out. Sweat soaks my clothes.

The sign for the next exit appears.

West Oaks Wildlife Refuge.

I have to get off the freeway. Away from the rest of traffic before I crash and a lot of people get hurt.

I swerve onto the exit ramp. The sedan cuts off another car, tracking me. Honking and squealing brakes follow us off the freeway.

Almost immediately, it's just the two of us on a deserted road. I drive straight through a stop sign without slowing. The rolling landscape of the wildlife refuge opens up around us. Tall grasses wave in the sea breeze.

Getting away from the crowds means less likelihood of collateral damage. But now that we're isolated, there are fewer witnesses. I have no idea what this wacko is going to do.

I keep the 911 operator updated on my location. I just have to stay ahead of him until backup units respond.

An engine revs behind me.

Oh, shit. He's going to ram me from behind.

Wrenching the steering wheel, I turn onto a branch in the road at the last minute. But I hit a pothole. The car shakes and fishtails as my back right tire blows with a loud *bang*.

I glance at the rearview mirror.

The last thing I see is the front grill of the gray sedan racing toward me.

Then the world turns topsy-turvy into chaos.

18

Matteo

"*H*ey, Matteo," Danny calls out. "What does a leek look like?"

I cock my hip. "Really? You've never seen a leek before?"

"You're the one who made this list, not me."

We're at the grocery store getting food for the station. The truck's parked out front at the curb, while firefighters in navy WOFD uniforms traipse the aisles filling our carts.

Danny and I are on produce. And my friend needs more lessons in high-quality cuisine, it seems. I don't consider myself an expert in fine dining, but I specialize in comfort food, and that's all about flavor.

"Come on," I say. "Let me educate you."

It's been a busy day. Fire inspections, then a training. No emergency callouts today so far. I'm looking forward to finishing chores and getting some quiet time to call Angela.

I could FaceTime her from my bunk tonight. Not exactly private. But I'm creative. Maybe I could sneak into a storage closet somewhere.

Better yet, invite her to come down and sneak her into the closet with me.

Maybe I'll get online and order her some knitting supplies to replace the ones she lost. I wonder if Emily knows anything about knitting, because I sure don't. But I can just imagine Angela's smile when she opens the package.

I whistle as I stroll past parsley and cilantro. I show Danny the leeks, then work on collecting the rest of our greens and fruit.

"You're in a good mood today," he says.

"What are you talking about? I'm always in a good mood."

"Except when we've gone out lately." He taps his chin. "What happened after you stormed off the night of your birthday? Did you meet up with some chick?"

I can't subdue my smile.

Danny slaps my shoulder. "You *did*. Happy birthday to you, man. Have you seen her again?"

"This morning. In my bed."

He crows. "Nice!"

I sneak a peek at my phone. Angela didn't write back to my last text. She said she was going shopping too, and I had hoped I'd run into her, as unlikely as that would be. West Oaks has no shortage of grocery stores.

"Tell me about her. What's she like?"

I don't know what to say. I don't want to spill much because this thing with Angela is only temporary. But I also don't want to make her sound like some anonymous hookup that doesn't matter to me.

If anything, she matters too much.

"I like her. We're having a good time together. But I doubt it'll go anywhere."

"Do you *want* it to go somewhere?"

That question stops me in my tracks.

Do I? I've never had a relationship last longer than a weekend, and that was in high school.

I glance around, but our teammates aren't nearby. "It's complicated. She's a West Oaks PD detective. The one that article was about."

"Angela Murphy? The cop? The ex-mayor's *daughter*?" he shouts, and I clamp a hand over his mouth.

"Can you keep it to yourself? I don't want to announce it."

"Detective Murphy could be facing criminal charges for corruption."

"That's all bullshit. I've gotten to know her, and that isn't her. At all."

"You just can't resist a woman with problems these days. Is that it?"

"No. That's *not* it." But I haven't hesitated to insert myself into Angela's life and problems, despite my other commitments. "I like her, and I want to help her if I can."

"*Help* her? How are you helping her?"

"With the investigation against her. A little." I grab a few bags of spinach and toss them in the cart.

Danny's looking at me like a leek has sprouted from my head. "Emily made it clear she doesn't want you busting your ass for her. You're the one putting that pressure on yourself. Now you're getting involved in a West Oaks PD investigation, after Chief Ross warned us to stay away from it, because you're sleeping with the subject? You don't have to save every woman who's in trouble."

I shake my head. "I don't need the lecture."

"You don't have to pay penance because you're alive and Brent isn't."

I pivot on my heel, pushing him up against a table of avocados. A couple topple onto the ground. "Careful what you say next," I growl. "It better not be about my brother."

"All right," he says softly. "I'm sorry. I was out of line."

I move away from him, then bend to grab the fallen avocados. "I'm not paying penance," I grind out. "But is it so awful if I want to do the right thing for people? Make Brent proud of me?"

"I get that you've changed since Brent died. I'm not saying that's bad. But what do you really want, man? You're trying to make captain, work three jobs, *and* save all the women in your life. When is it going to be enough?"

"If you're trying to ask where I see this going, I don't have a clue. I want Emily and Natalie safe and provided for. It might be nice to work two jobs instead of three. But beyond that?" I can't answer my own question.

The truth is, I've never planned much for the future. For most of my life, I've preferred to live in the present moment. In contrast, Brent's entire life was built around his dazzling future. And then it was stolen away.

Where does that leave me?

My deal with Angela is just right. A few weeks, I can handle. And even if I wanted something more serious with her, Angela still won't let me in.

She still won't even admit we're *friends*.

So I'll do exactly what I'm doing now. Trying to be a good guy. And I'll have some mind-blowing sex along the way. Could be a helluva lot worse.

Our phones ding with a notification, and we both groan. An emergency call just came in. So much for our groceries. But that's how we have to roll. *This* is why we're always ready.

We race back to the truck and gear up. The sirens blare through our ear protection as we zoom toward the scene.

On the way, Captain Bucanan briefs us. "We've got a car crash. Wildlife refuge. We're the closest EMS available."

The wildlife refuge is a narrow stretch of land that runs along the coast. I like to go out there and run the trails sometimes. Natalie loves watching the birds. It's peaceful.

We get closer and see a small car overturned just off the road. It's unclear if there was another vehicle involved, but I spot the telltale signs of tire tracks digging into the dirt.

"Probably a hit and run," Buc says. "West Oaks PD is on its way."

Danny and another EMT-trained teammate are the first out of the jumpseats. The rest of us assess the danger. The car's smoking, but not actively on fire. It's a Honda, lying upside down on its roof. Crumpled all over like a used tissue.

Looking at it sparks something in the back of my mind. Recognition.

How do I know this car?

Then my stomach jumps all the way up into my throat.

No.

My feet carry me closer while my brain's catching up. "One female inside," Danny's saying. "Bleeding from her forehead. She's conscious. We need to get her out of there and get her stabilized. Ma'am, can you hear me?"

The driver is hanging upside down in the cabin. Blood streaks down her dangling arm. I hear a groan, and my heart's instantly choking me, trying to vomit out onto the dirt.

"Angela!"

I dive toward her, but Captain Bucanan holds me back. "De Luca, do you know the victim?"

"Angela Murphy." I know how freaked out I sound, but I can't rein myself in. "Get her out of there!"

"You have to let them work."

Someone cuts the door free from the body of the car. They slice away her seatbelt, get Angela out, and lower her onto the ground. Her eyelids are fluttering. Her mouth's trying to move.

"Let me go," I tell Buc. "I can help." I wrench away from

his grasp and go to her side, keeping away from Danny as he works.

"Angel, hey. You're going to be all right." I want to touch her, comfort her. I hover instead, hoping she can see me.

"Matteo?"

"Keep her head steady," Danny barks at me. "Don't let her move."

"A car…" Angela murmurs. "Chasing me… Hit me."

Rage fills me. Blinds me with fury.

I keep trying to ask her questions, but Danny ends up pushing me out of the way.

A West Oaks PD squad car arrives, and I head over to them. I practically accost the patrol officer when she gets out, holding her arms. "Listen to me. The crash victim is Detective Angela Murphy. West Oaks PD. She said someone was chasing her and hit her car. A hit and run. Call it in, *now*."

The officer speaks into her radio, but she's not moving fast enough. I grab the radio out of her hand. "Hey!" she shouts.

I spin away. "Get Detective Holt here," I say to the dispatch.

If Angela trusts Holt, then that's good enough for me. But shit, I can't remember his first name. I've never even met the guy personally. "Detective Holt," I repeat into the radio. "Get him to the wildlife refuge now. The car crash scene."

Somebody's been targeting Angela, but she thought they wouldn't hurt her physically. She thought she was *safe*. So did I.

We were wrong.

"De Luca, the victim keeps asking for you," one of my teammates says. "Who is she?"

"A friend."

An ambulance has arrived—a third-party company runs

them in West Oaks—and the paramedics are now strapping Angela onto a back board for transport to the hospital. I go and find Captain Bucanan again. "Buc, I need to go with her to the hospital."

"And why is that? What the hell is going on, De Luca?"

I know this is unusual. I have to justify my actions. There's no way around it.

"The victim and I, we're close."

Buc grimaces. "Does that mean you're sleeping with her? She's the detective who's been in the media, right? Who Chief Ross warned us about?"

Danny steps in beside us. "We're supposed to be reporting who we're sleeping with, Buc? If so, I owe you a list."

I know Danny is trying to defend me, but I'm in no mood for jokes. I'm about to fucking lose it.

Seeing her like that, bloodied and confused, barely conscious.

"She doesn't have anyone else," I bark, "and I'm not leaving her to deal with the hospital alone."

They're loading Angela into the ambulance. I have to be in there, and the paramedics are not going to want to let me, so I have to clear these obstacles as quickly as I can.

"Please, Buc." I can't think about the trouble I might be in. All I know is that I can't abandon her.

Buc's face could've been carved from stone. "Fine. Go. Let us know how she's doing."

"*Thank you.*"

I rush over, stopping the paramedics just as they're about to shut the ambulance doors. As predicted, they refuse to let me board. But Danny knows one of them, and Danny pleads my case to his buddy.

"Fuck it, hurry up and get in," Danny's friend says.

I jump inside and crouch next to her. "I'm here, angel. Right beside you." I kiss her hand as gently as I'm able, then hold on while the ambulance roars away.

19

Angela

For a while, everything's a blur. The shiny interior of the ambulance. The pastel walls of the hospital. The faces of the nurses and doctors. The sharp pain when they stitch up my forehead.

And Matteo's voice. I can't figure out why he's here.

When the orderly wheels me into my room after a CT scan, there he is. Matteo jumps out of his chair. His hair is wild, sticking up like he's been running his hands through it. He's wearing his WOFD shirt and heavy pants with suspenders.

"Angel."

I look up at the orderly. "You see him, right? Big guy? Tattoos?"

"Yes, ma'am. Sure do."

Matteo cocks his head, lifting a thick, dark eyebrow. "I told you I'd be here when you got back."

"I know, but I thought I might've imagined it. Glad I'm not *that* out of it." I'm mostly kidding.

"Hey, I'm happy to be the man of your dreams."

When I arrived, they asked me all kinds of questions and

ran tests, and despite the pain in my head and some dizziness, my brain seems to be functioning.

And Matteo kept appearing, like some kind of guardian angel. But I missed the part where he explained how he found me.

He sweeps over to me and lifts me right out of the wheelchair. He's impossibly gentle as he lays me on the bed.

"I can walk by myself," I complain.

Matteo fusses over arranging my pillows and fluffing them.

"You've got a lot of people looking out for you," the orderly says. "There've been cops guarding your door."

I didn't even notice. Are they guarding me like I'm a *suspect*? I must look panicked, because Matteo is quick to fill in more details. "Holt sent a unit to make sure you're safe. You were attacked. Do you remember?"

The orderly slips out. I settle back against the pillows. "I think so. Yes." It's both vivid and unclear, but I grasp at those memories, terrified they'll vanish.

When I was shot almost two years ago, I had no idea what had happened or who'd done it. I could only remember the dark figure, the gun.

I start to tremble, and Matteo rests a comforting hand on my thigh. "This okay?" he asks. "I'm not hurting you, am I?"

I place my hand over his to keep it there. "No. I'm glad you're here." He smiles so sweetly it makes me ache. Like a spoonful of honey hitting my teeth. "But how did you...?"

"Our truck got called to respond to the crash. I realized it was you. Damn near had a heart attack."

"They let you come with me in the ambulance?"

He cringes. "I may have threatened to make a scene. Danny knew one of the paramedics, so they didn't fight me on it."

"You just left? Even though you were on duty?"

"Don't worry about it. The captain gave me permission to go."

I can't believe he did that for me.

Being in the hospital again, I can't help but think of when I was here last. How alone I felt despite my fellow officers surrounding me.

Cops band together when one of us is hurt. We do everything we can to support the officer and his or her family. But when it happened to me, there seemed to be an invisible barrier between me and everyone else. Between my recollections and the truth of what had really happened.

This time, Matteo's here. I want to cling to him like he's a life raft in the darkness. Keeping me from sinking.

Just for a little while. Until I can stand on my own again.

Matteo's free hand goes to my face, thumb gently stroking down my cheek. "How are you feeling?"

"Still pretty dizzy. Achy and stiff. Were you there when I got the stitches?" I ask.

"No, we were separated for a bit. I did my best to give them your info. The hospital had your profile already. Neve's your emergency contact, which isn't very useful when she's out of the country."

"Guess not."

Other than the stitches, I think I'm in decent shape. I didn't lose consciousness during the crash. Despite the panic and confusion, I'm fairly sure my memory is intact. Not full of black holes. Not like before.

Matteo's hand moves down along my face and goes to my shoulder, gently resting over the scar on my collarbone. As if he knows that's exactly what I need right now.

The sensation grounds me. I sigh and sink against the pillows.

"Can you tell me what happened? If you're not ready to, I understand. But if somebody hurt you, I'm going to find them. I'm going to make them regret it." He's still smiling, but there's a razor-sharp edge beneath his words. An intensity in his dark eyes that I've never seen before.

The door opens, and Sean Holt pops his head in. "Hey, can I come in?"

I sit up, separating by a few inches from Matteo. "Sure. Just waiting on my test results to see if my brain's still there."

"Eh, thinking's overrated anyway." Sean walks in and nods at Matteo. He holds out his hand. "I'm Sean Holt."

"Matteo De Luca."

"I understand I have you to thank for the heads-up about Murphy's crash?"

Matteo nods. "I guess. I did my best."

I look from one man to the other. I hadn't heard about this.

Sean points a thumb at Matteo. "This guy was laying down the law after you got hurt. Made sure I was notified ASAP about your crash. I wasn't on call today, so I appreciated it." Sean gestures at Matteo's shirt. "You're WOFD?"

"I am."

"I would've been here sooner, but I was at the scene. We're taking imprints of the other car's tire treads. We put out a BOLO based on your description to the 911 operator, Murphy. Gray Buick?"

I nod. "I'm sorry you had to come in for this."

Sean frowns at me. "I'm sorry that you're here. That's my only concern." He pulls up a stool to my bedside. "Do you feel up to answering some questions?"

"I can go, if you'd rather," Matteo says under his breath.

I hold tight to his hand, letting that be my answer. Sean doesn't trust easily. But if I tell him to bring Matteo in on this, he won't fight me.

"Matteo already knows a lot of what's going on," I say. "I've been staying with him. He's been... helping me."

Sean grins. "Helping you, huh?"

I would roll my eyes, except I think that would make my headache worse.

"I just want to do whatever I can for Angela," Matteo says. "If she wants me here, then I'll stay. Tell me what to do, and I'll make it happen."

Matteo and Sean regard each other, like they're coming to some silent understanding.

"Cool," Sean says simply. Then he switches his focus to me. "Murphy, let's start at the beginning of your day. Take me step-by-step."

I backtrack to this morning, starting with the interview with Cassidy Diaz. Then lunch at Beau Grayson's house. "I was going to head to the grocery store next, and I decided on one across town. I was on the freeway. That's when I noticed the car following me. I tried evading him, and he got aggressive. That's why I took the exit to the wildlife refuge. I was afraid we would hit someone else."

Sean listens impassively, but Matteo squirms and breathes heavily as I speak.

"What caused the crash?" Sean asks.

"I took a sudden turn, hoping to get away. Hit a pothole. He slammed into me, and my car flipped. I'm not sure if that was his plan or not. If he was hoping to intimidate me, and it just got out of hand, or..."

"That asshole wasn't just trying to scare you," Matteo hisses. "He could've killed you."

"I'm lucky I wasn't injured any worse."

"Fuck that," he seethes. "We're going to find that sick fuck and make him pay."

Sean rubs his jaw, thinking. "I agree. So let's figure out who he is. We're running the plates, but I bet we won't get anything. Probably stolen. I've got our people checking surveillance and traffic cam footage. His car must be in bad shape after the crash. With luck, we'll grab him before he ditches the vehicle. Any chance he looked familiar? Have you seen him before?"

"He had a dark hoodie. Sunglasses. I think he was the same person who I saw leave my apartment building the other day."

Sean tilts his head questioningly. I haven't told him the details about that. Matteo's expression goes even darker.

I quickly tell them about what I saw outside my apartment building that day. Chasing the man in the hoodie, losing him.

"And you reported this to Chief Liu?"

"I did, but he's turned over anything related to my IA investigation to Cassidy Diaz. And Cassidy's taking a narrow view of my case. Basically, that I'm already guilty."

Sean's face twists up, and he grunts. "I'm sure the chief would appreciate knowing that."

"Maybe, but I'm not going to tattle to him. Cassidy already accused me of using my connections to cover my ass."

"Then *I'll* tell him," Sean says. "These people are a lot more dangerous than we thought."

"*These people?*" Matteo asks. "You think there's more than one?"

"I'm not making any assumptions. We know it's someone with access to West Oaks PD evidence. But they could have others working with them."

"Then she needs twenty-four-hour protection." Matteo stands up, leaning his bulk against my bed like a sentinel. "I'll be around as much as I can, but I have my rotation. I'll have to go on shift again in a few days. And a West Oaks PD unit won't cut it since the people targeting her have connections inside your department."

"My thoughts exactly. I had a few ideas."

"I don't need a babysitter," I say to Sean. "The guy in the hoodie followed me from the station. Nobody knows I'm staying with Matteo except you, Jake, and Matteo's sister-in-law. If I stay out of sight, I'll be okay."

That's what I did after I was shot. Hid under my covers. It worked *just fine*.

I press my palm over my collarbone.

"Murphy," Sean says, "whoever's going after you has escalated to violence. Ruining your reputation isn't enough for them anymore. Let's not find out what they're willing to try next."

He's being too rational. I want to stay inside my bubble of denial.

But I already knew this was personal. Whoever is doing this wants to destroy me in every way, and the confirmation of that fact has made everything more visceral. More frightening.

Since moving into Neve's room, I've told myself that I wasn't putting Matteo, Emily, or Natalie in danger. But *I am*. They aren't safe around me.

"I'll leave town. Stay somewhere else until we find out who's doing this." My instincts tell me to withdraw. *Hide*. Even if it means shutting out everyone that I care about.

"Not happening." The mattress sinks to one side as Matteo sits. He takes both my hands in his. "You're going to stay with me. I'm not leaving you to deal with this alone."

I can't look at him. I can't cry. I will not be the woman who bawls in front of her colleague. And Matteo? No. I don't want him to see me that way.

"I'll move out when Neve gets home anyway," I say.

"You think your best friend is going to put you out on your ass when you're in trouble? She'll stand by you, just like all of us are trying to do. When are you going to stop being so stubborn and accept the help that people want to give you?"

I scowl back.

Sean coughs and stands up. "I'll let you two discuss that alone. But I'm going to look into personal protection for you, Murphy. I'll make some calls, and I'll be in touch."

He sweeps out of the room just as a doctor comes in. "Ms. Murphy. How are you feeling?"

Matteo hovers so close the doctor has to ask him for room. He only steps back slightly, his face flushed and defiant.

The doctor tells me my CT scan showed no signs of brain swelling, bleeding, or skull fracture. My symptoms suggest I have a mild concussion.

"That car accident shook you around. You need to heal, which means you'll be resting your brain for the next couple days. You can go home, but you'll need someone to watch over you and make sure your symptoms aren't worsening."

"I'll do it." Matteo eyes me like he's daring me to disagree.

The doctor gives Matteo the instructions and says I'm cleared to head home.

After he's gone, Matteo turns to me, arms crossed and bulging over his broad chest. "I was serious, angel. No matter what else is happening between us, you mean something to me. We *are* friends. So don't sit there and say to me that *I don't know you* and *you don't like me*. We both know that's all bullshit now."

"I wasn't going to say any of that."

"Good. Because you're stuck with me."

Do something different, my best friend said, and I'm trying. Even though it isn't easy.

I've spent almost two years since getting shot hiding from the world. I'm still struggling with the instinct to withdraw and lick my wounds in isolation.

But the truth is, I don't want to push him away. I feel better when Matteo is around. Having someone to lean on has been a relief.

My fists tighten on the blanket. I swallow down my rising tears. "I want to stay with you. As long as it's safe for you and Emily and Natalie."

He sits beside me again and wraps me in his arms. I rest my head on his shoulder. I still ache all over, but it's instantly blunted by his presence. His strength.

"We'll figure that out. I said I'd be here for you. All you have to do is let me."

"For…" I try to remember what day it is. "Two more weeks or so. Right?"

He pauses. "Sure. Until Neve's back, I'm your emergency contact."

"How can I repay you?" I don't like this being so one-sided.

"It's pretty obvious. You'll owe me a *ton* of sexual favors. Once you're better, I'll put one of those collars on you and lead you around. Blow jobs for days."

I snicker and poke him in the side.

He leans over and nuzzles his nose to my temple. "Don't worry about it." His tone has dropped to a lower register. "Just let me take care of you."

My breath catches in my chest. "Roommate with a lot of benefits."

"You got it." He kisses my hairline. "All the benefits you want. And then some."

～

ABOUT AN HOUR LATER, I'm discharged from the hospital
and heading home. Matteo's truck is still at the fire station,
so we take an Uber. He instructs the driver to go nice and
slow. *She's got a concussion. Take it easy.*

"Are you hungry?" Matteo asks. We spent all afternoon
at the hospital, and the sun's starting to sink. So much for
my big plans to make dinner tonight and tomorrow. "I could
ask the driver to swing past a drive-through. I'll pay him
extra."

"I just want to get back."

On the drive, I get a text from Sean. But I'm not allowed
to read it. Matteo has confiscated my phone because the
doctor recommended I avoid screens for twenty-four hours,
so long as my symptoms don't get worse.

"Sean wrote that he's going to meet us at my place,"
Matteo says. "I just gave him my address. And my number,
so he can write me directly."

"Oh, good. God forbid I have a conversation with anyone
on my own. Or lift a finger for myself."

Matteo nudges my knee with his. "One of the many benefits of our deal. I'm at your beck and call. Full-service roommate. In case it's unclear, I mean that in the dirtiest way
possible."

The Uber driver snorts. I strangle my smile, but I lace my
fingers with Matteo's on the back seat. "Did I get any other
messages?"

"No, but I'm going to use this opportunity to delete your
profile on the hookup app."

"Ha, I already deleted that app from my phone."

He gives me one of those sweet smiles. "Because you're
getting such good nookie already, and nobody else could ever
compare?"

"More like, if you could recognize me on there, anybody
could."

He shrugs. "I'm still gonna take it as a compliment to my skills."

When we reach the house, Matteo actually unbuckles my seatbelt for me. He's over the top. But I don't mind. It's nice to be cared for. I give him a hard time about it, but I doubt I'd accept this much fussing from *anyone* aside from him.

Just something about him, I guess. Those pheromones.

Matteo keeps an arm looped around my waist as we walk up the sidewalk. Sean is waiting on the front porch, and he's not alone. He's with another man I've met before but haven't seen in ages.

Matteo doesn't budge an inch when Sean gives me a hug. "Murphy," Sean says, "this is Devon Whitestone. From Bennett Security."

Devon is the same height as Sean, though he stands more stiffly than my fellow detective. Devon's a former Army Ranger, if I remember correctly. Overprotective of his family, which is a trait I run into often among law enforcement and ex-military men.

"We've met," we both say at the same time, and smile. I shake Devon's hand. "Nice to see you, Devon."

"Likewise. Though I'd prefer this was a social meeting, and you didn't need my employer's services."

Devon and I have had a few clashes in the past. The company he works for, Bennett Security, operates like an independent government agency, though they lack any such authority.

I'll admit, I'm territorial. I don't like private companies rolling in and stepping on my turf.

But several of my friends have close ties to the company, including Sean. And the newly appointed district attorney, Lana Marchetti, is married to Max Bennett himself, the company's owner. Max has volunteered his company's resources to help people in trouble more than a few times.

Serving the wealthiest citizens of West Oaks has made him rich, but it doesn't seem that money is the only motivation that drives him.

Bennett Security has come through in the past where West Oaks PD failed. I'm not too proud to admit it.

"Let's go inside," Matteo says. "Angela should sit down."

Sean cuts an amused glance at me, and I just shake my head, though I keep the movement small. But I feel no need to explain what Matteo is to me. He's clearly more than a roommate. Friend, lover, protector? Anything I'd say would make me cringe, so I'd rather keep it to myself.

Inside the house, we all sit in the living room and finish the rest of the introductions. Matteo stays right next to me, barely leaving an inch between us on the couch.

"Holt said you're in need of a bodyguard detail?" Devon leans forward, elbows on his thighs, hands clasped loosely. Despite his now casual demeanor—which I assume is for my benefit—everything about him screams clean-cut soldier, from his side-part to the spotless shine on his shoes.

"Sean told you someone's targeting me?" I ask.

"He did. But I'd like to hear it from you, if you don't mind?"

"Sure. I'll start from the beginning." This is how it is to be a crime victim. Telling your story over and over again, no matter how much it hurts.

Matteo keeps his tight grip on my hand, and I subtly lean into him. After I share everything I can, Devon explains how this will work. He's a co-captain of their bodyguard team, and he's going to arrange for a two-man detail to be placed outside the house at all times, switching out with other teams in shifts.

"I'd like to set up a camera on all the entrances to the home as well so the team can keep an eye on things."

I look to Matteo, and he nods. "It's Neve's call as the homeowner, but you know she'll say yes."

"I'm happy to send our bodyguards' credentials for your approval," Devon adds.

"I'm sure they'll be fine." While I've had my doubts about the legality of their actions in the past, I've never doubted Bennett Security's dedication. "But I think my salary is too low to afford your usual price range."

"Don't worry about that. I've already discussed it with Max. Lana has spoken highly of you. So have Holt and Jane Simon. And I'll take Jane's opinion as gospel after all she did to help my sister. You're part of the Bennett Security extended family, so this will be free of charge."

"I won't accept anything free. But a discount, sure. I can live with that."

"Then pay what you can."

"Thank you." Those words aren't adequate. I'm humbled.

Devon goes through more logistics. Matteo and I share our schedules, and we arrange for a tech to come by later to install the cameras.

"I'll have a two-man team here in a few hours," Devon says. "We'd also like to offer our investigative resources to help find who attacked you."

Sean nods. "That would be fantastic. Since we believe someone inside West Oaks PD could be involved, we'll need outside assistance. I'm going to get a copy of everything we have on the Volkov case. Hopefully Cassidy Diaz won't object to that."

"Volkov?" Devon asks.

"A murder investigation that Murphy led," Sean explains. "We believe it's tied to the efforts to target her. I can tell your research and investigation team everything we know. Which sadly isn't much at this point."

"What about Chief Liu?" I ask. Alex might not appreciate

Bennett Security getting mixed up in this. Especially if the media finds out.

"Liu authorized me to run a separate investigation. He wants to hunt down the people who hurt you as much as we do. He just needs to be quieter about it. Internal Affairs will continue with their side of things under Detective Diaz."

"That's good news," I say. "Usually we have to run around and ask the chief's forgiveness later."

Sean smiles. "I do think that way is more fun. But you never know. Chief Liu might claim he had no idea what we were doing and leave us high and dry. So there's still risk involved."

"Glad you're getting some entertainment out of this," I tease.

Devon shakes my hand again and excuses himself to get his team together. Sean walks him to the door, then returns to the living room.

"Matteo," Sean says, "if you don't mind, I'd like to make a profile of every firefighter who was at the scene of the fire at Angela's apartment. I have no reason to suspect any of them of planting the heroin. But I've been taking a close look at everyone who could've had access to her apartment. Ashamed to admit I haven't made much progress yet, given all that's going on."

"Happy to. But nobody on shift with me could have been driving the gray sedan that attacked Angela today."

"Still, we need to be thorough. Like I said, we don't know how many people are involved in this."

Matteo turns to me. "You okay here for a bit?"

"I could use a nap."

"Not for too long. I'll check on you in a while."

"Yes, doctor."

He puts his lips to my ear and whispers, "Just wait 'til we're alone, and I'll doctor you up *real* good."

I smile.

Matteo lays a blanket over me, then goes to talk with Sean. I stay curled on the couch and close my eyes. But my thoughts are restless.

Somewhere out there is a gray Buick sedan. A driver in sunglasses and a hoodie. Who is he? What does he *want*?

Then, that image vanishes. And the face of Stefanie Rossi appears in my head. Not of her in life, but her death. Skin drained of color. Eyes staring without focus.

It feels like forever before I manage to sleep.

20

Matteo

As soon as Holt leaves, I go check on Angela. She's snoozing with her cheek smooshed against the couch cushion. Chips is curled against her side.

I kneel beside Angela and stroke her cheek until she opens her eyes. "How's your head?"

"Not bad." She sits up, and I run through the checks the doctor told me to do. She's still achy, a little off balance. Her stitches are bothering her.

"You can have more Ibuprofen," I say.

"I'm good for now."

I'd like to keep playing doctor with her until we're both naked and sweaty and she's feeling as *good* as possible. But I need to be gentle with her. So I sit beside her instead and brush my lips over the baby hairs at her hairline. I love how delicate they are.

"What do you need next? More rest? Food? Remember, full honesty. Terms of the deal."

She grumbles. "Then I want my phone back."

"This?" I take it from my pocket and hold it up, wiggling

it in the air. She tries for it, but I easily hold it out of her reach.

"Ugh. You're mean. I've been getting texts and emails, haven't I? I need to know what they are."

I unlock it. I'm still surprised she told me her code. "Hmm. Let's see. Neve wrote to you. Which was very naughty of her, because I told her you couldn't use your phone." I snort when I read the message. "Oh, she addressed it to me."

Neve: Matteo, are you taking care of our girl? You are the best guy in the world. I owe you! Whatever Angela wants, please get it for her? I will pay you back and then some.

"Have you told Neve about our 'benefits' deal?" I ask.

"No. She doesn't need to know everything I do."

I'm not sure why, but that chafes me. Neve wouldn't have a problem with it. But it's not my call. At least Angela seemed okay with Sean Holt and that bodyguard guy knowing we're close. I'm no longer in "dirty secret" territory.

She's finally accepting my friendship. And she's clearly got friends in high places, so I'm in good company. Angela might play the loner at times, but her friends prove she's a stand-up girl.

Brent would have liked her. My brother never took the easy route through life, and that's exactly how Angela is. She's struggled to overcome her fear, but when it comes to helping others, I doubt she would ever back down if she had a choice about it. She deserves people in her life who are equally loyal.

I scroll to the next message and frown. "Somebody named Grayson texted a few times. Who's that?"

"My partner."

Ah. That makes sense. He was texting her the other day, too. Asking why she hadn't written him back. "He heard what happened," I say. "Wanted to check in. Should I respond?"

"Not right now."

"Do you not like him?" Maybe I'm just being protective, but it bugs me that this guy keeps sending unwanted messages. Dude, if she doesn't respond, then stop texting. I'm persistent, but if Angela had flat-out ignored me, I would've backed off.

"Grayson is *fine*. He just wants to help, and I need him to focus on our cases since I'm not able to. And on his wife, who's about to pop out a baby. He doesn't need to be worrying about me." She exhales and rubs her face. "What I need is a shower. And then I want to lie down and bury myself under the covers."

I stand, offering her my arm. She takes it, and I help her up. She's wobbly on her feet.

"Do *not* carry me," she says, reading my mind. "I can walk."

"All right." She's ruining all my fun. "But which room are you headed to? Mine or Neve's?"

She's standing in the center of the living room, looking undecided.

"Your room," she finally says.

I'm being cool about this, but inside I'm pumping my fist. I didn't even have to argue with her.

"Could you get my things?" she asks. "My underwear is in the top drawer. And my toiletries are on the bathroom counter."

"You're the boss." I steer her to my bed and leave her sitting while I run to the other bedroom. After gathering up everything I can carry, I return. Some quick organizing, and she's got her own shelf in my bathroom.

I switch on the water in the shower for it to warm.

When I turn around, she's trying to take off her shirt. And almost careens into the bathroom mirror.

I grab hold of her. "Arms down. I'll handle the sudden movements."

I sit on the closed toilet and stand her between my knees. It's probably not necessary to take off each item of clothing this slowly. Then kiss the newly uncovered skin.

But I do it anyway.

"You know, Neve didn't mention any of these roommate benefits when she told me about you before."

"She doesn't get this deal. This is only for very special ladies. No offense to Neve, but we're not this tight."

"So you don't break out these moves on every new girl you want to impress?"

"Just you."

"Good," she whispers. "While we're doing this, I'd rather not share."

A giddy feeling lights up my veins. "It's just you." I run my finger down the middle of her belly, and she bites her lip, sucking in a breath.

When she's down to her bra and panties, I stop. "Should I let you do the rest?"

"You promised full-service."

"I did." I reach behind her and unhook her bra, then let it fall to the bathroom floor. Steam billows from the shower, but you'd think it was freezing in here by the way her nipples tighten. I move my hands along the curve of her hips, pushing her panties down as I go.

The outline of my cock in my pants leaves no doubt how I'm responding to this view.

But this isn't about me. I want her to feel safe and comfortable. After the day she's had, I don't want her to feel a single ounce of stress or obligation. So I grab a towel and wrap it around her, even though I'd much rather trace the map of her with my tongue.

"Tie up my hair?" she asks.

Angela tells me to grab a scarf, and I wrap it around her soft curls, covering the bandage over her stitches as well. After that, I hold her hand and help her step under the water, removing the towel at the last moment. I keep the shower curtain partly open and stand there, my clothes getting damp from the spray.

"Should I wash your back first, or the front?"

She chuckles at me and turns around, pointing that curvy ass at me. I lather my hands in body wash and smooth it all over her back, tracing the slope of her spine downward. Then over the smooth globes of her cheeks. She arches her back, pushing her ass into my hands. So damn tempting.

"Matteo," she sighs. "Touch me? Please?"

"I am touching you."

"Between my legs."

Ungh, my cock is throbbing and trying its best to break free of the confines of my pants. I want to slide my fingers into that soft cleft between her legs. Tease and stroke until she's whimpering. Then push my hot length into that sweet, dark-pink heaven as deep as I'll go.

But I won't.

"You have a concussion. We're taking it easy."

"The doctor didn't say no orgasms."

"He didn't know the kind of orgasms I deliver. I can't be responsible if your brain explodes."

She turns around to face me, and I wash her breasts, taking my time. Water sluices down her body. Her skin glistens. I can't resist giving the pointed buds a few tugs, and we both moan.

"Want to join me in here?" she asks.

"I want to, sure." In fact, I want to lick up every bead of water from her skin. Perhaps I could wash her better with my arms wrapped around her so she wouldn't be at the slightest risk of slipping and falling. I could hold her right up against my naked body.

But I'm still not going to.

Angela doesn't easily trust other people to care for her. So I'm proving to her that, with me, she can. She can trust me to be serious and responsible.

It's important to me that she believes it. That she doesn't have one single doubt.

The rest of that day and the next are pretty much the same. I take care of her, and she actually accepts my efforts. Even basks in the attention.

It feels like something is shifting between us.

I don't know if it's all in my head. Maybe she just knows that she has to heal before getting back to work and tackling the people who are against her.

Either way, I'll take it.

The Bennett Security bodyguard team shows up, and a tech installs our new cameras. I place an order for groceries as well so we'll be stocked up. Then I speak to Emily, who offers to stay longer in Bakersfield given the threat against Angela. I'm not happy about that. But it's the best way to handle the situation for now.

Until that psycho who attacked her is caught.

The next morning, I bring Angela herbal tea instead of coffee. She complains so much that I end up calling Danny. He says caffeine is okay as long as she's not having trouble resting. Angela demands that I put him on speaker, and they both agree I'm being way too paranoid.

"All I've been doing is resting!" she says.

So I make the damn coffee. Sheesh.

When I get back with her mug, Danny and Angela are chatting on the phone like old friends. "Aren't you still on shift?" I ask my friend.

"We can't all beg off work when we feel like it."

"Is Matteo in any trouble for coming to the hospital with me yesterday?" Angela asks.

I frown at Danny, but he's on speaker, not video. Angela's watching me. I glance over and meet her eyes.

My friend sighs through the speaker. "It's a good thing the chief isn't filling that captain spot tomorrow. I'm sure you can make it up. There's time."

"Captain spot?" Angela asks.

Great. "We're gonna go now," I cut in before he can answer, and I hang up.

She gives me a look that says I'm not fooling anyone. "Are you going out for captain?"

I rub my forehead. "Maybe. A spot will open up soon. One of the guys is retiring."

"But getting involved with me and the West Oaks PD investigation will make you look bad. Won't it?"

"I can *handle it*." I'm working hard to keep the testiness out of my voice. I don't want to talk that way to her. Not when she's injured.

"You sound like me. Claiming you've got everything under control even when the building is burning down."

"So you admit you don't have everything under control?"

"Isn't that obvious?"

"Do you want to talk about it?"

She goes quiet. But I feel that need inside of her. It's *right there* below the surface.

Tell me, I want to say. *Show me what you're hiding.*

But she doesn't. Not yet.

∼

THE REST of the day is low key. Grilled sandwiches for lunch, and I make Spaghetti Bolognese and garlic bread for dinner. Angela gets dressed in another of Neve's colorful dresses, and the Bennett Security bodyguards who are on-duty join us at the table.

Their names are Leon Kozinski and Rex Easton. They're nice guys, polite and professional. Leon is the chatty one, a little like me. Rex is older, the silent type. They ask Angela about her biggest cases and share stories about their toughest bodyguard assignments. She and I hold hands beneath the table, our legs pressed together. And Pretzel and Chips hover nearby, excited about the new people and the attention.

But I see it when Angela starts to fade.

Once they've left, I scoop Angela from her chair and carry her to my room. She doesn't complain. Soon, we're ready for bed and back under the covers.

"C'mere," I say, opening my arms, and she burrows against me.

"I should've known. The plants," she mumbles.

"What about the plants?"

"Neve's plants all look so happy. Because of you."

"I guess plants like me."

"I like you."

My grin is impossible to keep down, so wide it makes my cheeks ache. I gently run my fingers along her scar until her breathing gets deep and regular.

We haven't known each other for long, and for a lot of that time, we've clashed. But it seems that the worse things get outside of us, the more we turn toward one another. I don't want to question this connection we've made. I just want to lean into it.

I know how little time we get on this earth. You can make

big plans for the future only for them to be ripped away. So I'm going to enjoy her while she's here in my bed.

Especially because it won't last.

21

Matteo

When I wake, the house is dark and quiet. And I'm alone in my bed.

"Angela?" I ask softly.

There's no answer.

I swing my legs off the bed and go out into the living room, but there's still no sign of her. Pretzel lifts her head. I stop to rub her ears. "Go back to sleep." She lies down on her paws, blinking at me.

I try Neve's bedroom next. And there she is, sitting by the window, her silhouette dark against the bright moonlight.

Angela turns her head slightly, and I see her profile.

Tear tracks streak down her face.

"What's wrong?" I sit beside her on the padded window seat.

She sighs, trembling. "I can't get the images out of my head."

I pull her into my lap. "Images?"

Tell me, I think. *Just tell me.*

"The car coming toward me, hitting me. And... the person who..."

I don't know what it is about this moment. It could be the fact that I've been taking care of her nonstop for the past day, or that it's the middle of the night. Or it could simply be the darkness that's covering us, making it easier for her to say things she wouldn't in the daylight.

She finally gives me another glimpse of what she's been concealing inside.

"The man with the gun," she whispers. "The man who hurt me."

I hold on to her. Just trying to be here for her. "It's okay. You can tell me the rest."

"I want to. You've been so good to me." She looks up at me. Presses her palm to my cheek.

I don't know what this is. What she's feeling. What she's trying to tell me without words. For a long moment—it could be five seconds or five minutes—she stares at me.

Then she gets up, takes my hands, and walks backward toward Neve's bed. She sits on the mattress and lies back.

I follow and crawl over her, hovering. She slides her hands under my tee. Up and over my pecs, my shoulders, down my abs. But when she dips inside my sweats and strokes my soft cock, I stop her hand.

"We shouldn't. I don't want to hurt you."

"I *am* hurting."

Her voice is cracking. Like her heart's suddenly splitting open. And God, hearing that almost breaks me.

I've never seen her like this. Heard her like this. I wish I could pull her inside my chest. Pump my blood through her veins to warm her. Fucking *anything* to take away what she's feeling.

"What can I do?" I ask.

She reaches inside my pants again. Her delicate fingers pull and stroke my cock, my shaft thickening and swelling. Lust is turning my thoughts fuzzy.

This feels like a dream. Barely even real.

Still hovering over her on my knees and elbows, I hold her face and kiss her. My tongue searches her mouth. I want to soothe her. Give her what she needs. We're both panting for breath when I pull away.

"Please, Matteo. *Please*. Be with me. I'm so tired of being alone."

A spark ignites within me, burning me alive.

I tug at her clothes. I know I'm being rougher than I should be, but I can't stop myself. I want to show her I'm with her in every way she needs, every way she's begging for.

Anything to take the hurt away.

She's only wearing a sleep shirt. Nothing underneath. As soon as she's naked, my mouth is on her, sucking her tits. My hand pushes between her legs. She's wet. The heat of her makes me delirious with need.

Working my fingers inside of her, I latch my mouth onto her soft stomach. "Yes," she hisses, holding my head against her. "Mark me. Please."

I keep sucking her skin, but I force myself to stop before I leave a bruise. Finding that willpower isn't easy.

I'm barely holding onto rational thought as it is.

I scoot off the mattress and stand. Her gaze traces my every move as I grab my shirt by the collar and tug it off. Then slide down my pajama pants. I'm not wearing under-wear, so my cock pops free instantly, long and hard and aching. I wrap my hand around the base, giving it a squeeze. Precome pearls at the tip, glistening in the moonlight.

"Please," she whispers again.

Take care of her, my better side reminds me. *Don't hurt her.* "I need a condom. I'll have to go to my room and get one."

She bolts upright. "No. Don't go."

Shit. I go to Neve's nightstand instead and rifle around until I find a square wrapper. I'm being a terrible roommate.

An even worse employee. But if Neve was calling right now warning me not to do this or she'd fire my ass, I'd hang up the damn phone.

I'm going to fuck Angela just how she wants. Right here in her best friend's bed.

I knee-walk across the mattress toward her, still stroking my shaft. My thumb swipes over the moisture at the head, and then I bring my hand to her lips. She doesn't need any more encouragement from me. Her tongue darts out and slides over the pad of my thumb. Tasting my desire for her.

"Get me ready?" I ask, kneeling in front of her, my cock jutting upward. I hold out the condom.

She's not acting like herself, and I have to make sure she's in this with me. That she knows exactly what she's doing.

With shaking hands, she opens the wrapper and rolls the latex onto my shaft.

I lay down beside her so I'm facing her. I nudge her with a hand at her hip to get her into a similar position. We're lying face-to-face. My hand traces the curve of her hip down to her thigh, then travels inward. Toward the sweet, hot juncture between her legs.

Then there's a glint in her eyes, a sliver of her fierceness reappearing, and she grabs my hand, pressing it to her center again.

"I'm wet for you," she murmurs. "I'm wet all the time for you. I was even when we hated each other."

Her confession makes me shudder with anticipation. "I can't wait to feel you stretched around me. If you want my cock, then it's yours." I position her top leg so it's draped over my hip.

"I want it. I do."

My cockhead lines up with her opening. She gasps when I push inside.

Tightness envelops me. Heat.

I stop a moment as we both adjust. Her body wraps so tight around my swollen length. My arms circle around her, holding her against me. My shaft throbs inside her, and she whimpers.

"You feel…" she breathes.

"How do I feel in you, angel?"

Her eyes are shining, dancing back-and-forth across mine. "So good. Filling me up."

I thrust tentatively. "Do you feel me deep inside you?"

"*Matteo*," she moans. Her head tips back, exposing her throat. "I feel you everywhere."

I dip my head to kiss and lick the skin over her windpipe. I feel every pant, every breath she takes. We're completely tangled up together. Holding each other impossibly close.

I start rocking into her. Slow strokes. Her head nestles against my shoulder, her cheek to my chest. I lean over and drop kisses everywhere that I can reach. My hands rove up and down her body. Squeezing, caressing.

This isn't a position for vigorous, athletic fucking. It's far more intimate. A sex-charged hug. But I'm sweating, burning up like I'm sprinting through a marathon.

Intense pleasure circles the base of my cock, the best kind of ache growing in my balls. I need to come. I'm so close. But I need to get her there. I need to hear her moaning and finding the simple yet profound release that she craves. That she *begged* me for.

"You ready for more?" I ask her. "Can you take it?"

Angela's eyes were closed, but now she opens them. I see the fire that I'm feeling inside. That intensity. Not a trace of hesitation or pain.

The way she's looking at me is intoxicating. Steals the breath right out of my lungs.

Yesterday, she said she trusted me. But now, I can actually

see it in her eyes. Feel it in the way she's giving herself to me, taking me inside with such tender vulnerability.

I've never felt more like a man than in this moment. Like the man I want to be. And damned if I'm going to let down her faith in me.

"More," she says.

We both need this. To abandon ourselves fully to this incredible connection between us.

I roll her onto her back, propping up onto my hands and pushing her thighs open wider with mine. I thrust wildly into her, my cock dragging out before surging forward again, over and over.

"Do you love my cock in you?"

"Yes. *Yes*." She holds onto the back of my neck, her hips bucking into mine.

"Then come for me, angel. Show me how good it feels when I fuck you. When I take good care of you."

She opens her mouth on a primal moan, her cries going ragged, and I'm right there with her. "I'm coming in you, baby. So fucking hard." I grunt and groan through every pulse of my cock. She whimpers and shudders along with me.

We're both panting for breath when I rest my weight to one side of her. I hold on to her, keeping us connected until I have to slide out and discard the condom.

Then we trade long, slow kisses. We just lie there in each other's arms. Content. Quiet.

Darkness envelops us, the night ticking by.

Finally, she speaks again.

"I didn't have many friends when I was a kid. I was alone a lot."

I push a few curls from her face so I can see her better. "Yeah?"

"I was an only child. Classic introvert. I watched old movies and read books. I loved old mysteries. Suspense."

"Hitchcock?"

"Yeah." A faint smile. "That's how I decided I wanted to be a cop. Seeking out the truth, putting away the bad guy. Solving the mystery. The real life of a police officer is completely different from what I had in my head back then, but I've never wanted to do anything else."

"I admire that." For most of my life, I had no idea what I wanted to be. Even as a Marine, it felt like I was treading water. I couldn't see past being Brent De Luca's little brother.

"When I graduated and joined West Oaks PD," she says, "my dad wasn't the mayor anymore. Murphy is a common name, so most people didn't realize. I worked my ass off on patrol. Studied like crazy for my detective exams. I moved up fast. But it had nothing to do with my father. Even if some people now would rather believe that's the case."

"Some people only want to see where we came from. Not where we're going."

She burrows even closer to me, though I didn't think that was possible. "Exactly. When I'm working a case, I try not to fall into that same kind of trap. Lord knows I'm not perfect, but I've seen plenty of times how a first impression of a case can be wrong. Someone you think you know... turns out different."

She touches her scar.

I can feel it coming. What she's been working up to. I don't push it. I just wait.

"That day," she whispers, "I was helping Sean Holt with a case that involved him personally. We didn't know who to trust. Just like now. And I... made a mistake."

I kiss her. Hold her.

"It's been almost two years since it happened, and I'm... I..."

She's gasping. Shivering.

"Angel. I'm here with you, okay? Breathe for me. Breathe."

Slowly, her chest draws in air. In. Out.

"There was a figure coming toward me. A gun. I can only remember pieces. Then lying on the ground, feeling like something was being sucked out of me. I thought it was my soul. I know I was bleeding. Dying."

I'm still holding her gaze. I won't look away. I won't leave her alone with this.

"It's the parts I can't remember that haunt me the most. When I woke up in the hospital, I had no idea who'd hurt me. I still can't see his face, even though we solved the case and the person is in jail. I don't talk about this with *anyone*. I saw a therapist at work, and I tried to stop thinking about it. I *tried*. They don't know it's still an issue for me. And it's like it's all coming back, even stronger and even worse."

She hinted at all of this the first night that she moved in here. But I didn't realize it was this bad. "I'm so sorry, baby."

A tear slips down her cheek. "I didn't want you to see me like this."

I haven't known her for long, but Angela gives the impression of being one of the strongest, most stoic people I've ever met. Reserved, careful.

I hate that she felt she had to hide her pain.

"What I see is a strong woman who's more than willing to risk herself for other people. And who's fighting like hell to save herself. How could I think any less of you for that?"

She hides her face against my neck.

"But you don't have to bear this all on your own," I say. "Share the burden with me. I can take it. I want to." I feel dampness on my neck. I cup her cheek, wiping the tears with my thumb. "Are you okay?" It's a foolish question because she's just shown me she's not. But I don't know what else to ask. I'm out of my element here.

I've got so much pain inside my heart too. Doesn't mean I know how to deal with it.

"I will be," she says. "Just stay with me. Please?"

The fear and uncertainty in her voice rips me down the middle all over again. "I will. I'll be right here with you. You don't have to be afraid."

I don't know if she's asking me for tonight, or for the next two weeks. Or something more. If she's asking for the future. For things we've both been adamant we can't face.

Relationships. *Commitment.* I can't pretend I'm not freaked out by the possibilities. All the ways I could mess up. She knows how I've fallen short in the past. I've made no secret of that.

But if a future is what Angela wants from me—if she has that much faith in this connection we didn't look for but somehow still share—I'm willing to try.

For her, I have to try.

22

Angela

I wish I could report that I fall into a blissful post-orgasmic coma until the sun is up.

Sadly, that's not the case.

I cry myself to sleep in Matteo's arms. Then I only manage to sleep fitfully for about an hour at a time.

So sexy.

But every time I wake up, Matteo's right there. Sometimes his eyes are already open. If not, I wait as long as I can bare it before brush my fingertips against the soft whiskers of his beard, and his eyelashes flutter and he pulls me closer and smiles.

Hi, angel. C'mere. Tell me what you're thinking.

Nights are hard for me, especially when I can't get my mind out of the dark places it tends to go. But incredibly, I don't want this night to end. I want to stay right in this bed with Matteo. Maybe forever.

Around three in the morning, we talk about my favorite classic films. Then his days as a Marine. Which leads to making out like teenagers and then kissing down each other's bodies, trying to explore every curve and sensitive spot. Every goosebump. We spend at least an hour admiring each other. Pointing out all our favorite things.

He kisses every last edge of my scar. I study the small details of his tattoos, the veins in his muscles, the small scar on his stomach.

He's beautiful.

With the men I've usually gravitated toward, I enjoyed being the object of desire. But with Matteo, that infatuation goes both ways. When I first met him, when I didn't even like him, I thought he was hot. But now that I know him better, I can't believe how gorgeous he is. How did I miss it? I've never been with someone that I'm this enthralled with.

Matteo is a work of art. A sculpted vision of masculinity. And the way the early morning light shines through the window, hitting him in that gentle, illuminating way.

His dick is hard and leaking after I've been paying that gorgeous physique so much attention, so what can I do but take him into my mouth? Worship him a little more, until he's thrusting and moaning and his cock erupts onto my tongue.

He returns the favor and then some, making me come twice with his tongue and then his fingers after an equally thorough exploration of my entire body.

Finally, I get a couple of hours of solid sleep. When I wake again, sun is streaming bright and full through the window. Matteo's lying next to me, head propped on his hand, watching me.

"That's what you do while I'm asleep? Just hang out waiting for me to wake up?"

"I'm weird like that." He leans over and kisses me, and I grunt, pushing him away.

"I have morning breath."

"We've been kissing all night. We have the exact same morning breath."

He's not deterred, and I decide that I'm not either. Our lips touch in soft nibbles that turn more fierce and needy. We've been naked so long, I can't remember what clothes are like. Matteo's erection rocks against my center. My legs wrap around him and hold him right there while we make out.

Matteo separates from me just enough to grab another condom and roll it on in a swift, well-versed movement. He scoops his arms beneath me and flips us so I'm on top of him.

"This okay?" he asks. "Is your head hurting?"

"Nope." It's been almost two days since my accident, and pain is the furthest thing from my mind.

"Then ride my cock, angel. Use me."

I bite my lip and smile down at him. Should I like it this much when he tells me what to do? That commanding, scratchy tone to his voice. I never like taking orders from anyone, but for him, I'm making an exception. And it's a relief. A wonderful taste of freedom to let him take the reins. Even just for a little while.

Share the burden with me, he said. *I can take it.*

I want that. I really do.

My eyes roll back when I sink onto him. Inch after glorious inch fills me. He cups my breasts, rubbing my nipples with his thumbs.

Since our first time fooling around, I've been shedding my inhibitions with Matteo one by one. And there's nothing left now. The man saw me bawling last night. Saw me weaker than I've let *anyone* see me. So I don't think about anything now except our bodies, the pleasure we're giving one another.

I lean over him, touching his face and feeling the bristles of his beard beneath my palm. He takes my hands and laces our fingers together. Bucks his hips upward to meet mine.

Our bodies are slick and sticky, the scent of sex already heavy in the air.

I love his dirty talk. But this time, he doesn't say a single thing out loud. Yet I *hear him*. Everything his eyes are saying. *I'm here with you. You're not alone.*

We reach our climax together, staring into each other's eyes.

Sex has never been like this for me. Stripping away every defense I usually hide behind.

Afterward, the sun's shining insistently through the blinds. It's bittersweet that our night is over, but I'm ready to face everything that I've avoided in the last day. The people who are targeting me. The IA investigation against me. The Volkov connection.

All of it.

Also, I need to wash Neve's sheets and comforter. And maybe offer to buy her a new bed.

Matteo's stomach rumbles. "I should make breakfast. And let Pretzel out."

"Okay," I mumble.

He slides out of bed. Instantly I'm colder. He took my personal heater away. But it's the encouragement I need to get moving.

Matteo tugs his sweats on, then goes out to the living room. I hear Pretzel's collar jingling and the back door opening.

I head to Matteo's bathroom and start the shower. I'm halfway finished washing when he pulls back the shower curtain and looks in at me.

"We're back in my room now?" he asks.

"We already massacred Neve's bed. I don't want to defile her shower too."

He grunts. "But you make it sound so sexy."

I finish rinsing and shut off the water before grabbing a towel.

"Not even going to wait for me to join you?" He's pouting. It's cute. But I won't be swayed.

"It's already late morning. I need to accomplish a few things today. Not just having orgasms." I turn back and give him a soft kiss. "Thank you for last night. It was fun."

The word feels disingenuous the moment it leaves my tongue. And Matteo must have the same reaction from the way he flinches, so fast I almost miss it.

Last night was more than *fun*. It meant a lot to me. I showed Matteo pieces of me I've never shown anyone else. I don't regret a moment of it.

I'm not running from him.

I just need a tiny sliver of space.

"Can I have my phone?" I ask. "I need to see if Sean or Jake wrote." The doctor only said to avoid screens for twenty-four hours, and even that was more a suggestion than a strict rule.

Sighing, Matteo points into his bedroom. "I left it on my dresser."

I go to grab it, and Matteo stays in the bathroom to take his own shower. Then I'm in multitasking mode, throwing on a dress of Neve's, making coffee, and scrolling through my messages. In between, I strip the sheets from Neve's bed and shove them into the washing machine.

A few minutes later, Matteo is making scrambled eggs and I'm sipping coffee at the kitchen counter. There's silence between us again, and I'm trying to focus on my email inbox instead of noticing.

It's for the best that this arrangement of ours has an expiration date. When Neve returns, everything will change. And that's okay. Something this white-hot, this intense, is never meant to last.

I'll have to get back to my real life. My work.

There's a knock at the door, making us both look up. "I'll get it." I set down my coffee.

"Check the peephole."

"I *know*." When I do, I see Rex, the bodyguard. He and Leon must be back on duty now that it's morning.

I open the door, and a small figure darts inside past me. She shouts, "Matteo!" with her arms up in the air.

It's Natalie. Emily's standing behind Rex, laughing.

"Visitors for you?" Rex says with a grin.

I give Emily a hug. I wasn't expecting her and Natalie back already, but I'm glad to see them. Especially since we have Bennett Security keeping an eye on the house.

"I'm so sorry about what happened," she says. "How are you feeling?"

"Much better."

"Did they catch the guy who ran into you?"

"Not yet."

She squeezes me, then heads inside, and Rex holds out a bundle of envelopes. "Got some mail for you. Detective Holt dropped it off."

"Thanks." Some of this looks like generic work mail that my desk must've been accumulating. But there's also a large manila envelope with *West Oaks PD Evidence* stamped on it. It has my name scrawled on the flap.

It's not Sean's handwriting. I wonder who else from West Oaks PD knows about our side investigation.

"Coffee?" I ask Rex. "Just made a pot."

Rex is in his late forties, hair threaded with silver. He's standing in front of me with his hands clasped behind his back, every bit the distinguished bodyguard. "No thank you, ma'am. I should get back to my post."

Rex has a voice like some late-night radio host. Yikes. That man could talk just about any woman out of her panties. Not *me*, obviously, because that's Matteo's job. But some lucky lady.

In the kitchen, Matteo is holding Natalie on his hip like she's a toddler while he scoops scrambled eggs onto plates. Natalie's rambling about the adventures she's been having in Bakersfield. Emily leans against the kitchen counter.

"Didn't know you were coming back today," Matteo says.

"Needed to get the rest of our stuff," Emily explains. "And Natalie was dying to give Uncle Matteo a hug. She's been talking about nothing else. She didn't get a proper goodbye when we left a few days ago."

"A proper goodbye?" Matteo's spoon lands in the pan with a clank. "What does that mean?"

Emily scratches her nose. "We're going to pack up our things and stay with my parents the rest of the summer."

"*What?*"

Guilt floods me with nausea. This is my fault.

Matteo sets Natalie on her feet. "When will you be back?"

"When it's time for the new school year."

"That's almost two months!"

Natalie grabs my hand and pulls me into the living room. Pretzel and Chips trail after us. Natalie runs her hand down each animal's back while Emily and Matteo still bicker in the kitchen.

"I don't like it when they fight," Natalie says. "I don't like Grandma and Grandpa's house either. It smells funny."

I set down my envelopes, cross my legs, and sit beside her. "I'm sorry."

"But Grandpa took me to see his friend's coin collection. And Grandma showed me how to make candles. When we get back, Grandma's going to help me make a pink one."

"That doesn't sound so bad." I smile, even though my heart's twisting. Natalie is such a sweetheart. It's obvious how much she loves Matteo, how much he loves her. How hard Emily is trying. How Brent's death is still ruling over their lives.

And then I arrive and provide a spark for all that tinder. At least, that's how it feels.

Emily walks over. "Natty-bear, please help pack up your things. And get Pretzel's water dish and food."

"You're taking the dog too?" Matteo asks, following on her heels. "What about Chips?"

"You know my dad is allergic to cats."

"Fucking—" He presses his lips together on the rest of that sentiment. He spins around and storms out the back door into the yard.

Emily clears her throat. Her face is red. "Please, Natty-bear. Pack up and then you can play more before we have to go."

Natalie gives me a forlorn look. Then they both head into Matteo's bedroom.

I get up and go to the back yard. Matteo's sitting out there in a lawn chair, elbows on his knees, glaring at the grass.

He doesn't look up when I step outside.

"I'm sorry," I say.

"Why?"

"If Emily doesn't feel safe here because of me, then I don't blame her. I told you I'd stay in a hotel, and that offer stands." We already had this conversation, but I feel obligated to bring it up again. Having Natalie gone a few more days was one thing. All summer?

I won't even be here that long.

"It isn't because of you. It's because of me. This would be an issue regardless of whether you were here." He drags a hand over his beard. "When Brent was dying, right at the end, he asked me to take care of Emily and Natalie. I promised I would. Emily's never been comfortable with that.

She wants to do it herself, and I understand it. I do. But that was my last fucking promise to my brother, and it's fucking important to me."

He takes a heavy breath.

"Come here," I say. That's what he always says to me, but right now, he's the one who needs comfort. I tug on his hand until he slides off his seat into the grass. I kneel behind him and drape my arms around his neck, resting my cheek on his shoulder. He sinks back against me. Just a little.

"Can I have a hug too?"

I look back and see Natalie there in the doorway.

"Absolutely," I say. "There's room."

Natalie gets in Matteo's lap, and I stay behind him, hugging them both. It's nice. I could stay just like this for the rest of the day.

Maybe even longer.

LATER, we head back inside to eat cold scrambled eggs. Matteo, Natalie, and Emily pull out a board game to play for a while, making the most of their time together before they separate again. They ask me to join, but I feel like the odd woman out.

I grab my stack of envelopes and head into Neve's bedroom instead.

I've got a few emails to return, so I do that now. And I check in with Detective Grayson, assuring him that I'm fine. There was another local news piece about my car chase. The media is implying I'm a criminal mastermind who's run afoul of the mafia and that hit men are targeting me for vengeance.

I certainly hope that's as fantastical as it sounds.

It's all so surreal. I try not to think about how this will

affect my career even after my name is cleared. But my work is my life.

I won't let these assholes destroy me without a fight.

I spread out my stack of envelopes on the newly made bed, pushing aside the junk mail and making note of the items I'll need to deal with later. The big manila envelope keeps catching my eye. The one stamped *West Oaks PD Evidence*. Which is odd in itself, now that I think about it.

Would Sean use a stray evidence envelope to send me something? When I've already been accused of *stealing* evidence? Just having this envelope could make me look guilty in Cassidy's suspicious eyes.

Threads of doubt make me hesitate.

Did Sean send this at all?

I pick it up. There are papers inside. Stiff and thick. They feel like photos.

Carefully, I break the seal and open the flap. Peek inside.

Crime scene photos.

I tip the envelope, sliding the contents out, but my hand freezes when I get the first solid glimpse. My heart stutters and my lungs cease to work.

Garish pictures scatter over the bed. My lap. The floor. And there's a handwritten note taped to one of them.

Her blood might as well be on your hands.

For endless seconds, I can't move.

Then I rush into the bathroom and throw up my breakfast.

23

Matteo

*F*ar too soon, Emily says they need to go. I carry their suitcases out to their car. Emily has Pretzel by the leash, and the dog is whimpering like she knows something's up.

"Are you sure you can't take the cat?"

"*Yes*, Matteo. I'm sure. This isn't ideal, but I'm doing the best I can."

"Aren't we all?" I grumble.

I get that Natalie doesn't want to be without a pet all summer. I don't want that either. But taking just Pretzel, and not Chips? I don't know why those two like each other so much, but they do. It's cruel to separate them. And it's cruel to force Natalie to do it when she loves both of her pets with her whole heart.

I'm trying to shake it off. Not be the grumpy bitch that Danny likes to accuse me of being. But sometimes, it's hard.

Emily's arranging things in the trunk. "Can you tell Natalie it's time to come outside?"

"Yeah." A few minutes ago, my niece was putting away the board game we were playing. She's not happy about this situation either. Aside from those first few minutes when she jumped on me like a baby kangaroo, she hasn't been anywhere near her usual buoyant self today.

Maybe that's my fault. I should've acted thrilled that she and her mom would be staying hours away from me for the rest of the summer. I should've modeled a *positive attitude*. That's probably what Emily would say. But then Natalie might have assumed I didn't care about not seeing her. And it's the exact opposite.

Parenting is hard. But so is being an uncle who'll be missing his family for months on end and can't do a damn thing about it. I can drive out and visit them, braving Emily's parents. But not every day.

And way too soon, Angela won't be here either.

Inside the house, I find Natalie hugging on Chips, whose meows sound even grumpier than usual. "Careful," I say. "Don't want her to scratch you."

"I know she doesn't mean it." Natalie sets the cat down, and Chips darts away, dashing straight for the window that overlooks the front yard. Like she knows exactly where Pretzel has gone.

"Your mom asked you to come outside. It's time to go."

"I have to say goodbye to Angela first." Natalie goes over to the closed door to Neve's bedroom and knocks. "Angela? Are you there?"

There's no answer.

"She might be napping," I say, even though the words ring hollow in my ears.

With Angela, I still never know if she's going to pull me closer or push me away. I thought last night changed everything, and yet this morning, she was putting up subtle barriers again.

Maybe it's part of a process. She's slowly figuring out how

to open up. Let me in. I'd like to think she doesn't feel the need to hide from me after all the progress we've made.

But just because I want things a certain way doesn't make it reality.

Natalie raises her little fist to knock again, but I stop her. "We should let Angela rest. She's still healing after her car accident."

"Give her another hug for me?"

"I will. But I want another hug for me first." I scoop up my niece and squeeze her. "I'm gonna miss you so bad."

"Let's talk every day."

"Deal."

I carry Natalie outside. Chips tries to follow us, but I'm quick to shut the door before she can escape. Pretzel is in the backseat of the car making the saddest damn doggy eyes you've ever seen. Emily has to hold on to the dog's collar for Natalie to get in.

Once she's all buckled, I give Nat one last hug and a kiss on the cheek. "Love you, Uncle Matteo," Natalie says.

"Love you, too. Love you both."

Emily nods at me with a tightlipped smile.

I stand on the lawn and watch their car until they turn at the corner. Then I head back inside.

I go to Angela's and knock softly. "It's me. They're gone. You okay?"

Still no answer.

This really doesn't feel right.

I try the knob, and it opens. "Angela?" I glance inside, then push the door wider. I don't see her, but there are photographs scattered all over the bed on the floor. Weird.

There's a sound in the bathroom. Like a moan.

I head in that direction, but as I do, my eye catches on the photos. They're of a crime scene. A *murder* scene, clearly, because there's a dead body. A dark-haired woman, her clothes charred, her eyes staring. I've seen things like that before in real life, but this is still awful.

And then I reach the bathroom. Angela's crouched over the toilet. The sharp scent of vomit hits me.

What the hell *happened*?

I crouch beside her. "What's going on? Are you all right?"

She shakes her head. "The photos…"

"Did you find those photos in one of the envelopes you got?"

She nods.

"Did Sean Holt send you that shit?"

She swallows. Wipes her nose. "I'm not upset because of the pictures. I've seen them all before. I saw that scene myself. It's—"

She lurches for the toilet bowl and retches. I smooth back her hair to keep it away from her face. Nothing comes up. When she's done dry heaving, I help her get a drink of water from the sink. She rinses her mouth. I support her with an arm around her waist and take her over to the bed, where we lie down.

I try to wrap myself around her. Protecting her.

Fuck, I keep trying to protect her, and shit *keeps happening*.

"It's Stefanie Rossi's murder scene," she says in a hoarse whisper. "I remember that house. At the end of the street, all alone. Charred by the fire. The smell. Stefanie was lying in her bed. On her side."

Like Angela's lying now. She clings to me, fisting my T-shirt.

"I've never forgotten any of those details, so seeing the photos wasn't much worse. It was the note taped to one of the photos that got to me. It's from *him*. Or *them*. I don't know. Whoever's doing this to me."

"What did it say?"

"Just look."

I don't want to let go of her, but I have to in order to see. One particularly gruesome photo has a torn sheet of paper attached to it. Blocky letters.

Her blood might as well be on your hands.

Jeez, this is screwed up.

As I look at the photo, I realize Stefanie Rossi bore a resemblance to Angela. Curly dark hair. Sharp cheekbones and striking features. Angela's skin tone is a deeper bronze, but the similarities still stand out.

I feel *ill* noticing that. I have no idea what it means. But I really don't like it.

I crawl back to Angela and pull her into my arms again. "We need to find out who sent this. Did they drop it off here? Do they know where you live?"

"I don't think so. Rex told me Sean brought the mail. It must've been in my office. Someone blames me for Stefanie's death. They want to punish me, and I have no idea why. I'd never even heard of her until I went to her murder scene."

"Someone blames you for not finding this alleged 'real' killer."

She blinks. Her eyes are red, and tiny droplets dot her eyelashes. "Maybe. But I did everything by the book in that case. I even looked into his mystery man claim, and there was nothing solid to support it. Nothing but speculation. I didn't do anything wrong."

"I'm sure you didn't. But whoever's doing this, they don't care about what makes sense." I kiss her hairline, careful to avoid the bandage. "Let's call Sean and find out how the hell this stuff got in your hands."

Angela uses her phone to call Detective Holt. She puts him on speaker and explains what happened. Her voice is much stronger than it was a moment ago. I don't like what's happening right now, not one bit, but I'm glad that she didn't hide how upset she was when it was just me.

With Holt, she's back to being Detective Murphy. Unflappable.

Holt curses under his breath. "The envelope was with the others in your office. I barely looked at it, and that was foolish of me. The photos must've come from the Volkov casefile. Don't touch them again. We'll need to check them for fingerprints."

"I doubt the person behind this left any prints," Angela says. "They've been careful this whole time. I'm so *sick* of this."

I think of the guy she's described seeing multiple times now. The one in the hoodie. Is he a cop? Or working with one? "There must be cameras at your station, right?" I ask. "There has to be a way to find out who put this in Angela's office."

"I'll follow up on everything," Holt says. "But I need to get Jake Shelborne in here, and probably his sister too, because I'm swamped. The chief is trying to keep his hands clean, and I can't trust anyone else at West Oaks PD with this."

Angela closes her eyes. "And you've got enough extra work with me being out of commission. You can lean on Grayson when it comes to my cases."

"I'm juggling everything. You know me. But it isn't going to happen at light speed, unfortunately."

"I get it," Angela says. "Believe me."

"Just sit tight, and we'll work through everything we've got. Piece by piece. We're going to find the clue we need that'll crack this open. You've got Bennett Security there, and it doesn't seem like these people know where you live. I'm sure I haven't been followed when I've been there, and I'll keep being careful. You do the same."

Angela ends the call and tosses her phone on the bed. She scowls at the photos that are still strewn over the room. "You know, I distinctly remember trying to tell Holt to lie low when it was his life on the line two years ago. Did he listen to me?"

She pauses like she's waiting for my answer.

"I'm guessing no?"

"*Hell*, no. But I should listen to *him*?" She scoffs. "Whoever's targeting me just keeps on coming. They won't stop. So I won't either. I'm a detective. I'm going to do what I'm good at. What I've been trained to do. Investigate. Find the truth."

Her eyes lift to mine, shining with defiance. As if she expects me to fight her on this.

But everything she's saying makes perfect sense to me.

I don't want her hurt. But it's like she confessed to me last night—she's *already hurting*. I want to make that better. Whatever it takes.

"Okay," I say. "I told you I'd help you. I'm not an investigator, but I can be your muscle. I'll be the brawn to your brains." Though maybe I can help with both.

"Really?"

"Really." The uncertainty in her expression makes me pull her close and kiss her. "Who needs those guys from Bennett Security? I can be your bodyguard. If you'll let me."

She kisses me back. Slow, tender.

"Partners?" I smirk as I say this, but I'm not kidding. I want her to say yes. I need to keep her safe.

And I also need to know she's willing to accept what I'm offering. If she's not? I don't know where we go from here.

She gives me a hint of a smile. "Is this another benefit to being your roommate? Crime fighting skills?"

"I'm a man of many talents."

"All right. You're hired. But we *do* need Bennett Security. We need all the help we can get."

"Noted. Now that we're officially crime-fighting partners, where do we start?"

WE START by reviewing everything we can get our hands on about the Volkov case. But there's a big problem.

I have a shift to work.

I head to the fire station the next morning. There's no question about me showing up. I may have bailed to go with Angela to the hospital, but I'm not the kind of guy who shirks off my duties without a compelling, life-or-death reason.

But it also feels like turning my skin inside-out to leave her alone.

Thankfully, she's not truly alone. The Bennett Security guys are there. Otherwise, I don't know how I'd manage it.

I head in for the shift change after Angela promises she'll stay at the house doing background research. She won't go anywhere else without me. But I also check the new cameras a few times, just in case.

No more than two or three… dozen times.

"How's Angela doing?" Danny asks while we're washing the truck after lunch.

Captain Bucanan asked the same thing when I got in. But while Danny seems genuinely interested, Buc was far more wary. Chief Ross hasn't said anything about my trip to the hospital. Buc covered for me. I don't even know why he's being so nice to me. But thank goodness for small favors.

"She's feeling better."

"Any leads on the guy who crashed into her?" Danny asks.

Holt already let us know the gray sedan turned up at an abandoned lot on the outskirts of town. Stolen. No sign of the driver. A dead end.

"Not yet. We're working on it."

"*We?*"

I stare back at him. "Yeah. Me and her. Along with a

bunch of other friends of hers. We've got bodyguards sitting in a car outside the house twenty-four-seven just in case the fucker figures out where she lives."

"Damn. What does Emily think of that?"

"She took Natalie to stay with her parents for the rest of the summer." I take out my frustration on the truck, scrubbing at the shiny sides. "Her parents are giving her a loan, too, to pay off Brent's med school debt. Swooping in to the rescue."

Emily dropped that bombshell via email this morning.

"That's amazing. But why are you beating up the truck like it insulted your manhood? Gonna wear a hole in the paint."

I should be grateful for the reprieve. This loan from Emily's parents will put us in a far better position. They even promised to defer payments so that Emily could handle paying it herself. *Without me.* It would mean that I don't have to bar-tend anymore. I wouldn't have to worry about making captain and the salary that would go along with the promotion.

But it's a damn insult added on top of injury. Just a reminder that I'll never live up to my brother's memory.

"I'll miss Natalie. I'd rather have her close."

"I have no doubt. But if you're so determined to play everybody's hero, you might have to settle for taking them one at a time. Fix Angela's problems now. Then take on Emily and Natalie later."

I laugh. "That might be the most sensible thing you've ever said."

"I have my moments."

That night, while I'm lying in my bunk, I text Angela to ask how she's doing. The only response I get is, *Working.*

I'll bet this is how she usually is when she's on a case. Intensely focused. Unwilling to step away until she's made a breakthrough. Brent had that exact same work ethic. It's no wonder Angela is one of the top detectives in town.

She's incredible. She really is.

Finally, a million years later, it's morning. My shift is over. I don't think I've ever been this anxious to see someone. Certainly not someone I'm dating.

Not that we're dating.

But I wouldn't mind if we were.

I set those surprising thoughts aside and jump in my pickup, racing toward home while keeping to a reasonable speed. I wave at the Bennett Security bodyguards on my way in, then jog my way up the steps.

"I'm home," I say, closing and locking the door behind me. Angela is sitting at the kitchen table working on a laptop, and she barely glances up at me. She's got on a pair of chunky-framed glasses. I wonder where those came from? They're adorable.

Chips is curled up and sleeping in her lap.

"I found something," Angela says. "A lead."

"Tell me." I stand behind her and rub her shoulders, which are tight with tension.

"A website where prisoners can post about their cases and experiences. It looks like other people post on their behalf as well, trying to drum up public outrage and support challenges to their convictions." She pulls up the site. It's called *Justice For All*. "A lot of the activity on here looks legitimate, and a few prisoners have had their names cleared after new DNA tests, that kind of thing. Actual miscarriages of justice. But there are others who use the site to harass prison guards, prosecutors, cops, even defense attorneys."

She scrolls through the posts and comments.

"I found a lot of posts about Volkov, authored by someone with the handle LukeisInnocent. She claims to be his girlfriend. I spoke to the head of research at Bennett Security, and they hooked me up. Found all the info on the new girl-friend by tracking her IP address and doing a background check."

"Is that something the police can usually do?"

"If we have a warrant, sure. But here, we don't. I might be in trouble if anybody found out that Bennett Security helped me with this. The methods they used weren't completely above board. I'm hoping you'll keep my secret."

I kiss her neck, sucking gently at her pulse point. "Unless I use it for blackmail later."

She turns and gives me a quick kiss. "Bennett Security sent me a full dossier on her. The girlfriend lives here in West Oaks. I want to talk to her. See what she'll tell me."

"When?"

"How about right now?" She scoots her chair back, and I have to move to let her up. She sets the cat on the floor.

I was hoping for some private time with Angela first, but I'm not going to bring that up. Priorities. I'm supposed to be helping her solve this case, not coaxing her back into my bed.

"I just need to change first. If we'll be breaking some rules, I might not want to sport West Oaks Fire logos while we're doing it."

24

Matteo

*W*e take my truck. But I'm no fool. I ask the Bennett Security guys to trail us.

For me, priority one is keeping Angela safe.

"Her name is Katrina Katalsky." Angela's sitting in the passenger seat, reading from the dossier about Volkov's girlfriend. "She's twenty-two years old from Reno, Nevada."

"Twenty-two? How old is Volkov?"

"Late forties. He prefers the younger ladies, not that I'm judging."

"Right. I forgot you like 'mature' men."

She smirks at me. "Katrina and Volkov met each other through a website that connects single women with prisoners."

"A different website from *Justice For All*?"

"Oh, yes. Believe it or not, some women are into prison guys. The longer they're in and the worse the crime, the better. Volkov is serving twenty-five to life for killing his ex, so that makes him a decent catch, I guess? Can't account for what turns people on. But Katrina has a criminal record herself. Arrested for theft on three separate occasions, as well as assault. She was fighting with other women over different prison guys."

"Okay, so this isn't her first prison-boyfriend rodeo."

"Apparently not." We go beneath the freeway overpass and enter an industrial area of town, where warehouses and factories dominate. But there are residential pockets here too. Mid-century apartment buildings with crumbling stucco sides and missing address numbers. Reminds me of where Brent and I grew up in Missouri. A neighborhood that had seen better days.

The GPS tells me to take a right turn, then a left. I pull up to a three-story apartment that looks like it came straight from the 1950s. It's in better shape than a lot of the buildings around here. The first level is all open spaces for parking, with the apartment units above.

I put the truck into park at the curb. Leon and Rex have stopped on the other side of the street, and I wave to them in acknowledgment. They know we're here to question a possible witness. They're here as backup, ready to step in if Angela or I call.

Angela leans toward me, showing me the screen on her phone. "This is Katrina. A recent photo."

Large dark eyes. Dark hair. It seems Luke Volkov has a type.

"She's been dating Volkov for the last six months. Her posts on *Justice For All* started not long after they got together. She claims the police falsified evidence and conspired to blame Volkov instead of the real killer. Who knows, she might believe it. She started a fundraising campaign on GoFundMe to raise money for his appeals."

"Was she successful?"

"Only got about $1000. Which isn't going to buy very much if they're looking for a high-priced private attorney."

"So Volkov claimed that somebody else killed Stefanie

Rossi. And now, his girlfriend is saying that corrupt cops concealed evidence to ensure his conviction? Sounds like a motive for her to go after you. Since you were the lead detective."

"Yes. But I'm not sure where the photos I received yesterday fit in. It's hard to imagine that Katrina cares about Stefanie's death."

"You never know. Maybe she's really the crusader for justice that she claims. Is it possible that a woman drove the gray sedan that hit you? Not a man?"

She thinks about it. "I guess anything's possible."

We get out of the truck and start toward the staircase. Katrina lives in a unit on the third floor.

"Are you going to tell Katrina who you really are?" I ask.

Angela couldn't look further from a cop right now. Her hair is a mass of beautiful curls, and she's wearing one of Neve's sleeveless dresses with a pair of flared jeans underneath. I resist the urge to run my fingers down the tattoo on her arm.

"I'll claim to be a journalist. I'll only identify myself as a cop if I have to. I'm not supposed to be a part of this investigation anyway. But maybe Sean will be able to use what I find to bring her in for a more formal interview. Or even a search warrant."

"Did you tell Holt what we're doing today?"

She smirks at me. "What do you think?"

We climb the stairs. The metal rattles with every step. On the second floor, the curtains on all of the apartments are closed. We reach Katrina's unit, and Angela knocks.

"Ms. Katalsky?"

I edge in close behind Angela, wanting to keep her within easy reach so I can protect her if needed. Katrina didn't look like a bruiser in her photo, but she's been arrested for assault. If she drove the car that ran into Angela? She could be capable of anything.

I told Angela I'd be her bodyguard. Maybe I don't have martial arts or special forces training. But I was a Marine. I can do plenty of damage.

We're both quiet, listening. But there's no sound from inside. Angela knocks again.

"I don't think she's home," I say.

Angela glances in the window, trying to see through the crack in the curtain. "The dossier didn't say anything about a job. I guess we could wait around and see if she turns up. A good old-fashioned stakeout." Angela takes out her phone. "I'll let the Bennett Security guys know to settle in."

"We might not have to do that," I say. "Look." I nod at the next apartment over, where a face is peering out between the curtains. She vanishes when she sees us looking.

But then the door to that apartment opens, and the same woman looks out through the gap, narrowing her eyes at us. A chain bars the doorway. "Are you folks here for Katrina?"

"We are. Maybe you can help us." Angela holds out her hand. But the woman sneers at it.

"I don't want anything to do with Katrina or her *friends*. You'd best be on your way before I call the authorities."

Angela gives her a disarming smile. "We *are* the authorities. Trying to keep a low profile, but we'd like to ask Katrina some questions about a recent incident."

"About time. I've complained about Katrina plenty, but nothing ever changes. Do you have any ID?"

I expect Angela to say no, but she dips her hand into the small purse she's carrying. She holds up her badge. "Never leave home without it." She winks at me.

"Who's he?" the woman asks, eyeing me.

"My bodyguard."

The neighbor abruptly slams the door shut.

But then it opens again with the chain disengaged, and her entire demeanor has changed. "I'm Lola. If you want to know what Katrina's been up to, you can come in. I'll tell you everything I've seen."

"Nice to meet you, Lola. I'm Angela. And my associate is Matteo."

Lola's blue eyes wander over me. "A bodyguard, huh? Must be a perk of your police job. I never heard about that one."

"A *big* perk." Angela grins at me as she goes inside, and I follow.

"The kettle's already heating. I was about to make tea. Hope you like mint." She bustles into the kitchen.

The apartment is covered in sunflowers. In framed prints on the walls, on the sofa pillows, on the dishes and glassware in the china cupboard. There are vases of silk sunflowers on the dining and end tables.

I glance around while Lola pours hot water into three sunflower mugs and drops a tea bag into each one. She hands them out to us and gestures for us to sit at the dining table. The chairs are so small and delicate looking, I'm not sure it'll hold me. The thing creaks when I sit down. Angela looks perfectly comfortable in her tiny chair, while I feel like a giant in a kids' playhouse.

"Is Katrina gone a lot?" Angela asks.

"The opposite. She's usually skulking around here, though she comes and goes as she pleases at all hours. Usually she prefers her *friends* to come here. *Strange men.*"

"Strange men?" Angela repeats. "What do they look like?"

Lola waves her hand. "Average. Young. Katrina invites them in and they listen to loud music. I've asked her to turn it down, and she screams at me. That's why I've complained to the city. I was a West Oaks School District bus driver for twenty-five years and I don't tolerate that kind of language.

I'll bet she and her boyfriends are abusing substances, too. This used to be a nice building."

"Do any of the men wear hoodies?" I ask.

Lola sips her tea. "Yes, I think some had the hoods of their shirts up. That's what I meant by shifty. Trying not to be noticed. Is that why they're called *hoodlums*?"

"Um, I'm not sure." I try not to laugh, looking to Angela for help.

"Did you notice the cars any of them drove?" Angela asks.

"I don't think so. But I've noticed Katrina's car. She has a new one, fancy. A gold Mercedes. And new clothes and jewelry too. Thinks quite highly of herself despite her behavior. I wish she'd move on out of here and leave us respectable people alone."

"When did she get the new car?" I ask.

"A month or so back. Before that, she could barely make rent."

Angela glances at me. If Katrina's GoFundMe campaign was such a dismal failure, and she's been scrambling to get money for her boyfriend's legal defense and has no job, where's she getting cash for a new car and wardrobe?

Angela finishes her tea and sets it on the table. "Thank you, Lola. This has been very helpful. Would you mind if I give your name and number to my colleague at West Oaks PD? Detective Sean Holt?"

"I would be happy to. I also have some suggestions for neighborhood safety. Do you think Detective Holt would like to hear them?"

"Entirely possible."

We thank her again and head for the door.

But when we step outside the apartment, we're met face-to-face with a young, dark-haired woman who's unlocking the next-door unit. She's wearing designer logo jeans and a silky bomber jacket.

Katrina.

She takes one look at the both of us and bolts.

Shit.

"Katrina, wait!" Angela says.

Katrina goes for the stairs. I take off after her.

Angela's footsteps pound behind me. I hear her yelling into her phone at Leon and Rex. "On foot in pursuit of a possible suspect. Coming down the staircase."

Katrina jumps down the last bit of the staircase, darting away. The girl is fast. Wiry.

And the look on her face when she saw us? Saw Angela? Pure panic.

"Suspect heading north," Angela says into the phone. She's falling behind. I keep going. Katrina climbs over a chain-length fence. It rips her jacket, but she doesn't pause. I vault over the fence, gaining on the girl.

We're in an alley that runs behind a strip mall just off the main road. Katrina's still booking like a triathlete at a qualifying meet.

I spot Leon running down the street parallel to me. Then Rex appears up ahead at the mouth of the alley. Katrina's running straight toward him.

They're outflanking her.

Katrina skids to a stop when she sees Rex, arms flailing. Her gaze darts around for an escape. I see her mind working. She might try to go through the back door of one of the strip mall businesses. Leon will be waiting on the street on the other side.

I've slowed down, and I carefully approach her. "*Katrina.* We just want to talk."

She doesn't make a move. She's frozen there with indecision.

I close the distance. Grab her arm. Then the girl takes a swipe at me.

She's holding a damn *knife*.

"Take it easy!"

She takes another swipe at me. "I'm a free person! I won't be oppressed by the government!"

"I'm not a cop. But if you don't quit it, you're going to wind up in jail anyway." I manage to get hold of her wrists. I squeeze until she drops the knife.

She turns and freaking *spits* at me. *Gross.* Some lands in my beard and on my neck. Leon and Rex converge on my position in time to see the bodily fluids fly. The disgust on their faces matches mine.

Angela catches up just as I'm whipping off my shirt to wipe my face.

But at least we've got Katrina cornered. I step back so I'm out of the splash zone. Leon and Rex can take one for the team. I'm done.

Angela strolls the last few feet like this is a casual, pre-planned meeting. "Is there a reason you're half naked?" she asks me.

"This hellion just spit on me!" I'm still scrubbing at my beard.

Angela turns to Katrina, who's glaring at us with her arms crossed. "You can either have a calm discussion with us," Angela says, "or I'll call the police and the tattooed gentleman will press charges against you for battery."

"She tried to stab me too," I add. Rex slides the knife further away from Katrina with his shoe.

Angela's fighting back a smile. I don't think it's funny. "Then assault *and* battery," Angela says.

"I don't have to do anything," Katrina snaps.

"You're right. The choice is yours." Angela takes out her phone.

Katrina's eyes widen. "Fine. I can talk to you. But only if somebody will change my tire."

"Your tire?" Angela asks incredulously. "We're not AAA."

"That's the deal! I have a flat, and the tow truck guy said it would be hours. And I just got my nails done, okay?" She holds up her hands. Her nails are long, pointed, metallic blue. "I'm parked in a lot half a mile away. I had to walk all the way back here. This is the worst day *ever*."

Angela shakes her head. "Okay." She points at Leon and Rex. "You two, if you don't mind, walk with us to the nail salon parking lot? Run her down if she tries to take off again." Then Angela turns and points at me. "*You*, find a shirt to put on."

25

Angela

Leon and Rex get started on changing the tire of Katrina's Mercedes. We've walked down the street to a parking lot that serves a convenience market and a smattering of other local businesses, including Katrina's preferred nail salon.

The Mercedes is so new it still has the dealer plates. It's this year's model. Yet there are multiple scratches and dings on the fender and doors.

"Had it long?" I ask.

"That's none of your business," she snaps.

There aren't many trees around, and the concrete is baking in the sun, but we've found a small corner of shade cast by a nearby building.

Matteo disappeared to go to his truck, where he said he has a gym bag. He's going to get a new shirt. Part of me wished he could keep parading around shirtless. Both because it's an excellent view, and because I think it was distracting Katrina. I don't love that this girl had her eyes on my man.

But the interrogator in me was salivating over any kind of

leverage I might have in this. I'll just have to use my other skills.

Wait, *my man*? That's how I'm thinking of him now?

Not the time, I tell myself. I'll freak out about that later.

"Why did you run from us?" I ask.

"Because you were at my neighbor's. I don't like her, and she doesn't like me. She's tried to call the cops on me before."

"What makes you think we're the cops?"

She glares at me. "I know who you are."

"Oh, good. I figured you did. But I'm glad you can come out and admit it."

Her lip curls. "I saw those articles about you online. You're a dirty cop. I don't know what you want from me, but you're not going to get it." She looks down at her long blue fingernails.

"Have you been talking to the media about me?" I ask.

"I don't have to. You've shown your true colors. Everybody knows what you are."

"But you've posted online on other topics. *Justice for All?* You use the name LukeisInnocent?"

She smiles wickedly. "All I post is the truth. That's what Luke tells me."

"You believe that a convicted felon, whom you've never seen in the outside world, only tells the truth? A convicted murderer and drug trafficker?"

"He's a beautiful person who was wrongfully accused and convicted. You are the one whose heart is full of lies."

I sigh. So far, this has all been predictable. I need to get more specific. Show her what I know.

Katrina keeps saying she doesn't want to talk, and I'm sure she'd prefer we never showed up today. But I'll bet some part of her wants to tell me her story. That's the thing about people. In the end, everybody wants to share. Even when it would be wiser to stay quiet.

I'm strategizing when Matteo jogs up wearing a fresh T-shirt. Somehow, this one's even tighter than the last. His nipples are visible through the thin white fabric.

I force myself to stop ogling, only to realize Katrina's doing the same thing.

Ah ha. There we go. Leverage. Just what I need.

"Remember how I was telling you about Katrina's GoFundMe campaign to help her boyfriend?" I say to Matteo. "I told you those things are never successful. But you said she might've been doing it for some other purpose. Not just the money."

Come on, Matteo, I think. *Work with me.*

He looks thoughtful before responding. "Right. I thought she was sending a message to Volkov. That she supports him." A grin teases his lips. "Just what a woman should do for the man she loves."

Katrina lifts her chin. "Exactly. I will do anything for him."

"You're a fighter," he says. "I'll give you that. I wasn't thrilled about you going after *me*, but you're devoted." He shrugs. "Most guys could be so lucky."

She preens at Matteo's compliment. Hard to believe she was spitting at him a quarter hour ago.

He takes a step closer to her, folding his arms and flexing his chest. "But I hope Volkov is taking care of you in return?" He's turning on the charm. Eyes flagrantly checking out what Katrina's got.

I'm not a fan. Turns out, I'm a touch possessive when it comes to Matteo.

But Detective Murphy? She's loving this.

"Luke does all kinds of things for me," Katrina says. "He's the best."

"Did he get you that sweet ride?" Matteo nods at the Mercedes. Rex and Leon are really slow-playing the tire change to give us time to talk.

Katrina's proud expression goes back to squirrelly. But I see how much she wants to show off for Matteo.

"Luke helped me. Sure. He wants me to have everything in the world, and I want that for him too."

"But how does Luke afford it?" Matteo asks, all innocent curiosity. "He doesn't make much money in prison."

She shrugs. "We have connections. *Both* of us. We know the right people. *Important* people." Katrina's eyes narrow at me, and goosebumps raise all over my skin.

"What people?" I ask.

"I'm sure you'd *love* to know. Detective *Murphy*."

I'm losing patience. "You wouldn't be sleeping around on Luke, would you? Your neighbor told us men have been visiting your apartment."

Her glare is murderous. "I'm allowed to have friends."

"But does Luke know that?"

"I see what you're trying to do. And it won't work. You can't turn me against him, and you can't trick me. I don't have to talk to you at all."

I go for one last shot. "Does Volkov blame me *personally* for his conviction? Does he want revenge on me?"

She grins knowingly. "Guess you'd have to ask him that yourself."

ON THE WAY back to Matteo's house, I call Sean. He's quiet as I tell him what I've been up to today.

"Katrina was definitely hiding things," I say. "She hinted she has important friends. That could mean West Oaks PD.

But so help me, Holt, if you start lecturing me about following rules—"

"I wouldn't dream of it. There are things I have to share with you as well. I was just on the phone with Jake. I'm swamped today, seriously underwater, so Jake's going to stop by to fill you in. I'll video conference."

An hour later, we're back in Matteo's living room, sitting with Jake Shelborne. Sean is Zooming-in using Jake's phone. I've just finished updating them about my conversation with Katrina Katalsky.

Leon and Rex are back at their posts outside. But I bought them both a late lunch on the way home as a thanks for their hard work. They deserved it.

"I can add a bit more to the story," Jake says. "Katrina was trying to find a new lawyer for Volkov, right? Well, it looks like she succeeded. I found out from my contacts at the US Attorney's Office that Volkov has a new attorney of record, and he's just filed a slew of new cases challenging his conviction. These are in federal court, but I'm guessing the state ones aren't far behind. It's a scattershot strategy. File everything under the sun, then see what sticks."

"But the GoFundMe campaign failed," I say. "Where did the money come from?"

"Your guess is as good as mine. But I doubt it's a pro bono case, given the lawyer. He's not known for doing these cases for free."

"What are Volkov's grounds for challenging his conviction?" Sean asks from Jake's phone.

"He's making a bunch of claims, including that police misconduct prevented him from presenting an adequate defense. In other words, that West Oaks PD hid evidence that showed another person killed Stefanie."

Similar to Katrina's online posts. Though I'm sure the

lawyer has presented it with all the legal trappings. It's still ridiculous.

But now? If a judge grants a hearing on Volkov's claims, I would need to testify. And Volkov's new lawyer would have plenty of fresh ammunition to use against me.

A corrupt cop who steals evidence.

There's no way it's a coincidence.

Everything I've been through the last few weeks suddenly makes a lot more sense. And I'm shaking with fury while my lunch churns in my stomach, about to send me into my second vomiting session of the day.

"That's what this is *all about*," I say. "Volkov has been trying to destroy my credibility to get ready for his court challenge. He thinks he'll be able to convince the court that I'm a corrupt cop and get a new trial. Or maybe even overturn his conviction altogether."

This is just what the news article said would happen. Defendants would challenge their convictions for cases where I was the investigator. Volkov's case might just be the first.

But he created this situation. He's to blame. I'm sure of it.

Matteo's gripping my hand. "This is fucked. There has to be something we can do to prove Volkov's part in this. To stop him from what he's doing to Angela."

"The good news is that the courts don't move quickly," Sean explains. "It's going to take time for a judge to even consider Volkov's filing. I'm going to get Janie in on this. She can help consult with the legal side of things and get a game plan together for us."

I nod. I have my union lawyer, but I'd prefer Jane Simon at this point. I might be facing criminal charges of my own, civil suits. I never could've imagined that I'd hire a defense lawyer to represent me. But what other choice do I have?

Matteo jumps up and paces, dragging his fingers through

his hair. "But the guy who flipped Angela's car and tried to *kill* her wasn't waiting around for the courts. And he wasn't just destroying her reputation. He was trying to hurt her. Frighten her by sending those crime scene photos of Stefanie Rossi."

"Which doesn't fit with the rest of our theory," Jake says. "Hard to believe it's the same person doing all those things."

We've suspected for a while that multiple people could be involved. But what if they're not working together at all? They're different actors with different motives?

My dizziness is back, but I don't think it's the concussion.

"We'll keep investigating Volkov," Sean says. "Katrina was a key discovery. Good work on that, Murphy. I'll see if Bennett Security can drag up anything else on her. Let's keep working and check in again tomorrow. I've got to run. I have about fifteen other meetings to get to."

Sean's image disappears as he disconnects from the video call. Jake tucks his phone away.

Matteo sits down again and hugs me to him. "What're you thinking?" he whispers.

"That I hate feeling so powerless," I murmur back.

"Me too. So we plan our next move. Right?"

I inhale a whiff of cedar and woodsmoke. Having him here grounds me. Helps me to push away the fear and the fury.

He really *does* make a good partner.

"Could I see the envelope you received with the Stefanie Rossi photos?" Jake asks. "I'm going to take it for finger-printing."

"Sure." I get up, and Matteo stands with me. We show Jake into Neve's room. I haven't touched the photos since earlier.

Jake kneels, studying the handwritten note, as he puts on a pair of nitrile gloves he just pulled from his pocket. "There's anger in this note," he says. "Desperation, too. This wasn't sent by someone who just wants to make you look bad in court. Matteo was right about that."

"It's personal," I say. I've felt that for a while. But now it's undeniable. "Someone believes I prevented justice for Stefanie's real killer."

Matteo rests his hand on the small of my back.

Jake gathers up the photos and replaces them in the envelope, then stores all of it inside a larger plastic bag. He snaps off his gloves when he's done. "We need more on Volkov. To get a sense of what he knows, his motivations. Who he's working with. Whether this conspiracy begins and ends with him, or if it's bigger. More… messy."

"Can we talk to him?" Matteo asks. "He's in prison, so he can have visitors. We go and question him. Rattle his cage. Then he might call his man—or woman—on the outside, and you can get a recording of his phone call. That's how it works, isn't it? Those calls are all recorded."

I share a glance with Jake, raising my eyebrows.

Matteo's onto something. I'm annoyed I didn't think of it first.

"True," Jake says. "I like the idea. But we'd have to be very careful what we ask him. Nothing about Stefanie Rossi."

Matteo looks confused, so I fill in the blanks.

"Volkov has a lawyer challenging his conviction for Stefanie's murder. We can't question him about that case without his lawyer present. Jake and I are law enforcement, so his lawyer would have a fit. But we can ask him about the fire at my place, the car hitting me. Katrina. Anything recent."

"What if *I* question him, then?" Matteo says. "I'm not a cop. I want to ask him, to his face, if he killed Stefanie or not. If this is all a legal sideshow or if he really believes what he's saying." He shrugs. "Besides, maybe Volkov will be more receptive to me. Katrina seemed to be."

I snort. "That's because she saw you without a shirt on."

"You can tell me what to say."

"I love that you'd do that for me, but it won't work. As a civilian, you'd have to get prior clearance, fill out forms. Volkov would have to agree ahead of time. It's not practical. But Jake and I could still go." The more I talk this through, the more it seems promising. "We'll ask our questions about the plot against me. Then wait for Volkov to call his friends on the outside, just like you said, Matteo."

We'd be going on the offensive. *Finally*.

"What do you say?" I ask Jake.

"I'm in." Jake unlocks his phone and taps around a bit. "Prison Locator says Volkov is housed up in Sacramento. The drive from here is around seven hours. I happen to have an informant there, so I could stop by and meet with him as well. Provide a fig leaf for this little adventure, since we're still pushing the boundaries with this."

"If that bothers you—" I start.

"No, I don't care. You've done plenty for me. And Harper, too. I can take some heat from my bosses if they don't like this. It's nothing to what you're dealing with."

I want to tell him thanks, express how much this means to me. But Jake smiles and nods at me like he already knows. He's low key when it comes to work colleagues. He saves his stronger emotions for the bad guys he's targeting.

And, of course, for his wife.

"When can you go?" I ask him.

"We can drive up tomorrow, interview Volkov. Then head back here the next day. I'll book us a hotel."

"I'll be there too," Matteo grunts. "The whole time."

Jake smiles. "No problem. You'll have to wait in the car at the prison, though."

"That's fine. The rest of the trip, I'll be Angela's personal security."

"Got it," Jake says. "Separate rooms? Or…"

"One for you. One for Angela and me. Because that's where she'll be. With me."

I hold back my laugh. Matteo's possessiveness is so damn endearing. I never liked that kind of thing before, but when Matteo gets feisty and protective, it makes me all warm and tingly.

We go out into the living room, and when Matteo is distracted, Jake leans into me. "He does know I'm married, right? I'm hardly a threat."

"He's being ridiculous. It's his thing."

"He's attached to you."

I look over at Matteo. He's opening a can of food for Chips. "The feeling is mutual."

"I figured. You look happy for somebody in this much trouble."

"Shut up, Shelborne. See if I do you any more favors."

"Ha, after this? You'll owe me a big one. But I'll transfer it to Harper. She'll probably make you volunteer for her elementary art classes. I can see it now. Model for finger-painted portraits. Play-Do sculptures."

"Go home. Say hi to her for me."

He salutes and heads toward the door. "Until tomorrow. Gotta love a road trip. Especially an impromptu one."

"Volkov isn't going to know what hit him."

26

Angela

*L*uke Volkov looks different than I remembered. Thinner. His face has aged in the past year. Yet he's still handsome.

I hate that I noticed that.

He walks slowly into the interview room, rattling chains from his wrists and ankles. The guard leads him to the table. Secures him in place. His eyes are impassive until he gets a good look at me.

"Detective Murphy," he says, voice lifting with surprise. "Well, well. Didn't expect to see you here."

"Until a couple of weeks ago? I never would've expected it either."

We set out this morning, taking Matteo's truck since he insisted on driving. But it worked, because it gave me and Jake a chance to strategize on the way here. The Bennett Security bodyguards followed us out of West Oaks, checking to make sure no one was tailing us, before they circled back. They're going to keep an eye on Matteo's place while we're gone. Plus, they said they'd feed Chips. Those guys are the best.

Once we reached Sacramento, it took a while to get cleared to see Volkov and meet the prison's strict rules. But we're finally here. I dressed in one of my suits, leaving my piercing behind. The only thing that's different from how I looked at his trial is my hair.

Yet Volkov is studying me like he finds every detail fascinating.

I stare back, filled with a hundred different emotions. Anger that Volkov thought he could screw me over for his own ends. Anxiousness about whether we'll get what we need to prove it.

And underneath, way down deep, the terrible fear that I did something wrong. That the worst I'll face is still yet to come.

"I'm Agent Shelborne," Jake says. "From the DEA."

"A drug agent to see me?" Volkov seems mildly surprised but disinterested. He doesn't take his eyes off me. "That hasn't happened in a while."

"Do you know why I'm here?" I ask.

His chains clank. "I would think it's that new lawsuit I filed. But you're not allowed to harass me about that without my lawyer present. And I would've thought you were too busy to think about me, anyway. What with your legal troubles."

He's completely nonchalant. But I struggle to contain my furious response. I can usually hold myself together during the most stressful of interrogations.

But not this time. I'm raw on the inside. And the only person who soothes me is stuck outside the prison, waiting for us to finish.

Thankfully, Jake seems to notice my frustration and takes over. "We're not here to discuss your lawsuit. Or your murder conviction."

"*Wrongful* murder conviction," Volkov says.

Jake doesn't take the bait. "We have questions about more recent events."

"Something that happened here at the prison?"

Jake smiles slowly. He's been through plenty of difficult interrogations himself. In fact, I suspect he did a lot more in the Army than your typical soldier stuff. Though he's never admitted it.

"We know exactly what you've been up to lately, Luke." Jake's voice is low. Dangerous. "We know about Katrina. About the plan to plant heroin at Detective Murphy's apartment. We know it all."

Volkov considers this for a moment. But he's got a decent poker face. "I don't know what you're talking about."

"You're not involved with a woman named Katrina Katalsky?"

"She's my girlfriend, sure. She helped me get my lawyer."

"How did she pay for that?" I cut in.

"I didn't ask her. We have a trusting relationship. But the rest of what you were saying has nothing to do with me. The heroin? I don't touch any of that stuff anymore. Anything found at your place is on you. You can't pin it on me. Not this time." His pale blue eyes latch onto mine. "It's all coming back around. How does it feel?"

My teeth clench so hard my jaw creaks. "Someone working under your orders set fire to my apartment building. Chased me down on the freeway. Nearly killed me."

There's a slight movement around Volkov's eyes and mouth. But is it surprise? Or an attempt to hide his glee?

"Katrina said that you both have important friends," I tell him. "Who was she referring to? Someone inside West Oaks PD?"

Another flinch. Then he just shrugs.

He barely even reacts when I report that Katrina's been seen with other men. He goes on about how in love they are, how much they trust each other. And I just can't take it anymore.

"We know you're involved in this," I snap. "It's just a matter of time until somebody else talks."

Volkov folds his hands on the table. "Detective Murphy, you can believe whatever you want about me. But I'm not the same man I was. I made mistakes in my past. It cost me Stefanie. Cost me nearly *everything*."

Jake leans forward. "What about your Bratva friends? Aren't they trying to get you out of prison?"

"I have nothing to say about my former associates. I never have. I don't snitch. When I say I'm not the same man, I mean *inside*. My soul. I've repented for selling drugs. Doing things that were hurtful. But I've never had a need to repent for Stefanie's murder because I *never did it*. I'm innocent."

I stand up, my hands going flat on the table. "Do you know the problem with this claim of innocence you expect everyone to believe? There was never any evidence to support you. No mystery man was ever there. It was *you*, Luke. *You*."

"I never had a chance to prove what happened. You condemned me as a drug dealer, even though I wasn't even in West Oaks the day Stefanie died. Do you deny that?"

Jake is frowning at me because we're not supposed to be discussing this. But Volkov is the one who brought it up. And I can't keep from responding. "Your alibi had no corroboration."

"What about the fact that no fentanyl was ever found in my possession, even though Stefanie overdosed on a combination of heroin and fentanyl?"

"This was all discussed at trial. The jury didn't believe you."

Finally, Volkov raises his voice. "Because they believed you instead of me. The cop instead of the dealer. But it was still a lie. I loved Stefanie."

I laugh. "Sure, enough to hit her the day she broke up with you. Witnesses testified. They saw it."

His eyes cut away from me, and I see shame there. "I did things I regret. But I'm not the man who killed her. And even if I was, why would I wish to harm you? If your theory is correct, I'm trying to both destroy your reputation and kill you. How would that help me?"

The exact questions we were asking yesterday. But I'm not going to tell him that. "I have no idea. I can't see inside your sick mind."

"I want you to sit in court and testify about the real evidence against me. But not just you. I want everyone involved to look me in the eye, look a judge in the eye, and tell the truth. Why would I just go after you?"

"Maybe it's because I'm a woman? Do I remind you of Stefanie? Do you want to punish me the way you punished her?"

Snarling, Volkov tries to jerk upright, yanking at his chains. Jake throws his arm in front of me, leaping halfway out of his chair.

The guard by the door shouts a warning.

Volkov settles, and Jake slowly sits back down in his seat.

My heart is beating like a runaway train in my chest.

"If I've got it wrong," I say, "then explain it to me. Maybe you just wanted to plant the heroin in my apartment. Make me look dirty. It could be somebody else who came after me to hurt me. You don't want to be blamed for that, do you? Tell us what you know. Tell us who you're working with."

"You're wrong about everything," he seethes. "Every fucking thing. And you have *no idea*. You're looking in all the wrong places, and when somebody comes for you and you realize what's really going on, you'll know exactly how I feel."

27

Matteo

The heat is blistering today in Sacramento. I pace outside my truck, waiting for Jake and Angela to return. I don't like that she went in there without me. She's speaking face-to-face with the guy who tried to kill her. Or at least, who started the plot. A man who's already a convicted murderer.

This was *my* idea?

I trust that Angela can handle a guy like Volkov. That's not my issue. I can think she's strong and also want to protect her at the same time. Plus, Jake will be there with her too.

I'd just prefer to be the one by her side. All the time. And that impulse is getting harder to deny.

Finally, Jake and Angela emerge from the gate and cross the concrete toward me. Jake has his usual easy-going smile, the kind that probably conceals hidden depths that he keeps in reserve.

But I'm far better at reading Angela, and she looks stricken.

"What happened?" I ask when they reach me.

Jake waits, but Angela doesn't answer.

"Volkov claimed to know nothing about the attacks on Angela. If he's lying, he's extremely skilled at it."

"He admitted Katrina is his girlfriend?"

"Oh, yes. Without a doubt. But he claimed not to know how she's getting her money or how she afforded to hire him a new lawyer."

I glance at Angela. She's got her arms crossed over her middle, eyes glassy and down on the concrete. I rest my hand on her hip, and she doesn't pull away. But she doesn't come any closer either.

"Maybe Katrina is behind everything?" I say. "And she's doing it without Volkov's knowledge?"

"Possible." Jake reaches for the back door to the truck. "He might call Katrina and ask for an explanation. We'll have to wait for him to make the next move."

That was my plan, but it's still not what I wanted to hear.

Jake gets in. I turn to Angela. "Are you okay? Because it doesn't seem like you are."

She blinks. "I'm…"

For a split second, I see everything on her face. Fear and dismay and a thousand doubts and questions.

And then, she buries it all. "Let's go. I just want to get out of here."

WE GRAB takeout on the way to the hotel. After checking in, we retire to our separate rooms. Jake says he needs to write up his report on meeting with his informant at the prison, which he handled before they saw Volkov. And Angela still isn't in the mood to talk.

I polish off my burger in about three bites, while Angela paces the room with her food untouched.

It's taking everything in me to keep my mouth shut. I don't want to push her. From the beginning, Angela hasn't reacted well when I get demanding. Except maybe when we're in bed together.

But if I had never gotten pushy with her—never stormed home on my birthday to confront her about the hookup app, never insisted on being a part of this investigation—then there's no way we'd be where we are now.

So I get up and block her path, taking both of her hands in mine. "Hey, talk to me. What happened with Volkov?"

She opens her mouth, and then her phone rings. Damn.

Angela takes the device from her pocket. The number isn't in her contacts.

"It could be a journalist," I say.

But she shakes her head. "I think I recognize the number. It's Grayson's—my partner's—wife." She answers the call. "Nora? Is that you?"

I'm standing close enough that I can hear every word on the other side of the line. "Angela, have you heard from Beau? Or seen him at all?"

Angela glances at me. "No, I'm out of town. Beau and I texted… Yesterday, I think."

My partner, she mouths. I nod. I remembered.

"He didn't come home last night," Nora says. "And he's turned off the GPS family share on his phone. I'm getting really worried."

"Did you contact West Oaks PD? I'm on leave. I'm not plugged in to everything that's going on."

Nora's voice shakes with barely concealed panic. "I did, yes. Nobody seems to know anything. He hasn't been to the station either. What if something happened to him?"

Angela sits on the bed, rubbing her forehead. "Do you have someone else you can call if the baby comes? Someone to help you?"

"My sister's here staying with me. But Beau has been acting strange lately. Getting home late. Not sleeping in our bed even when he's home. I'm scared. What if he's having second thoughts? What if he doesn't come back?"

"Let's assume he's fine until we hear otherwise. Okay? Maybe he just needed some time to himself. He wouldn't be the first guy who's panicked right before his first kid arrives. But Nora, he loves you. I know that for sure."

She sniffles. "Okay."

"I'll be back in town tomorrow. He'll probably have turned up by then, but if not, I'll help track him down. And don't hesitate to call everyone else at West Oaks PD if I'm not back and you need help. We're a family. We take care of each other." Angela frowns as she says this, a look of pain crossing her beautiful features.

After a couple more minutes, they end the call. Angela puts her phone down, her shoulders slumping.

I sit on the edge of the mattress next to her. "Do you really think Grayson took off because he's nervous about becoming a father? That's a shitty thing to do to his wife." I certainly would never pull a stunt like that, not even in my more irresponsible days. What kind of an asshole leaves a pregnant woman in the lurch?

"I hope that's all it is." She shakes her head. "I need to text Holt. We need to get people looking for Grayson to make sure he's all right. Volkov could've sent someone after him."

"What do you mean?"

She doesn't look up from texting. "Grayson was my partner when Stephani Rossi was killed. Our first murder investigation together. His first *ever*. I remember all the notes he was taking at the scene. How hard he was trying to get each detail right. Jotting down everything I said like my word was gospel."

Angela tosses her phone aside and takes a stuttering

breath. Her hands press to her collarbone, right over the scar. "What if I got it wrong?" she whispers.

"Got what wrong?"

"*Everything.*"

I sit beside her and wait until she tells me the rest.

"When Volkov testified at the trial, he denied each allegation. His mafia connections, being a heroin dealer. Even roughing up Stefanie when she broke up with him. He seemed like a man who would lie about absolutely *anything*, so it wasn't hard to believe he would lie about killing her too. But that wasn't the same guy I spoke to today. He admitted the rest of it was true, more or less. But he still swore he was out of town when Stefanie died."

"I thought his alibi wasn't convincing."

"You didn't hear him today. He was so sure of himself."

"Are you saying you actually think he could be innocent?"

Her lower lip trembles. "I don't know anymore. I just don't know. The more I think about it, the less sure I am. Like Stefanie's diary. The missing pages. What if those pages said something crucial? Something that could've changed the entire picture of the case?"

"There are always going to be lingering questions. Different ways to twist the truth."

"I *never* doubted that Volkov was guilty. Not for one minute. But back then, I was working so hard to convince everyone, *especially* myself, that I was okay after being wounded. What if I screwed it all up? What if I shouldn't have been back on duty at all?"

Her eyes are unfocused. She's letting these doubts swallow her whole.

I kneel on the floor in front of her, forcing her to look at me. "You don't cut corners. You're never careless. Did you conceal the fact that the journal pages were missing?"

"No."

"Did you conceal anything that would've helped Volkov's case? Were there any leads you chose not to follow?"

"No. The man's prints were on the murder weapon. There were things I couldn't explain, but not because I didn't try. But—"

I don't let her finish that sentence. "Exactly. You wouldn't do that to someone. Not even someone you believed was guilty."

"How do you know?" she whispers.

"You try to keep your heart locked down, but I see it. I *see you*. Doesn't matter if we met a few weeks ago or a few years. Doesn't matter how much you try to deny me and pretend this is just some convenient roommate thing between us."

She tries to look away from me, but I gently hold her chin. "I know *you*," I say again.

"How can you be so sure?"

"Because, angel, you're already mine."

I cup the back of her neck with my palm and kiss her. My other hand goes to her collarbone. Rests over her scar. I need her right here with me, not trapped in the past. Trapped in her terrible memories and corrosive self doubt. Those are places I've been before in my own head, and it never helps.

People always say, believe in yourself. Like that's easy. But it sure as hell helps for somebody else to believe in you first. Especially during your worst moments, when you can't see anything good.

"Baby, everything about you is beautiful. Scars and all. Will you let me show you?"

28

Matteo

I pick her up from the bed. Her arms clasp at my neck, legs wrapping around my waist. We're still kissing, building up a hypnotic rhythm with our lips and tongues.

I need to show her what I see when I look at her. How brave she is. How caring.

This is the woman who climbed up the balcony of a burning building to save a dog. Who cares deeply about justice. The truth. Right and wrong. Who's more than willing to chase down bad guys and risk herself while she's at it.

She should feel nothing but pride when she looks in the mirror.

So that's where I take her. I set Angela down in front of the full-body mirror that's on one wall of the hotel room. I turn her to face it, positioning myself behind her, hands on her hips.

"What are you doing?" she asks.

"I'm showing you who you are." I kiss her neck, keeping my eyes locked on her reflection. "A beautiful, brave woman."

"Matteo. This isn't necessary." She tries to walk away, but

I keep her in place.

"Nope, we're doing this. Because it is *clearly* necessary. You need to acknowledge who you are. So we're going to stay right here until that happens."

She frowns at me, but she stays there. Waiting to see what I'll do next.

I slide her jacket off her shoulders. Then unbutton her shirt. She's all business today, dignified and proper. So I take extra pleasure in taking off her top and tugging her bra cups down, exposing her breasts. My cock gives a jolt at that mouthwatering sight.

"You see what I mean?" I whisper in her ear. "Beautiful."

I unbutton her tailored pants and push them down. The panties go next, and the bra, which I unhook to toss it aside. And now she's naked in front of the mirror.

I'm fully clothed behind her, my cock like granite inside my jeans.

"Look at you. Look how incredible you are. I don't just mean your body. I mean your heart and soul and integrity, because I can see all of that when I look at you, too."

My hands cup her breasts. "But in addition to all that, you are *really* fucking sexy, angel. Do you have any idea how hard I am for you?"

Angela leans back against me. Her ass brushes the thick bulge in my pants. I bring a hand between her legs and stroke her sensitive folds. Her head falls to my chest, eyes closing as her arms reach up and clasp behind my neck.

I wish I could take a picture of this. All her naked glory, my hands on her, the relief on her face as she begins to let go of her stress.

"I want my skin against yours. Should I get naked, baby?"

"Why aren't you already?"

I step back slightly to pull off my clothes. My erection points upward, so eager for her. Angela doesn't move an inch while she waits for me. Just stands and watches me in the reflection.

I drop to my knees behind her and run my hands up her legs.

"I like *this* view," I say.

I trail my fingers up the inside of her leg until I reach the hot, wet juncture between her thighs. A growl rumbles from my chest. That's what I need, right there. I drop kisses onto the curve of her hip and then her plump ass cheek. My fingers stroke and caress her most sensitive spaces.

Her hands go out and land against the mirror as she braces herself, bending forward.

"If you want me, you need to tell me."

"I need you, Matteo. Please. I need you inside me."

I reach behind me for my jeans. There's a condom in my wallet, and I pull it out and roll it on as quickly as I can. I can't wait any longer. The need to claim her is far too strong. I told her she's already mine, and I meant it. But if I had my way, I'd claim her every single day so neither of us could ever forget it. She'd feel safe and cared for and protected.

If you let me, I will.

I stand up behind her, holding my shaft at the base.

"Now I'm gonna fuck you in this mirror and make you come, and we're both going to watch, because that's exactly what you deserve. To have nothing but pleasure and admiration." I drop a kiss to her spine. "But only if you let me. You gotta let me in."

Her eyes meet mine in the mirror. She arches her back for me. "I'm waiting. I'm yours."

I find her wet opening and guide the tip of my cock there, pressing inside. She whimpers. I keep going, pumping with gentle thrusts, going deeper each time. She stretches around me inch by inch. Welcoming me.

"You feel me, angel?"

"So good," she gasps. "More. Don't ever stop."

"I'm not being too rough?" I'm still conscious of her concussion and the stitches on her forehead.

But Angela says, "Not rough enough. Fuck me harder."

Pleasure blooms in my body, in my brain, like a better drug than any ever invented. I lose track of time as I move inside her. Pulling out and thrusting back in. She's way up on her tip-toes, and her tits bounce in time with my rhythm.

It's a little unfair. I'm getting the view from the front and behind, a filthy panorama of this gorgeous woman while I ride her with my cock.

One of my palms lands flat on the mirror above hers while I hold her against me with the other. My hips pump into her hard and fast. Her feet aren't even touching the ground anymore. She pushes against the mirror, leaning over as she cries out.

"Watch yourself come, baby. You're stunning."

Her eyes open, and she follows my command. She watches herself in the mirror while she orgasms, her channel squeezing my cock. And that's it for me. I pulse my release into the condom inside of her, groaning through the intense sensation.

When I pull out, her knees bend. I grab hold of her so she doesn't fall. Somehow I get us both to the bed. We're gasping for breath. A quick cleanup, and I return, pulling her on top of me.

She stretches out over my body, her cheek to my chest. My palm rests on her bare back. Feeling her breaths and her heartbeat come back down.

"Angela, I meant what I said. You're mine. I need you with me, and I'm tired of pretending there's an expiration date on that."

"I need you too," she whispers.

We both know we're not talking about just sex. Not

anymore.

"Then let me be here for you. Be *with* you."

She touches the tattoo on my chest. The words *Semper Fidelis*, which mean *always faithful*. The motto of the Marine Corps.

In my life, I haven't had that much to hold on to. My brother was my constant. The one thing I could count on. But he always thought I should want more for myself.

I like to think I'm faithful to my friends and to my duties, and I love Emily and Natalie. They're my family. But I want the kind of faithfulness that calls a man home at night to the one place he wants most to be. What Brent had and lost. What I hope Emily will someday find again.

And I want the woman I care about to be just as faithful to me in return. To truly need me down to her core. It feels like my heart's been calling out for it, and I didn't understand until now. Didn't ever think I could have it.

I don't know if Angela and I can have that together. It's still early to say. But it seems possible.

I want to find out.

"No expiration date, huh?" she asks. "You want to change our deal again?"

"Hell yeah, I do. But I need to know you're right there with me. No more pushing me away."

She props her chin on her hands to look at me. "The deal doesn't mean anything if it keeps on changing."

"Or maybe it means *everything*. It's whatever we want it to mean."

She crawls up my body until we're face to face. Brushes my messy hair back. "Okay."

"That's it? Okay?"

She nods.

Seems that's all the clarity she'll give me. But for now, it works.

29

Angela

*A*fter a night tossing and turning in the hotel bed, I manage to fall asleep on the drive back. But I don't let go of Matteo's hand. Or maybe I should say he doesn't let go of mine.

When I wake up halfway back to West Oaks, before I even open my eyes, I feel his touch. Know that he's right there next to me. Just like he promised.

I'm lucky he's so stubborn. He's insisted on caring about me even when I made it difficult. Despite everything that's going on, I feel like the luckiest girl in the world. He said that I'm *his*. God, I want to be. And I want him to be mine.

He kept saying last night that I deserve his admiration, and I'm not sure about that. But it feels incredible. I want to do just the same for him.

Also, when he fucked me in front of the mirror? *Hot*.

I'm still reeling from that interview with Luke Volkov. I don't want to believe that I missed something crucial. It guts me to think that Stefanie's killer has gone free while I helped send an innocent man to prison. But somebody out there believes it, and I'm starting to think that Volkov truly believes it too. So unless he's managed to block the memories or split off another personality, then it must be true.

It really could be true.

The only solution is to go back to the evidence. Sean told me he would pull everything from the file on Stefanie's murder. So I'll go back to the beginning. Pour over every inch of that file. If there's something else to be found, then I'll find it. I'm on leave anyway, so this is the perfect time. I'll bet Matteo will help me. I'm the detective, but he has insights too. I value his opinion. I want to lay out the case for him, see what he thinks.

If this did happen, if Volkov is innocent, then I have to make it right. I have no idea what that would mean for my career, yet the truth matters far more.

Being with Matteo makes me feel like I can face anything, even the parts of myself—of my past—that I've been trying to hide from. I don't want to hide anymore.

But there's still my actual partner to think of as well.

Grayson.

When I checked in with Nora first thing this morning, he was still missing. I'm worried that he's gone off the rails because he can't handle the stress. Not just of becoming a new father, but trying to manage our caseload. He and Nora have already been through a lot in their marriage, so I hope they can weather this storm too. And I'll try to be there for Grayson, no judgment. Both as a colleague and as a friend.

This entire experience has made me realize how much my friends mean to me. When I've needed them, they've been there. I'm going to return the favor. I'm tired of being cut off from so many people. Matteo has shown me that I don't have to be.

I must be staring at him, because Matteo asks, "What?"

"Just admiring you," I murmur, hoping Jake won't overhear.

I've always enjoyed looking at Matteo. But now it means so much more.

If Jake wasn't in the backseat, I'd probably try to climb into Matteo's lap while he's driving. Which would be extremely dangerous and not at all the kind of thing Detective Murphy would usually do. I can just imagine those headlines.

But that's what Matteo does to me. Makes me crazy in the best possible way.

"What should we do when we get back?" Matteo asks quietly.

There's so much I can barely get my head around it. "Check in with Sean. Try to find Grayson."

He tips his head in my direction. "You did notice I said 'we,' right?"

"I noticed, and I have no objection. In fact, I insist on you helping me."

"So demanding." He grins at me. "I'll try to make room for you in my schedule."

"When are you due back at the fire station?" I've just realized it's been more than forty-eight hours since his last shift ended. I hadn't been keeping track.

"Not until tomorrow. I had an extra day off between shifts this time."

We hold hands and make mushy eyes at each other as he drives.

We're about an hour out from West Oaks when our phones start blowing up.

First, it's texts coming in from Sean and several more of my West Oaks PD co-workers.

Then I hear Jake cursing.

Instantly, I'm filled with dread. I don't want to look at the messages. I don't want to know. I just want to hold on to these brief happy moments for a little bit longer, because I've had so few of them in the last two years.

"Murphy," Jake says. "There's another article about you."

Shit. "Another takedown piece from the local media about me stealing evidence?"

"It looks like more than that. It, um, mentions Chief Liu. And... Matteo."

Matteo's forehead creases as he glances over at me.

He pulls over the truck so we can all see the article. I'm already choking on frustration and shame, imagining what this latest piece of tabloid journalism could have said.

And then I actually read the thing.

It's worse than I even imagined.

West Oaks PD Senior Detective Angela Murphy has recently been accused of an extensive scheme of police corruption, including wrongfully removing and concealing evidence. But newly discovered information suggests the chief of police himself has helped provide cover for Detective Murphy's illegal activities.

According to sources, Detective Murphy had a previously unreported sexual relationship with Chief Alex Liu. Chief Liu promoted Murphy to senior detective over other qualified candidates, despite not disclosing their prior relationship. The chief has also warned West Oaks PD officers not to discuss the charges against Detective Murphy, suggesting they could be disciplined for speaking out against her.

"It's like there are two standards," an anonymous source reported. "One for the chief's favorite, and another for the rest of us."

But the new allegations against Detective Murphy do not stop there. She is currently living with a West Oaks firefighter, Matteo De Luca, who is a witness against her in the pending investigation of her actions.

"She's having a relationship with one of the witnesses to the internal affairs inquiry," the anonymous source said. "It looks like

witness tampering and undue influence. How much more can she get
away with?"

West Oaks PD has so far declined to make an official comment.

I'm getting lightheaded. I can't breathe. I push open the door to Matteo's truck and lurch out onto the side of the road, leaving the pavement. Cars keep roaring past on the freeway.

I reach a tree and lean my back against it.

Matteo has gotten out of the driver's side. He walks toward me, hands in his pockets. "So. That wasn't the best thing I've ever read."

"You *think*? They used your name."

I wish I knew who's been talking to these reporters about me, because I'd love to give them a piece of my mind.

Who would know that I had a previous relationship with Alex? That I'm with Matteo now?

Is it Cassidy Diaz?

I guess I'm lucky it said Matteo and I are "having a relationship," not just using each other for sex. Technically that was true until, what, last night?

No, even when this started between Matteo and me, it was more than I pretended it to be. But some of those details would've looked ugly. And because I'm the woman, it would've reflected worst on me. The dirty cop who sleeps around to get her way.

Who am I kidding? That's exactly what they're saying already.

I wrap my arms around my stomach, almost bending over. I'm nauseous.

"I'm so sorry," I choke out.

I knew my past was a minefield. I just never thought it would all be exposed like this. Everything out there for the world to see. To judge me by. My father's previous position, my intimacy with Alex. And now, the report about Matteo. It makes me look every bit as corrupt as they claim.

But it's not just my reputation being tarnished now. It's Matteo's.

He stands in front of me, hands out like he's afraid I'll topple over. "I don't care what anyone thinks of me. People have talked plenty of shit about me before. It's my actions that should matter. You and I haven't done anything wrong." He pauses, and I can't see his grimace, but I can feel it. "Except maybe looking at Detective Diaz's notes that one time, but you would've found that stuff out anyway."

"You know that's not how this works. You look bad just being associated with me."

"I don't care. I'd rather be associated with you than the alternative." He holds my face in his hands. "Having the world know I'm in a relationship with you is hardly the worst ding I've had to my reputation."

I cringe and look away.

"Hey, that was a joke. I don't even know if we're in a relationship."

He waits, like he's hoping I'll fill in those blanks. But I can't right now. I don't know what to say.

"Angela, I said I'm with you. Whatever that means, I'm proud of it, and I'm not going anywhere. This shit can't scare me away." He laughs, and I hear the nervousness there. "You're not going to let it scare *you*, are you?"

My phone rings, and it's like nails against a chalkboard. What could this be but more bad news?

I glance at my screen and curse.

It's Alex.

"I have to take this. It's the chief." I swipe my thumb across the screen and hold the phone to my ear, walking a few feet away.

"Alex?"

Matteo stands stiffly where I left him, crossing his arms.

"Angie." Alex sighs into the phone. "How the hell did this happen?"

"I have no idea. You know I don't talk about… us. It's ancient history."

"But that doesn't matter, does it? Not now."

My chest squeezes like it's a vise around my heart. Yet I can't bring myself to apologize to him. Because really, what do I have to be sorry for? The fact that Alex and I dated years ago shouldn't be a strike against me. And if it somehow is, it shouldn't be mine alone.

"Is it true about you and the firefighter?" Alex asks.

Matteo watches me. I wonder how much he can hear.

Jake is out of the truck now, too. He's leaning against the door, watching us.

"Yes. Matteo and I are seeing each other."

Matteo's shoulders lower as he exhales.

"But you know that has nothing to do with the corruption claims against me," I say. "It's a coincidence."

"Well, it doesn't look like a fucking coincidence. He's a witness. And this makes the stuff about you and me look far less innocent."

Matteo must hear that, because he opens his mouth and takes a sharp step toward me. I hold up my hand. If Alex hears his voice, this will just get worse.

"It *was* innocent, right?" I find myself asking. "My promotion to detective?" Because I've always wondered, and I've never been brave enough to ask. "It had nothing to do with our history? Or with my dad being Waylon Murphy?"

"Of *course* not." I hear his chair squeaking. He must be in his office. "Look, I've got no choice here. I need to suspend you without pay. Just until this blows over."

"That's bullshit," Matteo hisses.

Thankfully, Alex doesn't hear. "I need to send a signal

that you're not getting any special treatment. And anything Detective Holt has been working on the side needs to stop now. We can't afford more publicity at this point."

"What about the guy who ran into my car? Who sent me to the hospital?"

"I'll assign that to Cassidy Diaz. Anything pertaining to you, it's in her purview."

I'm so angry I'm shaking. But do I want Sean to get dragged through the mud in the media next? No way.

"I didn't want things to be this way, Angie. You know I didn't. But if we're both going to weather this storm, we have to be careful."

"Right," I manage to say.

"I'll talk to you soon."

He hangs up, not even waiting for a response from me. At least I know the article is truly nonsense. This doesn't feel anything like special treatment.

SEAN TRIES TO CALL, but I don't answer. I can't deal with it. As we drive the rest of the way back, Jake brainstorms what we can do next. But there's no way around this.

I'm toxic right now. Jake and Sean shouldn't try to help me. They should take some lessons from Alex in self-preservation.

We drop Jake off at his place, and Matteo drives us home. I feel like I'm sleepwalking as I go inside.

Neve's house has been a comfort to me since I moved in here weeks ago. All the plants, the sunlight. The feeling of a warm and cozy place where I might be able to bloom despite the disruptions in my life.

And Matteo. The best, warmest part of this place.

Now, I feel like a blight. Like I'll spoil everything I touch.

"We'll get past this," Matteo says. "This media stuff always calms down when the next juicy story hits. Think about the progress we've been making. We just have to wait for Volkov to make that phone call and give something away, and we can keep working on the investigation ourselves."

He's saying all the right things. I want to collapse into his arms, let him hold me and make me feel better.

But instead, I go toward Neve's room.

"Angela?" he asks.

"I need a minute. Just a minute to breathe." I close the door, flop onto her bed, and close my eyes.

What am I going to do?

The first thing on my list should probably be to turn off my phone. But I don't move fast enough. Because it rings again.

And this time, it's my father.

30

Matteo

I sit on the couch, unsure of what to do. It's probably not a good sign that Angela ran into Neve's bedroom and shut the door the minute we got home. Just when I thought things were finally going in the right direction between us.

But having our fledgling romance blasted in the news wasn't the ideal start to a relationship.

I'm sure Angela just needs a breather, like she said, and I shouldn't overreact. That article was brutal. It would've been hard for anyone to read that about themselves, but for someone like Angela? Who's so incredibly private?

I hate that some asshole is using me against her. Not because of anything I did wrong, because I'd stand by every single choice I've made. Even the times I've pushed the boundaries. But it still sucks.

My phone buzzes. Danny's been texting. Sounds like that article is making the rounds of the guys on our shift. I think there's a group text going, everyone jumping to my defense and brainstorming what they can do. I glance over the messages quickly without trying to engage. Their concern is nice to see.

These guys are my family, and I'm grateful that they didn't assume the worst.

But that article didn't say anything untrue about me. It made insinuations, sure. But the facts regarding me were accurate.

I decide to bite the bullet and make the call I'm dreading most. The one that's unavoidable at this point.

"Chief Ross?" I say when he answers. "It's De Luca."

"Man, what were you thinking?"

He's just as pissed as I expect. This is far more controversy than WOFD has dealt with before. I do my best to explain myself, but I've never been known for my eloquence.

"There's nothing improper going on," I say. "Angela and I like each other. She's innocent of what they're saying."

"But I told you from the beginning to stay away from that detective. Not to get involved."

"I know, sir. It wasn't my intention. I couldn't have predicted how we'd end up in each other's lives. But she *did* end up in my life. When someone needs help, it's not right to wash my hands of them because it's not convenient."

"But did that have to include shacking up with her? Being her *boyfriend*?" He spits the word out.

I know not every battalion chief is as uptight as Ross. Why couldn't I have gotten one of those?

"Uh, well. Maybe not."

"We're getting calls from journalists asking for comment. I've heard from the Fire Chief, and he wants to know what the hell our problem is at Station Two. First that scandal over the pictures of our guys on social media a month ago, and now this?"

I hate making excuses. But the other controversy wasn't my fault. "Sir, that past incident wasn't—"

He bowls right over me. "I'll need you to stay home for your next shift. This is too much of a distraction."

I swallow the lump of indignation that's growing in my throat.

"After that, you're back on shift, but you're on probation. I can't spare you any further. I'm sure the union will get involved in this, as is your right. But so help me, if you keep making this station look bad, you won't have a spot anymore."

There's certainly no need to mention the potential captain promotion. There's not a chance in hell he would consider me. Not after this. I should probably be more disappointed. But I've spent years jumping through hoops, busting my ass even through Brent's illness, only to have the chief believe the worst of me? After one news article?

If it came down to choosing between Angela and all of that, I don't even have to think. There's no contest.

"Do you understand me, De Luca?"

"Yes, Chief. I understand."

I turn around and find Angela standing in the now open doorway. I lower the phone. "How much of that did you hear?"

"Some." Her voice is as brittle as cracked glass. "Just got off the phone myself. *Again*. This time it was my dad. He finally heard how his name's been getting dragged through the mud."

"I'm sorry." I go over to her and try to wrap her in my arms, but she edges out of my grasp.

"Please don't say sorry. You shouldn't have had to…" She trails off and shakes her head. Her hand moves to her scar, then drops. "My father offered to call the current mayor for me. Which is exactly what people have accused me of all this time. I've never taken a favor like that from him. But you know what? I was tempted. So tempted."

"Anyone would be."

"But the worst part is, my father never offered before. That's how bad this situation is." She paces across the living room. "What did your chief say?"

I glance down at my phone, wishing I could make it disappear. Make the outside world go away so we could return to how things felt last night and this morning. Not perfect. Not by any means. But not like the fragile connections we've built between us were suddenly at risk of caving in.

"Please tell me, Matteo."

"Chief Ross said I'm suspended from my next shift. And after that, I'm on probation."

Her eyes close, her face crumpling.

"I've had setbacks at work before. I always come back from them." I reach out for her again, but she keeps moving. Anxious energy bleeds out of her.

"The first day I moved in here, you said you didn't want anything to do with my problems. It would've been a lot better for you if you'd stuck to that."

"That is not true. And it's not how I feel."

"But I'm dragging everyone else down with me, especially you."

"Then so be it. We'll be down there together." I step into her path, holding onto her shoulders. My fingers knead at the tension there, and she relaxes in my grip. "You've had a very rough few days. A rough few weeks. But this isn't you. Letting that article get under your skin? Letting them win? That's not your style. At *every step*, you have pushed back when you're challenged. Even against me. That's the Angela Murphy I know."

She tenses up again. I can feel the knots bunching in her muscles. The panic under her skin. Her eyes dart around the living room before landing on the front door.

"I need to take a walk. I just… can't be here right now."

Can't be around me? Is that what she means? "Why deal with this alone if you don't have to?" I ask.

I'm right here. I'm right fucking here.

"Because maybe I *should*." She goes toward the door.

"Angela, don't walk away from me." My tone is harder. As sharp as the pain inside me. "Not when I *know* you want to stay."

She slips on her shoes. Grabs her keys.

My fists clench, and anger flares at my center. A spark that's quickly catching. As if the wreckage of my heart—all that was left after my parents' neglect, after losing my brother, after Emily driving away and taking Nat—is nothing but dry kindling.

And I'm one moment away from it all burning down.

When Brent was dying, I did absolutely everything in my power to save him. I gave him my kidney. If the doctors had let me, I probably would've given him the other one too. Because he was the better man.

But no matter what I did, no matter how much I fought, it wasn't enough to keep my brother here.

At some point, a guy needs to learn his lesson. Scrape together what he has left before it's nothing but ashes.

So I don't chase after her like I've done so many times before.

I watch her walk out the door.

31

Angela

The moment I step outside, I almost turn around. But my head is a mess right now. I don't want to say anything else that's going to hurt Matteo.

I *do* want to be with him. But at this specific moment, I can't.

I start down the sidewalk. I don't know where I'm going. Just... not here. I'm drowning in self pity, and Matteo was right. That isn't me. So I refuse to do it around him. I just need some space. Time to think.

I'm not hiding. Not running away. Even if it damn well looks like it.

But when I reach the end of the block, I stop. My feet won't carry me any further. Every step I take away from Matteo just makes me feel more broken.

It all comes rushing at me. I almost double over. The ache in my chest, the wrenching of my stomach. The things that article said about me. The disappointment in my father's voice. It piles on top of the past months of loneliness. Of fearful images and dark memories. And even before that, my insistence that I didn't need anyone else inside the high walls of my heart.

I crouch there on the sidewalk, staring at the concrete. Suffocating. While Matteo is back at the house waiting for me. After begging me not to go.

He's the one refuge I've found who always makes me feel safe. Cared for.

I'm making the same stupid mistakes. Aren't I?

Maybe I still want to protect myself from the world, but not from *him*. When I was scared and crying, he was there. More than willing to take the risk of coming near. He earned my trust time and again. Came back, no matter how much I pushed him away.

Admitting how much he means to me might be the scariest thing of all. Yet I did it last night. I meant every word.

I need to go home.

Home. And I don't mean Neve's house. I mean Matteo.

I turn around and see the Bennett Security car idling not far away. The guys must've seen me leave and followed. They're diligent, all right. I give them a weak smile and a wave. I must look ridiculous to them, crouching on the sidewalk, and then turning around to go back home after just taking off.

But hey, it's like Matteo said. He feels crazy around me too. We can be crazy together.

I want that. More than *anything*.

Then another car turns onto the street. It pulls up to the curb right next to me, and the window buzzes down.

It's Grayson. My partner. And he looks like absolute hell.

"Murphy?" he croaks.

I go over to his open window. I wonder when he last showered. It smells like it's been a while. "Grayson, where on *earth* have you been? Nora's been calling me."

His eyes squeeze shut. His knuckles are white on the steering wheel. "I know. I feel like shit."

"You should. What have you been doing? You haven't been drinking, have you?" He should know better. A DUI would be the end of his police career.

"No. I just need somebody to talk to. I was hoping you would have a minute. Please. I was going to go knock on your door, but then I saw you out here."

I frown. "Wait, how did you know where I live? I've been keeping that quiet."

"The article. I looked up where Matteo De Luca lives."

Shit. I didn't think about that. The entire world now knows exactly where I am, including whoever's been targeting me. I look over again at the Bennett Security car, where Leon and Rex are watching me closely. I nod at them. Trying to show that everything's fine.

"I know you're going through a lot right now," he says. "But I don't know where else to turn."

Just a moment ago, I was having a pity party for myself. And here comes Grayson, reminding me that some people might have bigger problems, even if he hasn't been suspended from work without pay.

In a way, Grayson's doing me a favor. Making me think about somebody other than myself. I want to get home to Matteo, but if Grayson needs me, I can't turn my back. I'm sure that's not what Matteo would want.

"I have a few minutes. Sure."

A new voice speaks behind me. "Detective Murphy? Everything okay?" It's Rex. He's out of the car, keeping a polite distance, but his stance is protective.

"I'm fine, Rex. Thanks. This is my partner, Detective Grayson. He just needed to talk for a bit."

Grayson is scowling at his steering wheel.

"I'm going to talk to him for a while," I say, "and then I'll head back home."

"Would you like us to stay nearby, ma'am?" Rex asks.

Given everything that's going on, that's probably wise. "Sure. We'll just drive around the block. Or park somewhere to chat. Won't take long."

I get into the passenger side with Grayson, and Rex goes back to the other car.

"I didn't realize you had a tail," Grayson says.

"And I didn't realize you were nearly falling apart. Have you told your wife you're alive?"

He shakes his head.

"*Beau.* This is not okay."

"I know that," he mumbles.

He drives us to Ocean Lane and parks in a public lot over-looking the beach. Sunbathers frolic on the sand and in the waves. It's as busy around here as it gets. The height of summer. We're lucky we found a parking space at all.

I send a quick text to Nora. I don't care if Grayson has a problem with that or not. She at least needs to know he's in one piece. Then I put my phone away. "What's going on?"

He rubs his jaw, which is dark with several days of stub-ble. His eyes are bloodshot, and his hair hasn't seen a comb in a while either.

"I can't do this."

"Do what? Be a good husband? A father to your child? Nora could go into labor any day."

He digs his hands into his hair. "You think I don't realize that?"

"Something brought this on. Is this because the baby's almost here?"

"It's *everything*. I'm so scared I'm going to fuck it up."

"I'm sure that's normal. You've been stressed. Believe me,

I get that. And part of it is probably my fault. Or at least, not yours. But you're a good guy, Grayson. Nora adores you."

He shakes his head. "You don't know. You don't know what we've been through. What I've done."

A chill runs through me. "What have you done?"

He stares hard through the windshield at the people on the beach. "I cheated on Nora."

"*When*?" I blurt out.

"Around the time I moved over to major crimes."

I curse. Ugh, I don't want to know this about him. I glance around the parking lot until I spot Leon and Rex idling in the next row over. My chest moves as I exhale, realizing I was holding my breath.

"Is that what you were talking about the other day? The rough patch you went through in your marriage?"

He nods.

"Does your wife know?"

He nods again.

"So she forgave you. That says something. I'm sure you've been trying to earn back her trust. But this, what you're doing right now? Flipping out? This is the exact opposite way to go about it."

He turns to me. "But what if I don't deserve her forgiveness?"

I don't like the look in his eyes. It's harder, *meaner*, than I've seen from him before. "Why would you say that?"

"Because you've done things you aren't proud of. Right? You understand."

"I really don't like what you're implying."

Suddenly Grayson's hands are on me. Pulling me to him. His mouth lands on mine, rough and forceful. His fingers dig into my arms, and his tongue shoves its way past my lips. The taste of him is sharp. Repulsive.

I try to break the kiss, but his tongue prods deeper.

Invading my mouth. Like he doesn't even *care* that I don't want this.

I shove him away from me so hard his head bangs against the glass of his window. "What the *hell*?" I spit out. "What was that?"

"I thought you said I was a good guy. But not good enough for the mayor's daughter?"

I wipe at my mouth. "You have lost your damn mind," I hiss at him.

"You'll sleep with Chief Liu and that firefighter you just met, but you turn up your nose at me?"

"That is nobody's business, especially not yours."

"You've always acted so high and mighty. Untouchable. Better than everyone, making the rest of us feel like the leftovers. But it was all a lie, wasn't it? You're just like the rest of us. Compromised. Selfish. Just admit it."

Every one of his words hits me like a physical blow. "I'm going to assume this is temporary insanity on your part. But I don't have to put up with it. I'm done with this conversation."

I reach for the handle of the door, but he slams down the automatic locks.

"You're not going anywhere. We're not finished."

I've known him for over a year and a half, and I've never seen this side of him. The Beau Grayson I know is gentle. Funny. Never cruel. I don't want to believe this is the true self he's been hiding.

For Nora's sake, I hope it's not.

Then Leon is on the driver's side, glaring at Grayson. One hand is on his gun holster. He knocks hard on the glass. "Open up."

Rex appears outside my door and yanks on the door handle.

"Let. Me. *Out*," I say to Grayson.

My partner hits unlock. His face is bright red.

I push open the door. Rex steps back to let me out. Before I slam it shut, I lean over and look down at my partner. At the man I thought I knew.

"Go home to your wife and child. Beg Nora to take you back. And pray for the strength of character to deserve it."

32

Matteo

*I*n the days after my brother's death, I didn't leave Emily or Natalie's side. But during the nights, while they slept, I would drive up to the overlook in the West Oaks Hills that had been Brent's sanctuary. I felt closer to him there, in the place where he'd found peace when life got too stressful even for him. The guy who could seemingly handle anything, whether it was a demanding career or providing for his wife and daughter or being a hero to his screw-up little brother.

So that's where I go now.

I park my truck on the abandoned road and walk out as close as I can to where the slope drops off to the ocean. The sun is sinking toward the horizon, boats and birds silhouetted as I squint.

"Brent, I miss you," I say into the wind. "I don't know what I'm supposed to do."

A bit ago, I texted with Leon and Rex to make sure they stuck with Angela. And of course, they were already on it.

You're not needed, Matteo. They didn't say that, but I felt it in my bones. *You think you can do this, but you can't. Your efforts are not needed.*

Maybe I've been chasing all the wrong things. I wanted to prove something. Show the world I could live up to Brent De Luca's legacy. Perhaps even make up for his loss.

But maybe I've just been paying penance, like Danny accused me of. That's not a way to live a life. The fact that I'm standing here *alone* is proof of that.

My phone rings in my pocket.

You'd think with all the shitty phone calls we've been fielding today, I would have shut the thing off. But I couldn't do that. Because what if Angela called? If she did, I'd still be there for her. I wouldn't hesitate, even now. That's how stubborn I am.

But my heart falls once again when I see it's not Angela. It's Emily.

With a sigh, I sit down in a patch of wild grass and answer. "Hey, Em."

"Hey." I'm expecting to hear some kind of judgment in her voice. But it's soft. Sympathetic. "I heard from Danny about that article. How are you? How is Angela?"

"We're both pretty bad. At least, I assume so. She took off."

"Matteo. I'm so sorry."

"It's not that surprising. That's what usually happens around me. I'm the fun guy, not the one people stay with. And I'm not even that fun anymore."

"Wow, you're really wallowing."

"Am I saying anything that isn't true? Look where you are. You left too."

"I didn't leave you. Not the way you're saying."

"That isn't how I see it."

"You really want to have this out right now? With the day you're having?"

I pick up a rock and toss it toward the cliff. "Today is perfect. Go ahead. Tell me what you really think of me. I'm already feeling shitty. Might as well get the rest of it over with."

"You are impossible, you know that?"

"Keep going. Lay it all out. All the ways I fall short of Brent. All the ways I will never be able to measure up." Fuck, I sound like a real prize right now, but I can't stop. "You and Natalie lost the best guy in the world, and I'm all that was left."

"That's really how you see yourself?"

"That's how *everyone* sees me."

Then Emily makes a sound I've never heard before. She *roars*. There's a loud crash. My whole body seizes. For a moment, I'm afraid she just had a car accident or something. I didn't think she was driving.

God, what did I do?

But then she speaks. "I just threw my phone at the wall. I'm lucky the screen didn't crack. That's how frustrated I am with you. But not for any of the things you're thinking."

"Well, I—"

"No. Shut your big mouth for once. It's time that you listen."

Chastened, I shut my mouth. I listen.

"Matteo, Brent was not perfect." Her voice cracks. There's a long pause before she keeps going. "I loved him so much. But not because he had no flaws. He worked *all the time*. Even when we were supposed to be on vacation, he always had his face stuck in a book or a research proposal or a spreadsheet. He was so serious. He had the whole world's problems riding on his shoulders, and he intended to solve them. I adored that about him, but sometimes he could be a little... arrogant. Convinced that he knew best. I'm not criticizing him. I know that he loved me, and he loved Natalie more than life itself. He was the love of my life. But he could be difficult to live with sometimes. Okay? It's just true."

I pick up another rock and squeeze it in my fist. "Why haven't you ever said any of that before?"

"Because he's gone. The day he died, my heart died too. I could barely keep going. I should have been able to do it for Natalie. But the truth is, I almost fell apart. But do you know what got me through?"

"No," I mutter.

"*You* did. You were there. Every single minute. You picked me up off the floor. And somehow, you made me smile. Laugh. Inside, I was still black and blue, but you helped me get myself together enough to be Natalie's mom. And you were there for her, too. You kept her spirits up. Took her to get Pretzel and Chips. You surrounded her every day with so much love, even when I felt like I was falling short."

"Because I reminded you both of Brent. Even if I was the shitty, lesser version."

"*No*. You're right that nobody could replace Brent. But we never wanted you to. You saved us by all the ways that you're different from him. You gave your heart to us, every single day. With your silly jokes and dances and the ridiculous things you would say to make us laugh. You and I fought, I'm not denying that. But you brought us *joy*."

I drop my head onto my hand. "Then why did you leave West Oaks? Why didn't you want my help anymore?"

"Because you *do* remind me of him," she says quietly. "You're maybe even better than him at certain things. You're so free with your love and affection. I think I may have been using you as a crutch, and I can't keep doing that. I need to move on. I don't want to put distance between you and Natalie because you're probably her favorite person in the world. But *I* need distance."

There's a twisting in my gut. "Are you saying that you have… feelings for me?"

"What? Ew. *No*."

I snicker nervously, and that turns to full-out laughter when she joins in. "Don't think so highly of yourself," she says. "Not every woman wants you."

"I mean, I wouldn't blame you."

"Gross. Anyway." She laughs again. "We're coming back to West Oaks at the end of the summer. I promise. And we should schedule times to get together in between. You could come here. Bring Angela with you."

"I don't know. I'm not sure what's going on between us. She runs hot and then ice-freaking-cold."

"She'll see the light. How could she not? You're amazing."

I huff. Never thought I'd hear those words from my sister-in-law. "Thanks. That means a lot."

An engine approaches, and I hear tires throwing rocks on the unpaved road. I stand up.

Leon and Rex, the Bennett Security bodyguards, are in the front seat.

"Sorry, Em. I gotta go. Later?"

"Yeah, of course. Later."

I get up and start walking to the car. The back door opens, and Angela bursts out. She runs straight for me, curls bouncing.

She launches herself into my arms. I don't have time to think. I just catch her, holding onto her with everything in me. Then she's kissing me. My nose and my cheeks and finally my mouth, her lips lingering, tongue brushing out like she's searching for mine. I open up and take control of the kiss.

Our mouths connect like we need each other's air to breathe.

Finally, when she pulls back to look at me, I say, "Hi, angel. That was quite a greeting."

My eyes flick over to the car, where Leon and Rex are staring hard at their phones, trying to hide their grins.

"I'm so sorry I left," she says. "I turned around almost the minute I walked out the door, but then something came up." A scowl mars her features, then it's gone. "When I got back to the house, you weren't there."

"How'd you know I'd be here?"

"A lucky guess. If you weren't, I was going to try the firehouse. And then The Shore Lounge. Or that pub where you sometimes work."

"You were chasing me down?"

"Yes." She says this with utmost sincerity. Not a trace of sarcasm. "You deserve to be chased. I wasn't going to give up until I found you."

Damn. That's nice to hear. "All you had to do was call."

"That wasn't good enough." Her hands cup my face. She strokes my beard. Drags her thumb across my lips. "I think I've been running from a lot of things since I was wounded. But with you, I feel like I'm *home*. I'm still not sure how to do this. Be with you the way... the way you deserve. But I want to. I want you *so much*. You're the sexiest, kindest, best guy I've ever met."

My face is heating. "Way to stroke a man's ego. Don't stop, though. Feel free to keep going."

Her hands move to my chest. "And you're the most heroic. Since we met, every time I've needed you, you were there. Even when I was a pain about it."

I chuckle. "That might be. But I don't want to be just *anyone's* hero. I want to be yours."

"You are," she whispers. Another slow, aching kiss. "I'm falling for you."

Our lips are still touching as she speaks. Brushing with each syllable.

"Then I have bad news. I can't catch you this time. Because I'm falling right along with you."

Her eyes glisten. A tear overflows and cascades down her cheek. I kiss it away, which leads to more kissing, touching, until we're breathless and my cock is getting big ideas. "I should take you home," I say, "before Leon and Rex get more of a show than they bargained for."

"I don't care who knows. Or who sees."

"Wow. It's good you took that walk to sort out your head, because I'm loving everything you say." I pinch her chin affectionately. "I don't want to share our moment, though. I want all of you to myself."

Angela rides with me, while the bodyguards follow. I hold Angela's hand and kiss her knuckles and lean over to make out at the red lights. I can't stop smiling. Neither can she, though she's still wiping away tears.

"You said something came up after you left the house," I remind her. "What was it?"

There's that scowl again. "My partner. Grayson. He turned up."

"Is he okay?"

"Physically, I think so. Mentally? No. He's not okay. I don't know what's wrong with him. But that conversation, messed up as it was, put everything in perspective for me. I was running from the best thing that's happened to me. And if you think I'm worth..." She waves her hands. "All the mess you're having to endure right now, then I'd be a fool not to hold on to you."

"Remember what I said? Nobody tells me when I've had enough." I lean over to kiss her shoulder. "Especially when it comes to you. There's no such thing as *enough*."

Somehow, her smile gets even bigger and brighter. "Not when it comes to you, either."

At the next green, I step on the gas. I want to get this woman home and show her just how insatiable I am for her. But she must have a lot on her mind too, given the day's events. "Angela, you know I'm with you, right? Whatever happens next. I'll fight back against that news article however you want to. And I'm more than happy to keep investigating with you. I don't give a fuck what our chiefs have to say about it."

"Thank you. I'm grateful for that. For *you*. Maybe we can take a breather the rest of today and strategize tomorrow, because I'm tired of dealing with everything else. I just want to be with you."

"Then you will be. Ask, and I'll deliver."

"If I ask for ten orgasms?"

I grin. "Then buckle up, baby. 'Cause it's gonna be a wild ride."

We get home, and Angela jumps out of the truck, heading over to Leon and Rex's car. She knocks on their doors and gives each of them a hug, then meets me at the front door to the house.

"What was that about?" I ask, trying very hard not to sound possessive. She's my girl, and everybody knows it. I mean, it was in the news.

"I owed them an extra thank you. They've gone above and beyond."

"Thought that was my job," I grumble, winking to show I'm teasing.

"Take me inside, and you can go above, beyond, and anywhere else you want."

I can't unlock the door fast enough. I slam inside like a stampeding animal, tugging her along with me. "Do you want my tongue in your pretty pussy first? Or do you want my cock pumping inside you when you come?"

She moans, lips pressing together. "Both. Everything."

"It's *that* kind of day, huh?" I whip my shirt over my head as I plan which surface I'm going to fuck her against first.

Then I get an idea. I pick her up and carry her into the kitchen, where I set her on the counter. "I'm going to lay you out here and eat you up like a five-course meal."

"Well, *hello*. You two are doing just fine without me, I see."

Angela shouts in surprise. I spin around.

Neve is standing there grinning, leaning her shoulder against the doorway to her bedroom.

My roommate. My *boss*.

She's back.

33

Angela

My best friend is wearing the most self-satisfied grin I've ever seen.

"Uh, Neve." Matteo subtly adjusts himself and grabs his shirt from the floor. "You're home early."

"And you weren't expecting me? I guessed that much. I wrapped up all my shoots and decided to head home to support my poor, unfortunate bestie. Matteo, I asked you to take care of Angela, not make moves on her while she was homeless and vulnerable. Have you been molesting my plants, too?" Her eyebrow arches as she tries not to laugh.

"Oh, stop it. You're enjoying this way too much." I hop down from the counter and put my arm around Matteo, just in case he has any doubts about me wanting to own him as mine.

Neve crosses her arms, sticking out her lip in a pouty frown. "Matteo, what are your intentions toward my best friend?"

He opens his mouth. Glances at me. His eyes say, *Help*?

I give Matteo a kiss on the cheek. "I will handle her."

"Would you?" he murmurs. "Because honestly, she scares me a little."

"Should we start shopping for wedding gowns? Baby booties?"

I grab her hand and drag her into her room. She's cackling. I shut the door and glare. "You didn't see the article that came out today?"

"Article? I was in the air, and then I came straight here. You know I hate reading news."

"A lot has happened while you were gone."

"I can tell. I thought you two might hook up. I encouraged it! But I was getting some hot and heavy vibes in there. Are you chewing up my poor roommate before you spit him out? That might be a touch awkward for me."

I rub my forehead. "It's not like that."

"Be honest, how big are we talking." She holds her hands apart. "Like, nine inches?"

"Would you quit?"

"*Bigger*?"

"Stop." I push her hands down. "It's not *like that*."

"You're not riding that pony?"

"Good Lord. Why am I friends with you again?" I sit next to her. "Hot and heavy is accurate. But it turned into more. This is special. Matteo is special. To me." Wow. I'm explaining myself so well.

"Hold on. This sounds serious."

"It is. I told you that you'd missed a lot."

"Wow. Okay. Do you mean relationship serious? Isn't that fast?"

I struggle with how to explain this. How much has changed. How *I've* changed.

"The night we celebrated your birthday, and you said I was struggling, you were right. I was so lonely. So terrified to get out there and live my life. I thought if I had my career sorted out, the rest didn't matter. But in the past few weeks, I've lost that too. The only thing that saved me was Matteo. He's... *amazing*. Funny and generous and so damn persistent. He takes care of plants and animals and kids. And..." I hold my hands apart. "*Bigger* is right."

We both collapse into giggles.

"Angie, I've never heard you talk about a man like this."

"I think he could be it for me."

She gasps, hand to her mouth. "I just wish I introduced you to him sooner. He didn't seem like your type."

I laugh. "I know. I didn't think so either, but it turned out he had a profile on that hookup app you made me join. That made me realize he's *very much* my type."

"What about the underwear I bought you?"

"Oh, that helped too."

She crows with laughter. "I'm a mastermind and I didn't even know it! I will take every ounce of credit!"

"And I'll let you have it. I have Matteo, and that's all I need."

"Lady, who even *are* you?"

"I'm happy," I say, surprising even myself. Because it came straight from my heart.

My career is in shambles. Terrible things have been happening, things that shake the very foundations of who I am. I'm worried for Nora and Beau Grayson. And I have a lot of work to do on the Volkov case. But I'm *happy*. For the first time in a while. I have Matteo. I have plenty of friends who've stood by me, even if some haven't.

There's so much tragedy and sadness in this world, too much, and I intend to grasp what's *good* and hold it tight. Cherish it.

"And I'm so glad for you." Neve hugs me. "There's another reason I came back early. I wanted to help you find a new place. But now, I'm not sure what you have in mind.

How serious is serious? Are you and Matteo moving in together permanently?"

That's a question I'm not ready for yet. "This was only supposed to last three weeks. Until you were back. It's still so new. We want to be together, but the details are sketchy at best so far."

"Just let me know."

"What about you? Did you meet your future Italian husband on your trip?"

"Oh honey, no. I met and rode many stallions, but I'm the one who can't be tamed."

WE SPEND that evening catching up with Neve. We sit in the living room, sipping glasses of red wine, while I cuddle up to Matteo. His arm stays around my shoulders, and my hand rests on his thigh. After a while, Neve even stops staring and shaking her head. This feels good. Like something I could get used to.

My best friend. My *boyfriend*. Not a bad setup, really.

We FaceTime with Natalie for over an hour. She puts Pretzel in front of the screen, making the dog wave her paw, and Chips darts right up to sit in my lap and stare at Matteo's phone.

Then we check in with Emily. There's a gentleness to how she and Matteo talk to one another tonight. It's a contrast to their constant bickering before. I wonder if they had a chance to work some things out earlier today while Matteo and I were apart. He seems more accepting of them being in Bakersfield, at least for the time being.

When FaceTiming is through, Matteo makes dinner while I give Neve the short version of all that's been going on. She knew about my car accident, but not about my security detail.

And when she hears about the bodyguards, she insists on them coming inside. Leon and Rex are at the tail end of their shift, but they stay for dinner. From the way Neve eyes Leon, I'm guessing he'll end up a conquest. I'd go for Rex myself—if I hadn't met Matteo, obviously—but he's too old for my friend's tastes.

By the time Matteo and I head to his bedroom, I'm falling asleep on my feet. We cuddle while brushing our teeth. Then undress, turn off the lights, and slide into his bed. We kiss and caress each other for a while, just enjoying the simple pleasure of being near one another.

I must have a late rush of energy, though, because now I don't want to fall asleep. This has been a roller coaster of a day. Yet I'd live through it again just to end up here next to Matteo and see him smile at me.

"You didn't get your ten orgasms," he says.

I giggle. "That's okay. That can be another night. We have time."

"We do, don't we?" He wraps one of my curls around his finger.

I wonder if I should mention Neve's question about living arrangements. Now that she's back, I'm either sleeping here in Matteo's room or the couch.

Unless I get my own place, which was always the plan.

While I love my best friend and I love her house, I'm not so sure I want to be her roommate forever. But this is Matteo's home. Would he want to... with me...

Wow, I'm getting so far ahead of myself. So I decide not to mention those runaway thoughts.

"You and Emily seem to be getting along better," I say instead.

"You noticed?"

"I notice a lot of things about you."

He drops a kiss onto my hairline. "We had a good talk. I

understand better where she's coming from. Why she went to Bakersfield."

"Yeah?"

"She made me realize something. Brent asked me to take care of Emily and Natalie before he died. I promised I would, and it's been awful to think that I failed at it. But there's more than one way to take care of someone. You know? Emily said that I saved them." He licks his lips. Glances away. "But it wasn't about providing for them as far as money is concerned. It was just by being there for them. I needed to hear that."

This man. Every time I think I can't want him more... "See? You are a hero. You're wonderful."

He cocks his head thoughtfully. "I like that. Never heard that I'm wonderful before."

"Good thing I'm here."

"Very good thing." He rolls on top of me. But I stop him before he kisses me.

"Matteo, there's something I need to tell you."

He pauses, looking down at me with a slight frown. "Yeah?"

"I told you I saw my partner today. Grayson. That he wasn't well. He kissed me."

Matteo doesn't move, yet every inch of him tenses.

"I was furious. To say the least. Leon and Rex showed up almost immediately and got me out of there."

"Okay." The muscle in his jaw ticks. "Do I need to have words with this Grayson asshole?"

"I'll handle it. But I needed you to know what happened. Because I don't want anyone else."

"Good. You're mine, angel." He presses the pad of his thumb to my lower lip. "This is just for me."

"Only you," I whisper.

"And this." He cups my breast. Squeezes. "And this." His hand trails down to the cleft between my legs. "All for me."

"Then take it."

Our lips come together in slow, sensual kisses. Matteo's cock is still soft at first, and the feeling of him hardening against my leg is decadent. All the signs of his arousal shoot fire through my veins. Seeing his dark brown eyes dilate with lust, feeling his breaths quicken in his chest above me. The heat of his body rising like I turned up the thermostat.

His thick thigh rubs between my legs, and I shamelessly rock my clit against him. I'm so hungry for this man. Desperate for him. I drag my nails down his back. Not hard enough to hurt, but enough for him to close his eyes and grunt at the sensation. I just want *all* of him. All of him on top of me, around me, inside me. Claiming me.

"You ready for me?" He takes a condom from his nightstand.

"Let me?" I ask. I don't know why it turns me on so much to sheath his cock. Maybe it's the way he looks at me while I do it. Like he's having wicked thoughts and can't wait to pounce and act them out.

And pounce, he does. He grabs each of my thighs in his big hands, pushes them open, and watches as his cock enters me. I reach for him, my fingers digging into his hair, and tug the rest of him down onto me.

"You like when I press you into the mattress?" he asks. "You want me to pin you down?"

"Yes. And never let me go."

I need to feel as much of him as possible. To feel that I'm his, and he's *mine*.

Matteo's swollen shaft glides in and out of me. The rhythm, the heat where we're joined, the smear of our sweat and friction of our naked skin—it makes me delirious. I suck his tongue into my mouth, wanting him to fill me in that way too. I've never been with any man without a condom, but now I'm longing to get rid of that final barrier. Maybe soon, we will.

Just thinking about his hot come shooting inside of me pushes me over the edge. His hips pump faster as I shake and moan against him, his tongue still muffling my cries.

After, we cuddle and enjoy the afterglow.

"Neve seems okay about us," Matteo says.

"She's more than okay. She's thrilled. She wants to take all the credit and for our firstborn to be named after her." I add an eye roll to show I'm kidding, but Matteo's smile turns all syrupy and he rests his palm over my heart.

"Unless it's a boy."

I snort, though a million flutters are cascading through me.

"Did you tell her what we did to her bed?"

"*No*. Absolutely not. I cleaned every inch of that room, and my secret goes to my grave."

I'm not sure what instinct makes me grab my phone from the nightstand to check my messages. Maybe it's that I don't want to hide from anything anymore. Except for telling my best friend the sex acts I engaged in on her bed. *That* is just too much information. But aside from that, when it comes to real danger, I've got a sexy firefighter-hero to back me up. My usual bravery quotient has gone through the roof.

Yet what I see on my phone still chokes me up like a softie.

Messages from dozens of colleagues. West Oaks PD detectives, patrol cops, admins, and staff. Even people I know from some police departments in nearby cities. All showing their support for me. They say, in various ways, that they don't believe my personal relationships have any relevance to my credibility as a detective.

"What is it?"

I turn the phone toward Matteo. It's hard to even know what to say. Especially without crying.

"They might've been unsure how to react to the previous articles," he says. "But this one, those kinds of personal attacks, were just too far. They know you. They care about you."

It feels so good to see the evidence.

But my heart falls a little when I see Nora Grayson's message. She thanked me for letting her know her husband spoke to me, but he hasn't been home. I hope that he's in a hotel somewhere getting his head straight. And doing that *alone*.

As I'm holding the phone, a new text comes in from Sean. This morning, I wrote to him saying I wanted to review every scrap of evidence regarding Stefanie Rossi's murder and Volkov's conviction.

Sean Holt: I have updates regarding the Volkov/Rossi evidence. We need to meet tomorrow. ASAP.
Me: I've certainly got the time. But I'm now suspended without pay, and Chief said all investigations except Cassidy's are barred.
Sean Holt: That won't be an issue. There have been other developments. Will explain tomorrow.

I set up a time to meet, making clear that Matteo will be coming with me. Sean doesn't comment on that. He just says he'll see me then.

Something major is up.

I set down my phone, and Matteo pulls me into his arms again. "Ready to get back to work?"

I like that he put it that way. "Yes. I want to find who's responsible for what's been going on. And what really happened to Stefanie Rossi. No matter what it means for my career."

"Right on. I'd say I'm proud of you, but I'd rather you be proud of yourself."

"I will be. After I see this through."

I'm going to do whatever it takes to find the truth.

34

Matteo

olt offers to come to our place for his meeting with Angela. But at the appointed time, I open the door and do a double take at who's there with him.

Detective Diaz is on my porch. She locks eyes with me, shaking her head slightly like a disappointed schoolmarm.

"Cassidy?" Angela appears at my elbow. "What is this?" she asks Holt. "You're working together now?"

"Let us come in," he says. "You'll understand when you hear what we found."

Angela nods, but I'm not so willing to forget how Detective Diaz has upset my girl. And Diaz doesn't look the least bit contrite.

Yet I can't imagine Sean brought her here to arrest Angela on criminal charges of corruption. So I step aside to let them pass.

"Mr. De Luca," Cassidy says when she gets inside. "I'm guessing there are a few things you omitted from your interview with me."

I cross my arms, partially blocking her way. "Not really. I

was only getting naked and nasty with Angela *after* that interview."

Sean snorts, and Angela elbows me. "Word choice?"

"What? I thought that was polite enough. If she's coming here to make more accusations against you, then this meeting isn't going to last long anyway."

"I'll second that," Neve says from the kitchen. "I was just making coffee, but not for anybody who's got a problem with our girl."

"Sorry, who are you?" Sean asks.

I point my thumb at Neve. "Our other roommate. Angela's best friend."

"And self-appointed Mama-bear," Neve adds.

Cassidy holds up her hands in surrender. "I wish we could continue with this delightful repartee, but we actually have something serious to discuss. Angela knows I was only doing my job by handling the IA investigation. But new information has come to light, and I'm the one who contacted Detective Holt about it. Angela is no longer the target of my inquiry."

"Then spit it out. What's this new information?" Angela's hand goes to her shoulder, right above her scar. That's the only clue to betray her anxiety. But I see it. I touch the small of her back, and she leans into me.

Sean waves us into the living room. "Maybe it's best if we all sit down for this."

Once we're settled and Neve has passed out the coffee mugs, Cassidy speaks. "As part of the Internal Affairs investigation, I was looking into evidence that has gone missing from several cases. Angela is already aware of that."

"I think the whole world is aware of it after those articles about me. But you refused to share the details."

Cassidy shifts in her chair. "That's what I'm trying to do now. First was the heroin found by the firefighters at your apartment. It came from the evidence seized from Luke

Volkov's home after he was accused of Stefanie Rossi's murder."

"Because he was a drug dealer," I say, and Cassidy's eyes cut to me. She looks annoyed at my interruption. But she nods.

"Yes. But that heroin isn't the only stolen evidence that we found at Angela's apartment. We were delayed in executing a formal search warrant, but when we did, we identified more items that tied to cases where Angela was the lead investigator. Some of it from archives, but some from pending cases too. Mostly jewelry, all pretty easily identifiable. As if the items were intended for us to find."

Angela grabs my hand. "They were planted there. Please tell me you realize that?"

"I had to do my due diligence. I couldn't just assume my colleague was innocent. But yes, we now believe someone else was trying to frame you."

I bite the inside of my lip to keep myself from interrupting again. I would love to get my hands on whoever did this. I'm sure Angela is thinking the same thing.

"I started to piece together who had access during the relevant times," Cassidy says. "I was able to narrow down when the evidence was likely stolen, but of course whoever did it made efforts to cover their tracks. So it took a bit more work to narrow down the culprits. But there were still too many possibilities. The break came when I learned that Detective Holt had pulled the full casefile and evidence inventory for the Rossi murder."

"Because I asked him to," Angela says.

Detective Diaz gestures for Holt to take over the explanation. "I had an idea," Holt says. "I decided to pull the logs for who accessed the Rossi murder files in the last year. When Diaz asked what I was doing, the cat was out of the bag. So we pooled our resources, which made it all go faster. We found a common thread." His gaze moves to Angela. "Your partner. Detective Grayson."

"What?"

"Grayson has accessed the file and evidence for the Volkov case multiple times in the last few months. Long after Volkov's conviction was final."

"And knowing that," Cassidy says, "I confirmed that Grayson had recently accessed the evidence for every case where items went missing. For every case where you were lead investigator, Grayson was on it too. As your partner."

Angela is practically vibrating beside me. Her hand feels like a live wire, coursing with electricity. "I saw Detective Grayson yesterday. He's falling apart. I thought it was because his wife is having their baby soon. You really think he planted that evidence in my apartment?"

"He could've been driving the gray sedan that ran you off the road," I say.

"The man in the hoodie." She covers her mouth, swallowing. Like she's choking back bile. "Who I chased outside my building."

My gaze meets hers. "And who might've been visiting Katrina Katalsky. Her neighbor saw a guy in a hoodie, too."

"Katrina who?" Detective Diaz asks.

Angela waves that question away. "She's Luke Volkov's new girlfriend. I don't know how she fits into this. I don't understand why Grayson would try to frame me."

"Unless he needed someone else to take the fall for stealing all that evidence," Holt says. "Because according to Diaz, only a small fraction of it was found in your apartment. There's more that wasn't recovered, particularly items from the cases that are still pending. Jewelry, drugs. Things that would've been easy to sell on the street. This was a money-making scheme."

And Katrina had a new source of income. How she

would've hooked up with Grayson, we don't know. There's obviously a lot more of this that we're missing.

"Motives aren't the priority," Detective Diaz says. "We all know that. Right now, our focus is on means and opportunity. And Grayson had it. We don't know how and why this started, or why it's so tied up with Luke Volkov. Grayson had to know we'd notice the evidence was missing, especially from the pending cases. He needed someone else to take the fall."

Angela closes her eyes. "So he picked me."

"We've been trying to get in touch with Grayson to ask him questions, but we can't find him," Holt explains.

"His wife told me he hasn't been home." Angela details her encounter with him yesterday, but I'm less focused on her words and more on how she's feeling.

From all the things she's told me, it's clear that being betrayed by someone she trusts is one of Angela's deepest fears. Something she's struggled with since getting shot. And here it is happening again. I want to hold her and make sure she's okay. This is probably eating her away on the inside, no matter how skilled she is at hiding it.

"Our department has already been rocked by those news articles and the claims about you," Diaz says. "We're going to make sure we're certain before taking any of this to the chief. Heads are going to roll after this kind of scandal."

I scowl. "Would've been nice to keep the suspicion against Angela quiet in the first place. Until you were *certain*."

"I didn't leak a word to the media," Diaz retorts. "I don't know who did. But this time, I'm going to make sure nothing gets out until we're ready. The people standing in this room are the only ones who know what we've found. Not even the rest of my team."

"What about Jake Shelborne?" Angela asks.

"I'll bring him in if we can use him," Holt says. "But for the moment, it's just us."

They head out, and Angela retreats into my bedroom. I go in behind her and shut the door.

She sinks onto the edge of my bed like the weight of all we've just learned is too much. "Grayson said such cruel things to me yesterday. Has he hated me this whole time? And I just didn't see the signs?"

I sit and wrap my arm around her. "The guy's got issues. It's not your job to understand."

"But I need to. Cassidy was right that motives aren't the most important part of developing a case. But motive is the kind of thing that keeps me up at night. Wondering why."

I chew on that for a bit.

"The link to Katrina is strange," I say. "If she was really working with Grayson, and he's where she got the money, how did it happen? Did she find out that he was the junior detective on Volkov's case, and thought she could get info from him?"

Angela rubs her eyes. "Grayson cheated on his wife before. Katrina would've made an attractive honey pot. She could've tracked him down to get info on Volkov's case. Got her hooks into him. She could've blackmailed him."

"And forced him to help with their scheme to ruin your reputation and make you look so corrupt that Volkov could challenge his conviction."

She gives me a wan smile. "You're good at this, you know. Brainstorming."

I tap my forehead. "Figures. It's practically a hurricane in here."

She laughs, and I kiss her, drawing her against my chest.

We both sit and think for a while longer. Letting all these disparate facts drift around in our heads, turning the pieces to make them fit.

Angela speaks next. "So... Katrina approaches Grayson. Gets the ammo to blackmail him. He agrees to help her undermine Volkov's conviction. And steal some evidence for her to boot, a little icing on the cake. Enough money for the new car, the clothes. And a new lawyer for Volkov. Then Grayson sets me up, both to take the blame for stealing the evidence and to support Volkov's lawsuit. It makes sense."

"But why would he try to hurt you?" I ask softly, even though inside I want to rage that someone would do that to her. "Why would he send you those crime scene photos of Stefanie Rossi?"

Angela stands up and walks back and forth in front of me. She does it for so long, I think she's going to wear a hole in the rug. Then she freezes in place.

"Angel? What is it?"

When she turns around, she has a look of pure horror on her face.

"Yesterday, Grayson kept saying he didn't deserve forgiveness for what he'd done. What if... Oh my God, what if he killed Stefanie? He admitted that he cheated on Nora around the time he became my partner. That was when Stefanie told Volkov she'd met a new man. And she wrote about him in her diary. The guy who had promised to take care of her."

I stand up and go to her, resting my hands on her arms. "The missing pages from her journal."

"*Yes.* Grayson was *there*. At the murder scene in Stefanie's house. And there for every search warrant we carried out. He could've ripped out those pages. Tampered with other evidence."

I try to puzzle it out. Stefanie was working as a call girl. Grayson was unhappy in his marriage. He met Stefanie. Became involved with her. She fell for him. Left Volkov for him. But Grayson's promises were hollow. Did she threaten to tell his wife?

"Grayson was the mystery man Volkov was talking about the whole time," Angela says. "Grayson made sure that Volkov was convicted instead. But then, Katrina found him, thinking he was just a detective on the case. I'll bet Katrina has no idea what Grayson really did. She would've reported him otherwise. But Katrina's scheme to get Volkov free made it more likely that Grayson would be found out."

"It put pressure on him. No wonder he's falling apart."

"But it's more than just fear of being caught." Angela's eyes dart across the room as her mind works. "Guilt is eating him alive. Especially now that his wife is about to give birth. He feels like he deserves to be punished. But he won't turn himself in, so that guilt and anger and blame has to go somewhere."

"So he decided to punish you instead?"

"Because I didn't catch on to what he was doing. He blames me for letting him get away with it."

"That's why he sent you the crime scene photos."

She gasps as she inhales, then buries her face against my chest. "How did I miss this? The whole time, I had no clue. It was right there in front of me."

"You were struggling in your own way. You did the best that you could. You trusted your partner."

"Just like Stefanie trusted Grayson. And he killed her."

Nearly killed you too, I think.

The thought of Grayson's hands on her, his *mouth* on her. Adrenaline makes me lightheaded, makes my vision go fuzzy.

"We have to stop Grayson from hurting anyone else," I say.

Especially you. I will not let him hurt you again.

"I have to call Sean," Angela says. "It's all the more urgent that we find Grayson. He must have some sort of endgame in mind, and we need to move before he reaches it."

35

Angela

Jake finishes adjusting the hidden microphone at my collar. "Testing, one, two."

Another DEA agent across the room gives him a thumbs up.

"And there you have it. We're good to go." Jake pats my arm.

We're inside an empty storefront on Ocean Lane. I've been through sting operations before, but never one quite like this.

Not one where I'm trying to catch my own partner.

I barely slept last night between making plans and agonizing over Grayson's betrayal. It's almost too much to contemplate. Part of me keeps praying I'm wrong. That my partner didn't kill Stefanie Rossi and use his position to frame an innocent man. But if it wasn't Grayson, then none of the rest of what we've found makes sense.

After I realized how dangerous Grayson could be, Sean arranged for a West Oaks PD unit to sit outside Nora's house, just in case. Then I texted Grayson this morning, asking him to meet me to talk. I told him I had new information about the Rossi murder. We're hoping that's enough to tempt him.

I still haven't heard back from him, but we're proceeding under the assumption that he'll show.

Officer Evans walks over next, holding out a small earpiece. He's the brand new, baby-faced patrol officer who's on Cassidy's Internal Affairs team, the same one who tattled on me about climbing the balcony the night of the fire.

I guess he got the memo that Grayson is now the target instead of me. But we're all friends now, and I'm not one to hold a grudge.

"This will be your radio receiver," Evans says. "Detectives Holt and Diaz will be able to speak to you while you're outside."

Sean is in a corner, setting up the mobile command center, while Cassidy stares at a screen over his shoulder.

Meanwhile, Matteo is prowling the room like a caged tiger. He's not even supposed to be in here since he's a civilian. But Sean gave the go ahead. Matteo was upset that he won't be by my side while I'm meeting with Grayson. But it's not possible. Besides, Grayson might be terrified of him and run the other way, like he backed off fast when Leon and Rex showed up the other day.

We have to be careful and get this absolutely right.

My job will be to chat with Grayson and get his guard down. Then Sean and Cassidy will make their appearance and convince him, with strong words if necessary, to come down to the station and answer some questions.

Since we've had to keep this mostly quiet from the rest of West Oaks PD, Bennett Security is providing extra manpower. They'll be placed strategically outside in plain clothes while I meet with Grayson. Jake and some volunteers from the DEA have joined in too.

We don't have nearly enough for an arrest warrant, so we

need to get Grayson to come in willingly. Unless he tells me something incriminating, which is why I'm wearing the wire.

But given how dangerous he could be, we're not taking any chances. We've got highly trained bodyguards, agents, and operatives on standby. This is a patchwork, fly-by-night operation. Built of alliances and faith. But I've never been so confident in the team that I'm working with.

And that includes Officer Evans, even though I had some doubts about the young patrol officer before.

Evans helps fit the radio receiver into my ear. Like everyone else, he's dressed in street clothes to remain inconspicuous once we're outside. With his baby face, skateboarding T-shirt, and shorts, he looks like a high school kid on summer break.

Evans scratches under his Dodgers cap. "I've never worked with Grayson, but he seemed like a good guy." He glances around as the others continue bustling to get the command center ready. "It's a shock to find out a detective could do things like this. I don't even know what to think."

"You and me both. But you thought I was capable of plenty too," I point out.

He grimaces. "I'm sorry about that."

"You were the one who told Diaz that I tried to get into my apartment building the night of the fire, didn't you? I remember you were there that night."

"I just reported what I saw. I wasn't trying to cause any trouble for you. Just get to the truth."

"That's exactly what I want as well. Hopefully, when we get Grayson in to be questioned, that's what we'll get."

Evans smiles sheepishly. "When you're back on duty, I hope we have a chance to work together on a different case. One that doesn't involve anybody from West Oaks PD as a suspect."

"I'm looking forward to that."

Evans notices Matteo looming right behind his shoulder, and the young officer scurries away.

"Don't scare the kids," I murmur.

"What are you talking about? Kids love me." There's no privacy here, but Matteo pulls me off to the side. He drops his head, forehead touching mine. "I'll be out there where I can see you the whole time. But please be careful, okay? Because if Grayson touches a curl on your head, I'll have to rip him apart limb from limb, and the rest of your cop friends might not appreciate that."

I give him a quick kiss on the cheek, wishing it could be more. But not when I'm surrounded by work colleagues, even now that I've left my hermit shell behind.

"I've got a lot of backup," I say. "And I'm not afraid of Grayson." It's been terrible to realize what he's capable of, yet it's easier to have a face attached to the man who's been targeting me. The faceless unknown was far more frightening. "When he's not hiding behind a disguise, or going after a woman alone, he's a coward. I'll be fine."

Matteo's large hand cups my face. "You'd better be. I have plans for you."

"Do you?"

I expect him to whisper something sexy, but instead Matteo says, "I want a future with you. I don't know what that'll look like. I'm pretty flexible. But having you with me? That's non-negotiable."

I'm about ready to dissolve into a puddle of tingles and flutters. "I want you in my future too."

"I'm not a bad roommate."

"You're not. I might even want to continue with that arrangement. But just us, not with Neve. She's my best friend, but I don't need her mothering me."

He tucks a curl behind my ear. "Our own place? How mature and grownup. I like the sound of it."

"With room for Natalie and Emily when they want to visit?"

His grin is bright enough to carry me through the rest of this, no matter how stressful it gets. His eyes are doing that thing where he says more just by looking at me than speaking out loud.

I lace our fingers together, smiling back at him, and then Sean and Cassidy head over. While I want to keep basking in Matteo's glow, I have to let go of him and focus on my colleagues.

"Murphy, we're just about ready to start." Cassidy glances at her watch. "I heard from the officer I sent to check on Katrina Katalsky. There's no sign of her at her apartment, and the place has been cleaned out. She may have skipped town."

"Which suggests she was in on it with Grayson," I say. "Maybe Grayson tipped her off that things are unraveling for him."

"For her sake, I hope that's what happened, and that he didn't decide to silence her," Sean adds. "We need to get Grayson into custody before this can turn into something worse." Then he looks over at Jake. "Shelborne, are we all set on Murphy's wire?"

Jake gives him a thumbs up.

Then Devon Whitestone, the co-head of the bodyguard team from Bennett Security, strolls over. "My guys are ready to go whenever you are."

We all wait for Cassidy to issue the final go-ahead. She's officially the head of this operation, so the order is hers to give.

She nods. "Let's get out there and bring Grayson in."

～

I PUSH out of the storefront and walk along the sidewalk. We've chosen a quiet stretch of beach where innocent bystanders will be minimal.

There's a breeze coming off the ocean, ruffling my dress around my legs. I've worn one of Neve's sundresses. I never used to dress this girly, but her clothes have been growing on me. I just might go and pick out a few of my own.

And maybe some more colorful shirts to wear with my suits too, for when I go back to work.

Back to work.

It's funny. When I was recovering from being wounded, that was all I wanted. To get back to my job. But now, I'd go for a real vacation if Matteo could get the time off.

Maybe we could go to Mexico. Hole up in a casita on the Gulf side, where the water is warm. Or anywhere, really. Just as long as I get to share it with him.

Hopefully downtimes with Matteo will be just as wonderful as the stressful times have been. But how could they not? I'll bet there's never a dull moment with him, even if the world around us is nothing but peace and tranquility.

While I appear to be walking alone, I've got dozens of eyes on me. I pass by the public parking lot, which I know is full of Bennett Security bodyguards. A car drives in, and I recognize Jake behind the wheel. He's wearing a fedora like a noir detective. That's a look I would've pegged for Sean, with Janie as his Girl Friday.

"No sign of Grayson yet," Sean says in my earpiece. "We have lookouts on all the roads that feed into the parking lot, as well as on the footpaths."

I reach the sand and check my phone. Grayson still hasn't written. But he'll come. I just can't imagine he would pass on the chance to find out what I know.

Now, I just have to wait.

The more I glance around, the more I spot familiar faces.

Like Leon and Rex, who've donned backward baseball caps and are sitting on a tailgate of a truck, sipping cans that are probably soda rather than beer. Matteo's with them, pretending to be staring at his phone, yet I feel his eyes on me.

Seeing my backup centers me, yet it also pulls me into the moment. To how *real* this is.

Grayson—my partner, my friend—could be a killer. I have to bring him in. And once I do that, once this is *finally* over, I can go home with Matteo and plan that getaway.

But a few minutes turns into half an hour. Then more.

After a solid hour of waiting, all I've done is soak up the rays of the sun. There's been no sign of Grayson. If he approached and spotted a bodyguard or someone else he recognized, our lookouts would have seen him.

I get out my phone and call him. It goes straight to voicemail.

Then Sean says in my ear, "Murphy, just got word. Grayson showed up at his house. Our unit there stopped him, and he's agreed to come down to the station. I'm heading there now. Same with Diaz."

"What about me?" I ask.

"We're calling the op. It's done."

"*Obviously*, but I want to be there when you question him."

Sean pauses. I hear background noise on the line. It sounds like he's in the car, probably already racing toward the station. "Go back to base. You did great, Murphy. You put together all the pieces last night. Now let me and Diaz finish it."

Not what I wanted to hear.

I curse, walking toward the parking lot. Jake gets out of his car. Matteo jogs over on my other side.

"What's going on?" Matteo asks.

"They found Grayson," Jake says. "We're standing down."

We all hurry to the command center. Everyone's packing up, getting ready to leave. The Bennett Security guys, the DEA. They're fine with moving on to their next task for the day. West Oaks PD now has it covered.

But I feel like Cinderella if she got dressed up but didn't get to go to the ball.

"So we're heading home?" Matteo asks, brow wrinkling. "Just like that?"

"*No*. I'm going to the station for the interrogation." I don't care if I've been suspended. Let the chief take it up with me. I'm going to be on the other side of that one-way glass seeing what that bastard has to say for himself.

Officer Evans steps over, hands tucked into his shorts. "Detective Murphy, I could give you a ride to the station if you want. I'm heading there next."

Matteo frowns. "I can do it. I'm Angela's ride anyway."

I've already talked about this more than I want. I'm still smarting from Sean's comment. *You did good, Murphy*. Like I'm no longer needed.

I still want that vacation with my sexy firefighter, but *after* I've taken care of business. Seen this through.

Grayson didn't just betray Stefanie and his wife. He betrayed *me*.

"It's okay," I say to Matteo. "This could take hours. You go home, and I'll call you when it's over."

He hesitates, glancing between me and Evans. Then nods. His arm snakes around my waist, pulling me in for a quick kiss. "Let me know if you need anything. Doesn't matter what it is. Just call."

"I will."

"I'll be waiting."

He lets me go, and I follow Evans out to his squad car.

ALMOST IMMEDIATELY, we hit a snarl of traffic.

West Oaks can be like this sometimes. One minute the roads are quiet, and the next, everyone in Southern California is here for the beach or a night out. I tap my fingers impatiently against the driver's side door while checking my phone.

"Does Detective Holt know you're coming?" Evans asks. His window is open, and cool air blows through the cabin. He's resting his arm on the top of the door.

"Not yet. He already told me to go home. If I show up at the station, it will be harder for him to refuse to let me stay."

The light changes, and we inch forward. *Come on. Come on.*

"My name's Braden, by the way," he says.

"Braden," I repeat. "Right, I remember." He's watching me while we're stopped at a red light, so I smile back politely. "How do you like being on patrol with the property crimes department?"

He's chewing his lip so much I'm surprised it's not ragged. "Property is pretty good so far. Maybe not what I expected."

"No?"

"I thought I'd have more chances to help people. Save lives."

"I understand. I was frustrated being on patrol too. It's important work, crucial, but I wanted to be solving crimes single-handedly. That's not how it works."

His eyes slide over to me again. He has an odd expression. I can't tell what he's thinking. "Is it better now? As a detective?"

For some reason, I stumble over my answer. "Not always. Sometimes, I still wish I could do more. There are unanswered questions."

"Does that happen a lot?"

"Not a *lot*. But some questions are bigger than others, if that makes sense. They stick with you."

There's finally a break in the traffic. Wind noise fills my ears as Evans accelerates.

"Is Stefanie Rossi one of those?" he asks. "The questions that stick with you?"

"She is. Yes."

"But you claim to care about finding the truth?"

I glance over at him. "Of course I do. I thought I said that earlier." And that's not the kind of question a patrol officer usually asks a detective. It's borderline insulting. I huff a laugh, because honestly? I have no idea if he's being serious. Though he sounds like it. And his vibe has been getting stranger as the minutes pass.

Evans is sweating. A red flush has inched up the pale skin of his neck. Something is definitely up with him. I'm wishing I insisted on driving. I look down at my phone again, wondering if I should tell Sean I'm on my way after all. And that Evans doesn't seem well.

"She ran away from home," he says.

"You mean Stefanie?" I guess he's been reading the case-file. Is that what this is? He's upset over a tragic death? He wouldn't be the first newbie patrol officer to struggle with the ugly reality of violence.

I relax my grasp on my phone. "Yes, she ran away. She was a kid, caught in a terrible situation. She wanted someone to save her."

"And the guy hurt her instead. Killed her." He grips the steering wheel like he's strangling it.

"Evans? *Braden*? Are you all right? Do you need to pull over?"

He doesn't respond to that. Instead, he turns the car at the next intersection.

"This isn't the way back to the station," I say, trying to keep my voice calm. "Shouldn't you have made a left instead of a right?"

"I'm trying to avoid the traffic." He's breathing heavily, as if he's trying to rein in his emotions. "I heard your theory about Detective Grayson. That he... he framed Luke Volkov for murder and then decided to frame you."

"Yes." I swipe my thumb across my screen, holding it up subtly to unlock it. Do I call someone? Is Evans behaving erratically, or is this nothing?

"And if your theory falls apart?" His voice has gotten sharper now. Thinner. "What then?"

"You're talking like you know something I don't."

"What if I said I do?"

I narrow my eyes at him. "I'm sorry? You do *what*?"

"Know something you don't."

Cold lances down my back. "Then tell me. Right now, because I don't like being jerked around."

No response.

We're now going through a neighborhood. Cars are parked along the curbs, yet there are none driving on the street. No pedestrians or residents out either.

I stare at the door handle. The next time he stops, I'm going to get out of the car. It seems wild to even consider it. But this guy is giving me creepy vibes, and I've had enough of it.

"Evans," I bark at him in my most authoritative tone. "Stop the car. I'm getting out now."

"Stefanie wanted out too. But nobody came to help her. *Nobody*."

Enough of this. I unlock my phone to call 911.

Suddenly, Evans grabs the phone from my hand and launches it through his open window. Then he guns the engine. Swerves into a turn, entering another street.

"What the hell are you doing?" I yell, grabbing onto the dashboard. "Evans. *Stop*."

We're tearing down a residential road and going way too fast. Houses fly past in the windows. My heart whirrs in my chest.

We lurch to a sudden stop, brakes squealing, and I'm thrown forward against the chest restraint of my seatbelt. My thumb immediately presses the seatbelt release, but it's locked out. *Shit.*

Evans turns to face me.

He's holding his service weapon. Aiming it at me.

My vision feathers with darkness. *A figure lurching toward me…*

"Don't," I whisper, fighting back the fear. I go to reach for my weapon, but I'm not armed. I didn't bring my gun to the meeting with Grayson.

I certainly didn't think I'd need it here, in a squad car with a patrol officer barely old enough to shave.

Who is this guy? Because he's far more dangerous, freaking *unhinged*, than he ever seemed.

"We're here." Evans nods at the window. "Look."

My eyes move to follow his gaze.

We're at an abandoned house. It's alone at the end of the street, just minutes from Ocean Lane, and yet it could belong to another world. Overgrown weeds surround the place. Black scorch marks snake up the siding to a caved-in roof, and there's a tilted for-sale sign forgotten in the yard.

A tattered piece of yellow crime-scene tape hangs from the shuttered doorway.

This is the house where Stefanie Rossi died.

"She was my half-sister," he says.

36

Matteo

I know I told Angela I'd go home and wait for her call. She said this interrogation could take hours. But when I'm halfway to the house, I turn in the direction of the station instead.

What can I say? When it comes to Angela, I go with my gut. And my gut is telling me I should stay close. I don't like the thought of Grayson being closer to her than I am. I know that's overprotective. Possibly even irrational, given that she'll be surrounded by other officers, including Holt. But I told Angela that if she ever needed me, I'd be there.

Maybe it's selfish, because keeping her close is just as much for me as it is for her. This need to protect Angela seems to be a vital part of me that I can't overcome or deny. Could be a problem given her line of work and my complicated schedule.

But hey, I never claimed I was perfect. She's known that from the start.

I pull into the station parking lot and jump out of my truck. Instead of stopping to message her and let her know

I'm here, I just head to the reception desk. The officer on duty gives me the usual spiel.

No, he can't let me back there. Yes, he can try to see if Detective Murphy is available.

Thank you.

I walk back and forth across the reception area, ignoring the curious stairs of officers and people I assume are witnesses going by. It was like this the last time I was here too. A constant level of activity. I try to smooth out my features and dial back the tension in my muscles, because if I seem threatening, I'm more likely to end up arrested myself rather than ushered to see my girl.

Finally, the officer at the desk waves me over. "Detective Murphy isn't here. You'll have to try later."

"She's not here? You're sure?"

"Yes, sir. I'm sure."

That *sir* sounded a lot more sarcastic than respectful.

I take out my phone and call her. She doesn't pick up. I try texting, but it doesn't look like she's reading her messages.

Where is she?

I try Neve next, but she hasn't seen or heard from Angela either.

I return to reception. "Then what about Detective Sean Holt? Or Cassidy Diaz? Because Murphy said she was on her way here, and she wouldn't have gone anywhere else." Not with the mood she was in. Angela was determined. I know how single-minded she can be when she's got her sights on something.

"Detective Holt is unavailable," the officer says immediately.

"Well then let me talk to *somebody* who can help me find Murphy. What about Officer Evans? He was going with her. Where is he?"

"Sir—"

"Everything all right out here?" Holt strides toward us, forehead etched with tension. "I thought I heard your voice, Matteo. Is Murphy here?"

"She was heading this way. You haven't seen her? Officer Evans was giving her a ride. They should've beat me here."

Sean pulls me aside. "I don't know. Maybe they took a detour? I doubt Angela wants to be here anyway." He rubs his face and lowers his voice. "This is going to take a *lot* longer than I was hoping."

"The interrogation? Why? Grayson won't talk?"

"The opposite. Grayson's been talking since before Diaz and I even got here. He won't shut up. He's in there bawling like a baby, saying how sorry he is. But he claims not to know anything about the missing evidence or planting it in Murphy's apartment. He swears it wasn't him. Says he hasn't been to the evidence archives in months, despite the logs."

I'm surprised Holt is telling me this. But it probably has something to do with how exhausted he looks. "Isn't that how everybody is at first? They just deny?"

"A lot of the time, sure. Except Grayson is in there confessing all kinds of other things. Cheating on his wife, cheating on his damn taxes. Next I expect he'll admit to taking money from the collection plate at church. He's clearly got a lot to get off his chest."

"Like kissing Angela?" My stomach and my fists clench just thinking about it.

"Yep, that too. He says he's embarrassed and ashamed. But nothing about the actual crimes we suspect him of. When I asked if he knew Stefanie Rossi when she was alive, he just seemed confused."

Alex Liu appears behind Holt. "Detective, shouldn't you be in there with Grayson?" Alex looks from Holt to me, frown lines appearing around his mouth.

"We're taking a break," Holt says on a sigh. "Hoping some time to sit and think will jog Grayson's memory, because none of this makes sense."

"I'd rather you and Diaz keep working on him. As long as he's talking, we need to be listening. Eventually, he'll slip up."

Holt digs his hands into his hair. Then he nods and heads back down the hallway. "All right. You're the boss."

But Alex remains. "Is there something I can do for you, Mr. De Luca? I'm not sure what Holt's been up to, but we don't usually invite civilians to interrogations."

"Angela was supposed to come here with Officer Evans after the sting operation was called off, but I can't find her. I'm getting worried."

"Were they taking his cruiser?"

"I think so, yeah."

Alex taps something on his phone, holding it to his ear. "Connect me to Officer Evans, please," he says.

Then waits. Shakes his head.

"No response from Evans. But I can look up the GPS location of his vehicle. Come with me." He nods his head and starts down the hall.

I follow Alex to his office. He sits in his chair and types rapidly on the computer. "Go ahead and have a seat," he says.

I sink into the chair across from his desk. "I didn't expect this warm of a welcome from you. You didn't seem happy to see me and Angela together the last time I was here."

Maybe I shouldn't be saying that to the police chief. I shouldn't be thinking of him as "Alex" either because I just might say that out loud. But I've never been so great at keeping my mouth shut, not even to my *own* boss. And my nerves are wound tight as hell with stressing about Angela.

"Because of my history with her?" Alex asks. "Is that what you're thinking?" He flashes a quick, sardonic smile. "I do care about Angela. But I want to see her happy. If that's with you, then I can accept it, despite the fact that you were a witness in the internal investigation."

"Especially since it now looks like she's innocent? You didn't seem so concerned for her happiness when you suspended her without pay."

"That wasn't personal."

I cross my arms, widening my stance. "Maybe not, but if you claim to be her friend, she needs to know you'll stand by her. I don't mean giving her some unfair advantage, but at least defending her when she's unfairly under attack."

"I wanted to. This job isn't easy. I have a lot of people I'm responsible for, not just her. But I would still do anything for her."

"You say that, but I actually mean it. I will *never* let her down if I can help it."

For the first time since Brent died, I know what I'm supposed to do, where I'm supposed to be. I'm supposed to take care of her, and she's willing enough to accept that from me. But the even better part? Angela takes care of me, too. In all the ways I need it. She's opened up to me, given me her hard-won trust, and that is the most precious gift I ever could've received.

I *will not* fail her.

And if anybody out there is hurting her right now, I'm going to hunt him down—through hellfire if that's what it takes—until the end of my days.

Alex bows his head slightly. "That's probably why she chose you. You're a lucky man. Maybe someday, I'll find a woman who sees me the way Angela sees you." He taps at his keyboard, then curses. "Damn it. The GPS locator on Evans's squad car isn't functioning. But I'll see if I can track his likely destination from when it was last operating. In the meantime, I'm notifying available units to be on the lookout for them."

"Is the GPS broken?" I grind out. "Or did Evans switch it off?"

"I'm not sure."

"Who is he? Could he have some reason to harm Angela?"

"Not that I'm aware of." Alex taps his fingers on the desk, staring at his screen.

I can't stand here waiting for some computer to spit out answers. Adrenaline and anxiety are creating a potent mix in my veins. Commanding me to get out there. Look for her. *Do something*.

This situation is all wrong. I feel it like a change in pressure, like the very air is about to ignite.

"I need to get out of here," I say.

"Do you have any idea of where she might be?"

"Not yet. But I'm not just going to stand around."

"Maybe you should head to your place in case Angela goes home."

Yeah, that's not happening. I'll scour every inch of West Oaks if that's what it takes. "I'll figure it out."

I head out to my truck, racking my brain for where she might've gone.

But if this Evans guy took her someplace... what if she didn't go voluntarily?

Somehow, I have to find her.

37

Angela

"Lift that panel," Evans says. "It's loose."

We're behind Stefanie's house. Black streaks stain the wall, and bits of brick have crumbled into the overgrown yard. We've waded through the weeds, and my thin dress has the tears to show for it.

Evans is behind me holding the gun. I can't see the weapon, but I can feel it. The yawn of the muzzle. Evans has been careful to stay out of my reach.

I'm hoping he just wants to talk. To tell his story and share his grief over Stefanie. If he wants something else with me? I guess I'll figure that out when it comes. I'm functioning one moment at a time.

I pull aside the panel, opening a gap in the plywood over the back entrance. "I didn't know Stefanie had a brother," I say.

"Another detail you missed?"

"I was careful with the investigation, Braden. I *tried*."

"Be quiet. I don't want to hear your excuses. Go on. What I want to show you is inside."

Trembling, I turn sideways to go through the gap. Evans

follows behind me. We come into a room that might've been a kitchen. One wall is burned. It looks like the flames skipped here and there, claiming some parts of the house, leaving others untouched. Horrible in its randomness. Makes me wonder why it didn't simply burn.

It's like my darkest memories. Vivid in some places, absent in others. And I don't know why.

Why is Evans doing this? What does he want?

"Keep going," he says.

I edge forward. There's debris everywhere. Littering the floors. Dishes, artwork that fell from the walls but wasn't replaced. There's a thick layer of dust and dirt over everything, but with a trail of footprints running through the middle of it. Like someone's been in and out of here a lot, including recently.

I look back at Evans. His eyes are on the detritus of his sister's life. Her death. I contemplate lunging for him, trying to get the gun, but it's too risky.

His eyes dart back to me.

"I was living in Oregon with my dad when she died. Stefanie..." He shakes his head. "Before everything got bad, she went to that fancy private school here in West Oaks. You'd think our mom would be proud, but she was glad to pass off Stefanie to someone else. Like she'd done to me with my dad."

"I remember speaking to your mom," I say.

"And she didn't care much, did she? Not even when Stefanie was gone. Certainly not about me. But my sister cared about me. She called me on my birthdays and Christmas. Sent me gifts. She was always kind. Always wanted to hear how I was doing."

He gestures with the gun. "Keep going."

I walk beneath an arch into another room. The living area. I remember being here when I surveyed the crime scene.

Stefanie's body was found in the bedroom, and that was where the fire was most intense. But out here, in the living room, was where the murder weapon was found. The syringe, which had Volkov's fingerprints.

Was it really Grayson who planted that evidence? Who killed Stefanie?

Or was I wrong about that, too?

"I didn't hear she had died until weeks afterward," Evans says. "Nobody called me. Not even our mother. One of my friends from college saw an article about Stefanie's murder online and recognized her name because of how much I'd talked about her."

A look of acute pain crosses his face. His eyes squeeze closed, but they open again too quickly for me to make a move.

"I followed the trial in the news. I assumed everything that you and the prosecutor said was true. That Luke Volkov did it. I thought after he was convicted that justice had been served. But it wasn't *enough*. I wanted to look Volkov in the face and ask him why he killed my sister. A girl who just wanted to find a home. To have people she could love and trust."

"Did you visit Volkov in prison?"

He nods. "But Luke wasn't the heartless mobster you made him sound like. He felt terrible about what happened to Stefanie. And the more we talked and I listened, the more I started to believe him. He wasn't the one who killed her at all. So I decided I would solve it."

He points at something across the room, and I follow with my eyes.

There's a display tacked up on one wall. I go closer. I recognize pictures from the crime scene, reports from the casefile. It looks like a copy of the entire murder book. But there are also hand-drawn notes on the photos and papers, overlapping onto the stained drywall.

This must be the work of months. But it looks more like a visual depiction of a conspiracy theory than a logical, methodical crime investigation.

And below the murder book display, there's a shoebox with a framed photo of Stefanie atop it. A teddy bear, a few items of costume jewelry, and a fancy-looking men's watch. Like some kind of shrine.

Evans stares at all of it along with me.

"You applied for the police academy?" I ask.

"Yes. I wanted to learn everything I could about her murder. But I hoped I could help other people, too. People like my sister. It was useless. *All* of it," he spits out. "A pipe dream."

"Why not come to me or the chief? Talk to us. Share your story and your concerns, instead of this… *whatever* this is." I wave a hand at his conspiracy wall.

"How would that have helped find Stefanie's murderer? You still haven't found him. You've decided every step who to blame, and then only paid attention to the evidence that matches."

"Then show me," I say carefully. Not trying to challenge or provoke him. I need him to open up. See me as an ally. "Where did I go wrong? I do care, Braden. If I messed up, I want to be able to fix it."

I might be trying to win him over to get myself out of this safely, but I'm speaking from the heart. I need to know what really happened to Stefanie, too.

But he scowls.

Evans storms over to the small shrine and points at it. "I found this shoebox hidden under one of the floorboards of this house. *After* you and forensics were supposed to have done a thorough search. I already knew that after Stefanie dumped Luke, she got rid of anything that belonged to him. She talked about it in her journal. Yet these things were left. These must've been some of Stefanie's most prized possessions, and you didn't even find them."

"Why didn't you bring these items to West Oaks PD?"

He ignores me, instead picking up the men's watch. He brandishes it, waving it in front of me. It's a Rolex. I see the brand name on the face. I'm shocked she kept it instead of selling it. This watch is worth thousands of dollars.

"Stefanie wrapped this up in a handkerchief like it was important to her. Like it meant something. But it wasn't Luke's. Do you know what? I'll bet it was *his*. That bastard she trusted who took *everything* from her and then threw her away. Do you know why I didn't bring this to you or the chief? Because I didn't trust you! I didn't trust *any* of you. I sent it to a lab myself. Paid for it to be analyzed for DNA or whatever else."

"What did the lab say?"

"There was no DNA but Stefanie's." Evans squeezes the watch in his fist. "The one clue I found, and it still lead nowhere."

"It might not be too late. We could figure out where it was bought. A watch like that is going to have a sales history."

He laughs bitterly. "I thought so too. Except it's *fake*. Not even a real Rolex. It came from some flea market or a cheap cart downtown. Just as fake as your investigation and Luke Volkov's trial. Fake as the promises of the guy who killed her. Fucking useless."

He tosses the watch onto the ground by my feet, and I pick it up.

Could this really have belonged to the killer?

It's a beautiful watch. I've seen ones like this before. A black face, white hands, a silver metal bracelet. The circular piece around the watch face is half blue, half red. A distinctive, high-quality fake, assuming Evans is right. I'm certainly no watch expert, but this has the heavy feeling that an expensive item of jewelry would have.

Yet there's damage to the metal that a pricey Rolex wouldn't get. And when I flip it over, I see a long scratch across the back.

That scratch strikes a chord inside me. A feeling of déjà vu.

Don't worry, it's not a real Rolex.

I've heard those words before. But where? I don't know where that thought came from.

But Evans has no idea my brain is wandering.

"Whoever owned that watch and gave it to Stefanie, he's long gone. And it's because of *you*. If you hadn't been so focused on Volkov, you might've been able to pick up the trail before it went cold."

"What makes you so sure the killer wasn't Beau Grayson?" I ask.

"Because he had nothing to do with anything!" Evans explodes. "He was your partner, but so what? Your theory was based on him accessing the evidence archives, but that was all bullshit. Now, Stefanie's killer will never be brought to justice. And her blood might as well be on your hands."

I remember the note attached to the photo of Stefanie's body. The words written in blocky letters. My name scrawled on the envelope flap. "You sent me those crime scene photos."

"I wanted you to know what you'd done."

"And it was you in the hoodie, wasn't it? You were in my apartment. You ran me off the road."

I'm so furious I almost rush at him, but he's still got the gun. I clench my fist around the watch instead. My palm slicks with sweat.

"You accessed the archives. *That's* how you know it wasn't really Grayson."

"When I was trying to investigate Stefanie's murder," Evans says, "I found the heroin still in the archives, even though the drugs should've been destroyed. An administrative error. But I thought it was a sign. I took the heroin, and nobody even knew it was missing. I didn't know yet what I wanted to do with it."

My blood curdles. It was Evans behind all of it. This whole time. "When did you decide to use the heroin from evidence against me?"

"Not until a month ago. When I finally realized there was no hope left of finding Stefanie's killer. I wanted someone to discover that heroin and blame *you*, and you'd know that it was karma coming back around to you. The world would find out just how corrupt you really are, how you frame innocent people and let the guilty go free. I picked the lock to your apartment to plant the drugs. Then I set the fire in your neighbor's unit, just like Stefanie's killer had done. Couldn't set it in yours because it might have destroyed the heroin."

My neighbors saw him skulking around that day. The suspicious man in a hoodie and sunglasses. "You could've killed someone with that stunt."

"Not likely. I'm the one who placed an anonymous tip about smoke coming from the building. I was the first West Oaks PD officer on the scene. I didn't want anyone to get hurt. Not even you, not then."

"And then Cassidy Diaz invited you right into the investigation."

"I volunteered. She already knew me and liked me, so she was happy to have me."

"Why did you go to my building the day the search warrant was executed? That *was* you, right? The guy I chased?"

He nods. "I took off my hoodie and threw it in a trash can right before you ran into me. I had my uniform underneath. I was adding more evidence to your apartment because it seemed like the heroin hadn't been enough. I thought I would finally see some kind of justice for what you'd done, letting Stefanie's murderer get away. But you used your connections with the chief, all the advantages you've had as the mayor's daughter, to squirm your way out of it. Diaz kept insisting we had to take our time. Be *absolutely sure* before charging you. But it was moving too slow. The world should've been *outraged*."

"You leaked stories to the media?"

"Everyone had to know. But it still wasn't enough. I wanted you punished." He grabs at his hair. Waves the gun around as he gestures. "I... I just felt so helpless. I saw you at the station that one day, and I followed your car after. I thought I'd explode, I was so angry."

"So you ran me down on the freeway? Tried to *kill me*?"

"It got out of hand! I wanted to scare you. Make you feel just as powerless as me."

"You succeeded. I was terrified. You claim I'm corrupt, but you're the one who's stolen evidence."

Evans scowls at the ground.

"Did you use Grayson's ID at the evidence warehouse?"

"Yes," he says in a monotone. "He looks a bit like me. Blond hair. I found an old ID in his desk from when he was in the property department, and whenever I used it, I made sure the person working the evidence desk wasn't anyone I knew. I dressed in a suit, wore a Yankees baseball cap like the one Grayson sometimes wears. Nobody gave me a second glance."

"What about the rest of the evidence? The jewelry and drugs from pending cases. A lot of it's still missing. Were you selling it?"

He flinches. "It was Katrina's idea. She knew I was Luke's friend, and when she realized I'd joined West Oaks PD, she came up with the idea. Skim evidence from cases and resell it to make money for Luke's legal defense. I thought Katrina was like Stefanie at first, someone who needed help, but she's not. She doesn't care about me or even about Luke. She's only out for herself."

"Did Katrina know about your plan for revenge against me?"

"I didn't tell her or Luke what I planned to do to you. It's not about them. It's about Stefanie. Making somebody acknowledge that she was important. That she meant something in this world."

Suddenly, his voice is breaking. He looks like he's about to cry.

He's no older than twenty-one. An adult, yes, but in some was still a scared child grieving for his big sister. And in my rage at what he's done, I nearly forgot that.

Slowly, I walk toward him. I've still got the watch in my hand. The one clue Evans found to the real killer. Maybe he's right, and there's no way to tie the watch to its true owner. But it represents *hope*. And that's what I need right now if I'm going to get out of this.

"Braden," I say. "Stefanie does mean something to me. Before I investigated her death, I was wounded. Someone I trusted hurt me. I'm not claiming I know what Stefanie went through, but I do know what it's like to feel scared and betrayed."

He seems like he's listening. He's still holding the gun, but his finger is no longer on the guard. He's holding it loosely. Looking at it almost thoughtfully.

"Did you know I went to see Luke Volkov a couple of days ago at the prison?" I ask.

He nods.

"I decided right after that to go back to the beginning. Look at all of the evidence again. And that's the same promise I'll make to you right now. I will do everything I can to figure out who owned this." I hold up the watch. "And bring him to justice."

A tear streaks from the corner of his eye. "It's too late."

"It's never too late. Not when it comes to murder. Some cold cases don't get solved for decades, but there's always a chance that—"

His anger boils over again, and his face turns to a snarl. "There are *no more chances*. Not for Stefanie, and not for me."

He raises the gun.

A shot rings out. I scream. Then two more shots in quick succession.

Evans falls to the floor.

I turn and see Alex in the doorway to the room, holding a Glock in his hand.

My heart's beating so fast I can scarcely breathe.

Alex doesn't glance at me as he crosses the room and kneels over Evans, stripping the gun out of the younger officer's hands. Blood wells from Evans's chest and his forehead.

Three expert kill shots. It's been decades since Alex was a Force Recon operator, but he still has those instincts inside of him.

"Is he…" I choke out.

"He's dead." Finally, Alex rises. Brushes off his suit. Walks over to me. "Are you all right?"

I can't bring my feet to move. I feel like I'm standing on the edge of a knife, and one false step could still end everything.

Which doesn't make sense. Because Alex is here. He saved me.

"Angie?" he asks.

He opens his arms, and I walk toward him. Let him hug

me. Yet it feels wrong. He's not the man I want. Alex always holds himself stiffly, with so much control. He feels nothing like Matteo.

My man is warm and passionate and comforting. He's who I need right now.

"I need to tell Matteo where I am," I say.

Alex chuckles. As if we ran into each other by chance here, and there's not a dead man on the floor a few feet away. A man Alex just shot. "You really do have a thing for him. He's certainly enamored with you. He came to find me, telling me he was worried about you. He's the reason I knew you were missing."

"Matteo came to you? Where is he?"

"I'm not sure. He wanted to look for you. But after he left, I had a hunch that maybe Evans would've taken you here. Lucky I was right. Did you want to call Matteo, tell him you're okay?"

"I would, except Evans tossed my phone out of the car window. He was Stefanie Rossi's younger half-brother. He joined West Oaks PD hoping to find her killer. When he couldn't, he decided he wanted to punish me instead. He used Grayson's ID at the evidence warehouse. Grayson never did any of it."

Alex shakes his head, glaring down at the prone body on the floor. "I'm so sorry, Angie. I should've seen it. I'm responsible for every officer under my command. I never should've allowed this to happen."

"Can I use your phone?" We can play the blame game later. Right now, I just want to talk to Matteo. Hear his voice.

"Sure. Let me call this in, get forensics here and processing started. We'll be in for a long night going over what Evans left behind."

What he left behind.

I look down at my hand and realize I'm still holding the

watch. At the same time, I get a faint whiff of Alex's cologne mixing with the scent of the gunpowder.

And suddenly, a memory surfaces.

Something I haven't thought about in *years*.

A watch on a nightstand, morning light glinting off its shiny band after a night of making love.

Watching the metal bracelet snap onto his wrist, his hair still damp from the shower.

A watch just like this one. The dual-colored ring, blue and red, with white hands.

Red, white, and blue, I joke. How very patriotic. Perfect for an ex-soldier.

"You had a watch like this," I say without thinking. "Didn't you?"

Then, another memory. Of me sitting on a bathroom counter, Alex kissing my neck, his shirt unbuttoned. That day, I held up his watch to slip it onto his wrist. I saw the scratch.

Don't worry, it's not a real Rolex.

A dazzling grin, a wink.

I gasp. Lift my eyes. And I meet Alex's gaze. His eyes are cold. So cold.

Why would Stefanie Rossi have Alex's watch? It can't be that they... That he...

My lips move. Pretending to smile. "What a strange coincidence."

"It is. Very strange." Alex is holding his phone in one hand, the gun in the other. He puts the phone away. The floor squeaks as his polished shoe takes a step toward me.

"Where did that watch come from?" he asks softly.

I take an equal step back. "Evans said he found it here. In the house. It was hidden in a box under the floorboards."

Alex's gun taps against his tailored pant leg. "Interesting. Did he have a theory about it?"

It belonged to Stefanie's killer.

"Not really," I force out. "No. He thought maybe Stefanie stole it? Or found it. I don't know."

Shit, I sound exactly like someone making things up on the spot. I'm usually a better liar than this.

But Alex... How is this possible? How can this *be*?

He sighs. Long and heavy. Like a man with the weight of the world bearing down on him. "Angie. You know, I've always regretted how things ended between us. Somehow, I thought we'd have another chance when we were both ready. When our careers weren't so demanding."

I slide my foot to the side. From the corner of my eye, I see Evans's gun on the floor. But I don't look at it. I can't risk it.

Not yet.

"We weren't a good match," I say.

"But you and the firefighter? You really think that will last? He doesn't have the mind that you do."

"No offense Alex, but you don't know Matteo. Or me, for that matter."

And I don't know you. God, I don't know you.

His eyes are hard, as if he heard exactly what I didn't say aloud.

"I can tell you have questions." He says this so quietly, I barely hear him. Especially with my ears still ringing a bit from the gunshots. But I hear him in my bones. The truth of it.

I'm squeezing the watch in my hand.

"Alex, what did you do?" I whisper.

38

Matteo

I watch the police chief round the side of a burned-out abandoned house. The lawn is overgrown with weeds. They're waist-height in some places.

I peer around the side to see Alex enter through a gap in the plywood.

What the heck is going on?

Just a few minutes ago, I was still sitting in my truck in the station parking lot when I saw Alex drive off in his Lexus SUV. I'd left his office not long before. Alex had claimed to have no idea where Angela was, yet now he was in a major hurry.

So, where was he going?

If it had something to do with Angela, then why hadn't he let me know? Just because I wasn't a cop? I decided I didn't care. If there was any chance I could help Angela, then I wanted to be there.

So I followed him.

My pulse was racing the whole way. I kept expecting emergency vehicles to appear, sirens blaring and lights flashing. Heading to some terrible scene. I thought the chief must've figured out where Angela was, and now he and the rest of the cavalry were rolling in. Hopefully to save her before it was… Jeez, I couldn't even finish my speculation. I refused to believe that we could be too late.

But Alex remained alone. He drove down a quiet street and parked. Got out and walked the rest of the way to this abandoned house. No back up.

When I saw him draw a gun from a holster at his lower back, I knew that some shit was about to go down.

He's just disappeared inside the house.

I hear gunshots. Screams. *Angela.*

I run toward the house, dialing 911 on my phone as I go. I tell the 911 operator that shots were fired and give the cross streets. "I saw the police chief go inside. Alex Liu."

"Do you know who fired the shots? If anyone's injured?"

"No. Not yet."

The operator is still asking questions, but I hang up the phone. I haven't got time to explain further. If Angela is in there, I have to reach her.

I look through the gap in the back door. I already hear voices coming from inside.

"He's dead," Alex says. "Are you all right?"

I'm about to charge in there because Angela could be hurt. I have no idea what I'm about to walk into, but that's what I do whenever I'm on duty and get called into action. I run *into* burning buildings instead of away from them. And if this could mean the difference between life or death for Angela, then I will risk myself every damn time.

But then I hear her voice. I can't make out the exact words, but she's okay. *Thank God.*

Logic breaks through my panic.

I have no idea what's going on in there, so I'm careful as I look and listen. Could someone else be in there with them?

Carefully, I step through the gap in the plywood and enter the house.

I hear Angela and Alex talking. Just them, no one else. "He was Stefanie Rossi's younger brother," she says.

The bitter aroma of gunpowder lingers, along with the older, stale scent of fire damage. Could this have been Stefanie Rossi's house?

I make the connection. This is where she must have died. There was a fire set at her murder scene.

Did Officer Evans bring her here? Is he the dead guy? Wait—Stefanie's younger brother?

And why the hell would Alex show up here alone when he told me, just minutes before, that he had no idea where Evans had gone?

I open my mouth to call out to them. Alert them to my presence so I don't freak them out. But for some reason, I don't speak. I'm stuck in place, just listening.

All my instincts are screaming that there's still danger nearby. I need to know what it is. Where it's coming from.

Angela says, "You had a watch like this. Didn't you?"

Every muscle in my body is poised to move. But I force myself to remain still. My heart thumps in my ears as they discuss this watch that Officer Evans found.

And then, the conversation shifts to their past relationship. To *me*.

"No offense Alex, but you don't know Matteo. Or me, for that matter."

"I can tell you have questions." His voice has gone low. Dangerous.

"Alex," Angela says, "what did you do?"

And then, he starts spilling his guts.

"I met Stefanie through a service. A discrete way for men with challenging careers, men like *me*, to meet women for an easy, no frills transaction."

"An escort service?" Angela asks. I can't believe how steady her voice is. Because I'm fucking *shaking*.

"Sure. I chose Stefanie by her photo. Dark hair, eyes, everything I liked. Stefanie was supposed to be easy. Someone I could spend a night with, a weekend, and then she'd leave me be. She reminded me of you, a little. All the idealism you used to have about your future. Stefanie was only a couple years younger than you were when you and I got together."

I edge closer until I can see them. Alex lifts a hand like he'll touch her. Angela shrinks away. It takes every single bit of control in my body—in my damn soul—not to race in there. But some part of my brain is functioning enough to keep me in place.

Alex isn't pointing his gun at her. He's not threatening her, not actively. Not yet. Instead, he's admitting that *he knew* Stefanie. Slept with her.

What would Angela want me to do?

I get out my phone and hit record.

"But unlike you," Alex says, "Stefanie wanted more. More money, at first. Then for me to marry her, which would've been impossible. You and I both know that. Someone like me, marrying a girl like her? An escort. The ex-girlfriend of a mobbed-up drug dealer. It would've been ridiculous. My career would've been over. I told her it couldn't happen, and she showed more backbone than I ever realized she had. Stefanie said she'd tell the media about our relationship if I was so ashamed of it. She'd destroy me. So, I did what I had to."

"You destroyed her first," Angela says.

"*Fuck*," I whisper. Bile is rising in my throat. I keep recording as I take careful steps toward the doorway.

"I never wanted it to happen that way," Alex goes on. "But once I saw I had no choice, the rest was straightforward.

Blame her ex. Set him up to take the fall. It wasn't hard to set up a syringe with his fingerprints on it, given how many times he'd been arrested. We had the prints on file. The fire helped wipe away any problems with the prints and any last traces of my presence here. Volkov was the first and only suspect. As I'd planned it."

"And you put me as lead investigator."

"Fresh from your leave. Yes. That way, I could stay closely involved in the name of supervising. When that diary of Stefanie's turned up, I was quick to tear out the pages that mentioned me by name or by my job title. When anything came up that pointed away from Volkov, I got rid of it. I had no idea about the watch." He laughs ruefully. "I thought I'd lost it. Stefanie insisted she didn't have it. The little brat must've kept it as proof that we were involved."

He's admitting everything. All the secrets that Angela's been trying to find for the last year and a half. The truth behind what happened to Stefanie Rossi.

Alex won't let her leave here alive.

But when is he going to strike? How am I going to get her out of there when he's the one holding the gun?

"You didn't realize she had a brother?" Angela asks.

"No, I told you the truth about that. I had no idea who was targeting you. I thought the plot was all about you, not about Stefanie." His thumb caresses the trigger guard of his gun. "But when Matteo told me you were missing and I checked Evans's location, I told your boyfriend the GPS in the squad car was turned off. That wasn't accurate. I saw that Evans was here. At Stefanie's house. I wondered."

That asshole. And I fell for it.

"You decided to save me yourself?" she spits out. "Play the hero?"

"Sure. And check what Evans was really up to." He shakes his head. "I never wanted things to end up this way, Angie.

Not for Stefanie. And *never* for you. But I'll do what I have to."

Oh, fuck. That is definitely my cue.

I drop my phone and barrel through the doorway.

Alex aims his weapon at Angela. She's diving for the floor, grabbing for another gun. I slam into him, throwing him hard into the wall as I bellow a war cry.

There are loud pops as fire-damaged wood snaps under our weight. Dust clouds into the air.

We fall to the floor, grappling with one another. I think he's lost his gun in the scuffle. But Alex isn't down. Not even close. His face is a vicious snarl, and his fist slams into my side. I block another blow aimed for my throat.

He doesn't want to disable me. He wants to *kill* me.

I'm a decade younger, maybe two, but the guy is strong and obviously well-trained. I'm a brawler. No finesse, but I make up for it with sheer ferocity. And this guy makes me see fucking *red*.

He's a murderer who kills women and hides behind a manicured facade. Who was going to hurt my girl.

He rolls us and lands a punch to my face. Hot metal and salt fill my mouth. I see a flare of satisfaction in his eyes just before I throw us both to the side with my entire weight. His head glances off the floor. I use his split-second confusion to get my arm locked around his neck as I rise onto my knees. He's laid out on the floor, while I'm straddling his back, my thick arm squeezing the air from his throat. Let's see him get out of this one.

"I told you I'd never let Angela down." I'm spitting blood as I speak. "And you are *never* going to hurt her ever again. You piece of shit."

Then I look up and notice Angela standing in front of us. She's got a gun in both hands, aiming it down at the chief's face.

"It's over, Alex," she says.

"Angie," he croaks. "Please. I loved you."

"I'm probably not going to kill you. But I am *this close*, so don't tempt me. I'm so sick of men I *trusted* pointing *guns* at me. I'd love to be the one pulling the trigger. Might even help work out some of my issues. Just try me."

I smile at her despite the pain in my jaw. *That's my girl.*

IT'S NOT long before the police cars and ambulances arrive. And chaos ensues.

Turns out, things get a bit messy when you're accusing the chief of police of murder and conspiracy.

Angela and I might have subdued him in that burned-out room, but within minutes, he's spinning stories to the responding officers about me and Angela being out of our minds. Luckily, I've got that recording of his confession.

Detectives Holt and Diaz show up to take over. An EMT treats me, and it turns out he's the same friend of Danny's who let me onto the ambulance with Angela after her car accident. Despite the blood, it doesn't look like my jaw is broken. I might have a cracked rib or two—Alex really could land a punch—but it's nothing I haven't lived through before. Most important to me is that Angela is unharmed.

I hold her as tight as I can and keep her close to me. That's all I need.

Since the police chief is now the lead suspect for a slew of crimes, a bunch of outsiders descend on the police station. Like the new district attorney, Lana Marchetti. And Jake Shelborne, along with his agent in charge from the DEA. Plus some people who say they're from the California Bureau of Investigation. I can't keep it all straight. Nor do I care who's got jurisdiction over this mess. I just care about my girl.

And finally, after endless hours of interviews with all these talking heads, we get to go home.

Neve's waiting up with homemade chicken soup and comfy clothes for Angela to change into. Even a mugful of plain broth and a milkshake for me after hearing my jaw is sore.

We crawl into my bed. "We made a damn good team," I say.

"I can't believe you recorded all of what Alex said. It was awful to hear him admit what he'd done, but to think nobody would know the truth, or believe it, made it that much more horrifying. I didn't know if I would make it out of that room." She clasps her hands behind my neck. "And then, there you were. Saving me. Just when I needed you. And I was *so glad* to see you. Not just because you were saving my life, but because the thought of never seeing you again was unbearable."

"I'm here, angel. Not going anywhere. You should know that by now."

For a long time, we just look at one another, even though we're both exhausted. I stroke the puckered skin of her scar.

"What're you thinking about?" I ask.

"You. I don't know how you found me."

"I told you. I followed Alex when he left the station."

We've both caught up on everything that happened. How Braden Evans was behind the theft of evidence and the attempt to frame Angela, plus the car accident that landed her in the hospital. Detective Diaz was furious to find out that the culprit was someone on her own investigation team.

But it was his older sister's murder that drove Evans to act so desperately. Now, we know the truth behind that too. Chief Alex Liu murdered Stefanie Rossi and made sure that Luke Volkov was convicted for a crime he didn't commit.

Detective Holt assured us he would call Volkov's lawyer

first thing in the morning and share everything they'd found. Hopefully, with the participation of District Attorney Marchetti, Volkov's murder conviction will soon be reversed.

As for Katrina Katalsky, we heard she was already picked up for shoplifting near the Nevada border. She'd tried to skip town after realizing the police suspected her. Evans may be dead, but Katrina will now have to answer for her participation in the evidence-theft scheme. So will Volkov, if he was part of it, but everything so far suggests he had no idea what his girlfriend and Evans were doing.

And Grayson? He was released from custody soon after Alex was brought in. We heard he's home with his wife, trying to fix what he's broken. They probably have a lot of couple's therapy ahead of them. For the sake of their kid, I hope they can find a way forward, whether they remain married or not.

"But I wasn't asking how you found me today," Angela says. "Or was it yesterday? I don't even know."

I keep caressing her, fighting back a yawn. "Then what did you mean, baby? You'll have to explain it because my brain is slowing down."

It's dark in my bedroom, moonlight bleeding through the blinds. It's just enough to show me that she's blinking away tears. Yet I don't feel sadness coming from her. Just relief.

"How did you find me *in life*?" she asks. "I didn't want to let anyone near. And even before I was wounded, the guys I dated were more like *Alex* than you. I was such an idiot."

"Good thing I'm persistent," I say on another yawn. "And loud."

"You're right. I couldn't ignore you. Not that I really wanted to."

"Neve probably *does* deserve the credit. Both for making you stay here and for creating your hookup profile. Because once I saw that, I knew I had to have you. Make you *mine*."

"That's exactly what you did."

I pull her in for some kisses. Gentle at first, because I don't want to push things if she's not feeling it. I may be persistent, but when it comes to whether we get sexy or not, my girl runs the show.

But it seems she's on board for more. I roll onto my back, pulling her on top of me. Kissing. Touching. Sharing our incredible relief that we've made it here. We're together and we're safe, and *nobody* can break us.

We take off each other's clothes, and I press myself against her, warm skin to warm skin. My hard cock against her soft belly. Her hand closes around me. Strokes me.

"You want this cock?" I ask. "It's all yours. I'm yours."

"I'm yours, too. All of me. Always."

"Is that a deal? 'Cause I'm gonna hold you to it."

"It's a deal."

EPILOGUE

Angela

"Happy birthday," Neve says, holding up her cocktail glass for a toast. "To my best friend. Who owes me for making her life so dang great."

"You're still milking that?" I ask.

"I'll only do it for forever."

We're sitting at the bar of the sushi restaurant on Ocean Lane, the same one as the night of the fire at my apartment building. It's been about five months since that night. My life is pretty much unrecognizable by comparison to who I was back then. And I love it.

All except for the nausea in my stomach the past few days.

Neve ordered us a bunch of sushi rolls and nigiri, but all I've done is nibble on plain rice. I ordered a club soda as well instead of a more festive drink. I wonder if I'm coming down with something.

But I'm determined to have fun tonight. I lift my soda and clink glasses with her. "Thanks for coming back to West Oaks to celebrate with me."

"I wouldn't miss it." She's been in New York City for the past month shooting the photos for some clothing website. "But why don't you look happier? I thought you were out here living your best life."

"I'm just feeling *blah* tonight. A stomach thing. Everything else is pretty much perfect."

While Matteo and I talked about finding our own place, that didn't end up happening. Instead, Neve moved out of the house. And I never left.

My best friend bought a new property with her fabulous photographer money, while Matteo and I pooled our savings —plus a hefty loan—to purchase the house from her. It was a stretch, but with our detective and firefighter incomes combined, we're making it work. Plus, Matteo is still working as Neve's property manager, even if he's no longer her house sitter getting free rent.

But my best friend, being the sweetheart Mama-bear that she is, left behind all of her plants for me. And my gorgeous boyfriend takes care of them and keeps them green and healthy.

Yep, pretty much perfect.

One of the best decisions I made in the last several months? Turning down the offer to apply for chief of police. Sean turned it down as well, only agreeing to serve as interim chief while the search for a permanent replacement goes on.

Our disgraced chief Alex Liu is under house arrest pending his trial. It's sure to be a media circus, and it probably won't even happen for another year. I'm sure District Attorney Marchetti has the case well in hand.

I suspect Alex will end up pleading guilty before jury selection is out. Because with that recording Matteo made, he's dead to rights. Alex is also as good as dead to *me*. While he's asked to speak with me since his formal indictment, I've refused. I want nothing to do with him.

I've been slightly more forgiving toward my former partner, Beau Grayson, if only for his wife and child's sakes. His baby daughter is a few months old now. While his wife banished him from their bedroom, they're slowly working towards healing their family. If Nora takes him back fully, then that will have to be her choice alone, no one else's. Maybe their marriage can't be saved. Either way, I'll support her. It's for the best that Grayson resigned from West Oaks PD and is now working as a county administrative employee.

But back to happier topics. After Neve moved out, Matteo and I bought new furniture for the extra bedroom and let Emily and Natalie decorate. The room is theirs for whenever they want to visit. They ended up returning to West Oaks earlier than planned, and the four of us, plus Chips and Pretzel, were one happy, noisy family for the rest of the summer.

Now that the school year has started, things have settled down. Emily found a new place not far away. It's close enough that we go over there for dinner, or they come to ours, pretty much every evening. It's especially nice for me on the nights when Matteo is at the fire house. That's when I tend to stay over at Emily's or Natalie comes over for a little slumber party, just the two of us. Matteo nearly bought out a yarn store for me, and I've been teaching Natalie how to knit.

That precious time with Natalie, and seeing how wonderful Matteo is with his niece, has made me start wondering about what *else* our future could hold. I've never been the type of girl who feels her biological clock ticking. Not even with my thirty-third birthday now upon me. And

Matteo hasn't mentioned us taking any big steps in our relationship, so I assume he's not ready for that either.

"I *am* living my best life," I say to Neve. But then my stomach gives another rambunctious twist, and I grimace. "I just haven't been feeling that good the past few days. I think I'm allergic to something. That must be it."

Neve sets down her cosmo and studies me. Then presses the back of her hand to my forehead. "What exactly has been going on?"

"Well, let's see." I list my random assortment of symptoms. I've been feeling more tired than usual, and I can't even blame Matteo for keeping me up late. He's been all about morning sex lately.

"Then there's this nausea. I don't feel like eating anything. All my favorite things, like sushi, are turning my stomach. But I haven't thrown up, so I don't think it's a stomach bug."

"Hmmm. When was your last period?"

"I don't know. A few weeks ago maybe? Or... longer." Now that I think of it, my menstrual cycle has been off too. "You see what I mean? It's weird. I don't know what's going on."

She levels a stare at me.

"Really," she deadpans. "And you're supposed to be the detective?"

"I'm the detective who got a commendation from the mayor, in case you forgot." I roll my eyes, because I really couldn't care less about the accolade. Though of course, I'm happy that Luke Volkov's murder conviction was reversed.

But I would much rather that Alex, a man I trusted and considered a friend, hadn't turned out to be a cold-blooded killer.

At least Matteo received a special commendation too. He got to wear his firefighter uniform and stand up with the mayor at a press conference and everything. It even made the news. *West Oaks firefighter and detective clear name of innocent man.*

"If you can figure this out," I say, "then feel free to share the results of your investigation. Or if you have a medical degree I didn't know about."

My best friend shakes her head. "Lady, we need to go to the drugstore. And you need to brace yourself. Because I think that lingerie I bought you may have worked a little too well."

~

Matteo

"UNCLE MATTEO, will you color with me?"

"Sure, Natty-bear." I pull up a chair to the kitchen table, where Natalie is crayoning-in every inch of her Encanto coloring book. We're having an uncle and niece night. The macaroni and cheese is baking in the oven—none of that instant powder crap in my kitchen—and we've got a Disney Plus marathon ahead of us.

Angela and Neve are out celebrating my girl's birthday, though Angela's birthday isn't really until tomorrow. She promised she would spend the official day with me and Nat.

I have so many plans. Starting with making Angela come with my tongue right when she wakes up. Happy birthday indeed.

Emily's off having a ladies' night too, along with a bunch of elementary school teachers. They're probably getting wild already. While I love the nights that Em and Natalie hang with us, these times with just my niece are extra special. Makes me think about how much I want some rugrats of my own.

I haven't spoken a word about kids to Angela because I don't want to freak her out. We've only been together for five months. But even though I'm biding my time, there's no doubt in my mind that Angela and I have a big family ahead of us.

I have the tendency to get my way eventually.

Just don't tell Angela I said that.

Aside from wanting to give Natalie some cousins, there's not much else I would change about my life. Angela and I have a sweet setup here. After we sorted through the belongings in her apartment, replacing the things that were damaged and moving all the rest over here, our lives have melded together like a béchamel sauce. Nice and smooth.

Our schedules are still hectic. She gets called out to major crime scenes more often than I'd like, and I still work my twenty-four-hour shifts ten days a month. We sometimes go way too long without seeing each other.

But she drops by Station Two when she can, and I've become a fixture around the police station, even though Interim Chief Sean Holt might prefer to get rid of me at this point. Not because he doesn't love me, but because I have strong opinions about the dangerous situations Angela winds up in.

It's her job to fight bad guys, but I also consider it my job to watch out for her. There's nothing either of us can do about that. It's an instinct for me.

One thing that's not my job? Being a captain. After a lot of thought and discussion with my girlfriend, I decided not to apply. I realized I didn't need a promotion to make Brent proud of me. And because of the loan from Emily's parents, I didn't need the extra money either. I'll keep giving my all *and* having fun, both as a WOFD firefighter and with my family. That's good enough for me.

But if I'd wanted that captain spot? Not gonna brag, but I would've had it all wrapped up. Captain Bucanan has become an advocate for me with Chief Ross and also a good friend. Turns out, Buc lost his dad to cancer. We've bonded over that. As for Chief Ross, he's given me nothing but praise since the mayor pinned that medal on my uniform. Station Two has had all the good publicity we can handle.

After a mac and cheese feast and way too many episodes of Bluey, I tuck Natalie into bed. A dozen bedtime stories and hugs later, and I'm back in the living room just in time for Angela to walk in the door.

"Hey, how was sushi night with Neve?" I head over to the door to greet her, but she doesn't say anything. In fact, she's giving me a glassy-eyed stare.

I run my hands down her arms. "Baby, what's up? Is something wrong?"

Angela digs into her purse. She hasn't said a word, and I'm really starting to worry.

Then I see what she's holding.

"Neve made me buy it. I took the test in the drugstore bathroom."

It's a pregnancy test. And I'm no expert here, but I think the two pink lines means it's positive.

"Is that what I think it is?" I ask.

"What *do* you think it is?" She's biting her lower lip, big dark-hazel eyes looking up at me with uncertainty. "Good? Or…"

I hold her face in my hands, beaming down at her. "I think it's the best fucking news I've ever heard. What about you?"

"The scariest news. But I think it's the best, too. I want this. With you."

"We're gonna have a baby." I pump my fist in the air. "My sperm wins. That birth control was no match."

Then we're both hugging and laughing and crying. And kissing. Lots of kissing. And I-love-yous.

"Guess we should get married?" I blurt out. Because I'm smooth like that.

She rubs at her eyes, smearing her mascara. "I don't need that. I don't need anything but us. And our family." Then she grimaces. "Though we'll probably still need to have a party so my parents can meet you. I already know they're going to love you, but my dad has really boring stories. And he never remembers who he's told them to, so get ready. You'll be hearing about the 1986 parade float fiasco a *lot*."

"I can't wait. We'll have to invite Emily's parents too. Get the whole extended family together."

Angela could tell me I have to sit through a hundred fancy, boring dinners with every ex-mayor and I wouldn't bat an eye. Absolutely nothing could bring this mood down.

I'm going to be a dad. And I *know* that'll make my brother proud.

"I love you, angel."

"I love you too."

We sit down on the couch, and she snuggles up in my lap. Pretzel and Chips join us, since they're staying over while Natalie is here. It's just a great big cuddle fest at Casa Murphy and De Luca.

"You do realize what this means?" Angela asks. "Neve still expects us to name our firstborn after her."

"Unless the little guy is a boy."

Angela looks up at me. "I was thinking about that on the way home. If it's a boy, what about Brent?"

I am head over heels in love with this woman. I've known

that for a while. I've been telling her for months, and she's always eager to say it back. But this kind of feeling? So big and bold that it feels like I'll burst at my seams with it? This is love on another level.

"Perfect."

That's all I need to say. Because that one word sums everything up.

The End.

Firefighter Danny Bradley's story is next!
Read THE TWO LAST MOMENTS,
book 5 of West Oaks Heroes.

ALSO BY HANNAH SHIELD

THE WEST OAKS HEROES SERIES

THE SIX NIGHT TRUCE (Janie & Sean)

THE FIVE MINUTE MISTAKE (Madison & Nash)

THE FOUR DAY FAKEOUT (Jake & Harper)

THE THREE WEEK DEAL (Matteo & Angela)

THE TWO LAST MOMENTS (Danny & Lark)

THE BENNETT SECURITY SERIES

HANDS OFF (Aurora & Devon)

HEAD FIRST (Lana & Max)

HARD WIRED (Sylvie & Dominic)

HOLD TIGHT (Faith & Tanner)

HUNG UP (Danica & Noah)

HAVE MERCY (Ruby & Chase)

ABOUT THE AUTHOR

Hannah Shield writes steamy, suspenseful romance with pulse-pounding action, fun & flirty banter, and tons of heart. She once worked as an attorney. Now, she loves thrilling her readers on the page in every possible way.

Visit her website at www.hannahshield.com.

Made in the USA
Coppell, TX
20 February 2024

29217982R00215